THE PUCK BUNNY

A HOCKEY ROMCOM

STEPHANIE QUEEN

The Puck Bunny
Copyright © 2023 by Stephanie Queen
All rights reserved.

ACKNOWLEDGMENTS

A Big Thank You

To **Dawn Castelli** for naming **Quinn James**, star veteran hockey player just joining the Boston Brawlers from L.A. and the hero in this story.

To **Kimberly Collins** for naming **Sara**, the heroine, a superfan of the Brawlers and the hero.

And to everyone who enters my *Name That Character Contest*, your creativity, enthusiasm and support is much appreciated!

PROLOGUE

SARA

*I*s it too weird that, at twenty-one years old, I, Sara Bellagamba, have a poster of Quinn James—arguably the most outstanding and definitely dreamiest hockey star who ever lived—on my bedroom wall, albeit turning at the corners because it's been there since high school? Of course I still live at home because I can't afford to move out since I'm paying student loans for my business degree from UNH—aka the University of New Hampshire, a premiere hockey school, of course. Did I mention that Quinn James himself is an alum? Yup, the most famous and spectacularly successful hockey player ever to come from the UNH Wildcats hockey program.

It's also weird that I'm working in a low-paying entry-level job after graduating summa cum laude.

In my defense, it's my dream job and I wouldn't trade it for a million bucks. Okay, *maybe* I'd consider a million bucks... And sure, the job itself isn't a dream because who dreams about staring at spreadsheets filled with ticket sales stats?

But who cares about all the tedium—I'm working for the *freaking* Boston Brawlers hockey team! (inner shriek!) Just walking in the doors to the corporate office suite at the Garden gives me goose bumps every single morning.

Besides, all the weirdness can be explained away by one single fact:

I'm a lifelong super fan of hockey and *especially* the home team Boston Brawlers.

So, when I find out Quinn freaking James just signed with the Brawlers at the last second in a stunning free-agency deal, I almost faint. Luckily, I'm sitting at my desk chair and can close my eyes until the dizziness passes.

"Did you see this?" I whisper-shout across the top of the cubicle to my co-worker and best friend from college, Billie Mae. She's from Arkansas and God-only-knows how she ended up at UNH as my roommate, but after dragging her to all the college hockey games, she joined me as an official fan of the sport, though not quite at my level.

She's enough of a fan to have finagled an internship with the Brawlers her senior year. Her dad is some kind of muckety-muck VIP in the business world with enough gravitas—or money—to pull some strings. Anyway, the rest is history because we now have our foot officially in the door, both having landed these horribly boring, low-paying jobs working for the best sports organization in the world.

"Have I seen what?" she says, only half-paying attention as she taps away at her keyboard at lightning speed.

"About the free-agency deal?" I whisper-shout a little louder as my eyes stay glued to the keyboard. "The online article describes him as—and I quote—the movie-star-handsome, hockey mega-god who played with the LA Shooting Stars for ten seasons, dominating the league and building a leading-man persona with his on- and off-the- ice glamorous-player lifestyle."

"Oh yeah," she says, still tapping. "I thought I heard someone in the elevator on the way in talking about a deal to get Quinn What's-His-Name." She turns to me, finally paying attention. "Isn't that the guy you had a crush on when you were a kid?"

Okay, maybe I exaggerated about Billie Mae being an official hockey fan. She still has a lot to learn about who the best players in the league are. Also, I may have fibbed to her a little when I told her about my old crush since it's not that old. In fact, it's still fresh as a daisy and blooming out all over me right now as I scroll down the article to the photos.

"Sure." I stay cool. "He's still cute."

She makes a face like she ate a lemon. "If you like old guys—whom, as it turns out..." She taps another key— "PR just sent me photos of to post on Instagram. Maybe you're right," she says, studying her screen for a beat. "He's not half-bad. Kind of a heartthrob vibe. I wonder if his teeth are real?"

"Yes, they are," I answer too fast.

She laughs, shaking her head as I finish reading the article.

Apparently, I'm not the only one stunned by the deal. It's also a shock to the sports world that he chose to go from the star power of the LA glam market to the cultural opposite with the notorious blue-collar Boston Brawlers. Not even his agent, best-in-the-business, Ham Jett would say any more than, "It's the right move for him at this time."

Some people—and, by *people*, I mean *me*—find that explanation a stretch when he was last seen in video clips in the off-season dating Princess Anica Romanova from Romaldestan.

But maybe, just maybe, he wanted the trade because he misses New England. He's the best player to ever play hockey at UNH, still holding a half-dozen records to this day, ten years later.

If only I'd gone there when he was there... What might have happened?

Get a grip, Sara. Not a goddam blessed thing would have happened because you're too average—possibly below average—to attract the likes of him.

My stupid reality check is right. I'd barely dated at all. At parties, I'd been *the* quintessential awkward girl, talking hockey instead of flirting. Flirting had never been my specialty. I've always been a numbers person and even though I'd ended up getting chosen as one of the student volunteer statisticians for the team my senior year, do you think I ever dated one single hockey player the entire season?

No. I did not.

I'd wanted to. I just couldn't manage to close any deals. They were too far out of my league—my league being the Pee-Wees C-team compared to their top NHL prospect status.

But I'm more worldly now, a college grad working in the city in a professional job and working on my wardrobe and my weight. Billie Mae made me promise to let her help me and we're making progress.

The first thing on her training list—yes, she's calling it training—is to build up my confidence with men. She says I have a body-image problem and insecurities that make me awkward when I try to flirt. Maybe it stems from too much time with two brothers who constantly tease me, or maybe it's because of the time my dad went away for a while. But today Billie Mae and I are going out to lunch and she'll coach me on what to eat and maybe to practice flirting.

And now I have something to practice for. Because, now that Quinn's here, there's no *way* I'm not going to do something about it.

What I'm going to do, I have no idea, but something...

Just, hopefully, *not* the kind of something that will make me look back someday and realize this is where I went off the rails.

CHAPTER 1

SARA

A WEEK LATER

"She's just a puck bunny. Who cares?" One of the Brawlers players says just before he guzzles his beer. The young lady in question retreats, weeping, to a table with her friends. Even though this guy plays for my team, he's clearly an asshole. Am I the only one in this crowded bar who notices? His words burn into my soul offending me and my margarita-riddled sensibilities.

I jump up from my seat because someone has to stand up for the girl.

"I care." My voice is loud and every Brawlers player at the table to my right faces my way. My gaze slides to Quinn's, but I dart it away to stare right at the offending asshole. "Aren't puck bunnies people, too, with hearts and souls and feelings? Who do you think you are to say that? You shouldn't be mean to people —*any* people—just because you can get away with it. You just shouldn't."

I stop talking and my corner of the bar goes quiet.

The guys from the team's table on my right stare at me, without saying a word. All the puck bunnies at the table on my left stare at me.

The beat of silence turns into two as a ball of seething embarrassment rises in me, the inferno heating my cheeks—now, no doubt, a bright red—and I want to crawl inside myself and disappear. This is not what I had in mind for tonight.

My gaze automatically goes to Quinn, and he's staring back at me. Like everyone else.

Great. I've just made an outrageous spectacle of myself, butting into a private matter so loudly and passionately that I feel dizzy, and he's here to witness it. He must think I'm a jerk calling out his teammate. I can kiss any hope of any relationship with this guy goodbye. I swear, this is the last time I drink tequila.

My heart thunders in my chest as I hold his gaze.

It takes another beat to register the expression on his face. He's not scowling, he's not shocked. No, he looks… *pleased*. Then he breaks the pause of shocked silence.

"She has a point." His voice is loud and clear and that famous one-dimpled smile makes me stumble.

Then he winks and I stop breathing, yet people keep talking as if something momentous hasn't just happened. *Maybe he doesn't think I'm an idiot.*

'Course, he obviously doesn't think anything amazing just happened either because after that wink, he just starts talking to one of his friends.

I need to get out of here before I literally die of embarrassment.

But I also need to get his attention back because I want more of that sweet sexy smile of his. It'd felt like having the best sex ever.

Well, not that I'd know because the best sex ever should come with an orgasm and since I've never actually *had* an orgasm I can't really compare.

But I can imagine.

I can also ask him to be the one to take my orgasm virginity—even if the likelihood of even the *possibility* of that just shrunk significantly.

Not that I'm really upset by it because, sure, I've always been a big fan of his but I've never actually aspired to... well, have *sex* with him. Not for real. I mean, it's not like I'd ever dreamed the chance would actually happen.

But then he got traded to the team and I work for the team and... well... This is no *dream*; this is an honest-to-God, for-real *goal*.

As I melt into the crowd, I notice the older puck bunny—the woman who was sitting at the puck bunny table, who looks like she's best friends with the crying girl. She slides out of the booth and shoots straight for me.

I dash for the exit. It's late and I need to get home. Mom waits up for me.

Once I'm out the front door I gulp the seedy air of Boston's Canal Street's car fumes mixed with stale beer like it's going to save me rather than kill me. Instead, it makes me cough.

But relief fills me because I escaped without further incident, without anyone knowing who I am.

If anyone found out I work for the Brawlers... Well, I don't want to think about that.

"That cough sounds rough. Maybe you ought to cut back on the cigarettes," a sexy female voice says from behind me.

I jump and turn around to find—holy mother of hockey—the older puck bunny right there talking to me. *Shit*.

Coming to the bar, The Tea Party, tonight and watching from my cocoon of obscurity with my hair dyed red and baseball cap pulled low, was like having my own private show, watching the team play their off-ice game as the puck bunnies do their thing. But now I've got the head puck bunny talking to me.

I had managed to stay under the radar, unnoticed like the

wallflower I am, completely obscured with no one paying attention to me until now.

"That was cool of you to stand up for Mindy back there."

My nerves calm because she sounds nice. And she's *thanking me* for butting in. "Oh, thanks. I guess I couldn't help myself. Mindy doesn't deserve to have her feelings hurt like that. No matter what." I feel my face flush with the same indignation from before.

The lady smirks and puts out her hand.

"I'm Sheila. Mindy should have known better. I saw it coming a mile away. Tried to warn her not to get her hopes up." She cocks her head. "And you are?"

"I'm… Lola." I cringe inwardly at the made-up name. No way can I let her know who I am on the off chance she'd find out I work for the Brawlers. My boss would have a kitten if she knew I came to this player bar after a game.

"Meeting the players at The Tea Party for fun and games is not supposed to turn into something real." Sheila shakes her head. "It's exciting, and of course, all about—"

"Fantasy." I totally get caught up in Sheila and Mindy's plight.

"Some girls just can't handle managing expectations, you know. It's only for fun. They don't get the deal."

"One night of bliss and that's all I'd need." I sigh.

She laughs. "Sounds like you're one of us. I haven't seen you here before. You new to town?"

I don't want to admit that I've been around all my life, that this was the first night I dared going out to a bar myself—in my defense I only turned twenty-one a few months ago—and only so I wouldn't have to watch the game alone. I definitely can't tell her I've avoided going places where the players go after games because I'm not supposed to fraternize.

I nod.

"I wouldn't mind having you join our crowd, maybe meet us after the next home game if you want," she says.

"Really?" My mind spins like a washing machine with an extra-large load, figuring out if I can pull it off. None of the players know who I am at work since I'm new. I'd have to make sure I keep up my altered appearance when I come out—I won't call it a disguise exactly. And definitely keep up my low profile at work so I don't run into any of the players—especially Quinn. Not that that's a thing. In fact, it's highly unlikely. "I'd love to. It would be so much fun. Do you go to late-night wild parties after the bar closes?"

She laughs. "Not usually, but there've been occasions." She looks me over. "You might want to dress up a bit. Especially if you have your eye on one of the guys."

"I do."

"Okay, it's a date then. I'll tell the girls. Want to give me your number and I'll put you on the group text?"

A grin takes over my face. This is like getting invited to the coolest sorority on campus only this is better because it's real life. Or... is it? We just agreed it's all about the fantasy, didn't we? My momentary confusion doesn't dampen the warm-and-fuzzy thrill that I get I rattle off my number.

After she leaves, I run down the street to the parking garage as if I'm Cinderella and it's about to strike midnight. After I finally reach my pumpkin—er, car— I drive home to Revere, just north of the city, replaying the events from the moment I'd jumped from being a wallflower to being on the stage with the players and the puck bunnies.

Then I remember Sheila suggested I might want to dress up a bit and I gulp. How far out of my comfort zone am I willing to go? I'm not built for luring men in with my looks.

CHAPTER 2

QUINN

O'Rourke's telling a story about having a third child and something about being surprised at the ultrasound yesterday when it showed up twins. That would normally get my attention and I'd buy him a drink—hell, I'd normally buy the whole joint a drink, except for two things.

One, I'm not in L.A. anymore and part of the reason for that is to cut back on the partying. The last thing I need to do is cultivate another entourage by buying drinks for the entire crowd at The Tea Party, even if I do get the sense that this crowd can't be bought as easily as the others were back at the Razzle Dazzle in L.A.

And, second, I need to control the unusually strong impulse I have to follow the cute and brave puck bunny as she escapes out the door, practically bouncing off patrons like a pinball being played by the wizard himself. But she is adorable and not just because her voice had a nervous quiver as she declared war on assholes in defense of puck bunnies everywhere—God, that was so real I wanted to give her a hug.

She was dressed so differently than the rest of the puck bunnies at the table, in an oversized Brawlers' jersey and baseball cap as if she were trying to hide her red hair that I'd bet my next endorsement is a dye job. And the way she looked at me before she left… Like I was a water mirage in a desert and she wanted to drink me up. *Fuck..*

A puck bunny who disses a player? That's something new and intriguing. And for a guy like me who's seen it all, had every kind of girl—every age, size, and level of crazy—throw themselves at me every which way, meeting or, rather, *almost* meeting, a woman who's different is like fucking butter, the kind that melts in my mouth and weakens my resolve, lighting up my interest meter as if the pinball puck bunny hit my jackpot good and hard.

Half-listening to the guys as I raise my glass in congratulations to O'Rourke, I watch one of the other puck bunnies—this one older and dressed like she's in the official puck bunny uniform of tight jersey with a low neckline that shows a lot of cleavage, a tight black skirt too short for the imagination, and black fishnets under her tall boots, as she goes out the door after my girl. Damn. I was hoping to sneak out myself and run into her.

Okay, so maybe I could be that creepy.

Stupid idea. Shaking my head, I return my attention to the guys. "This calls for a bottle of whiskey for the table." I drain my beer, then aim my glass in the direction of the server hovering close enough to see my move and scurry over. The guys nod and laugh, but they're not overly excited about the whiskey. Maybe because we have another game tomorrow night and, in spite of the fact that this is still pre-season, this is a disciplined bunch.

"One shot to the lucky father and then off we go home for our beauty rest," I don't want my new teammates to think I'm still that party guy from L.A..

Or, at least, not anymore.

O'Rourke nods. "Perfect, I could use the beauty sleep." He takes a gulp of beer. "All us old guys could use the sleep."

I point to my chest as if to say *who me* in mock denial. But he'd be wrong. Not that I'm *old*-old, but, in hockey years, anyone over thirty requires more care and attention than he used to. The margin of error for what I can get away with off the ice has shrunk down to exactly zero. Not that I learned the obvious lesson the *real* hard way, but I did experience an incident or two that drove the point home like the first nail in my professional coffin.

Glancing back at the door as the server delivers our bottle and shot glasses, I'm not surprised to see the flashy puck bunny return without her apprentice. She seems too real to be a game player. Is she even one of them? Though she was quick to speak up loud and clear in defense of all the ladies, and the one in particular who's still crying in the corner.

I groan inwardly. There's no way I'm going to let the incident go without having a quiet word with the offending asshole. Not that I needed the brave puck bunny to fire me up over his assholery because I don't put up with that shit when I see it.

I lift my glass with my new teammates. A sense of comradery hits me as we drink to O'Rourke. When I swallow the shot of golden fire, I know the warmth I feel is only partly from the whiskey, and only partly from the comradery. Some of the spark I owe to my brave little puck bunny.

Standing, I glance at the table of her friends and give an acknowledging nod. They respond with raised glasses and cheers, but I slip into my jacket, signaling my imminent exit, to calm them down. No way I want to start my tenure here by making a spectacle with a bunch of puck bunnies, no matter how lovely they may be. They're too high-profile, and, if they're anything like L.A. puck bunnies, they want the splash of attention from social media more than me.

"See you in the morning, guys."

"You still at the hotel? Want a ride to the rink in the morning?" Finn says. "I live downtown and can swing by."

"Thank you, really, but I think I'll walk."

More than one guy raises their brows and I get some shit about not being the pedestrian type. I laugh and leave the table after throwing down a few extra fifties because over-tipping is one L.A. habit I don't feel inclined to change. The servers here work just as hard to afford to live in a city that's almost as expensive.

None of the guys bat an eye at my excessive tip and that makes me smile wider as they all get their coats on. I feel the eyes of all the ladies at the puck bunny table on me as I walk by and can't help waving—which makes them break out in titters and shouts that include phone numbers and invitations that I bet would make my shy puck bunny blush.

As I pass by Jonas Bergman, the asshole player—or, to be fair, the guy who made the asshole statement about puck bunnies—I touch him on the shoulder and direct him toward the back exit of the bar. He follows, though with a skeptical furrow in his brow, a downturn at the corners of his mouth and his shoulders hunched and tense.

We reach the back door and he stops. "What do you want?"

"Let's talk about that puck bunny comment."

"You're not buying into the crap that loud-mouth girl spouted, are you? She had no business butting into my personal thing. She has no idea—"

"Suppose you tell me what the idea is. Like, explain why there's a young lady back there crying her eyes out in between giving you a stare down every few seconds like she wants to strangle you while she's jumping your bones?"

He narrows his eyes and clamps his mouth tight like he's a kid in the principal's office being asked to rat out a friend. He's so pathetic I temporarily forgive him for calling my brave puck bunny a loud-mouth.

"You may as well tell me or I'll find out from the young lady." Or one of her friends, like maybe the brave *loud-mouth* who'd stood up for her.

13

His eyes widen. "What do you care?" He stares down at his shoes and I wonder how old this kid is.

"Walk with me."

We step out the back door because it's my habit to leave through the back. Then I realize that maybe I don't need to do that here in Boston. We're in a back alley bordering a narrow side street with a few cars jammed in. I return my attention to the young man who needs to learn a lesson in respect.

"It's not going to get any easier holding it in—and don't tell me there's nothing because I know there's something." I've been around long enough to know a problem when I see one and I know there's something more than meets the eye going on here.

He sucks in a deep breath of city air, then talks.

"She said some things. She's trying to use me, to get money or something maybe." He doesn't look convinced, more like panicked.

Sadly, I don't have a chance to explore further because Finn is coming up fast behind us. I nod in his direction acknowledging him, then lower my voice.

"We'll talk more about this tomorrow. After practice. You're not off the hook."

He smirks. "Yes, Mom." He takes off for the street, headed who-knows-where, before I can do any more than scowl and give the finger to his back for the *Mom* comment as he trots away.

Finn joins me. "You walking? I don't mind giving you a ride."

Looking at the nearly empty street, I make a snap decision to take him up on the offer of a ride because it's more like an offer of friendship.

"Maybe I won't walk. It's been a long night. A long week if I'm honest."

He snorts and I follow him to his car parked at the curb near the mouth of the alley. I laugh because it's a decked-out, silver

14

Jeep Rubicon with so many bells and whistles it probably has *actual* bells and whistles.

We climb inside and I'm not surprised to find it's trashed as I pick up an empty pizza box off the passenger seat and toss it into the back with the rest of the randomly strewn stuff—including smelly hockey paraphernalia.

"I'll have to get me one of these heavy-duty beasts to ride."

He snorts. "What happened to your Ferrari?"

"When in Rome…"

He shakes his head. "You ready for the start of the season?" He presses the start button.

"Bring 'em on. We're playing Montreal for the season opener, right? Big rivals of the Brawlers. Let's make a statement."

Finn nods as he drives, the same easy smile that seems a permanent feature of his face. I like him more every minute I spend with him. Fun and non-judgmental—aside from the Ferrari crack—which I sold when I left L.A. Plus, he's serious as fuck when it comes to his hockey. My kind of guy.

"One more game, one more team event and then it's Go time," he says.

"Team event?" I search my mind, but I must have skipped over that detail on the two-week itinerary I was given when I'd arrived too late for pre-season training and in a rush to get back on the ice.

He looks at me as he pulls up at the curb of the Bostonian Hotel where I'm staying temporarily. I haven't had time to house-hunt and the places the team realtor chose were all sterile condos near the Garden and practice facility. My old self would have been perfectly happy with the sleek, high-end digs and their ultimate bachelor-pad style but I'm determined to walk the talk of getting away from the wild bachelor lifestyle and back to my New England roots, so I sent her to the suburbs to find something homier. Maybe with a yard for a dog.

"Yeah," Finn says. "It's the Brawlers' Pop-Up event for *More*

Than Words, an organization that helps kids in the system learn how to work."

"Pop-up event?"

"A pop-up store we're hosting at the Garden. The kids do all the work and we draw in the customers and sign merch. Last year, I got to know one of the kids and we've stayed in touch. He's into graphic design and I had him work with me on designing a collage poster for me to auction at the Brawlers' Foundation Gala."

"Sounds like a cool NPO."

"NPO?"

"Yeah, that's L.A. speak for non-profit organization. Sorry."

"No prob. Wait 'til you see this poster. I'm thinking I should buy it myself to put on the wall in my den."

"Is that right?" My smile is sinister.

"Don't even think about out-bidding me."

"Why not? That's what a charity auction is for, isn't it?"

He punches my arm. "Get out."

I laugh "Maybe I want a poster of you on my wall. Who says I'm not a fan?"

"I'll tell you what. If you buy it, you have to promise to give it away in a drawing to one of the *More Than Words* kids."

"Deal." I open my door. "See you in the a.m. Thanks for the ride."

"One more thing." He pauses and I wait for him to tell me his puppy died or something. "Don't encourage Jonas with his puck bunny activity. He can't afford trouble. He's not a superstar."

I hear the rest of his unspoken words—*like you are.*

CHAPTER 3

SARA

*H*ow is it possible that the next day is a normal, sunny, fall day with crowds of people going about their business on the way to lunch as if nothing ever happened? And I'm one of them, acting like my life didn't just change, acting as if I didn't actually meet my dream man and decide with scary-firm finality that he will be my big O-giver, the guy who will open up the heavenly flood gates to pussy ecstasy.

If only Mr. Potter, my poetry professor, could hear my thoughts now. He'd lose it in his pants and give me an A+ instead of that undernourished B-, the only grade below A- I ever got in college because I worked my tushy off for three and three-quarter years but had a lapse at the end of my senior year. It was, of course, guy related. But I'm over it.

Billie Mae snaps her fingers in front of my face and grabs my arm, steering me into the corner entrance of Pizzeria Regina in the north end of Boston, otherwise known as our favorite lunch spot and the reason I run the beach in Revere, rain or shine, every morning.

"What's with you?" She pushes open the door and I rush inside, heading straight for my favorite booth in the corner. It's worn and comfy in spite of the fact that it's made of wood and has no padding.

The waitress comes over without menus or a pad and pen like she does for other customers. "The usual?" She shifts her gaze between us, a semi-friendly smile on her face.

I'll have to up the tips again and see if I can get a full smile out of her. Friendly talk and asking about her family certainly didn't work and twenty percent tips haven't worked. But I am determined to make it happen—to get a big, fat grin out of that clearly overworked and unhappy woman.

"Yes, please. Thank you so much, Maria." Billie Mae smiles is extra bright.

Maria leaves, unimpressed.

I lean in and whisper, "We're going to have to tip big today. Maybe up it to thirty percent."

"If that doesn't do it, there's no hope." She shakes her head.

Whatever keeps Maria from utter happiness with her job doesn't slow her down at least, and she returns with two glasses filled with red wine that looks like grape juice because they don't believe in wine glasses here.

"Did you watch last night's game?" Billie Mae asks. "Sorry I couldn't watch with you, but I had to give Karl a try." She scrunches her nose.

"Another dud?"

She nods.

"Gotta give you credit for not giving up. How many swipe dates have you been on?"

"I prefer not to keep count any longer. It could be discouraging and I'm determined to stay positive." She arches a brow, but I don't question her.

It's a bone of contention between us because she's been trying to get me to try app-dating all summer and I can't bring myself to do it. Nothing says the opposite of romance like swiping through anonymous photos for a date.

But there's no question I need to do something before she runs off into the sunset with some guy and leaves me behind. Not physically, but every other way.

The waitress delivers our pepperoni pizza with extra olive oil, two red-and-white checkered paper plates, a pile of napkins, and no silverware, then leaves without a word or a glance. Once she'd told us to give it a minute because it was hot, but I guess that was a one-time warning we're trusted to remember at the risk of burning off the roof of our mouths. It's the extra olive oil that makes this a particularly dangerous risk.

As I'm about to delve in because I'm starving, having forgone breakfast in favor of running the beach so I can justify indulging in our regular Wednesday greasy pizza lunch, Billie Mae leans in to ask her question again.

"So, did you watch the game? What did you think of you-know-who?"

"You can say his name, Billie. It's not like he's Voldemort or something." I know she's caught my evasion when she doesn't scold me for calling her Billie instead of Billie Mae—a definite no-no because she doesn't want to be confused as some tomboy.

"Interesting. Who did you watch with?"

"A bunch of strangers at a bar." I figuring I have a fifty-fifty shot that she won't believe the truth because it's so unlike me. She knows very well that when I'm not at her place, I normally stay home and watch the games on TV, sometimes with my younger brother.

She freezes with her pizza halfway to her mouth and I'm kind of glad I saved her from certain mouth-sizzling pain. She slowly lowers her pizza back down as I meet her carefully controlled expression—because Billie Mae never loses her cool.

"You're not joking, are you?"

I shake my head, weighing the risk of hot pizza sizzling my mouth against the cruel judgment of my best friend accusing me of going off the deep end if I'm forced to tell her the whole story.

"My brother wasn't around and I didn't feel like watching alone."
It's half of the story.

"Soon we'll be eligible to request tickets and go to a game in person. In the meantime, maybe we could to go out to a bar together to watch the next game?" Her voice is too high and her smile too bright.

I'm digesting her words and ready to agree when she goes on, "I hear The Tea Party is a hopping place for Brawler's fans."

SAVED by pepperoni pizza from telling her the whole story, we leave the idea of going out to The Tea Party—where I'm pretty sure my new puck bunny friends would greet me like their own —up in the air. She's been wanting to get me out since she moved to Boston, and though I'm not cut out for flirting with strangers at a bar in spite of her recent training, I'm not strictly against going out for a good reason.

Either way, I'm chewing my lip (and dead pieces of skin off the roof of my mouth) on the way back to the Brawlers' corporate offices, when I should be telling her about my brief conversation with Quinn. Okay, conversation is a stretch of the meaning, but I don't know what else to call it. Exchange? Whatever, it's strange that I'm reluctant to share—or, maybe, I'm embarrassed because, let's face it, I didn't handle it gracefully.

In the building on our way to our cubicles, we're walking down the hallway and I catch a whiff of a dizzyingly sexy masculine scent and then I hear,

"Go, Wildcats!" From behind us.

It's him. It's Quinn James.

I stumble and look back, then, before I ask in total shock how he knew I went to UNH, I look down.

I'm wearing a UNH Wildcats hoodie over my sweater and skirt because it's cold in the office.

20

He smiles and gives me a thumbs-up.

I open my mouth but I can't speak. Thankfully, I *can* move, so I duck into the aisle of cubicles and dash for safety behind the half-walls. Shit. I can't let him recognize me as the girl from the bar. *Stop being paranoid.* If he finds out that girl works here, my fantasy will never come true. The Brawlers have a serious non-frat policy. It was the most important thing that was made clear to me and Billie Mae when we took this job—absolutely *no* hanky-panky with the players—or anyone at work, for that matter.

For me, it would be totally worth it. What's a stinky little admin job compared to a night of bliss with my man, Quinn James? Not a gosh darn thing. It's my dream job, but a possible night with Quinn is a bigger dream.

Unfortunately, it would be a disaster for him. Ipso facto, he would never do it or, more precisely, he'd never do *me*.

My cheeks heat up just thinking these deliciously naughty thoughts.

Is something wrong with me? Like, what makes me think it's a possibility—unless I continue to play Lola. I must be crazy.

But I don't have time to contemplate the cost of a good psychiatrist because Billie Mae tracks me down.

"What the hell?" Billie Mae whisper-shouts as she finds me hunkering in my cubicle. "Are you out of your mind?" She swings her chair over. "You can't act like a crazy fan-girl with players. You know the rules about behaving professionally?" I stare at her and she softens. "Are you okay? You look pale."

"I feel shredded." I grip her arms. "I don't think he recognized me. Did it look like he recognized me?"

"Recognize you?" She snorts. "How would he know you? Have you met him?"

"I turned my head for a second."

She shakes her head. "You took off fast."

Players and staff do not mix. Ever. They are off limits for

anything but a professional relationship. I can't let him know I'm the same person he saw at The Tea Party, the crazy big- mouthed girl he'd stood up for, saving me from even worse embarrassment by giving my objection legitimacy.

But I don't think he recognized me just now and I heave a sigh of relief. Cursing that I have no make-up on and my hair is a mess after being out in the wind, I realize I'm clutching Billie Mae's arm when she pries my hand off her.

"You sure you're all right? And why would he recognize you—"

"Where do you think he was going?" I whisper.

"I don't know. Not PR. He walked right past the office."

I scrunch my face. PR is where Billie Mae's boss lives. I'd say that's where she works, but it seems like she lives here because she's always here in the morning no matter how early I am and always still in the office when I leave since we started working here almost three months ago.

Billie Mae rolls her eyes and glides her chair back into her own cubicle to answer her phone. Her boss, Delaney—because no one ever calls her Ms. Delaney, or Miss Delaney or certainly not *Mrs.* Delaney because she doesn't seem to be married, or at least not to a person, having already married her job and I'm not sure what her first name is because no one ever uses it—is a piece of work. Billie Mae is afraid of her though she tries to pretends otherwise because she always gets a nervous look when she talks to her boss on the phone. Like she is right now. *Shoot.*

"Yes, ma'am. We'll be there in a minute." She gives me a look that says, *Save me.*

"Who's *we*?" I say, patting her back in comfort as she stands.

"You and me."

"*Me*?" A blast of nerves hits me. Beads of sweat pop onto my face. "Really?" We saw Quinn in the vicinity of Delaney's office.

My stomach plummets because I can't let Quinn see me at work. Ever. Face it, I'm not as much worried that he'll recognize

22

me as I am that I'll give myself away somehow. I'm no good at lying. Forget about acting.

I'm not ready to lose my job since I don't have another one unless I count my mom's promise of the waitressing job—which I don't because I didn't work hard to make summa cum laude so I could waitress. For now, I desperately need this job—and, even more, I desperately *want* this job—for the perk of hockey tickets and the cool factor on my resume. I have to stay at least a year.

Quinn can't see me, but I can see him, can't I? And Billie Mae and I can get free tickets to games starting next week when our probationary period is over—assuming I make it that far. Those tickets, alone, are worth half the fifty hours a week I work. Plus, my brothers will throw all my belongings into a dumpster and start a fire—exact quote—if I don't get them tickets to at least one game this season.

"Don't be so nervous. I need you to be the strong one," Billie Mae says, dousing the panic and forcing me to get a grip. "Whatever Delaney has to say, it's going to be abrupt and delivered with a scowl and we'll end up having to work late. It's only a matter of how late."

"Right." I make haste as I follow Billie Mae toward our VP of Public Relations, checking for a Quinn sighting or any whiff of his presence because I'd know his scent anywhere now—that earthy sexy spicy smell was intoxicating. It's probably some kind of crazy rare cologne that only billionaires can afford.

We get to Delaney's office and I beat Billie Mae to the punch, knocking on the door, because I'm here to take some of the pressure off her.

Delaney shouts for us to come in. Without asking us to sit. "There were some interesting videos posted all over social media last night."

I cough and my eyes start watering, but I swear I'm not crying.

Billie Mae's sliding me a look. She nudges me and I calm down, managing to meet Delaney's scowl.

Is it deeper than usual or am I being paranoid? Those videos could be anything, having absolutely nothing to do with me.

I straighten my shoulders.

The boss clears her throat. "The videos are about some puck bunny who made a scene at The Tea Party last night, accusing one of our players of being an asshole." She pauses and glares meaningfully—emphasis on the *mean*. "We need to counter this. Find out about the incident and get some positive clips on there."

Dizziness makes my brain fuzzy, and I would sink to the floor in despair, embarrassment and shame if I weren't frozen solid as stone as if Delaney had turned into the Medusa and nailed me.

"Right away," Billie Mae says.

"I just sent you the link to one of the posts on IG. I hope she's not talking about Quinn James. That's all we need."

"It's not him." The words shoot from my mouth like I'm a fire extinguisher shooting frozen air from my lungs to kill the nasty idea. "I mean, he's not that type of guy... Is he?"

I'm trying not to pee my pants with anxiety over the fear that they might discover the puck bunny in question is me. Fully thawed, I spout on.

"*No* one's that type of guy—until they are." Delaney scowls. She waves at her computer screen showing an IG clip starring little ol' me, the former wallflower who wishes she could jump back into the wallpaper right now.

"We'll find out all about what happened and make sure we post photos and clips of the offender kissing kittens, puppies, and babies." Billie Mae clutches my arm.

"Good. Sara you're on this detail too. We're officially moving you part time to PR as a general helper now that the season's starting. You okay with that?"

I nod, keeping my mouth clamped shut like it's the proverbial barn door and there are all kinds of horses now escaped and running around. Mostly in my stomach.

We leave Billie Mae's boss's office—though I suppose she's my boss, too, now—*crap*—and Billie Mae practically drags me back to our cubicles.

"What's wrong with you? It was *you* in that video, wasn't it? I took one look and I knew—"

"How?" I thought I looked pretty well disguised with black-rimmed glasses, the over-sized team jersey, baggy jeans, and ball cap. Not to mention the red dye job on my hair.

"Come on, Sara. I know you. I know that cap and those clothes and... *you.*"

As soon as we get back, she sits and rolls her chair over to my cubicle again as I plop into my chair.

She whispers, "What the hell were you doing there? What's going on?"

"Shhh." I glance around. Margaret, the lady who wears a wool Brawlers hat in the office all day. I think it's sometimes so she doesn't have to wash her hair. She smiles at me as she retrieves a stack of paper from the office's only scanner-printer.

Billie Mae resorts to torture to get me to talk, pinching my thigh hard enough that I'm worried she's going to penetrate my tights even though they're advertised as indestructible and I could write the testimonial—until now.

"Stop. There's nothing to tell. I stayed for a few drinks."

"A few drinks?" She stares at me, giving me the sinister arched brow treatment along with enough telepathic persuasion that I swear it would make anyone crack.

"Then some of the Brawlers came in. There were some puck bunnies. And Quinn James." I take a breath. "My puck bunny name is Lola and Lola is going for a night of bliss with Quinn."

CHAPTER 4

QUINN

*W*hile Ryan and Rafe have me corralled in the locker room, talking about our next opponent, an East Coast team I don't know as well as they do, for our last game of the pre-season, Jonas manages to slip out of the locker room. Shit. I won't let him get away after practice.

"Pappadue, their goalie, is hot but has a weakness in the upper left corner of the net."

"Who doesn't?" I say. Ryan snorts and Rafe glares, but annoyance forces my gaze to the door and I pick up my stick. "Let's get on with it. I'll test Finn's upper left corner and see how he does." I wink because I'm not out of that habit. There are a lot of L.A. habits I need to lose.

"Cocky s.o.b. aren't you?" Ryan doesn't move.

"I don't mean to be."

"Liar."

I laugh.

"You mean you have no reason to be," Rafe says.

He's right. In actuality, they both have as many stats to be cocky about as I do, and more wins. The only difference is that my rep comes with more glitz and my face happens to be out there in the media as if I'm the star of the league, though I'm more like the poster boy. My visibility is hard to understate since my cameo appearance in last year's Academy-Award-winning action flick—*and* the fling I had with a certain woman I refuse to allow any headspace.

"Guess I'm not used to playing with a couple of superstars of your caliber," I say.

"Not used to winning The Cup either," Rafe says. He's won The Cup on two teams and I feel like saluting to the icon.

"Touché. That's the reason I came here." Only a half-lie. But the last thing I want to talk about is how I've allowed my priorities to drift from important things like real people and relationships. I needed to leave L.A. and everything about it behind me.

"I thought it was to escape the clutches of too many—"

"Losses." I cut Ryan off because I have a premonition he's going to say *too many puck bunnies* and I don't want to hear it. Mostly because it's more truth than my half-lie.

I shove off the wall where I'm leaning and head for the door.

Ryan snorts and they follow.

The locker room empties out, then we jump onto the ice, shredding the good work of the Zamboni within two minutes. I work up a sweat as I skate circles, feeling the breeze ruffle the hair around my neck as I gaze up into the rafters.

The banners wave back, reminding me where my focus should be and that I need to turn the ambition of my half-lie—to win The Cup—into a reality.

The other half of the truth—that I need to find someone to settle down with, a woman who's authentic and honest and into me for *me*. After the season. Maybe next year. Or maybe by Christmas so I don't have to spend the holiday alone if my mom's warning is for real.

Okay, I'm a little reluctant about the settling down part, but I made a promise to Mom, and, besides, it's inevitable, right? I get a chill and not the good kind, but I shake it off as I skate around behind the net, circling Finn who's scraping up the crease with serious intent.

"Get ready to be bombarded. I'm coming for your upper left corner." It's only polite to give fair warning. Plus, I need the test of a prepared goalie.

"You and what army?"

I laugh.

Then the challenge begins and practice is a bitching whirlwind of skating, shooting, and yelling with sticks flying and more intensity than half my real games back in L.A. When Coach blows the whistle and shouts that it's break time, I try to swallow a swear because of course he's going to make us come back out here.

"What the fuck?" I mutter to no one in particular as I exit through the gate while Ryan and Rafe stand on each side like sentinels. Apparently, it's the tradition of these co-captains.

"The fuck is that we get a break and then do a cool down skate and a quick on-ice meeting," Ryan says.

I'm too beat to do anything but nod.

"Good job out there. You kept up."

Rafe sounds like he's surprised and I find I'm not too tired to give him the finger—which loses some of its bite with the glove on, but he gets the message and laughs.

WHEN THE PRACTICE ends for real and we get off the ice for a second time, I follow Finn. I let him go through the gate first because he's loaded down with goalie gear and could shove me aside if he has a mind to. I step onto the rubber like I'm a sailor who was lost at sea and has finally found land.

Finn stops and elbows me.

"Dude, Delaney's eying you. What the hell did you do?"

"Some viral video from last night," I say. She'd sent me a text with said video, asking for an explanation, but I haven't answered. Which has me doubly motivated to talk to Jonas —*before* I talk to her. I don't want to throw him under the bus, but I don't want to take the blame and let him get away with his behavior either.

"Last night?" It takes a beat and then it dawns on him. "You mean at The Tea Party when that crazy chick—"

"The young lady who stood up for the puck bunny," I correct him because it doesn't seem right to call her crazy. Bold maybe, but not crazy. Better yet, I'd call her brave, but I'm not going to mention that to Finn because that would make *me* the crazy one.

"Sure," he says. "She was a trip. So why does Delaney need to see you about that and in person, no less?"

We're standing at the gate and I glance in Delaney's direction to see her with folded arms waiting near the locker room door so there's no way to avoid her.

"Because I stood up for the young lady in question, which got me the starring role in the clip. And there were a few comments accompanying the video post that were more than suggestive. Now Delaney thinks I need to somehow distance myself because she doesn't want my so-called L.A. image following me here to Boston." I have limited control over that but I agree with her and she's a pro, so I'll go along with whatever she says.

"Your L.A. image, huh?" Finn grins wide and slaps me on the back. "Good luck with that. You know the saying; you can take the player out of L.A. but you—"

I give him the finger and walk away to him cackling behind me. When I reach the locker room, I step aside to join Delaney, not even pretending I don't know she's here to see me. Other guys give me looks as they file into the locker room.

"Sorry in advance for the sweat," I say as I take my helmet off and rivulets drip down my temples.

She waves a hand and deepens her scowl as if I'm talking

about a meaningless spec in the universe of problems. She's probably right.

"We've got a solution to your problem," she says.

"Is that right?" I can't keep the skepticism from my voice but she ignores it.

"Be in my office in twenty minutes—showered and dressed."

She looks me up and down and I know she's not undressing me with her eyes, thinking I'm a specimen. No, I'm pretty sure she's thinking I stink and look slimy and could probably use more than twenty minutes to get presentable. Not that she'll give it to me.

Jonas walks by me with a smirk as Delaney walks away and I follow him into the locker room right to the bench where he sits.

I lean in. "I won't have time today, but we *will* be having another talk. You're not off the hook."

He scoffs and gives me an eye-roll, but I can see it's for show. His heart isn't in it. Shit.

What's this kid's problem?

Then I get to my own locker and start undressing because I have no time to lose. Been there and done that and now I have my own problems to deal with.

DELANEY'S WAITING, sitting on the edge of her desk with her arms folded, and eying the clock as if she's the vice principle in charge of detention and I'm a school kid. But the idea only makes me smile because I was a regular in detention back in the day and those are fond memories. Mostly. Kid troubles are nothing like the kind of trouble a grown man can get into. Especially the girl kind. And especially in L.A.

"What are you doing Saturday? Cancel your plans," she says before I can answer. "We have a charity event scheduled at ten a.m. sharp." She reminds me of a drill sergeant, or what I imagine a drill sergeant would act like based on movies I've seen.

"Yes… *ma'am*." I almost stumble and say *sir*.

She gives me another squinty eye like she knows. "You have a reputation, glitter-boy, and it's the kind that plays all well and good in Hollywood, but doesn't fit well around here. No more puck bunny incidents."

I'm ready for her to go on with her lecture about my evil reputation—and honestly, I get it, though she doesn't seem to realize she's preaching to the choir—when I'm saved by a knock on the door.

I look up and there she is, Little Miss UNH—minus the hoodie, but an eyeful of the kind of unpretentious pretty you don't find in L.A. The kind of girl that reminds me of back home. The kind of girl my mom would love to meet.

Nope. Not going there. Mom can wait until *after* the season. Hockey first. Besides, as the girl walks in with her friend, I can see how young she is.

And there's something else about her, something familiar…

"Have we met before?"

CHAPTER 5

SARA

*C*rap.

I hold my breath, while Delaney introduces us, pretending he didn't just ask me that question, hoping to holy heaven that he doesn't really recognize me from the other night. If he does, so far, he's not saying.

"This is Sara—" She looks at me for my last name.

"Bellagamba," I spurt. Then in a gush of crazy-mouth, I elaborate, "It means beautiful leg. Of course, I have *two* legs so it should be Bellagamba*s*—plural—but apparently someone in my family tree must have been walking around on one leg, so...." I run out of steam abruptly and feel all the stares on me in the beat of silence. Uh oh, there's a bad déjà vu moment coming on... Until Quinn's dimple shows up as he gives up suppressing his smile,.

"But your ancestor's one leg must have been a beauty. I can see the family resemblance."

His dimple gets deeper and his blue eyes flash like a neon invitation to my heart which almost pounds out of my chest while I heat up everywhere. I don't care that I'm blushing until Delaney clears her throat in a way that intimidates me more than if she shouted at me to get a grip—which I finally do. I dart my gaze away from Quinn in an attempt to save myself further embarrassment since I'm supposed to be a professional, not a puck bunny.

But who knew the role of puck bunny would be so much easier, so natural for me to play?

"Enough of that," Delaney says. "There will be no admiring of legs around here." She stares down Quinn, but he doesn't look the least bit intimidated as he aims his dimple at the old ball-buster.

"I'm sorry, Ms. Delaney. I didn't mean anything by it. Only trying to be polite."

I cringe at his use of *Ms.* and I'm afraid to see her reaction, even more afraid I'll leap to his defense if she scolds him.

But all she does is squint her eyes. "Call me Delaney. Didn't I tell you that? Everyone calls me Delaney."

That's not all they call her. Ball-buster is more common—on polite days.

When my glance catches Quinn's, I notice he has that suppressed smirk look again and I'd bet my non-existent bank account that he's thinking the same thing.

"You and Billie Mae are going to assist Quinn at the *More Than Words* pop-up event on Saturday. Ms. Bellagamba, you'll be handing out team merch to the kids at Quinn's signing table. We're expecting he'll draw a larger than usual crowd."

"That sounds wonderful," I say, believing every word.

"Yes." She clears her throat. "Also, there will be press around and we want to make him look good. To avoid any more puck bunny incidents, you two need to keep any aggressive young ladies under control." Delaney gives him a knowing nod and my puzzle meter skyrockets. "Unless you have a steady girlfriend who can help out?"

He responds with a shake of his head like he regrets it. "No one special," he says, then slides a look at me.

Dizziness threatens, but I warn myself there's nothing to the look. No dimples. Only curiosity. Mild. Very mild.

Delaney jams her hands ono her hips. "Don't disappoint me. We need to get some good social media out of this." She glares at Quinn who appears totally unaffected. "Coach told management in no uncertain terms that he didn't want you and your glam reputation overshadowing the team moral. To be precise, he doesn't want some glittery puck boy from L.A. coming in here and ruining the locker room—his words, not mine." She smiles like she wishes they were her words.

"No worries, Delaney," Quinn says. "I'm 'hockey and family' only this season. I came here to get back to my roots and win The Cup."

She nods, but I only see her from my peripheral vision because I'm too busy staring at the object of my every desire. Lucky for me, my tongue is tied or I'd be saying something like, *Is it hot in here, or is it me?*

"Dismissed," Delaney says as if she's commanding a squadron.

Quinn gestures for us to go through the door first.

Billie Mae grabs my arm and drags me to the right, back to the Brawlers' corporate office cubicle-ville, the lowliest space in the sparkling empire, almost like a dungeon compared to the other offices and facilities.

"See you ladies Saturday." Quinn turns in the opposite direction, toward the most rarified place in the empire—the practice facility and rink.

I watch Quinn go. Of course he's not looking back at me. It couldn't have been interest I'd seen in that eye-sparkle. It was probably the reflection of all the sparkle coming off my eyes rebounding back at me. If it's possible, my insides go even more gooey as if I've reverted to my twelve-year-old fan-girl self. I need to snap out of this.

Back in my cubicle when some of the sparkle has worn off, I acknowledge that this assignment is the worst possible thing that could happen. Not because I could lose my job if my puck bunny status is found out, but because it's doubly likely that he'll recognize me as the puck bunny who plans to seduce him. Doubly hard for me to seduce him since he's pretty much said he's not interested in puck bunnies, or anyone for that matter—"Hockey and family only this season."

Is it possible for me to fall for him just based on one meeting? No—I'm certain that's my parched pussy talking and needing a drink of that tall glass of cool refreshing heaven that is Quinn James. The ultimate thirst quencher personified if I ever saw one.

"What is wrong with you? Have you lost your marbles? You looked more like a puck bunny than a polished professional back there."

"That's because I am," I admit. "Do you think he recognized me?"

"As what? A cartoon fan-girl?"

I nudge her arm. "For real, Billie Mae, this is important. I'm going for the brass ring here. I have an honest-to-goodness goal to make this mind-numbing pauper-making job worthwhile—without getting caught. Did it look like he recognized that I was the puck bunny in the IG video?"

"I don't think so. He would have said something, right?"

"Not if he wanted to be polite—and that man is very polite."

She snorts. "Yeah—*beautiful leg*, really? What was that? You're lucky he bailed you out of that awkward word-vomit."

I roll my eyes. "I can't help it if my name is Bellagamba." I prefer to move on from the whole one-legged relative conversation and hang onto the premise that he did not recognize me. Where that leaves me, I'm not sure since he's not going to be easy to wrangle now that he's avoiding puck bunnies.

Then my bestie does her mind-reading routine. "You don't need to worry about the whole puck bunny thing anymore," Billie Mae says, "now that we'll be seeing him professionally."

"One event is not *seeing him*. Besides, the key word is *profes-

sional. Which means no flirting, let alone *big-O, virginity-busting hook-up.* You heard Delaney."

It's her turn to roll her eyes. "That was all talk. She'd have to catch you doing it for it to be an issue—"

"Don't even think those words." I shudder.

Going to an event with him is the most fantastic assignment ever—and the worst at the same time because I can't be with him officially or I'll lose my job—which isn't really that bad. But the worst consequence is that it could hurt his career. So that's not going to happen.

The only way I can possibly achieve my goal is in my puck bunny persona. No one would blink an eye.

The only problem is he's not interested—not even in puck bunnies.

CHAPTER 6

QUINN

*W*alking back to the parking garage, I'm pissed at Jonas and myself because I didn't bother mentioning to Delaney that Jonas was the source of the puck bunny problem. I'm not sure I'm doing him any favors *not* telling her because he needs to be held accountable for being an asshole to the puck bunny—or, rather, Mindy. But in a fit of irony, I got myself involved in his reform while Delaney—and my mom—are focused on reforming me. Do I really need it? Maybe.

Puck bunnies are people too...

The words of my bold puck bunny run through my head. Without realizing it, I'd been looking forward to seeing her again.

Which only proves that Delaney is right because I can't afford to get involved with a puck bunny—no matter how innocent—if I want to stay out of the limelight and have a nice, quiet, low-key life in New England. I need a steady girl I can bring home to Mom to satisfy her *second* condition for the Christmas family reunion—that I need to heal my fractured bond with my brother.

As I open the door of my newly delivered Land Rover, a picture of Ms. Bellagamba of the lovely legs pops into my head. Meeting Bellagamba was... interesting. More than the fact that she's gorgeous in an understated way and obviously a fan because that sums up every puck bunny I ever met—except that she was... understated. Yeah, maybe that's it. She seems so... innocent?

And familiar. That niggling at the back of my mind kicks in as if I've met her before. Maybe she's from back home. If she went to UNH, she's probably from New Hampshire so maybe I know her family or met her once somewhere a while back.

All I know is that there's something familiar about her and that's exciting as hell if I'm honest.

And a problem.

I nod to myself because I'm not okay with trouble. Recent issues in L.A. cured me of that. But this is nothing like that. *That* was all about a very different kind of woman.

Okay. We're on.

I allow my curiosity to find out who Sara Bellagamba is and how I might know her—or at least have met her before—to take control. But I'll have to be careful that my curiosity isn't misinterpreted as anything more. Especially not by her.

Pulling out of my parking space, I dial up my new bud Finn because I sense a fellow mischief-lover in him.

He answers on the second ring. "Miss me already?"

"How'd you guess? Seriously, I have a question. No judgment."

"You got it. Let it fly."

"What do you know about Sara Bellagamba?"

"Who? She some super model I never heard of? An Italian starlet?"

I chuckle as I pull out of the garage and head for the tunnel to go meet the team's realtor to see a place north of Boston.

"She's a staffer for the Brawlers. Works for Delaney."

He blows out a long whistle. "I don't have a clue who she is, but if she works for Delaney, she's in the *hands-off* zone with a barbed-wire electric fence wrapped around her. And spotlights with dogs and armed guards with orders to shoot—"

"All right, I get it. Maybe it's not like that." I'm lying my ass off, but even with all the caution lights flashing, I'm curious about her and there's no harm in being curious.

"Oh yeah? What's it like exactly?"

I can hear his smirk. the glee in his voice makes me grin. "Curiosity—and don't say it."

"What? About curiosity killing the cat? I wasn't going to say a thing. No judgment. Of course, that doesn't make you any less dead—"

"You can't see it, but I'm giving you the finger right now."

He laughs. "Seriously, what do you want to know?"

I blow out a breath because I don't exactly know the answer to that.

"The usual. Who is she, where does she live, her family. I get the sense that I know her from somewhere, but I don't want to ask her because I don't want her to get the wrong impression like I'm hitting on her if I don't know her from somewhere."

"You sure you're not looking to date her?"

"Positive. But I do have to work with her at the *More Than Words* event on Saturday and maybe I want to make sure we get along."

"So that's why you need me to make the inquiries?"

I chuckle. "You got me." I pause. "I, uh, may have flirted unintentionally when Delaney introduced us. And Delaney may have called me on it."

"Jesus. You're a piece of work. Everyone knows flirting in the work-place is a no-no. Or does that rule not apply in La-La Land?"

Driving through the tunnel, I have to face up to the fact that the transition from Hollywood glam bachelor to down-to-earth quiet life is going to be tougher than I thought.

"It applies. I guess I'm used to living up to the persona I had back there, but I promise you I'm over it. Maybe I just need more practice." More focus on hockey.

There's a pause on his end as I emerge and head up route 1A to Revere, following the Waze app directions on my dashboard.

"Just so you know," Finn says, "there's no way I'd bother if I didn't know a lady in the ticket office—Margaret. She helped me out a couple of times and we clicked."

"Of course you did." I breathe in the sea air as I follow Revere Beach Boulevard around the curve to the oceanfront lined with luxury high-rises that were definitely not there when I'd been a kid coming here to swim.

"Turns out Margaret loves to share gossip, so it should be easy enough to find out a few things about your... Ms. Bellagamba, was it?"

"Yeah."

"Interesting name."

"You don't know the half of it."

"Do I want to know?"

"Not from me. I'm no gossip-spreader." I pull into the circular drive of one of the tall, shiny buildings and frown. "I want to know if there's some kind of connection where I remember her from. And to mend fences so she doesn't think I'm flirting. Listen, I gotta go. I'm meeting the realtor. Keep me posted."

"Sure. You keep me posted on where you end up living. Don't wander too far from the rink."

"I don't plan to. Later, man."

The realtor, a middle-aged woman with bleached blonde hair, waves her hand and runs toward me in heels and a black-checked tunic-like outfit. She beams a wide smile and when I meet her half-way, she gives me a hug. I instantly like her. Over the years in L.A., out of necessity, I developed a keen ability to size people up which is not a lot different than sizing up an opponent on the ice.

"Oh my God, I'm so thrilled to meet you. You're even more handsome in real life. I'm sorry I'm not behaving very professionally. I'm Edith Hanly, by the way. I'm so happy to meet you." She backs up a step and puts out a hand.

I shake it while she clears her throat, though her smile doesn't diminish. It's one of those well-used smiles with the creases dug in at the sides of her mouth and lines fanning from the corners of her eyes.

She's a woman of a certain age comfortable in her own skin. She reminds me of my aunt, Mary.

"Great to meet you too, Edith—you don't mind if I call you Edith?"

"I'd be sad if you didn't." She takes my arm and escorts me to the building. "We'll be looking at the penthouse. It has unparalleled ocean views and a roof-top patio. I know you wanted something laid-back, but this just came on the market and was too special not to show you. Besides, I think there's something about the ocean that relaxes the soul."

Breaking away from her, I open the door.

"Don't worry, Mr. James," she whispers. "The people here won't bother you. It's very low-key."

"Call me Quinn. Good to know." But I need some convincing. I want to go back to living a normal non-celebrity life, unlike how it was in L.A. The place is polished and the security in the lobby is impressive as Edith checks us in. She uses a key and we take the elevator up to the top.

"Your own private entrance," she says rushing off the elevator into a small lobby with one door straight ahead. It's lined with a tasteful vase-topped table and two chairs—the stuffy kind. I'm not sure this place is my style, but, to be polite, I'll take a look before I say anything.

"You were right about the ocean view, Edith." We walk straight for the wall of windows in the high-ceilinged great room and I take a long look.

She beckons me to the balcony and we step outside. The fresh shot of ocean air does its magic.

But when we go back inside and look around, the sleek modern architecture and all the bells and whistles in the very sterile kitchen are exactly as I expected. We could be in Malibu if the temperature outside was fifteen degrees warmer.

"The place is stunning—front-cover-of-Architectural-Digest-worthy," I admit, wanting to let her down gently.

"It would be terrific for entertaining," she says.

"Exactly. Unfortunately, that's exactly the kind of lifestyle I'm trying to avoid. I'm looking for the opposite—something more homey, more classic New England." Her face falls, but I swoop in for the rescue. "How about if we look at a house? Nothing too big, but updated and comfortable."

She nods. "I got you. I hope you don't hold it against me that I showed you this place. It was my duty as a realtor to make sure—"

I put up my hands. "No problem."

She escorts me out and we drive in her old-fashioned and extremely comfortable Caddy down the boulevard along the mostly-empty beach except for some dog-walkers. I used to have a dog. A very long time ago. Simpler times when I knew what was important.

We drive to an area called Point-of-Pines and pull into the driveway of a cottage-style ranch with impeccable landscaping like it'd been done by a sculptor rather than a gardener.

"Pretty, isn't it? But don't let the polished perfection fool you. The inside is just what you ordered—comfortable."

She's right. Off the foyer we walk into large warm rooms with tray ceilings and arched openings that flow from the fireplaced living room to the dining room with tall windows, and gleaming hard-wood floors throughout. The kitchen is a knock-out with an enormous double oven that looks like it ought to come with a couple of chefs to run it. I whistle. "What the hell is that?"

"Good eye. That, my young man, is a Bertazzoni Heritage series double oven."

"I vow to learn to use it if I buy the place. Mom would love it." Dad would have drooled over it.

Fuck. Don't go there.

"Better yet, you could invite a young lady over who can cook for you." Edith gives me a sly, smile.

I laugh. "Touché, Edith." Hmmm, does Ms. Bellagamba cook? Or maybe my brave puck bunny—whose name I need to find out so I don't have to keep thinking of her as a *puck bunny*. It doesn't seem right, especially given the circumstances of our almost-meeting.

WTF am I thinking? I meet exactly two interesting women and I'm already imagining having them over to cook for me?

"Quinn? What do you think?"

I've been staring at the stove a little too long and I turn to back to Edith. "I'm thinking that, either way, I can't lose with this masterpiece in my kitchen."

"You're interested in buying the place? You didn't even see out back yet. It's the best part."

I'm watching the waves roll up onto the sand from the window over the kitchen sink which is all I need to see. "Consider the place bought. I'll count on you to get me the best deal possible."

Edith transforms instantly into a canny business woman as if she were wearing a pin-striped suit and tie, and is smart enough not to delay an official offer by dragging me outside. She nods firmly.

Once the papers are drawn up at the kitchen island, I do take a walk out back. There's a pergola-covered patio area with a pizza oven and a small inground pool, then a lawn and then the beach. My nephews would love this place. The idea pinches my heart and a sense of urgency to have them over squeezes my chest.

I learned the hard way that life is short and you need to seize the day and all those clichés that are all too real when life punches you in the gut with an unexpectedly quick death of a loved one.

My dad deserved more from me. I barely saw him a dozen times in the past ten years because I was so busy gallivanting on the off season. He was a good man.

Edith is quiet and leaving me to my thoughts which are killing me. The rumble of the waves lessen the stabbing pain through my shoulder blades as I listen. It's high tide so there's a strip of pebbled sand that we walk along the hundred feet of beach frontage and I breathe in the salty air.

"I think you're right, Edith. The sea air is good for the soul."

CHAPTER 7

SARA

*N*ext day at the office, I wear my new outfit—very worker-bee, a gray-and-black plaid button-down dress with a belt, tights, and high boots. No bellagambas showing at all because it's important to keep my work persona professional. Especially now. Can't be too careful about not letting Quinn recognize me.

Maybe I should get some black-rim glasses—with plain glass —to emphasize the look.

With coffee in hand, I tap away at my computer, searching out all the latest social media posts on the Brawlers and especially Quinn James, who's now my official duty rather than the pin-up boy of my girlhood dreams.

"You're early." Billie Mae slides into her cubicle with her coffee and an overstuffed bag filled with the kind of goodies my hips would love a little too much. "The new outfit looks good. I'm glad you bought it."

"I promise I'll pay you back as soon as I get my next paycheck." I bite the inside of my cheek because that means my household contribution is going to be a little light this week.

Poor Mom. Looking like a young professional is no cheap matter. Maybe I could return the dress...

Billie Mae waves a hand and takes a bite out of her pastry, then holds it out in a gesture meant to share.

I shake my head ferociously and cross my fingers as if I'm warding off the devil or a vampire or something evil—like excessive calories glomming onto my body that was already rounded to the maximum marginally acceptable roundness.

"Your loss." She gives me a cheeky smile and I give her an eye roll and get back to the endless stream of IG posts using the Brawlers' hashtag. Quinn is featured in about half of them. I, using the @BostonBrawlersHockey account officially, like all the good ones and repost or comment on the most flattering ones. Then I'll need to get busy combing through the latest PR office clips to post something. Honestly, we're a little thin in relevant material.

That's one of the assignments we have is to come up with original material, take some vids at practice and eventually maybe the games if we're lucky. My belly ripples and I heat up at the prospect of being around Quinn on a regular basis. But in spite of his spectacular dark wavy hair, mesmerizing blue eyes and that deep dimple, it's not his looks that have me overheating.

There's something regular-Joe about him that I hadn't expected, something unpretentious and endearing, even gracious about his ease with relating to people—and by people, I mean me. I'm a tough test case and he cracked me in no time, rescuing me from my innate awkwardness on the only three occasions I encountered him.

She has a point. With those words said in my defense, It didn't take him any time or effort at all to lift me from nut case to hero —at least in my mind. How else could I react to a man like that besides falling madly and wanting more? It's not like men like him grow on trees—believe me, I've been searching all the trees as well as the forest of college guys at UNH but they were without another Quinn James.

An incoming email pops up on my screen, reminding me that I have a job. Lowly, dull, and pedestrian as it is, for now, I need it. The worst thing about this job used to be the low pay. Now the worst thing about it is that I'm taunted by the possibility of Quinn James.

My short-lived dream of becoming a puck bunny to seduce Quinn is all but up in smoke. My neurotic insecurities rise up and mock me. Even if I get up the nerve to go back to The Tea Party and he just happens to be there, he's going to reject me. He made a point that he wasn't interested in puck bunnies. That guarantees a big fat rejection.

But at least today I look professional, maybe someone he would consider, in case I run into— Crap. I'm still pathetic. It's two days until my hopefully-fateful, first, official, in-the-flesh assignment with Quinn. Fateful, because Billie Mae has convinced me that, if I'm discreet, Delaney will never find out about a quiet one-nighter. I mean, after all, it's not like I'm aiming to *marry* Quinn, I just want one night. One blissful, explosive, world-changing night. Even I'm not unlucky enough to get caught for one night. Then I'll be happy and I can quit this job and get a real job and buy season tickets to satisfy my fan-girl needs.

The only reason I took this job was to get the tickets and to have a cool job on my resume, because it sure as crap wasn't for the paycheck. If I had to pay for tickets, I'd have to come to work naked because I'd have no clothes. I can barely pay the dry-cleaning bill and fare for the T to get into work, as well as contribute a little something to our household because food and electricity aren't free, as Mom would say. She stops short of charging me rent because that's against the rules in any upstanding Italian family. But I put extra money in her cookie jar anyway.

Just before lunch, when I'm ready to bounce from my seat to escape cubicle-ville, my phone rings. Thankfully, it's not my work phone. Grabbing my unfashionably over-sized bag, I reach in to find my buzzing phone as Billie Mae motions for me to follow her out.

Margaret nods at us from her perch on a step stool as she rummages through an old metal filing cabinet as we walk by her and I wait to answer the phone when I'm past her earshot. Rushing ahead of Billie Mae, I push through the exit door to the stairwell and answer the phone on the fourth buzz.

"Hello?" I'm breathless as I rush down the stairs with Billie Mae who skips effortlessly ahead of me.

"Lol? You okay?"

I'd know that voice anywhere. "Sheila?" The head puck bunny is calling me? I stop where I am on the stairs in between landings, half a flight to the exit. "Sure, I'm good. I was on my way—never mind. How can I help you?"

She laughs. "Leave it to you to ask about helping me. You're a regular good Samaritan, aren't you?"

I laugh one of those nervous-fill-in-the-gap laughs because I have no idea what to say in response. Plus, it's probably a rhetorical question because she doesn't wait for an answer.

"As a matter of fact, you can do something for me, or actually, for Mindy. Can you come to the game Friday with us? We have a block of tickets and there's an extra one."

It's my turn to laugh. "I'd love to, but it sounds like you're doing *me* the favor."

"Oh, don't worry, there's a catch."

She waits and so do I, my heart beating fast as I remember Delaney and her thoughts on puck bunnies.

"We need your help," Sheila says, "because Mindy is real upset and it turns out she may be pregs."

I'm holding onto the railing with one hand or I'd have stumbled to the next landing. "Pregs? You mean *pregnant?*" I whisper

48

the words because they're the kind of words that speak of secrets and privacy.

"That's right. The little fool won't tell the asshole Bergman because he made it clear he wasn't interested in a relationship and she's no blackmailer."

I shake my head, still trying to digest the scenario, in particular the part where I might be of help. "No, of course not. But—"

"I need your help to fix things between these two. I know he has feelings for her. I've seen it a hundred times—"

"A hundred?" I ask. Did I mention I have a problem with being too literal sometimes?

"You know what I mean. Will you help?"

I bite my lip because every instinct in me is standing up and shouting *Yes! Yes! Of course I'll help*! I've always wanted to be the do-gooder heroine in a romance story, but I don't need Delaney finding out about my puck bunny alter ego.

Looking at my reflection in the glass exit door, I make my decision. I choose to believe in the power of romance and happy-ever-afters–and the power of a good disguise.

Even if it's not *my* HEA.

"Okay, I'll help. But… I'm not sure what I can do—"

"No worries; I have a plan."

That's exactly the moment I start worrying like a world-class Olympic champion worrier, like the gold medalist worrier who's about to break all the worrying records in the universe.

I might have drawn blood just now when I bit my lip.

Outside, Billie Mae tracks back, knocking on the glass door. She's mouthing, *We only have an hour for lunch.*

I nod and try to focus on Sheila while licking the blood from my lip.

"What's… the… plan?" I ask like I'm in a cartoon waiting for the anvil to drop on my head.

"You'll come with us to the game tomorrow night and, afterward, we'll go out and you can convince Jonas Bergman of the error of his ways—that Mindy is a good, decent girl and has real feelings for him."

"Me?" I squeak like a Minnie Mouse impersonator. I better watch it or my voice is going to stay like Minnie's older sister permanently. "I—of course I'll help." My underdog empathy strikes as if I've slugged down a gallon of margaritas. I feel a lot like Popeye after he eats his can of spinach. What does it say about me that my hero-inducing spinach is tequila-laced margaritas? Never mind. The puck bunny avenger is back.

"Great. Meet us at The Tea Party before the game for a costume check."

WTF? "Did you say *costume check?*"

"Yeah. Nothing personal, but you were dressed a little…"

"Never mind. I get it. Not exactly sexy." I stave off the blush even though we're on the phone and she can't see it because I have a feeling I'll need the practice. "Don't worry. I'll be prepared. Dressed for success."

"You sure?"

"Never mind me. How do we know Jonas will be at The Tea Party after the game?" My practical business-like-self kicks in, the *me* I'm comfortable with.

Billie Mae throws her hands in the air then brings them down to check her watch while tapping her foot like a fellow cartoon character.

"He texted Mindy—out of the blue—and said he'd be there if she wanted to talk. I think he might have an inkling what it's all about and that's why he blew her off last time. Thankfully, for whatever reason, he's manning up."

"Then what do you need me there for?"

"To keep him from fleeing as soon as she opens her mouth. You're as good as a guilty conscience personified."

I swallow her words, not sure if they taste sweet or sour, but, either way, I own them. I butted in to call Jonas out and now I need to finish the job. This must be how avengers feel.

"I'll be there at five-thirty for the costume check. Then I'll see you at the game."

🍩

ONCE I FLY out the door to the street, feeling like Superman busting out of the phone booth, I explain everything to Billie Mae as we high-step it to The King and I, my favorite Thai food place in Boston. She forgives me about the delay for the pure intrigue value of the phone call.

Two days later, Billie Mae helps me with the hair dye, but I dress myself which increases her already pouty mood because I banned her from going to The Tea Party.

All clothed, I emerge from her bathroom and stand in front of her, only mildly self-conscious.

"What do you think?" I say in a low, scratchy voice. I decided my voice needs a disguise too.

She circles her finger.

Spinning around in a short black skirt with textured tights—I couldn't bring myself to buy the fishnets—with a fitted Brawlers' jersey—Quinn's number 17—I get a little dizzy and stop to wait for the verdict from my fashionista bestie. Who also happens to be the owner of a championship poker face.

"Where did you get that jersey? Didn't they have any smaller sizes?"

"I guess the pro shop needed to save them for the charity event tomorrow."

I do another circle in front of the mirror. "But, seriously, do you think he'll recognize me?"

"I don't think so. You don't look like yourself at all with all that make up and red hair. Plus the super bra really pops your boobs. You should wear it all the time."

I hunch my shoulders, self-conscious about my size.

"He'll never know you're Sara. I've forgotten already. You're Lola to me."

"That's what I needed to hear."

"God, you're good at that husky voice. You sure you can keep it up for the whole night?"

"No choice."

"You sure it's necessary?"

"*Ye-aah.* He'll know it's me otherwise because he heard me at the meeting with Delaney. But he never really heard Lola-the-puck-bunny talk—except that crazy speech I made when I was half drunk and didn't sound like myself anyway since I was loud and crazy on tequila."

"Promise to take videos—with the volume up. I got to hear all the drama."

I snort. "Now who's crazy? *No* videos. You heard Delaney; we're supposed to be avoiding puck bunny videos of Quinn. Plus, I want to stay anonymous and plan to hide my face from every person in the place except our little group."

"Don't get paranoid."

"You weren't there. You didn't see how fast any little stir can bring up those cell phones, even in a bar where the crowd is notorious for letting the team be."

She shakes her head. "That's right, I didn't see it. But I'd sure like to. Are you sure I can't come and sit in the corner? I promise—"

"Absolutely not. I couldn't play the part with you watching. And don't even *think* of disguising yourself because I'll see right through it."

She laughs. "I told you, stop being so paranoid. You're the only nut who goes out in disguise around here. I'm me, myself, and I, the one-and-only."

It's true. Billie Mae is singularly self-possessed and sure of who she is. It's what drew me to her. And what I envy most about her. At the advanced age of twenty-one, I'm still searching and confused, still getting my footing, still coming out to the world and myself, not quite yet fully formed and comfortable in my skin. Whoever's skin that is.

She finishes spraying my freshly-dyed-red hair with a gallon of hair spray while I cough.

"I'll see you later," I say, checking my watch and scampering to the door with my heart picking up speed as this charade starts to get real.

Tonight the skin I'm wearing is Lola, the puck bunny avenger.

CHAPTER 8

QUINN

I arrive in the locker room three hours before game time. A group of the guys head toward me from the buffet. Jonas is with them.

"Hold on a minute," I corner Jonas at his locker. "It's time we had a talk."

"Not that bullshit again."

He takes a seat on the bench and opens his bag.

I sit next to him. "We need to clear the air. We're teammates and there's a problem between us."

He gives me a look like I've lost my mind, and frankly, I'm thinking maybe I have, because this thing with him and the puck bunny—or all the puck bunnies—has me bothered like I've been walking around with a sprained ankle.

"The only problem between us," he says, "is that you're getting into my personal business where you don't belong."

I sigh. "You wouldn't know a mentor if one rolled you up in a ball of dough and baked you in the oven at five-hundred degrees, would you?"

He stops with a sock in his hand and looks at me, brows knit. "What the hell are you talking about?"

"Never mind. It's something my dad used to say. He was a baker."

"*Was?*"

I nod without elaborating.

His face changes. "Sorry."

I shrug. "Meantime, you have a problem with a puck bunny—who is actually a woman—and who, for whatever reason, is broken up about you."

"No, she's not. Those weren't real tears. She's a good actor. She doesn't give a shit about me."

I don't bother arguing with him about the authenticity of her tears or her acting ability because I know something about crying women and actors, courtesy of my long stint in L.A. with the Shooting Stars and my brief interlude in the movie business. "You like her?"

"Not a chance. She's crazy. Has crazy ideas about us."

I lean in and lower my voice because we're getting somewhere. "What kind of ideas?"

"The usual. The kind I can't afford to listen to no matter what."

"I see." And I do. He's talking about a real relationship. I'd bet my pinky ring on it—the one I never wear because it was a stupid gift from a woman back in L.A. with more money than sense.

"There has to be someone else," he pauses, "besides me."

"Besides you? What makes you say that?" There's something more going on here and I get a pit in my gut—and a whiff of déjà vu.

He looks down at the filthy locker room floor and then drops his head to his hands, mumbling something.

"What are you saying, man?" I think I know, but this shit is real, so I need to hear it plain and simple from him.

He straightens, leans in and says in a low strangled voice, "We might have done it without protection once... Or twice..." He swipes a hand over his face, muttering some curses about being a fucking dick.

I can't agree more, but I bite my tongue. No good beating up on a guy when he's clearly doing a good job of it himself.

"So, what are you going to do about it?"

He looks miserable. "I'm going to talk to her tonight after the game at The Tea Party. Satisfied?"

I nod and give him an encouraging smack on the back. "Good man."

He nods, but his misery is undiminished

"I'll go with you if you want." I mean it, but I doubt he'll take me up on it. He takes off his other shoe in silence before looking up at me.

"Thanks, man. I appreciate it."

Shit. I stand because I need to re-focus on the game. Pre-season or not, I have a mission and it doesn't involve star-crossed hockey players and puck bunnies. I'll handle it. I've always handled multiple priorities haven't I?

Maybe not, or at least not well. Maybe that's been my problem.

"What's up?" Finn comes over and takes my seat. He turns to Jonas. "You look like an old man with no teeth sitting in front of a steak."

I laugh and Bergman eyes him, shaking his head.

"I'm fine." He says this in a tone that implies he's not the one with a problem.

Moving on, I get in line for a stretch with the trainer and get my head back into hockey. When my skates finally hit the ice in pre-game warm-ups, my mind is cleared of all but the puck, the stick, and the net.

"GREAT OUTING," Coach says, not exactly smiling. He nods in my direction and Ryan smacks me on the back. We're in the locker room after the game, still dripping with sweat and working off some adrenaline. Coach followed us in right off the ice, before taking his usual session with the press. My smile takes credit for the two goals and two assists, but I keep the pride tamped down because it was a pre-season game and our opponent wasn't at full strength. Still, we won and that's better than losing the game whether I scored a couple goals or not.

Coach says to the room at large, "Sleep in an extra fifteen minutes tomorrow and don't forget to meet here in the locker room by ten a.m. sharp, ready for the pop-up event. There'll be a lot of kids coming, so bring your energy." He nods one last time and we return with a chorus of grunts and *Yes, sirs* and *Go Brawlers*.

Before he leaves, he says, "I'll send for you if the press wants to talk to one of you reprobates."

After he leaves, Jonas laughs. "Reprobates?"

I'm not sure he knows the meaning of the word. But he needs to learn.

A couple of the guys joke around, accusing him of being the chief reprobate.

With my towel wrapped around my waist, I head for the shower. As I pass by him, I mutter under my breath,

Reprobate means incorrigible."

He gives me a slight nod and then a wicked smile, worthy of a reprobate. "If the shoe fits." When I turn to head to the showers, he touches my arm which stops me. "You're still on for tonight, right?"

I nod and move on. Going out to a bar tonight is not what I'd had in mind; I'd planned a quick quiet dinner—maybe with a couple of the guys, maybe alone—and then hitting the sheets early because it's been an exhausting week. On the other hand, I can't deny the building anticipation of returning to The Tea Party.

Maybe *I'm* the incorrigible one. Maybe it's a symptom of withdrawal from my L.A. lifestyle when I'd automatically gone out every night, because why else would I look forward to returning to the scene of the crime?

A picture of the brave puck bunny snaps front and center in my head without provocation. *Puck bunnies are people, too.* A smile follows that thought before I can banish the idea that I might be looking forward to seeing her again. There's no guarantee she'll be there, and, yet, as I dry off, my energy is up—along with maybe one stupid part of my anatomy—for no good reason, confident that there will be an encounter of the kind I'm trying to avoid.

Shit. It's definitely been too long since I've been with a woman.

When I've barely finished dressing, the assistant coach, Barney, opens the locker room door and calls my name. "Press wants to talk to you. Pronto."

Some of the guys give me shit, including and especially the chief shit-flinger, Finn.

"There goes Hollywood doing his *thang.*"

I give him the finger on my way by. We're both grinning. Giving him my middle finger is beginning to be our *thang* now.

I grab a towel from the pile near the door and swipe it over my hair, but it's no use. It won't be the first or last time I face the press with my hair a dripping mess, but at least it's not from sweat.

Pushing through the door, I expect to head for the press room, but I'm immediately confronted by cameras of all kinds and at least a dozen media types standing in the hall right outside the locker room. Coach is standing by with his game look in place and he tilts his chin in my direction. Taking a deep breath, I join him.

This scene is a little different than L.A. where even the media are as polished as the fans. Here the environment is earthy and moblike. My back is against a cement wall and questions are being thrown like bricks. Like the good old, old days back in high school when I first gained notoriety.

"Do you think you can have another hundred-point season?"

"How's it feel to be in Boston?"

Then, "Why did you really leave L.A.?"

Followed by the bolder, "There are rumors that you left a pregnant woman behind—are they it true?"

I forget to duck the brick question and feel the blood drain from my face in spite of my notorious poise and cool under fire. Shit. "No. It's not true."

"What the hell?" Coach says. "Hockey questions or I'm having you all thrown out."

"I'll try to get past a hundred points this season, but I'm really focusing on doing whatever it takes for the team to win The Cup."

"Is that why you came to Boston?"

"I came back to Boston to be near family and get back to my roots where I grew up. The Brawlers is my hometown team, the one I rooted for when I was a Peewee."

"What about the puck bunny?" yells a young woman holding her iPhone in my direction.

Good question. While I give her a puzzled look I weigh the possibility of ignoring her when Dick, a Boston Globe reporter asks me about my second goal. Saved by my now favorite reporter, I intend to give Dick a master's thesis answer for his reward.

As I get started, I notice Delaney-the-ball-buster swoop in and wave off the lady with the iPhone who's still lingering, leaving me to go on uninterrupted about my favorite thing—scoring. Goals, that is.

A couple of the other guys come out, including Rafe and Finn, taking some of the media attention. Finally, the questions die down and the media crowd thins, leaving a smattering of mostly friends and fans. Scanning the crowd is automatic, though I don't know why I'd expect to see any familiar faces, maybe I'm hoping to.

Maybe I should have gone home to see Mom and rallied a hometown crowd for the game, but I'll save that for the season opener. I promised Mom and Aunt Mary—and whoever else wants to come—tickets to that game.

When we spoke, she didn't give me crap for not finding the time in the past couple of weeks to drive an hour north to see her. My own conscience is doing all the crap-giving.

Sure, I've been flat-out busy, but I could have skipped the frat-ernizing with teammates and gone home. I'm procrastinating. I admit it. But it's for good reason. Why should I look forward to being rejected by my big brother yet again? Letting a sigh escape as I scan the area and the faces, I stop short.

I see my best friend from childhood, Lenny Derico, grinning back at me. We played hockey together since Peewees with his dad coaching. The Dericos lived next door—hell, I practically lived at their house, practicing shots in their back yard and sleeping over half the time to get up for early practices.

I head straight for Lenny's welcome grin, knowing he's here for me, not because he wants something from me. Guilt about my family and the virtual blow-to-the-gut disguised as a reporter's question about leaving behind a pregnant woman fade to a shadow.

"What the hell are you doing here, you old dog?" I slap Lenny on the back as I give him a real hug, the kind reserved for long-lost childhood friends who you never should have lost contact with in the first place.

He laughs and backs up, but there's a hint of nerves in his smile.

And then I see why.

"Mom? What the—what are you doing here?"

"Can't a mother come and watch her big shot hockey player son at a game?" She has a tear in the corner of her eye and her arms open.

Shit. My chest tightens, squeezing all kinds of emotions out like I'm a tube of toothpaste. I go to her, hugging her hard. I can't believe how much I needed to see her, to have her welcoming hug to reassure me that she's forgiven me because I haven't been home since before Dad died. Not that she ever said she had anything but understanding. Maybe it's me who needs to forgive myself. I hug her hard and feel her small sob as she clutches me.

"I missed you so much, honey. It's so good to see you."

Getting my cool back, I clear my throat and take a step back. "You too, Mom." There are a million other things I want to say— that I *should* say—but even if I didn't have a lump of emotion clogging my throat, the hallway outside our locker room after a game is hardly the time or place.

"That was some kind of game. Maybe next time you'll get the hat trick," Derico says.

"Sure, just don't put money on it."

"How about if we put money on you to have a hundred-point season?" Mom asks.

I laugh. She's been making outrageous bets on my perfor-mance since high school—albeit, the bets were usually for choco-late chip cookies. She would bet with Derico's dad, which was technically all wrong—or would have been if the bets weren't always ridiculous enough for her to lose.

"Do it, Mom. I have you this time. If you win, you bake cookies for the team."

She laughs and Derico says he'll take that bet.

"Let's get out of here," Derico says. "You can buy us a late dinner."

Shit. I lose my cool.

"What's the matter, Quinn? You have other plans, don't you?" Mom asks. "Don't worry. I know we surprised you."

"It's not that, Mom. But, yeah, you did surprise me. I thought we had a plan to get you and Aunt Mary tickets for the season opener."

"I couldn't wait and Lenny said he had tickets to this game, so…"

"You have other plans." Derico nods. "It's a woman right? Whoever she is, bring her along. We have a lot of catching up to do." He has an uncomplicated clear view of life, like always. His priorities were always in the right place; he never had any doubts or confusion about where he stood or what was important. Even now, after a couple of years that I haven't been in touch, he knows we're still friends. Derico, in short, carries no baggage. Me? I'm like an alpaca—and the biggest guilt at the moment is that I don't deserve his loyal friendship.

"If the problem was a date, there would be no problem." I swipe a hand through my hair and look around for Jonas. "I promised a guy on the team I'd help him out tonight."

"Help him out?" Mom squints her eyes wondering what the hell that means.

"Give him moral support. He needs it."

"You're such a good man—"

"I don't know about that," I say before Mom can get going. I can't believe she'd still sing my praises after… well, after everything.

"Dad says hello," Lenny says.

"How is he?"

"You should visit and find out."

"Touché. I will. Better yet, I'll get you *all* tickets to next Saturday's game—both families—and take you all out to dinner afterward." I shake my head. "I can't believe you two paid for tickets and didn't tell me—"

"Don't you worry," Mom says. "I can afford a ticket to your

game. I thought it would be fun to surprise you." She gives me a half worried-half apologetic look, pretty much accusing me of failing to come home. I bet she thinks that I've going out carousing, that I prioritized fooling around over coming home—.

"Look, tonight's not what you think. I really do need to help out a friend—"

"I believe you, sweetheart. Not that you owe me any explanation. I knew I was taking a chance surprising you like this." She smiles and pats my face like she always has, like the warm wonderful woman she's always been.

Shit. I feel gulty anyway. Because I owe her for all my absences in the past ten years.

I glance at Derico. His smile is genuine and without judgment.

He punches my shoulder the way he always did when we were kids. "Don't worry about it. You help your friend and we'll see you next week—if that works for you?"

"Thanks. It does."

"I'm not used to playing so close to home and didn't even imagine you'd be here. I'll get the best tickets they have for next week. Talk to the family, both of you, and let me know how many tickets you want and I'll have them for you."

Mom laughs and Derico grins. "Don't go Hollywood on us, big guy. This doesn't need to be a big production."

He's still smiling but my smile is forced now—because he has no idea what a bullseye he's hit right in my Achilles heel. Hollywood is the *last* thing I want to be.

"Maybe your brother and his family will come." Mom arches an eyebrow. "*If* you call him."

My gut churns and I nod. I *should* call him, but the last time didn't go well. I'd called to let him know I was coming back east to play in Boston and hoped to see him and get to know my nephews. He'd told me not to make any rash moves on his account. Even if the words were less than warm, his tone had left me frozen. And angry. But I was angry at myself not him, so I'd ended the call before I blew up and made things worse than they already were between us.

After one last heartfelt hug between Mom and me, I exchange a look with Lenny as he takes Mom's arm. He knows I owe him my right arm and left nut for tonight and all the other times he's been there for me.

With an understanding smile, a little sadness at the corners, he escorts Mom to the exit.

I watch them leave, then try to shift gears to an intervention at the Tea Party.

Spotting Jonas stuck with a reporter—the same one who'd asked me that crappy question. I'm about to rescue him when Coach shows up and sets him free. Good man, that Coach.

Jonas reaches me in a few strides and we don't say much as we escape through the garage and walk to The Tea Party. We're wearing ball caps when we walk in, trying to stay unrecognized if we can.

"Whatever you do," I say, "keep it low-key. No attention. No social media moments."

He grunts and leads the way to the back of the bar. There are three women sitting at the table closest to the back hallway near the exit. They have their backs to us, but I'd recognize that redhead anywhere. She's here, my earnest young puck bunny. That gut feeling I'd had about seeing her tonight was right. But I don't need that complication because I'm supposed to be here for Jonas' moral support, and the last thing I need to do is fuck up and involve myself in any more puck bunny drama. It's bad enough he's tangled up in it. This isn't supposed to be about me and some puck bunny.

Jonas greets the ladies. *She* turns around and stands up, and my priorities go haywire with just one look.

My earnest puck bunny has gone from shy to full-tilt in-your-face-sexy-as-hell puck bunny to out-play all puck bunnies. Fuck.

It's damn amazing what a short skirt and long legs will do to a guy. And ridiculous considering this guy has been around the block and been exposed to the best of the best Hollywood has to offer. I've been literally around the world and had every manner of woman thrown in my path, so I am not a man easily impressed. Not at all.

In fact, it's not her legs, or her impressive cleavage or her pretty face that impress me, though they're all nice. It's those eyes and the raw innocence sparking from them and hitting me right in the solar plexus as if she's reached out and grabbed me by the balls. Except I bet that's not something she would do and the idea is hotter than the reality of any number of starlets who've done just that.

"Quinn," she says in a deep, breathy voice, nothing like what she sounded like before, except there's that same shaky catch like she's nervous.

"What's he doing here?" Mindy says.

"Quinn, this is Mindy," Jonas says.

He pauses a beat and then adds in an afterthought when the older woman gives him a censuring look.

"And this is Sheila. Quinn came because I asked him to."

He doesn't introduce my brave puck bunny, but she doesn't seem to mind.

He takes a deep breath. "Say what you have to say, Mindy."

CHAPTER 9

"*W*hat I have to say is... I'm *pregnant*, you big jerk."

My hair almost blows back with the force of Jonas sucking in his breath and taking all the air in the vicinity with him.

"What the *fuck?*" Jonas looks on the verge of either hysteria or violence, as if Mindy had just pressed the big red start button on a big ticking bomb.

Quinn puts a hand on Jonas's shoulder and says in a low voice, "Take it easy. Just listen. Listening isn't going to change anything or cost you anything."

"That's right," Mindy says. "I'm not that kind of girl who wants your stupid money."

"What kind of girl are you?" Jonas grits out, not ready to give up his anger. I move closer to Mindy's side and Sheila grips her arm on the other side. I'm hoping it doesn't come to blows, but Jonas' boiling temper is off the charts, so much so that I'm surprised I can't hear the whistle on the kettle screeching through the din in the bar.

"I'm the kind of girl who wants a father to my baby."

Jonas laughs, but not the *ha-ha, that's funny* kind. No, it's more like the guy who's waiting for the hangman's knot to be tied around his neck.

"Children aren't so bad," I say. If I'd've realized how lame my words would sound, I'd have poured some whiskey down my throat or stuffed a puck in my mouth. Which… is what Jonas looks like he wants to do right now.

"I'm no one's idea of father material." He steps closer, aiming his murderous eyes at Mindy. To give the girl credit, she doesn't back down. No. In fact, she steps up toe-to-toe with him, dragging me and Sheila with her.

Quinn sticks close to Jonas, gripping his arm tight enough that it ought to hurt. Jonas might end up with a snapped bone if he doesn't start paying attention to his friend who's muttering something under his breath. But Jonas just tries to yank his arm free.

"How about if we all have a drink?" Sheila says.

"Yes. This calls for a celebration," I say. But the mood is all wrong based on the *Are you kidding me?* faces on all four of my fellow celebrants-slash-combatants.

Quinn recovers first from my outrageous remark, skipping over any response because what could he say that would make it better? Instead, he waves at the server and asks for a couple more glasses and a soda.

"You're drinking soda?" I ask. *Crap.* "Oh—Never mind. I get it. The soda's is for Mindy." I blush furiously because I'm pretty sure I've fully become master-of-the-art of foot-in-mouth repartee.

The server brings over glasses and pours us each a glass of whiskey. Mindy picks up the soda, shaking her head my way like I'm a lost cause. *Crap.* I'm supposed to be helping the situation.

"Why don't we sit down?" I say while everyone but me is drinking like they just came in from a month in the Sahara desert.

Sheila nods and we maneuver it so Jonas sits next to Mindy in the booth and Sheila sandwiches him in on his other side so he can't escape. I sit opposite them, next to Quinn. It's all very cozy and tense and I decide this is a good time to have a nice big swig of my whiskey.

Unfortunately, I've never drunk whiskey before, so when I take a big gulp like the others, it doesn't go well. And by that, I mean as soon as the Liquid-From-Hell hits my throat, I spasm automatically, spewing it all over the table toward Jonas and Mindy in an impressive spray as if I have a compressed air hose hidden in my mouth.

"What the hell?" Jonas puts up his hands to block the spray from hitting Mindy.

"Are you all right?" Quinn pats my back and hands me a napkin, staring into my watering eyes with real concern. He gets the server over to the table in a snap because, of course, she's been staring at him the whole time, just *waiting* to be beckoned.

"A margarita with Patron for the lady."

"Yes, sir, right away." The waitress gives me a wistful look and dashes away.

"How did you know?" Sara says.

"You mentioned something about tequila and I didn't figure you for the type to drink it straight up."

His dimple deepens, obliterating whatever sass I have left. But it's more than the dimple destroying me right now, it's him and the gold-medal attention he's showering on me that has me self-conscious about my non-gold-medal self. In fact, I'm so far from a gold medal, I never even dreamed of competing for the Olympics of flirtation.

Of course, that never stopped me from dreaming about the prize sitting in front of me. Maybe it's time I man up and jump in the game. I've already humiliated myself in front of this guy enough to know he's too nice to make me feel any worse.

Sliding my gaze over to check on Mindy and Jonas, I find them engaged in a tense conversation. I'm calling that progress, so I turn my attention to Quinn.

"You're too nice, you know that? Surprisingly nice because it's something people never talk about. They can rattle off all your stats and talk about how many starlets or princesses you've dated but—"

His smile falters on the mention of the princess and I stop my stupid ramble because making him feel uncomfortable is far worse than whatever humiliation I could possibly inflict on myself. "Sorry. Don't mind my ramble." I touch his arm as the server returns with my margarita in the nick of time. As I pick up my glass and she disappears, I lean in. "But you really are super nice."

Then I down the drink, bypassing the straw, not waiting to see if his dimple's returned because my strength to withstand his intense eyes alone is waning. Not to mention, all the girly parts are coming to life with a vengeance from my parched V right through my ovaries and all the way to my uterus squirming around and making me hot.

"Either you were very thirsty or you—"

"I was in need of courage," I say with daring honesty. "You may have noticed I'm nervous."

His dimple lights up—and everything in me lights up like a Vegas slot machine hitting the jackpot.

Sheila stands up, disrupting my moment, thank God.

"I'm heading for the ladies' room. No need for you to come with." She winks at me and sashays away.

He turns to me. "Thank you. You're right. I don't often get people telling me I'm nice. I think you're nice, too."

My blush is immediate and deep, probably enhanced by the tequila buzz running through my blood. I wave a hand. "Nah. How would you even know?" I ask. It should be a rhetorical question, but it's not and I stare at him waiting for his answer.

"You're here to help a friend, for one thing," he says.

"You have a point." I dare another glance at the unhappy couple. "And I think our scheme is working."

He chuckles. "How do you figure? They look like they'd be strangling each other if we weren't in public."

"That's nothing. They just need to get past those first bumps and they should be fine. Jonas cares about her."

He glances at his teammate, then turns back to me. "Are you sure?"

I don't get to answer him because Mindy stands and throws what's left of her soda in Jonas's face. "You can have your goddamn fucking paternity test if you want. But if you make me do that, I'm going to get an attorney and when it turns out to be a match, I'm going to make you pay."

Jonas turns whiter than my mom's bleached hair before he pulls her back down.

"I can't believe you just caused a scene," Jonas says, looking more panicked than I feel.

"Don't worry about the crowd. Keep your cool," Quinn says. He gives Mindy a cool look as if he's taking his own advice. "There will be no lawyers," he says.

My mouth opens and I'm going to protest on Mindy's behalf, but she looks contrite and nods.

"You're right. If this lug doesn't want to be a father to his child, no court is going to be able to make him."

"Who says I don't?" Jonas asks. "All I want to know is if this kid you say you're having is really mine."

The waterworks start in earnest, making Mindy's crying from last time we were here look like a puddle compared to this Lake Michigan.

"Shit," Quinn says under his breath. "Can you do something?"

I automatically reach out and pat Mindy's hand.

Sheila comes back from the ladies' room, rushing as soon as she sees Mindy's state, and jumps into the consoling big-sister role.

Jonas, in a panic again, tries to look cool, and, at the same time, pats Mindy's arm trying to console her.

"Someday—" I say, but I don't get any further.

"Just shut up," Jonas growls at me in a frustrated outburst. "I don't want to hear another word from you. Just leave."

Quinn stands and takes my arm. "We'll both leave," he says in that controlled voice that I'm not sure how to interpret. "As soon as you apologize." He glares at Jonas like he's an opposing player in a championship game.

Jonas glares back.

Sheila ping-pongs her gaze between them and I'm watching Mindy trying to control her sobs. I'm also watching the way Jonas has his arm around her and how he squeezes her shoulder and leans in. He shows very impressive tenderness especially considering he's glaring back at Quinn and hasn't flinched after several tense seconds I look around the bar to check for raised cell phones. So far, none. Amazing what lowered ball caps will do to keep people from recognizing someone.

Mindy whispers something and he still doesn't flinch or look away from Quinn. But after another beat, he clenches his jaw and nods.

"Sorry." He takes a deep breath and turns back to Mindy.

I'm confused and frozen in place for a moment, unsure what to do.

But not Quinn. He gives me a soft smile, the pre-dimple kind that's like a pat on the back for effort. He stands and leaves the table.

I rush after Quinn losing my avenger air and half my confidence, feeling like the kid in *Back to the Future* with the fading photo, identity being threatened. My hand shakes as I reach for his arm and he turns to me, those crystal blue eyes expectant.

He hails a cab, then turns to me with a frown. "That didn't go well."

"Sadly, no, it did not," I say in an almost normal voice as I smile back. Mindy's teary face returns to me.

My heart sinks for Mindy while my gut flutters at the nearness of my man, Quinn.

A cab pulls up to the curb and Quinn's dimple shows up with ironic timing, making my panties go damp in a Pavlovian reaction. I tighten my thighs and my lips, refusing to melt into a simpering fan-girl puddle this time. Where's that avenger-puck-bunny persona when I need her? Is that who I really am?

"It didn't go exactly according to plan, but all is not lost. They're still talking. Loudly, but still, they're talking. Maybe they just need some time."

"You had a plan?" he asks.

I nod then stop and force in a breath, commanding myself to behave like a normal adult. Maybe that's my problem. Maybe I'm *not* a normal adult. But I should at least act adult-like.

"I did—I mean, I do." I squint and squeeze my temples to stave of the headache that really wants to pound my skull. "See, we were going to start by remembering the excitement she and Jonas shared, the long, um, nights and how Mindy cured him of hangovers in the mornings. And then we were going to move on to how there was a connection or he would never have... uh... suggested they connect so intimately." The rush of blood to my face thankfully stops the onslaught of my nonsensical fairytale.

"You're a *romantic* puck bunny?"

I think he's teasing me, so I blush some more, then shake my head, unsure if I should be okay with all the labeling. "I'm a girl with a heart and hope in it."

"Touché," he says.

The cabbie beeps the horn.

"Let me get you a ride home," Quinn says, "You look like you're about to drop."

"Oh, don't worry about me. You're the one who just played a damn hockey game." I blush again. *Damn it.*

His dimple deepens. "How about if we share?" He opens the door before I can spit a word out of my stuttering brain.

"What about Sheila and Mindy and Jonas?" I look behind me at the closed door of The Tea Party. I should go back inside because leaving them there doesn't feel right.

"Didn't they just throw us out?" he asks.

"You have a point."

He smiles and this time it's a deep, meaningful moment where I know exactly what he's thinking. He's remembering when he said those exact words to me. I smile back, for once warm and not bothered by blushing or overstimulated ovaries.

"Don't worry about them," he says like he knows I'm still worried because I am. "They're big kids; they'll be fine."

And just like that, he sweeps away my worry and my tummy moves like it's made of jelly.

The cabbie rolls down his window and is about to say something until he recognizes Quinn. I can see the exact moment of recognition because his face turns from a deep scowl—the kind that precedes a string of swearing—to a surprised smile.

Quinn waves and helps me inside ahead of him.

We sit side-by-side and I'm light-headed from either his nearness or the tequila. Also, there's that heady sense of feeling taken care of because he's seeing me home. His nearness is having a warm-and- fuzzy effect on my brain. But, most of all, there's the idea that I just may be able to score my goal, to get my big O with the man of my dreams tonight.

"What's your address?" he asks.

Crap. I can't let him bring me to my *house*. The one where my parents and brother live... So I give him Billie Mae's address and the cab takes off. Thank God I have the key to her place. Double thanks to heaven and every god that ever lived that she's out with her latest Tinder date. I want to pray that she stays out all night, but I won't push my luck. If I get him inside, I'll try and make it quick. Çrap. I don't have a clue how to do this. Maybe I should have another drink to loosen me up.

I hope Billie Mae doesn't kill me.

"Where do you live?" I ask.

"Presently, at the Boston Harbor Hotel, but I'm looking to buy a house not too far from the city."

"Smart. You'll have more space and a yard in the suburbs. Do you have a dog?"

"Not yet. I'm thinking seriously of getting one. You?"

"Yes—I mean no." Crap. I can't tell him I have a dog if I'm pretending to live at Billie Mae's tiny dogless apartment. "I mean I used to. Before I moved to Boston."

"You from New Hampshire? Because I have this feeling I've met you before."

"No. Not me. We've never met. Believe me, I would remember, right?" I try a laugh, but we're both saved from exploring why I look familiar when the cabbie pulls to the curb at Billie Mae's building. My hand shakes as he helps me from the cab and tells the driver to wait.

Crap.

"Don't you want to come in? I mean I know you're tired and all..." We're standing at the door and I'm trying not to hiccup, trying to keep from shaking like a maraca being played by a maniac. Staring into his kind and sexy eyes could go either way, either excite me more or settle me down. I concentrate on the kindness and settle down as he stares back, his dimple faint, his warmth penetrating my coat with his nearness, and his intoxicating scent mesmerizing me. He's taking his time with his answer and I lean closer in case he wants encouragement.

"I don't think I should." He sighs.

But his dimple gets bigger, so I don't collapse with disappointment. "Why is that?"

"Because I find you far too attractive to not spend the night and... I'm trying to stay focused on hockey."

"You were going to say you're trying to stay out of trouble, weren't you? As if I'm trouble?"

"No, it's not you. It's the circumstances."

"And by circumstances, you mean a wild night in bed with all the fireworks?" I put on the most enticing smile I can imagine and wish I had practiced in front of a mirror because I have no idea how to entice or smile enticingly.

But he steps back.

Then coughs.

But I think he may be hiding a laugh, so I frown.

"No, those aren't exactly the circumstances I meant." Then he mirrors my frown. "Not exactly, but maybe indirectly. Either way, it's not about you... Hell I don't even know your name—and *that's* the kind of circumstances I'm talking about. Getting in bed with a woman whose name I don't know is trouble. I need to stop doing that."

"Okay. My name is..." I cast around my stupid over-crowded brain for my puck bunny name that I should know except my brain is Quinn-fogged. "Lola." I tilt my head and lean closer. "Now you have no excuse. You already admitted you're attracted." I bend down to get the key from under the loose brick, but he pulls me upright.

"Lola?" He drops his skeptical smile and lets go of me maybe because I'm trembling at his touch. "Look, I admit it, I'm attracted, but I... don't want to take advantage of you. You're—"

"What? Please take advantage of me. I really like you. I'm *begging* you to take advantage of me." I bat my eyes, all pretenses gone, going for the genuine girl who needs a good night of big O indulgence that I am. "I would consider it a great favor if you were to take me and fly me to the moon. You know—make me forget my name and what planet I'm from, give me the biggest O there ever was or ever will be."

He's looking at me funny so I dial it back.

"I mean—no pressure. It can be any kind of O. I mean, how would I know?" I slip my eyes from his and talk to his jacket which is very nicely filled out by his massive shoulders. "You see, I wouldn't exactly know a big O from a mini-O since I've never had any kind of O—I mean, orgasm." I look up because, at this point, I'm more curious than afraid to see what his reaction is.

And in that split second, I remember that in my urgency to beg for my big O virginity to be popped, I've forgotten to disguise my voice.

He looks at me funny and steps back. It's fifty-fifty odds that he's reacting to my announcement that I'm an orgasm virgin.

But the way he's looking at my face, as if he might know me from somewhere—because he does—I'm thinking the odds are shrinking.

Then he tilts his head and stares closer, so I turn away.

"Okay, have it your way," I say, breathing too fast and wishing I could take everything back because suspicion isn't the reaction I was hoping for. I back up a step.

"We could get to know each other better first," he says.

His words stop me and set off all kinds of alarm bells in my body, both the good kind where my panties are on fire, and the bad kind, where I know there's going to be a big bucket of cold water dousing my plan any second. If he *gets to know me*, he'll know I'm not Lola. He may figure out I'm Sara. Then it's all over. Crap.

He's already suspicious, so I collect myself and get my new Lola voice back

"Maybe that's not a good idea," I say, sanity finally winning out while I contemplate the craziness of my scheme.

"I think it is, Lola." He runs his fingers through my hair.

My nerve endings explode, sending a frisson of pre-orgasmic proportions rocketing through me. My body responds before my brain and I lean into him, needing to connect to him.

"Yes. I mean, let's get to know each other." The word is breathy and I can't think.

CHAPTER 10

QUINN

*S*he fumbles the keys as she tries to open the door and I take a deep breath to clear my head of the idea of her *big O virginity.* In spite of my noble words about getting to know her better, the instant her invitation hit me like a blow to the head, my dick latched onto it with a vengeance and I lost ninety percent of my brain power.

But I'm pretty sure, in spite of a less than clear head, that I've figured out Lola is not who she says she is. I've heard that voice and seen that face before. I'm almost certain, unless she has a twin sister—and so help me God, I'm hoping for the twin sister explanation—that my puck bunny is none other than Ms. Bellagamba, Sara-of-the-beautiful-leg-times-two.

"Come in. Please." She stands on the other side of the threshold, looking all kinds of vulnerable, her eyes big and innocent, holding her breath as if I hold the key to her future—or at least the key to unlock her orgasm block.

"I'll come in for a few minutes, but I'm not staying. I have a few questions for you that I'd like you to answer, *Lola.*"

Her smile freezes with guilt and she rushes to the kitchen area of the small apartment, mumbling something about getting a drink. She's confusing and young and I shouldn't be here, but I need to confirm what's going on.

"We don't need another drink. Come and sit with me a minute," I say. "I won't bite. I promise." It's a damn shame, but it's true. No way can I touch this innocent girl. She's adorable and a little crazy in a harmless way—and my mother would probably love her—all which adds up to the fact that she's untouchable.

"Are you sure?"

I nod. Her voice is different, like she's purposely altered it.

She comes over and sits next to me, raw hope mingling with raw desire painted all over her gorgeous, albeit over-made-up, face. She's putting up quite a charade if she's working for the Brawlers by day and playing puck bunny with the players by night.

"Tell me about the real Quinn James underneath the glamorous super star," she says.

"Funny, but I was going to ask you who the real Lola is underneath the outfit."

"I'll be happy to take it off for you so you can find out." She bats her eyes and moves to stand up.

I grab her hand and keep her at my side. "That's not what I meant. Not that I wouldn't love—never mind. I want to know who you really are because I know you're not Lola the puck bunny."

Her face pales and her mouth opens and you'd think I'd just kicked her puppy.

"No, of course. I mean of course I'm Lola, but I'm new at being a puck bunny. You can tell?" She clears her throat. "Of *course* you can tell." She exhales. "There's no mystery, really. I love hockey and…" She dips her head, looking away. "And hockey players." She looks back up at me, her chin at a defiant angle and her eyes bright with defiance. "Particularly you. What girl wouldn't? You're a specimen to behold." She puts a hand on my chest then takes it away. "Plus, you're nice to puck bunnies and a good teammate. I'd be insane if I didn't drool over you, right?" She looks me up and down and I feel the heat of her stare and then she darts her eyes to my face. "I don't mean to offend you. Did I? Oh crap, the last thing I want to do is objectify you or make you feel like—"

"Don't worry. You haven't hurt my feelings." I try not to chuckle because she's adorably awkward and one-hundred percent real for a girl who's hiding her real identity.

"Oh good. I should have known. You're a tough hockey player after all." She talks with her hands and brushes my chest.

I capture her hand and hold on.

"What's your real name?"

She freezes, her mouth open, her face paling and then pinking from her neck upward to a sexy shade like she's aroused rather than embarrassed, but I know better. Or I think I do. Because she's the girl who just propositioned me to give her first orgasm, right?

Shit. Don't even contemplate that. She doesn't know what she's asking for and has no idea what the fallout could be. My guess would be she'd get very emotional and things would get messy. Because the last thing I need right now is a relationship with a puck bunny. Even if she isn't really a puck bunny. Fuck.

"You know who I really am, don't you? I thought my disguise was perfect. Guess I'd never make it in the spy business. I better hold back on that application to the CIA."

"Yes, I know who you are. But it's not your disguise. It's me. It's a special skill I have. I never forget a gorgeous face, *Ms. Bellagamba.*"

Her face collapses into her hands and she shrinks away, muttering something about never showing her stupid face again.

I pry her hands away and tilt her chin up until she's looking me in the eye. Maybe that's a mistake because they're glittering and about to spill tears and my chest tightens until I can hardly breathe. Fuck. Last thing I want to do is make her cry.

"Don't cry, Sara. You're fine. I give you an A for effort. You're clearly a passionate and determined young lady , but hell, I can't hold that against you."

She laughs, then cries, but just a little, while she furiously wipes her cheeks.

"Of course you would be even nicer than you are hunky. What are you trying to do? Break my heart while I crawl away completely embarrassed and unable to face you ever again?" She opens her mouth and her eyes go wide. "How am I going to work with you—"

"Don't panic. We'll be fine. We'll start fresh. Like this night never happened." I want to take the words back because I make it a point never to lie to a girl, and the truth is, there's no way I'll forget this night. And I have a feeling it's not even close to being over.

I separate myself from her.

"I should leave," I say.

Her face instantly looks crushed, but she recovers and stands. "I don't blame you. I apologize for throwing myself at you like a... a crazy person. It won't happen again. I promise to behave professionally."

"No need to apologize. I didn't mean I wanted to forget tonight. It's been kind of fun."

She snorts. "You have a bizarre take on what's fun, don't you?"

"I guess I do. But I've had a lot of nights out and a lot of experiences and this was... unusual. Getting slapped by Mindy, having you proposition me—"

"Ooooh. I'm so sorry—"

"Don't be. Seriously. I've never had anyone disguise themselves to—"

She smacks my shoulder almost hard enough to hurt but only because I have a bruise there from a check to the boards. I flinch and she stops and her face goes serious.

"You have a bruise from that check to the boards, don't you?

I'm genuinely sorry for that. Let me get some ice." She jumps up before I can stop her and rushes to the kitchen.

"Thank you." I should tell her not to bother because I was about to leave, wasn't I? But ice on my shoulder would be perfect about now. It's what I'd be doing if I were back in my hotel room.

She returns with the ice and places it gently in the exact spot I need it and then holds it there.

"Your hand is going to freeze. I don't suppose you have an ace bandage to wrap it in place?"

"No, but I think I can dig up a scarf that'll work." She raises a finger to indicate one minute then returning remarkably fast with a long colorful scarf in hot pink and turquoise.

I laugh as she gets to work wrapping it around the makeshift icepack around my upper arm and then around my neck to hold it onto my shoulder.

"Perfect," she says, looking proud and happy and expectant.

"Yes," I say, close enough to be staring at the light spray of freckles across her nose, faint enough that I hadn't noticed them before. I clear my throat.

"I'll set my timer for fifteen minutes." She taps her watch.

"You go full tilt at everything you do, don't you?" I ask. This is something I can identify with. Getting to the NHL required me to be single-minded from a young age.

"I guess." She stares at me like she wants to go full tilt with me again, but as tempting as she is, I'm convinced about it being a bad idea.

"How old are you?"

"Plenty old enough. Don't worry, I'm not a minor."

"Answer the question." I narrow my eyes at her.

She's trying to look offended and miffed. "Twenty-two. I graduated last May from UNH." Her face lights up in a smile. "Tell me about your time at UNH. It must have been so much fun. I've heard it was an exciting time to be there, to get swept up in the Wildcat fever, all the wins and the Frozen Four Championship. We didn't win during my time there."

"It was the best time of my life," I admit, realizing it for the first time. "I haven't been part of a team like that since then."

"Until now," she says confidently.

I nod. She's right. Her face lights up in that same smile, but she doesn't seem like the same awkward would-be puck bunny she did an hour ago, all flustered and unsure.

"Tell me, Sara, as a mischief-maker, what were your college days like? Did you plot elaborate schemes to meet guys back then?"

She laughs and covers her face, but just for a second. "Okay, I had that coming, but no. I was too chicken to carry off any of the schemes I might dream up in my head—and I admit there were a few. Billie Mae always talked me out of anything I'd actually mentioned out loud after a few tequilas—my kryptonite, by the way. She was my best friend then and now, but she believes in more conventional methods of attracting men."

I laugh. "Tell me some of your secret plots."

"Not—I'm already working off the embarrassment from tonight. You tell me about some of your mischief-making escapades."

"What makes you think I was a mischief-maker?"

"Because you haven't called the men in white coats to take me away yet."

"Touché. You're right. I appreciate a good bit of outlandish behavior now and again. Of course, at my advanced age, I've grown out of it mostly."

She hits me with a pillow to my chest. "You owe me at least one story as consolation and I don't care how far back you have to go."

"Okay, here you go. When I was a kid, I was the mischievous one in the family, the kid who did dumb things to get attention. Maybe I needed to get attention from my parents because they favored my older brother who was perfect. But I got their attention all right. It worked so well that my mischief carried over to school, though I eventually realized I got more attention from playing hockey so I quit being a knucklehead."

"You still have a bold exhibitionist streak," she says, nailing me like she's known me forever. "Give me one story. I promise I won't tell."

"Since you're so irresistible, I will. Hmmm…" I rub my chin and pretend to think about what to tell her, but there's one story that leaps to mind. I'll share it, but not right away.

"In sixth grade my coach, Mr. Derico, had to intervene and put a stop to my mischief because I put hair dye in my friend Lenny's older sister's shampoo bottle and she had to go to school with green hair—way before it was fashionable to do so."

She laughs. "That's nothing. I know you have a better story than that."

She's right. "I'm saving the good story, but I want a reward. What will you do if I tell you?" I'm all too aware that I'm flirting with her now and I'm not sure if it's my natural instinct or if it's her who provokes me. Either way, it's dangerous and not what I need to be doing, so I reign it in and I'm about to shut it down when she responds by leaning in.

"How about a kiss?"

That short-circuits my thinking for a second. Maybe she's not as innocent as I assumed. Maybe I was crazy to ever assume she's an innocently-dressed puck bunny. Young and innocent are two different things and I should know better than to confuse them.

"The story for a kiss?" she prompts me, her mouth a breath from mine.

I nod and turn my head so I'm talking into her ear and watching her profile.

"The story is one of my best boyhood memories. It's about the time I got in trouble with my favorite teacher. It involves my exhibitionist streak." I pause. "By the way, how did you know about that?"

"I saw you in that movie."

I laugh. "You have a point. It's under control now, but back then I'd do crazy stuff to get attention."

"Tell me the worst best thing."

"This is it. Also in sixth grade." This is the story I've been warming up for.

"That was a banner year for the trouble-maker in you."

"My peak."

"We'll see."

I laugh again because she's right. I'm thinking of causing some big trouble right now—involving her. "I borrowed a guitar, found an old sombrero, and snuck outside this girl's class I had a crush on at the time and serenaded her."

"That's sweet."

"You didn't hear my voice."

She laughs. "What did you sing?"

"Who said I could sing? I bellowed out *I'm a Believer* Davy Jones-style and embarrassed the hell out of her. The teacher yelled at me, but her heart wasn't in it because I could see the laughter in her eyes."

"So what happened?"

"The girl never spoke to me again, but I developed a massive crush on that teacher and brought her roses and chocolates every day for the next week. I quit when I waited for her after school one day and saw her boyfriend picking her up." I shrug. "He was massive. Looked like he could bench me and three of my best friends."

"Wise decision."

"I found out he played linebacker for the NFL and that's when I got serious about sports. I started lifting and throwing myself into hockey with a vengeance."

Her eyes widen. "Wow. Guess he was quite the inspiration."

"No, it was my teacher. She was gorgeous and kind and had the best smile." I touch her face. "Kind of like someone else I know."

She blushes in an instant and my chest tightens.

"You're pretty good at flirting, aren't you?" she says.

I raise my brows, surprised by her sass, though I shouldn't be. Anyone with enough spunk to stand up in a bar and call out an NHL hockey player for his bad behavior definitely has a reservoir of guts, even if it is well-hidden under a layer of insecurity. Innocence, though? Not sure.

"Sorry—it must be the tequila talking," she says.

"Don't be sorry when you're right, Lola. I mean Sara."

She swats me, pinker than ever, but grinning. She should be giving me innocent-girl-next-door vibes, the kind that scream *Don't touch!* because she's the exact kind of girl I've avoided—the kind who could get hurt because they're too real, feelings and all. No matter how she's trying to come off tonight.

But I'm not that guy anymore, am I? Or I'm not supposed to be. I'm supposed to be the kind of guy looking for a real girl, the kind I can bring home to Mama, literally. Shit.

"You're a much nicer person than I thought you'd be," she says. "And I always thought you'd be pretty nice."

"No, I'm not. I'm terrible, really." I don't elaborate and wonder if she'll know the kinds of terrible ideas she's put in my head.

When she blushes that pretty pink and her eyes pool into dark invitations, I know she knows exactly what kind of terrible I'm talking about.

The buzzer goes off on her watch and she meets my gaze. She shuts the alarm without breaking eye contact.

"Don't look at me that way unless you mean it," I say in a hoarse warning because it's not a line, not this time.

"I owe you that kiss." She moves closer, and her breathing hitches with all kinds of tension. Our mouths are almost touching, but she hesitates.

I'd be kidding myself if I didn't admit I was turned on anticipating her kiss, wanting that kiss and finding her hesitation making my dick spark to life. So, I take her face in my hands and close the gap, touching my lips to the softness of hers, without insistence or greed, measuring her response and taking in the stunning sweetness.

When she moans and throws her arms around me, pressing her body to mine, that changes everything.

CHAPTER 11

SARA

"*D*on't stop there," I say.

He stops. Sheesh, it's like my invitation is like the opposite of a magnet *every* time, repelling him.

"You're kind of young," he says.

I back up and take a sip of my neglected drink. It gives me courage. "Not that young."

"Innocent" he says, running a finger from my jaw along my neck to my collar bone.

I shiver. "Not me. You're the innocent one."

He laughs. "What makes you say that?"

"Because you're hesitating and it's not because I haven't sent you anything but *please do me* signals." I'm on fire now, with boldness and a hot need down in my lady parts.

He laughs again, but it's not the *ha-ha* kind. It's a low sexy kind that makes me vibrate all the way down to my toes—especially the places that count most. I squirm and he notices. Crap. Maybe I'm too anxious and I ought to back off.

But then he takes me in his arms and moves his breath against the hollow below my ear sets me off. I shiver as tingles reverberate everywhere. I sigh as he nibbles on my ear, sending another wave of tingling circling through my body.

"You make it hard for a guy to behave. I only came inside to talk."

"I like the way you talk." My voice sounds funny—unsteady and hoarse. "The way your mouth makes me feel."

"Oh, Sara. We haven't even *touched* the surface of how my mouth can make you feel."

He trails kisses from my earlobe—which is so sensitive - my panties get wet—down the column of my neck to the edge of my jersey. His hands travel from my shoulders to my chest as his lips find mine.

And then, whispering something I wish I could understand, he kisses me again. This time I'm ready and kiss him back, catching his tongue and giddy with ecstasy when he sucks in a breath and deepens the kiss. He explores every part of my mouth, nibbles at my lips and I can't get enough of the taste of him, savoring the intimate heat of his mouth and tongue.

It doesn't matter that I can hardly breathe and his hands cup my breasts and his thumb finds my nipple—no kidding because it's twice it's normal size and reaching for him.

"You have no idea how wonderful that feels," I say into his mouth, sucking in some air. His breathing is heavy, too, and that knowledge spikes my passion to another level. Or maybe it's the heavy-lidded sexy look he gives me, or the way his thumb circles my nipple and then brushes over it, again and again. My eyes close and I let out a moan.

"I think I have an idea," he says.

I run my fingers through his hair, fulfilling at least one long-time fantasy from my girlhood. And, oh boy, does it fulfill me. Far beyond what that young girl could have imagined.

I run a hand down his chest and linger on his muscles. "Do you realize how wildly compelling your muscles are?"

"Is that right?" He trails his hand lower, dancing his fingers down my abdomen as I come close to seeing stars.

I almost protest until I realize where he's going. "I'm so hot for you." Breathless, I stare into his eyes as his hand stops at my waist and he stares back. "Don't stop. Please." I trace his lips with my tongue.

His eyes dilate to all black and he takes a shaky breath. "You really know how to make a guy forget about... whatever reason why I was supposed to leave you alone."

"No reason. Two consenting adults. Very attracted and hot and—"

"And one very sexy, if talkative, young woman." His mouth closes in on mine like he's starved for oxygen and my breath is his air supply. Then he sucks my lower lip into his mouth and a flash of stars appears as I squirm with a needy moan.

"I want you... to give me... an orgasm... so much." I'm panting more than talking and pushing my hips toward him.

"How much?" He slides his hand between my legs.

Thank God for the short skirt. I moan as his strong fingers find the V at the top of my thighs—only problem is, they're stopped by my indestructible tights.

He nibbles my ear. "I can feel you burning up."

He presses his thumb against my swollen pussy right through the tights as if they were invisible and, damn, I scream.

"Jesus, you're so sexy, so responsive, and so fucking wet. I bet you're dripping inside—"

"Take them off. We need to take my clothes off. Yours, too." Do I sound desperate or sexy? It doesn't matter. I'm that desperate that I don't even really care.

I reach for his crotch. *Jackpot*; he's as big and hard as a baseball bat.

He jolts like I've shocked him. "Jesus. Don't get too playful or I might lose it," he grits out through a clenched jaw. But he hasn't stopped cupping my pussy.

I press into him. "I think we should go to the bedroom. And undress."

"You've convinced me you're serious about this," he says.

I let out a laugh and push off of the couch. Slipping his hand from between my thighs, I lead him to the bedroom—well, to *Billie Mae's* bedroom.

Crap. I wonder how much time we have before she comes home.

"What time is it?" I stop suddenly at her bedroom door.

"Is it important?" He nuzzles my neck while his hands roam up and down my body, knocking the panic from me better than two shots of tequila. Why do I care about the time?

"No."

I kick the door closed behind us as he sweeps me up in those magnificently muscled arms, making me want to squeeze them.

So I do.

He chuckles as he carries me the few steps to the bed, then lowers me to the mattress.

He takes off his clothes and I watch him. He's big and powerful and exactly like I imagined in my fantasies. Except he's real and nice and decent and caring and polite. All those things I want in a forever guy. I almost forget to take my clothes off. But after I get my tights halfway down, I can't take the throbbing anymore.

"You are a piece of art." I exhale the words and finish undressing. I bring my hand between my legs to test my pussy. It's more than ready for him.

He moves fast, pulling my hand away. "No you don't, Sara."

He lowers himself, pinning my hand above my head while I relish the weight of him, of his heavy cock against my belly and… *oh boy.*

"That's my job."

I lick my lips. "Are you…" I can't think let alone talk as he drags his other hand down my body, trailing sparks along the way, as the fire inside me flares up to nearly unbearable as his fingers find the center of my pussy.

He runs a finger from the top to the bottom of my swollen folds, applying just enough pressure to make me squirm and cry out. Then his finger stills and he brings his mouth to mine, quieting me, for a brief sizzling taste of his addictive lips. Then he leans on his side and brings his hand up to capture my face and hold my gaze with his.

"Before we go any further, sweetheart, I need to know who I'm relieving of their big O virginity. Are you Sara Bellagamba or are you Lola the puck bunny?"

"I..." Honest to God can't think. I'm having a hard time answering his question because he's so close, every part of his hard, smooth body surrounding me, and his erection pressed between my hip and belly, dangerous and close to my pussy. My hips lurch in an attempt to connect and he sucks in a breath.

"Jesus, Sara..." He grits out the words in the kind of low voice that I can feel scraping against my pussy.

"I..." My eyes start to water because I know the answer's important.

He pushes himself up and I whimper because, let's face it, I'm a wimp, but he doesn't go further, just hovers there above me where I can still feel his heat, smell his overwhelming masculinity, and, most of all, feel the tension like he's wound his massive boner into a tiny tight ball of self-control.

I'm in awe all over again as I gaze into his eyes, melting for reasons other than the elusive big O. He's not a fantasy. He's a man and I like him.

"Don't you know who you are?"

I nod. "Sara Bellagamba." The words drain all the breath from me, all the need from me. Not the physical need, but all that goal-oriented urgency about the Quinn James of my girlhood poster-boy-days being the one-and-only man deserving to christen my pussy with my first real orgasm.

Maybe he sees it in my eyes or maybe he's a mind reader—or, heaven forbid, he has his own hesitations—because he moves away from me, only his eyes remaining on mine, lit with regret and recognition and so many other complicated things mingling in my head to keep me from reading him.

"Sara, you're an innocent." His words are a gentle accusation as he pulls a blanket over me then sits on the edge of the bed next to me.

I still want him, but when I open my mouth, I can't speak. My dream flashes through my mind. But this isn't it. He's Quinn and he's better than a fantasy. Shuddering as the fantasy evaporates into the reality of his rejection, I clutch the blanket and nod as if he needs me to confirm. I am innocent.

He leans forward and kisses my forehead in the ultimate heart-melting act of selflessness, cementing my humiliation.

There's nothing like humiliating embarrassment and shame to cut through the fog of desire and I realize what the word *innocent* may mean to him. He may think I'm an actual virgin. I clutch his hand before he gets up, ready to tell him that I'm *not* and that's not what this is about. I haven't been saving myself for him.

But, before I have a chance, the loud squeak of the front door opening stops me.

"Billie Mae," I whisper to the questioning look on Quinn's face.

"Sara? What the fuck?" Her voice cuts through the air like an iceberg and the bed suddenly feels like the *Titanic* relentlessly heading for disaster as Billie Mae stomps toward her bedroom.

"Crap," I gasp, sitting up.

Raising a brow, Quinn stays cool, going into serious-game-mode. He stands, then lifts me with the blanket wrapped around me. "I take it you have a roommate?"

Double crap. "She's not my roommate." That's all I manage to say as he moves toward the bathroom, naked, glorious as a Greek statue, and looks at me like I'm speaking Greek.

Before we make our escape into the bathroom, as I'm holding my arms around his neck and hanging on, Billie Mae throws the bedroom door open.

She squeak-screams then slaps a hand over her mouth.

I squeeze my eyes shut to hold back my tears—who knows what the tears are for because I should be laughing, right?—and Quinn says, "Excuse us," as he ducks into the bathroom with me and closes the door.

Relief and regret hit me as he lowers me to the floor. When my blanket slips, he secures it around me without so much as copping a feel.

He whispers, "Is that the woman you work with?"

"Yes." My face heats up because I'm going to have to tell him the pathetic truth about how I still live with my parents.

He waits a beat for my explanation and no sign of impatience as he puzzles it out. "This is her apartment?"

I nod.

"You don't live here, do you?" He smiles.

I aim my eyes at the floor, studiously avoiding the mirror behind him so I end up staring at the sculpted beauty of his naked abs and hips and oh-my-God… his glorious, big, O-busting cock staring back at me, tall and proud and not one bit deflated.

Billie Mae shouts from the other side of the door, "I'm leaving now—I forgot something—I'm going out for a… cookie! I'm going to Mike's Pastry! I'll be back later. Maybe a half hour. Okay?"

"Okay!" I shout back in a shaky voice, raising my gaze back up to his face.

And, dang it, he's smiling, that one dimpled, eye-crinkling smile that makes him look boyish and sexy and dangerous and as trustworthy as Captain America all at the same time. The kind of look that makes you forget whatever else there is going on in the entire universe and focus on one thing: having his babies. Well, that and having multiple big Os while you're trying.

"Billie Mae is a good friend," he says, of all things, forcing me to melt further, but not in that hot sexy baby-making way.

No, this is where the danger of Quinn James comes in because he's way more than a sexy hockey-playing hunk—which is devastating enough all on its own—but he's... *nice*. The thoughtful, appreciative kind of guy who gets you. The swoony kind of man who does the right thing even when it means his balls are going to turn blue. I resist taking a peek at said balls, though it's not easy.

I nod. "I think it's time for me to go home. For us to go."

"Let's dress first," he says, his dimple soft and understanding.

A crazy laugh bubbles up and I let it out as he follows me out of the bathroom. I collapse onto the bed in a fit of giggles, lost to the absurdity of the moment. The blanket slips away and I don't even care because I'm practically in tears with my laughing fit.

He joins me on the bed, naked and gorgeous and totally comfortable as he grins down at me, roving his eyes over my body, and even though I know I should feel self-conscious, I can't work up the anxiety because I think I've finally hit bottom, the lowest most embarrassing level of humiliation possible with nowhere else to go but up.

"We should get dressed," he says, amused, but not kidding as he lowers his lids at half-mast, forcing me to suck in a breath at his meaning. "I'll take you home."

Is there invitation in that line?

Then I sit up like a shot. Oh *crap*.

Take me home? Oh, sure. That'll go over great. Mom will see me coming home with a guy I work with—and give me hell for risking my job—and Quinn will learn I live with my parents. Yeah, *that's* a winning situation.

Not.

"You can't take me home." I scramble off the bed and pick up my skirt and jersey. Eyeing the tights, I decide to forego them because they're not worth the trouble.

"I don't mind. No strings. I insist."

"Oh no. It's not possible."

"Why not?"

I have to tell him I live at home. I am now lowering to the sub-basement level of humiliation.

"I... I... "

He slips on his boxers and pants in one smooth motion and comes to me.

I don't back away in fear. Quite the opposite; I vibrate in anticipation of his touch, of him.

"Sara, there's nothing you can say at this point that could possibly be more embarrassing—"

"I live at home. With my mom. And dad. And little brother."

He stares at me for a beat as if he's waiting for something more, and then he does that soft smile again and takes me into his arms for a hug and kisses the top of my head.

Meanwhile my body is all tuned up for his tongue on my pussy but a kiss to the top of the head? Now *that's* humiliating. Or it should be, but he's understanding and didn't laugh at me.

Whatever I thought I wanted before tonight, is gone. What I really want is him. The real life genuine version of him who tells stories about his mischievous childhood and doesn't laugh at misguided puck bunnies.

LUCKILY, the house is asleep when he pulls up to the curb. Back home in good old Revere where I'll die—the neighborhood cat lady, still living in my parent's house at a-hundred-and-one-lonely-years-old.

"I'll be moving to Revere soon," he says. "We'll be neighbors."

A laugh bubbles up, but I keep it under control.

"I'm sure you'll be far from my neighborhood, somewhere on the other side of the proverbial tracks. On the ocean, right?"

His dimple shows up. "Neighbors in spirit."

I get out of the car and I've almost escaped when he says, "See you tomorrow at the pop-up event."

Crap. How the hell am I going to face him in the light of day? At work.

CHAPTER 12

QUINN

*E*scaping the Night of the Puck Bunny Disaster, which is how I'm thinking of last night as I lie in bed, might have been a lucky thing. There should be no question about it after discovering Lola and Sara are the same girl. That shit is so wrong on so many levels.

She's not a puck bunny from a bar; I work with the girl. Fuck. There'd be no escaping the fallout of a fling when I see her at work. And there's no escaping the fallout from last night since I'll be seeing her today at the charity event.

This is something I should be dreading because she's an emotional lady whether she's Lola or Sara, and who knows what she'll say or what kind of scene she might cause? But, as I wait for my alarm to go off at nine, I feel the opposite of dread.

I pick up my phone from the night stand. It reads 8:59. I tap the alarm off before it blares, then shove the covers off me. Heading to the hotel bathroom, I get out my shaving kit. I should be avoiding her and all the trouble of getting involved with someone from the organization even if it's only a mild flirtation. Especially with Sara. She's young and my gut screams at me that she's vulnerable and naïve and so not ready for a spin with the likes of me in spite of her protests otherwise. In spite of her begging me.

Double fuck.

I have a hard-and-fast rule: never sleep where you eat. That's what my dad used to tell me when I was younger, though he was never one to spell out the gory details. My mom, however, *would* elaborate and tell me to never fool around with anyone from school or work.

Either way, message received and rule followed ever since puberty and especially over the past ten-plus years of my hockey career. Until now. *Fucking idiot.*

Shit. A small sting sparks on my jaw as I draw the razor up. *Note to self: never call yourself out while you have a fucking razor in your hand.* Tearing off a piece of toilet paper, I plaster it to the bloody nick on my jawline. My focus is crap. What has me so fucking messed up? Something besides Sara/Lola. She's only a symptom of my problem. A distraction.

My reflection stares at me like I'm stupid. *It's no fucking mystery what's messing you up.* It started with that incident with Princess Anica Romanova that I had to deal with—in Paris. Then my dad dying. And because I was in Paris then, I didn't get a chance to see him. Or my mom and family. I haven't really had a chance to grieve since with the free-agency negotiations and moving to Boston and now the starting the season with my new team.

It's no wonder my family's fucking pissed at me. I haven't seen them because that means dealing with my dad's death and I can't do it—not yet. I need to concentrate on hockey, don't I?

Mom's more disappointed than pissed, but it feels the same as pissed to my battered no-good conscience.

My normally excellent sense of self-preservation which has been almost flawless for all these years—until that fucking incident with the princess—is now turned off and broken. It may be partly because I'm supposed to be avoiding all women and concentrating on hockey, according to my coach—and my agent based on his latest text. Or I'm supposed to be finding a down-to-earth woman to settle down with, according to my mother.

It doesn't escape even my muddled mind that these two sets of expectations are the exact opposite. This is what it feels like to be squeezed from two sides by the forces that are most important to me, hockey and family. I want both, but that seems impossible from where I stand right now.

In the mirror, I notice the toilet paper patch on my face, something I haven't seen in years, and the dark circles under my eyes from sleeping poorly, which was never a problem for me until lately.

This is what it looks like to be between a fucking rock and a hard place. Nowhere to go to for escape. Except, apparently, into a fog so muddy that I start making bad choices about puck bunnies who work for my team.

The fucking kicker is that *knowing* she's a bad choice doesn't change how I feel right now because I am, in fact, looking forward to seeing Sara Bellagamba, aka Lola-the-puck-bunny, aka bad-choice-personified. Because I like her.

I should be running the other way from her crazy ass, because she's a distraction to finding any kind of success in either hockey or a stable relationship. She's about as opposite from stable as I can imagine.

But as distractions go, she's a tough one to ignore. Maybe even a necessary one. Keeps my mind off my baggage. I can't wait to see what she'll do or say next. I wonder what Dad would think of her... *Fuck. Do not even go there.*

Instead, the image of her laughing and sprawled on the bed last night moves everything else from my mind.

She's a beauty, but there are a lot of beauties out there. I feel like I've met at least half of them. So, why her? I look for the answer in the uninspiring hotel bathroom ceiling and wipe the excess foam off my face.

I admit to myself the basic truth about her, either in her puck bunny Lola persona or as Sara Bellagamba, she's a nice person. Kind and sincere in her caring and her emotions and not very good at pretense when it comes down to it in spite of how hard she tries.

In short, she's something I haven't encountered in a woman in a very long time—she's modest, even humble.

She has no idea how tempting she really is.

I take off my boxers. In spite of the semi-hard, Sara-inspired morning wood, I step into the shower and force myself to contemplate hockey pucks and Coach's face rather than give in to the temptation of getting off on the replay of last night's most tantalizing moments.

Turning the water to cold, I make the shower quick and dress in black jeans and a Brawlers t-shirt with my name and number provided by PR. Since I'm still accustomed to L.A. weather, I throw on a light leather jacket against the cool autumn day.

When I get down to the lobby, I throw on my sunglasses and a ball cap that says, *Keep It Lite*, a leftover from a promo I did with Miller Lite that I kept for some reason. It's my *Average Joe* look to keep a low profile for my walk to the Garden. Whether I need it or not.

ARRIVING AT THE LOCKER ROOM, I'm greeted by the team's equipment manager, Zeb Standish, and his assistants in the hall outside the locker room. They hand me the official team hat and my jersey to wear for the day. Zeb takes the hat from my head with a wry grin. A few other guys are there, throwing on their shirts without bothering with the locker room as others arrive.

"As soon as you're dressed, get up to the lobby. Find the table with your merch on it. Someone will be there to help you. Sign as much as you can ahead of time."

"You got pens for us?" Finn asks.

"They'll have them for you."

"Some operation, eh?" Rafe says.

Finn laughs. "You gonna sign yours *All the best, eh,* Mr.-I'm-from-Canada?"

"Fuck you. You're just as Canadian as I am."

"Not for a while." Finn shrugs. "When in Rome..."

I grin and notice that Rafe leaves it alone as the three of us head for the stairwell together.

The lobby has been transformed to a hockey gear shop of mega proportions, smothered in all things Brawlers. Even the sales assistants are covered from head to toe in Brawlers gear and colors.

"Knock 'em dead." Finn punches my shoulder. "But watch out for the flirty fans."

I laugh, not bothering to mention that I'm more than familiar with flirty fans. This isn't my first public relations rodeo.

Searching the sea of merch displays with tall banners at each showing a larger-than-life action pic of a player, I spot mine.

My heart kicks like an engine revving because... there she is, Sara Bellagamba, the ultimate distraction in the flesh.

Striding over with my genuine smile, I remind myself that she's kind and vulnerable and young.

She looks up and her gaze meets mine like there's a magnetic connection between us. Her whole body freezes, then she drops a jersey. She scrambles to pick it up. I reach the display and take off my hat and jacket, then throw them on a chair. She spends some time opening a box, acknowledging me with a silent nod, then hiding behind the curtain of her dark, no longer red, hair. I'm afraid she's going to cut herself her hand is shaking so bad.

With extreme caution, I take the utility knife from her hand.

"We need to clear the air between us—for safety's sake if nothing else," I say like I'm calming a skittish animal.

She gives a small laugh, but when my hand touches hers, a zap of acute awareness jolts me and I wonder who's going to calm me down.

Surrendering the knife, she takes a quick step back. "Don't worry about me. Nothing to see here. No air to clear. Everything's crystal clear. I'm good. No problem—"

"Sara, let's be friends, you and I." Running the knife along the seam of the box, I rip it open, then close the blade and hand it back to her. "I like you. You're a decent, honest person and fun. How about it?"

The slow smile that takes over her face as she takes the knife from me looks like a beautiful dawn, the kind that wakes up all my senses—especially the ones I'm trying to keep dead and buried. I smile back because I'm helpless not to.

"That's what I call an offer too good to refuse," she says. "You have nothing on The Godfather, you know that?" She returns to the business of getting the merch arranged on the display. "So, we forget about..." She waves a hand as if last night is unmentionable.

I have my work cut out for me if we're aiming for an easy rapport, the kind not loaded with pent up lust.

"Last night never happened," I say. "We start fresh as co-workers." *The kind with a very special, physical connection that draws us together like gravity.* Even though I don't say the words, I see them reflected in the expression on her face. *Fuck.*

This is going to be hard.

The buzz in the large space starts up and before either of us can work out the coil of lust clogging the conversation, Billie Mae rushes over from a nearby display. *Shit.* Her friend who caught us naked together—bringing a whole other level of awkwardness.

Instead of saying, "Hello" or standing between her friend and the Big Bad Wolf—*me*—she holds up her phone and starts taking photos.

I immediately adopt my Hollywood persona, with the camera

smile and pose like an automatic reflex, a reaction so deeply ingrained in me that it takes no thought and even though it's totally put-on, it feels natural.

"Hey, you're good. We should call you Hollywood Quinn," she says.

I try to hide my flinch because she's not the first person to call me that. My brother used the name on a number of occasions over the years, with less and less amusement until it was a nasty pejorative that cut deep. I haven't heard it in a while mainly because I haven't heard from him in a while, other than at Dad's funeral. We barely acknowledged each other's presence.

"You good?" Billie Mae asks Sara as she puts an arm around her.

"Great. All set for the crowds of kids. How about you?" Sara's voice is extra bright and Billie Mae looks like she bit into a sour apple.

"You're chipper this morning," I say to Billie Mae and she nods without a scintilla of judgment or awkwardness.

Sara elbows her friend and escapes her hold, going back to work.

I want to say more to her, want to truly clear the air and make her feel at ease, but I have no idea how to be friends with this girl, but I know I better figure it out. Quick.

Jonas strides in our direction and I'm mixed on whether I'm glad or not to see him.

"I see you got a prime placement," he says.

"Where are you?" I ask, heading him off before he reaches Sara. I don't know if he'll recognize her, but I don't want to take the chance. Not here. Not now in public. I don't want her getting in trouble with Delaney.

He tilts his head looking over my shoulder, eying Sara. Shit. "Way the hell over there in the back with a few other guys. Rookies." He smirks, still studying Sara.

I angle my body to block his view while she and Billie Mae

ignore us, moving quickly and efficiently, setting up the merchandise.

He steps around me. "Hey, don't I know you?" Jonas asks her. Shit.

She looks up, startled.

"No," I say at the exact same time Sara does.

She goes back to rummaging through a box.

Billie Mae says, "Maybe. We work for the Brawlers in the PR office."

"With that ball-buster, Delaney?" Jonas says.

"That's the one." Delaney says. We turn.

She showed up from nowhere, her arms folded across her chest and an evil smile in place.

Sara pops up and we exchange an uneasy glance. I'm worried for her job.

"You seem to be next in line for ball-busting, Mr. Bergman."

"Sorry, ma'am. I didn't mean anything by it," Jonas says.

"Just make sure you sign as many posters as you can—at least a hundred—and be very nice to the children."

"Yes, ma'am. I like kids."

"Sure, you do. I'm not surprised." She walks off after a shot that is more effective than a mic drop.

"Guess that's my cue to get to work," Jonas says and takes off.

"Damn." I shake my head. "She *is* the best of the best when it comes to busting balls."

"No argument here," Sara says under her breath.

"We learned that lesson early and hard," Billie Mae says. "I gotta go. I'm assigned to help Ryan O'-Flipping-Rourke, bless his DILF-able soul." She gives me a sassy look and squeezes Sara in a hug that looks sincere, not an L.A. air hug.

Sara waves and then turns to me as she drags in a breath.

I smile. I can do friendly without flirting, pleasant without teasing. It'll be real work to keep the lid on teasing because she's so damn tease-able, but I'll manage as long as I keep hockey and my family front and center in my mind.

"Don't mind her." Sara waves in the direction of Billie Mae. "She was only kidding about O'Rourke. She's a total professional. In fact, you should feel flattered that she feels comfortable enough around you to be so... casual and open." She picks up a jersey from the pile and hands it to me.

I snort, then lower my voice. "I'd say we're definitely past the formalities after last night."

She blushes and the familiar rush of lust pulses through me. *So* not helpful. And so not professional, non-teasing behavior. I clear my throat. "Sorry. Last night never happened."

She stares at the pile of jerseys. "Maybe you should start signing the t-shirts since you're likely to sell more of them than anyone else."

Fuck. She's doing better than I am at forgetting last night.

"Sure. All I need is a pen. They said sharpies would be provided."

"Yes." She reaches into a box and pulls out a handful. "Take your pick."

A whistle blows, reverberating through the high-ceilinged glass lobby and I look toward the front door to see Delaney poised with the damn thing near her mouth.

"Doors are opening. Put on your smiles and bring the energy!" she shouts.

"I bet she would have been a great coach in another life," Sara says, seemingly to herself.

"I bet she *was* a coach before she got this gig," I add.

Sara looks at me like she's surprised I heard her. Then she smiles and it beams. My chest tightens for no reason.

My table is close to the entrance, right after O'Rourke and Rafe, so when the crowd surges through the doors, it's no time before I'm inundated with fans wanting everything autographed, from shirts to posters to mugs. Sara takes care of the sales with a hand-held device and bags the merch while I sign and chat with fans of all ages, but mostly kids.

Not that there aren't a lot of friendly moms lined up who are ready to take photos, most of them jumping in with the kids, but there's no onslaught of aggressive female attention that Delaney was worried about. The place is loud and sounds like one of our games—fans cheering when one of them walks away from a table, holding a signed jersey high overhead.

The fans are great and I'm surprised by some of the lively and knowledgeable hockey talk. It's easy to get caught up in their excitement and I don't think the smile left my face for more than a second or two.

Watching Sara, I make sure I don't rush through the signing so she'll have a chance to close the deals. That's not hard with the fans all wanting pictures. One lady asks Sara to take a picture of just her and her sister—no.

"I'd be happy to. Turn a little to your left so I can see your pretty face," Sara tells the sister—the one trying to rub her boobs against me.

Thankfully, she takes the pic fast and moves them along better than a bar bouncer with a drunk. There are half a dozen security guards spread around the lobby, but, thankfully, so far, the crowd has been orderly and respectful in their enthusiasm.

Sara hands me an open bottle of water when the sisters move on, then resumes helping the next group of fans to find their jersey sizes.

"This jersey will look perfect on you," she says to a little girl, holding up a pink version of a Brawlers jersey with my name on it. "What do you think?"

"I love it. I love your jersey, too."

"Only a t-shirt today, sweetie," her mom says.

"How about if I put one aside for you and you can save up for it?" Sara squats down. "Quinn can sign it for you today and we'll take a photo and when you've saved up, the signed jersey will be waiting for you."

The little girl's head bobs up and down as she grins, showing a gap in her teeth.

Sara smiles at the reluctant mom. "I'll give you my card." She pulls one from her pocket and gives it to the woman, holding her hands and squeezing. "No strings attached."

"Are you sure? I mean, can you do that?"

"Absolutely," I say. "Let's get that picture.

"I'll take it," Sara says, "of the three of you."

We take the photo and I take the pen to sign the pink jersey. "This jersey really is perfect for you," I say to the little girl.

"*You're* perfect for me," she says and I laugh.

"You are, aren't you?" I say. "What's your name?"

"Sara," she says, her grin plastered, and my chest squeezes as I exchange a quick glance with the grown-up Sara. This little girl is like a miniature version of her, right down to the name, adorable and passionate and charming. And Sara sensed the connection, treating her with extra warmth. Not that she hasn't been great with all the kids—because she has, especially the little boys who seem to adore her, and the not-so-little boys whose minds I can read and whose faces I am prepared to punch if they step out of line.

But they didn't because Sara seems to know how to handle herself. Well, with everyone except me that is.

"Thank you so much for everything," the mom says, scooping up her girl and taking the bag with the signed t-shirt,

"I hope to hear from you soon. Please keep in touch." Sara winks at little Sara and adds, "Your pink jersey will be waiting for you." They wave at each other as they move away and the next family of fans takes their place.

Before we have a chance to continue the parade of fans, there's a commotion at the entrance. A hush follows and then an explosion of excited murmurs as the people pull in that direction with their phones up and aimed at whoever just walked in.

Several security guards rush to the scene, pushing back the wave of Brawlers fans leaving their ques for someone making an entrance.

"Who is it?" Sara asks, standing on her toes.

All the fans in line are watching and drifting toward the new star of the show, whoever it is.

"I can't see yet. Too many people."

"It's gotta be some kind of hockey god. Maybe Bobby Orr." A pop of excitement lights her face.

I laugh. "Maybe."

The security guards clear a path—which happens to be leading directly toward me.

The fans part like curtains sweeping open on a stage to reveal the new main attraction.

And she's no hockey god.

She's the devil. The bane of my existence. The woman who started the chain of events that toppled the foundation of my life. The one woman I truly would like to forget and have planned to never see again.

"Fuck." I don't realize I've said it out loud until Sara plasters herself to my side, holding my arm protectively and whispers.

"Isn't that Princess Anica Romanova?"

CHAPTER 13

SARA

"*Y*eah, it's her." His whole body tenses beside me, into fight-or-flight mode. It's like he feels the Princess is a threat.

I tense up too, going into protection mode. Am I being ridiculous? As I watch the princess walk over to us with her cold, regal gaze aimed at Quinn, I can't convince myself that he doesn't need my protection and I double down, clinging to his side and dousing any hint of a smile on my face. *Don't even think about it, Princess.*

She's gorgeous in a slick, magazine-cover-way and I feel like I'm in junior high compared to her sophistication. Her outfit is over-the-top—all red, from her cashmere turtleneck to her wide wool palazzo pants and the long fur coat open and draping around her like a seductive robe. She has the kind of poise and command that I don't even bother dreaming about.

When she stops in front of us and smiles, he stiffens even more so I wrap my arm tighter around his. I'm his friend, aren't I? This is what friends do. They protect each other from nasty princesses up to no good.

"It's good to see you, Quinn. You look yummy in your new

team colors. I never thought I'd see the day you'd leave the L.A. Shooting Stars to come here." She looks around at the fans aiming their cameras at her and Quinn and the rest of us like we're in black-and-white next to her technicolor presence.

"You here to buy a jersey?"

She laughs, then puts a hand on his chest. "I already own your boxers, baby. What would I do with a jersey?"

He doesn't move, so I squeeze my way in between them, pushing her back to give him some space.

She spares me a glance looking like she didn't realize I was alive, as if she thought I were a prop, before returning her implacable gaze to the equally implacable Quinn. I feel like I'm standing in the middle of a petrified forest. But my protective juices are revved.

"Hello, Princess. Maybe you'd like a nice autographed mug?" I say.

She pulls her gaze from Quinn's to glare at me.

By this time, the security guards have the crowd under control and the only audience we have is the line of Quinn's fans waiting to buy merch. But they gawk and listen like they're perfectly happy to be entertained by the princess drama. I, on the other hand, would be perfectly happy to drop through a hole in the floor—but only if I could take Quinn with me. I don't want a scene that could get either of us, or the Brawlers in trouble.

Quinn squeezes my hand.

"Who is this?" Princess Anica says to Quinn as she stares down her sculpted nose at me.

"This is Sara." He lowers his voice. "Watch what you say next, Anica."

Picking up a mug, I hand it to her. "Here. Take it. It's on me. Enjoy your stay in America."

She doesn't take the mug from me. She flicks a non-existent piece of dust from her fur then resumes her staring match with Quinn.

"I intend to enjoy myself very much. Speaking of which, I'm sure we'll run into each other again." She raises her chin. "I've joined the board of the Brawlers Charitable Foundation. Such wonderful causes."

Quinn remains the Strong-and-Silent guy. But my worrying about a scene ratchets up and I squeeze his hand since he's still holding onto mine. God, I feel so connected to him—deep down, not just his hand.

I take a deep breath into the momentary silence and just when I think the princess is through torturing him, she leans in to Quinn.

And kisses him.

And it's not one of those cheeky kisses, oh no. The witch presses those perfect lips of hers against Quinn's as her lashes flutter closed—and one of her entourage pops out a camera—not a cell phone, but a real camera—and takes several photos before Quinn pulls back.

He ends the kiss quickly, but not in an abrupt ungentlemanly way. No unnecessary drama from him. He knows how to create a scene and how not to.

"Good-bye, Anica." He says the ordinarily harmless words with biting finality, but only for those of us within hearing distance—which is me and Anica. *The princess.* Crap. *I'm tangling with a princess.*

She smiles as if she's touched by his tenderness. The camera doesn't stop as she turns and saunters out the same way she'd come in, though with less fan enthusiasm.

I lift the mug. *You forgot your mug, Your Highness*, I ought to call out, strictly to mock her, but Quinn's tug on my hand stops me from saying the words out loud. Thank the *bad choice-vs-good-choice* gods.

The kids from More Than Words are helping the fans, taking over my spot and I'm relieved because that scene exhausted me. They were observing in the background and keeping the line in order and hauling in merch earlier, but their organization's goal is to have them take an active role in every aspect of the event.

Quinn takes the mug from me. "Let me sign that. Then you can send it to her."

"What are you going to write on it?" There's real fear in my voice because he has an mischievous expression on his face.

"Not much." He takes the top off the sharpie. "Something simple, like, 'Go to Hell.'"

I snatch the pen from his hand as he's about to write, smearing a long black line across the picture of his face.

He laughs.

"You... you're naughty."

"Did you think I was really going to do it?" he whispers, still chuckling as he takes the pen back and signs a t-shirt for a young girl as he smiles at her.

I shake my head. Not really.

The parade of fans resumes and I take the photos as the staff handles the payments. We're like a well oiled machine. Quinn continues to give each fan his attention, accepting compliments graciously, and engaging them with quips and answering their questions even if he's answered the same one a hundred times before. He looks like he could go on forever.

"Are we going to win The Cup?"

I'll be answering that question in my sleep tonight, but Quinn finds a way to make it seem like he's giving the answer due consideration each time, coming up with a different way to say *Yes* with conviction over and over again.

What a man—that's what I call stamina. And dedication. I sigh.

THE END of the day seems to come abruptly since there was no slow down in the stream of fans as the doors shut down. Delaney pulls us from the room to instruct us on controlling the social media posts.

"Make sure you put up the most positive shots you have, especially the ones with the princess. What's her name?"

"Anica Romanova," I say automatically, wishing I didn't have her name seared in my memory—in the dark place reserved for enemies of the people who I care about. Crap. *I care about Quinn—as a person.*

THE NEXT DAY, work is blessedly quiet and I contemplate putting my head down on my desk for a nap the way I did in kindergarten. But these cubicles aren't private enough and, as much as I should call this quits and find another better-paying job, I don't want to. Everyone says you need to stay in a job for a year or people get suspicious about your rep.

Plus, even if I'm not normally a fan of self-inflicted torture, I want to stay so I can see Quinn. I'm not delusional enough to think I'd ever see him again outside of work.

I'm exhausted and confused. Luckily, I don't have to take the T home tonight and can relax back into the seat of Billie Mae's car and close my eyes.

Billie Mae is coming to dinner tonight because my older brother, Bobby, will be home. I'm pretty sure she has a crush. It's a big occasion in the family, of course. I try not to be jealous of all the attention he gets because… how can I be? I'm just as smitten and guilty of treating him like the second coming as everyone else is. He's a pro hockey player.

He'd been named for Bobby Orr and does play goalie for a minor league AHL team in the Midwest, but, other than that, he's nothing like the hockey great. He's got a slim chance of making it to the NHL. At twenty-four he's an old man on his team, and this year could be his last chance to make it.

Thank God Billie Mae isn't grilling me for details about Bobby's love life—not that I have any. Instead, she's trying to talk me down from the disappointment of my abject failure at accomplishing my big O goal the one night I had my chance.

"Maybe Quinn will still be up for a one-night-only rendezvous on the sly."

I don't tell her that my disappointment goes well beyond that because a big O dam-busting night is only the tip of the iceberg of the kinds of things I've now allowed myself to want. I'm way too big a dreamer. Way too non-action oriented. This is what happens when I act on making dreams come true.

What happens? Horrific crushing disappointment and an even bigger dream to take home, one even more impossible than the last. I'm not even going to admit in my head what that's all about no matter how much I feel the ache in my chest as if I'd done fifty push-ups last night.

"Why would he go to the bother?" I wave a hand in dismissal. "He's clearly playing in another league that is so far above my pay grade that I may as well be a kindergartener."

"That mixed metaphor makes no sense," she says.

"You know what I mean. Keep your eyes on the road." She's driving because she has a car and I, of course, do not. "Maybe I should quit and take one of those well-paying jobs I was offered last summer. Do you think OMD still has an opening?"

"Don't be hasty. You're a grown-up. You can handle this. The cure is for you to meet someone else. Someone not related in any way with hockey."

I give her a side-eye which is lost on her since her eyes are glued to the road.

"Besides, you wanted this job for a reason. We'll qualify for game tickets soon—we can't leave now."

"That's true. We didn't work this hard for peanuts the past three months to miss out on the one true perk that makes this job special." I pat her shoulder. "Thank you for reminding me and helping me keep a cool head. I'll just have to suck it up like an adult and stop dreaming about crazy fantasies and enjoy the job, stay for a year for the resume like we planned and maybe even meet some nice guy when we're out some time now that I feel more confident about flirting in bars."

She rolls her eyes.

"I'm holding you to the plan to go out to bars."

That reminds me of Sheila and Mindy and my conscience squeezes my achy chest. "Sure. Except I can't go back to The Tea Party or be a member of the puck bunny text group anymore. I hope Mindy and Jonas are going to be okay."

"If you want to still be friends with them, you should. Meet them somewhere else." Billie Mae shrugs. "But don't, whatever you do, let them know you work for the Brawlers. Who knows what they'd make of that?"

"What do you mean?"

"They might try to take advantage of you, Sara. You're too giving to people." She taps my arm.

I swat her. "Keep your hands on the wheel." I don't bother telling her she's wrong about Sheila and Mindy. I can't explain how I know.

I have every intention of doing everything I can to see that Jonas and Mindy get together because I know they belong. I have good instincts about romance—everyone else's but mine—based on years of observation. I'm not exactly sure what else I can do for them, but I'm a smart girl. I'll think of something.

WE ARRIVE at my house five minutes before dinner. The small driveway is full so Billie Mae parks by the curb in front of the gray, clapboard, double-decker and we jump from the car.

I'm in a hurry, but as I walk up the short walk I blow a kiss to the statue of Virgin Mary, who mocks me and instantly activates my guilty conscience every time I see her in our tiny front yard surrounded by a short chain link fence. I don't know if the fence is for protection to keep her oblivious of the sin-riddled outside world, or if it's to keep her from escaping. I identify too closely with that statue sometimes.

"We're here." Billie Mae walks inside ahead of me.

We're the last to arrive and go straight to the dining room where my two brothers, dad, mom, Aunt Yolanda, and Grandma Zanetti are already seated.

Bobby gives me a hug and then he helps himself to a hug from Billie Mae.

She tries to stay cool, but I know she's having a fit of giddiness on the inside.

What's more interesting is Bobby's reaction to Billie Mae. He pulls out her chair for her while I struggle with mine, jockeying for space at the over-capacity table.

My younger brother, Paul, has always had a crush on Billie Mae, but this behavior is new from Bobby. He stares blatantly at her as he takes his seat across from her.

If I didn't treasure my right arm so much, I'd offer Bobby a napkin to wipe his drool. But he'd rip my arm off for a lot less than that—although he insists that the time I'd ended up in a cast was an accident. It probably was. I don't hold it against him. He was a rambunctious kid.

"It's been a while, Billie. You're more gorgeous every time I see you," he says to her.

He's a rabidly-horny twenty-four-year-old on the make having gone through way too many girls since puberty to count and I don't want him to take advantage of my best friend. I step in to cool him off though I know she won't appreciate it.

"Billie Mae's been dating a new guy. Tell us all about him—"

She pinches my thigh. I swear I ought to start wearing pads there to keep my *bellagambas* from bruising.

"It's nothing." She smiles that flirtatious one I've seen her use before and does an accompanying eye-lash flutter. "I swear, app dating doesn't work anymore."

"As if it ever did," Bobby says, nodding as if he knows.

"I still say you girls are working in the best place to meet men," Mom says. "You ought to be taking home one of those hockey players by Christmas if you play your cards right." She gives me a look I'm sure that's meant to encourage me, except for the skeptical squint of her eyes.

The table quiets as our dishes are filled with pasta, and eating —or, rather, scarfing—commences. Meanwhile, I'm still suffering from my unrequited big O and something nameless making me feel sad and restless, so I barely eat a mouthful of my otherwise favorite pasta. Even my mother notices my mopishness under-neath the excitement about Bobby's homecoming.

"What's with you?" she asks in her usual caring way.

"Nothing. I'm fine."

"I just expected more excitement from you is all." She looks to Billie Mae for an answer.

"Maybe it's all the excitement of working alongside Quinn James that has her worn out," my former best friend says.

I try sending her daggers, but Mom grabs me by the shoulders and Paul, still young and energetic jumps from his seat to join the upcoming inquisition.

"F-ing cool," Paul says.

Dad eats his pasta and Bobby grins, mostly at Billie Mae. Aunt Yolanda fans herself and Grandma Zanetti chuckles, shaking her finger at me, mumbling about paying attention to my mother. Even Grandma is turning on me. I'm only twenty-two and the pressure of not ending up an old maid is already getting to me.

"You work alongside Quinn James?" Mom asks. "And when were you going to mention this?"

"No big deal, Mom. We worked with him at the pop-up event yesterday. The whole team was there and lots of staff. It's not like—"

"Did you get tickets to a game?" Paul asks.

"Did you get anything autographed?" Mom lets me go with an expectant smile.

"No. We ran out of merchandise so I couldn't get anything."

"You could have had him sign your shirt," Paul says. He turns to Billie Mae. "Did you get him to sign something?"

Billie Mae gives him the finger—but with a smile.

Mom laughs and shakes her head, then goes back to eating a meatball. "Next time you have a chance, you make sure you get us something. I thought you said that's why you wanted the crummy-paying job?"

She isn't wrong.

"You're right, Mom. I need to get something out of this job besides a pay check."

She smiles, pleased.

However... she might not be so pleased if she knew what I have in mind.

CHAPTER 14

QUINN

$\mathcal{T}$he first game of the season hits me like an out-of-body experience. . The reality of being on a new team not even remotely like the L.A. Shooting Stars is like the difference between a rodeo clown and a bull. The locker room, the rink, the press, the fans, the weather, and the sonic boom that slams me when my skates hit the ice, the banners hanging around the rink... This team is a legitimate contender for The Stanley-fucking-Cup.

Warm-ups flash by until I find myself standing at center ice, lined up around the face-off circle for the start of the game. No one was more surprised than me that Coach made a last-minute change, slotting me for the first line.

The puck drops, O'Rourke wins the face-off, then I catch the puck on my stick like it's a magnet. The three of us—O'Rourke, Rafe, and I—race into Montreal's end and we're off, caught up in the time-bending frenzy of an NHL hockey game.

With thirty seconds left in the second period, I sit, dripping with sweat, on the bench, with the score two-all.

"Which one of you reprobates is going to score the fucking go-ahead goal?" the coach asks.

Some of the guys volunteer by grunting even though I'm pretty sure it was a rhetorical question. But he stares each one of us down in a row, and when his steely gaze meets mine, I go for it and raise my hand. I'll play this game.

"I'm scoring the next goal."

The three forwards from the fourth line race to the bench. As they scramble over the boards, I jump onto the ice and race to the blue line. One of our defensemen shoves the puck up in my direction and I go. Rafe is with me and I deke around the defenseman backing up, then flick my wrist.

The puck whistles toward the goal. The goalie lifts his glove hand and it hits his arm then bounces off.

Rafe is there in front of the goal and beats the defenseman to the puck, swiping in the rebound under the goalie's pads. Score!

Okay, so maybe it wasn't me, but I had a glove in it.

The red goal light goes off and, a few seconds, later the airhorn ends the period as the team rallies mid-ice to celebrate the go-ahead goal. The crowd is deafening, transforming the arena into a play-off-like cauldron of energy.

Boston Brawlers hockey is intense. Making a run for The Cup is no joke, and, as I get battered by sticks and gloves and jostled by good-natured chest bumps and congratulations littered with four-letter words and emphasized with one-armed bro-hug.

"We still have a fucking period to go," I say as we finally skate towards the gate. "And I didn't score a goal yet."

"WHAT ARE you doing in the locker, old man?" Jonas says to me. "Maybe you should get back out on the ice and score that goal."

That's right. No goal. I got two assists, but that's not what I was shooting for. Literally. I give Jonas the finger and snort in disgust both meant for myself, but the little shit makes a good proxy.

O'Rourke walks by me, shirtless but still wearing his pads, and taps me on the shin with his stick. Without the pads, the gesture feels less friendly, but he grins.

"I don't mind if you keep dishing the assists. You can go scoreless all season and I don't care—*if* you get two assists every game."

I continue dressing and smile as I button my lavender dress shirt. When I reach for the dark gray, window-pane, plaid suit jacket, he raises his brows and Finn comes over and looks me over, too.

"What's the matter? Doesn't anyone dress up after games around here?"

"Sure," Finn says. "If we're on our way to a wedding or a funeral." He smirks and brushes my lapel.

I slap his hand away. "You're funny. You know, you wouldn't recognize a basement bargain from custom Italian suit if—"

"That's custom Italian?" Jonas lets out a whistle. "You really earned that Hollywood Hockey name—an Italian suit for a post-game—"

"I'm taking my family to dinner, shitheads. Do you mind?"

Rafe takes my side, bemoaning the lack of style from some people. Most of the locker room is embroiled in the playful battle over what makes good post-game hockey style and I don't know if there's more laughing or throwing down of the f-word.

Either way, in spite of the fact that I'm enjoying the banter, I put it on my list of things to do—donate the Italian suits to a men's shelter.

AFTER MORE BANTERING with the press outside the locker room, I look around for my mother, more anxious to see her than I expected, but I see Sara.

She's loitering around the hall, taking photos with Billie Mae.

I acknowledge her with a nod. Looking away without a smile goes against my grain and the strong inclination I have to talk to her, but I move on and find my family waiting.

Relieved that Chris isn't here, I exchange hugs and easy banter with my family. As we're talking, Jonas comes by and I'm in the middle of introducing him to everyone and when Jonas spots Sara.

He calls to her, snags her surprised attention.

All my ease disappears as he sweeps her up into the circle of our group. She looks like a wide-eyed child visiting the zoo for the first time—excited, beautiful, and like she doesn't fit in. The last thing I want to do is introduce her to Mom and my family because everyone—including Sara—will get the wrong idea. And who knows what Sara will say?

But since the only other option is to be unforgivably rude to her, I have no choice.

"This is Sara Bellagamba, everyone. Sara, this is everyone—my mom, Aunt Mary, and my buddy, Lenny."

Jonas stands there, grinning like he's watching a show. He set me up and doesn't care that he's making Sara uncomfortable. I'll have to deal with him later. Again.

"Is this your girlfriend, Jonas?"

"Me? No, ma'am. She's with Quinn."

Fuck. I give Jonas a look that says, *You're a dead man*, but he doesn't care. My mother's smile goes impossibly wide and I close my eyes for a beat to let the strong urge to strangle Jonas subside.

But Sara, the normally shy one, has one of her spurts of boldness and speaks right up. "No, no. Jonas has it all wrong," she says. "I work for the Brawlers front office. Quinn and I are acquaintances."

Jonas snickers.

Mom nods, one of those motherly, knowing smiles, the kind that crinkle the corners of her eyes and light her face.

"How nice," Mom says. "What do you do for the Brawlers?"

Sara blushes and I know she's embarrassed by her lowly position. "She's a public relations assistant and very good at her job. She's gotten me some good publicity in a short time I've been with the team. My agent says he got a call yesterday for another local promotion."

"That's wonderful. Seems like we owe you, Sara."

"Not at all. Just doing my job. Besides, it's a lot of fun." She leans into Mom and lowers her voice. "It doesn't even feel like work, really. I hate to admit it, but I'd do the job for practically nothing."

I hold back a snort at her inside joke about her lousy pay.

"Oh you're so cute." Mom turns to me and I manage a nod. "She's such a doll, Quinn. So sweet. I think we should invite her to dinner with us. Surely, we can add one more person to the reservation?"

"Of course," Lenny says. "Any *acquaintance* of Quinn's is a friend of ours. It would be great to get to know you, Sara." He gives her a sincere smile and I get a bad feeling about this.

"You all have a great night," Jonas says. "I'm meeting some friends—"

"What about Mindy?" Sara says, raw disappointment bursting through whatever previous polish she showed. She's really taking this Jonas-Mindy thing to heart. Probably because she has a very big heart.

"How do you know Mindy isn't one of the friends I'm meeting?"

"Is she?"

Jonas smirks, and takes off without answering.

"Is everything all right?" Mom asks.

"Yes," I say before Sara has a chance to give any kind of explanation. "Let's get to that restaurant before we miss our reservation." I turn to Sara. "Will you join us?"

She shakes her head. "I couldn't intrude on your family dinner." She looks around. "Besides, I don't want to desert Billie Mae."

"Looks like Billie Mae deserted you," I say, looking over her head and watching Billie Mae talking to the equipment manager, or rather, *flirting* with him.

Sara spins around to look, but I take her shoulder and turn her back around to face me. "Come with us."

It's a foolish thing to say, a foolish way to say it with my stupid pleading smile and damn dimple, like I mean it. It's especially foolish because I do mean it and insanely foolish because I'm saying it in front of my mother and the others. Mom will think all kinds of things—all the wrong things.

But I don't want Sara to be deserted. And I do want to look at her, to tease her, to watch her blush and hear her laugh. And I especially want to see her occasional brave outburst of raw emotion.

Just this once. Then tomorrow the team takes off for a string of away games and when I get back, we'll resume as nothing more than acquaintances, someone I might see around once in a while, wave hello to in the hallways. Someone I don't stare at and definitely don't talk to, let alone tease. Fuck.

Hockey. Stanley Cup. Focus. That's the reason I'll give my mother why I'm not seeing Sara when she asks me about her one day in the not-too-distant future. Seeing her? For fuck's sake, I never planned on *seeing* her. I don't want Sara to get that impression either. Even though she said she's only about the Big O, I know better than that. Her emotional outbursts tell a different story about who she is.

"I'd love to join you for dinner—if you think it's—"

"Please do," Lenny jumps in, taking her arm and ushering her toward the parking garage. "You'll be a breath of fresh air compared to any girl I've met who Quinn's dated."

I'm following behind him and tweak him on the back of the head, reverting to our twelve-year-old best-buddy status like no time or baggage intervened between then and now.

He laughs and so does my mom. Though I notice she has a rim of sadness around her eyes that never leaves. Her smile—and the dimple I'd inherited—never quite clear, like she's seeing us, the world, from under a lake of fallen tears. That's when I feel the slam to my gut like I've been hit by a slapshot. Dad's gone and Mom is grieving and I haven't been here.

Whatever state of suspension my emotions have been in these last six months disappears. My seeming immunity to the emotional toll evaporates and I stumble with the weight.

Sara turns, her effervescent smile faltering as she looks at me. I'm not sure what she sees, except that it's an undefended version of my face, reflecting the sudden vulnerability and hurt that churn inside me. I can't have that, so I muster up a smile, forcing the dimple into place.

She takes my arm, looping hers around me and bringing me up to walk with her and Lenny while my mom and Aunt Mary walk ahead of us.

"We're taking my car," Lenny says. "Christopher and his family are meeting us at the restaurant."

I stop. My brother? "I didn't think he came."

"Of course he did," Mom says. "He would never deprive his children of the chance to see an NHL game. Those seats you got us were fabulous." There's a note of encouragement and pleading in her voice.

"Great." Fuck. Last thing I'm prepared for tonight is the strain of keeping the peace with Chris. I glance at Sara who's watching me closely. Maybe it's good that she'll be at dinner tonight.

"Where's the rest of *your* family?" I ask Lenny.

"They'll be coming to the next one. My sister flew the coop and lives in the Berkshires now, so it's not a quick commute. And

Dad... He needs some preparation for an excursion to Boston." Lenny's voice tightens and I give him a nod of understanding and put a hand on his shoulder.

We reach Lenny's giant Suburban SUV, then pile inside. I sit up front with Lenny. Sara's in back seat with Mom and Aunt Mary. I'm not sure how she feels about sitting between two strangers, so I turn and wink at her, giving her a real smile of encouragement, then I turn on the radio with the volume cranked up to listen to sports talk. Maybe that will take the pressure off her and any need for conversation.

Lenny and I jump into our usual talk about the game as if we were still on the same team like high school.

"The Brawlers win their opener and the big question remains whether signing the former scoring star from L.A. will be worth it. What do you think, caller one?"

"So far he's oh-for-one and the so-called hot shot still has a lot to prove—"

"Is that guy stupid, or what? Lenny lowers the volume. "Where do they get these callers? Idiot. You set up two of the three goals, Quinn. What do they want you to do in the first game? A hat trick?"

I laugh and throw in my two cents, and we argue with the sportscaster and his callers, giving them shit for any criticism. But in the midst of all the fun—because I can't take the shit seriously, learning long ago the radio guys are paid to stir the pot—I keep an ear tuned to the back seat to make sure Sara is okay.

At one point, she says to my mom, half laughing, "Are they for real?" She's talking about me and Lenny swearing at one particular comment by a caller about Hollywood Hockey—my old nickname, the one I'm trying to ditch. It's the only comment that pricks my thick-as-a-puck skin.

Mom laughs. "Afraid so. They enjoy giving grief to sports journalists from afar. It started out as a defense mechanism for their fragile high school egos, but, now, the ritual is plain ol' fun. They love nothing more than giving grief, period."

Glancing in the rearview, I see Mom shake her head with a smile—amused and... sad.

CHAPTER 15

SARA

"I understand you recently lost your husband, Mrs. James. I'm very sorry."

"Thank you." She takes a deep breath and glances out the window while I stop breathing, wondering if I've said the wrong thing. But then, there's no right or wrong way to confront grief and I can tell Quinn's mom is a grieving woman.

She turns back to me, a fragile, yet real smile in place. "So, tell me about yourself, Sara. Where are you from?" Mrs. James' eyes show that same uncanny deep-down interest as Quinn's eyes do, and I feel that same connectedness, like I'm the most important person in the world at this moment.

"Quinn's lucky to have a mom like you." Crap. No filter.

She blinks and then chuckles. "Thank you. I'm not sure what brought that on, but I'll take it. Be sure to mention it to Quinn."

"I will. First chance I get."

"Now, about you," she says, forcing me to do the thing I hate most, talk about myself.

"Oh, not much to tell. I'm just your typical recent college grad in the city trying not to get overwhelmed while I live on a poverty-level salary, working for my ultimate dream team. The

Brawlers are awesome—but I don't have to tell you that, do I? I'm a certified—maybe certifiable—fan from way back."

She's smiling, almost laughing, but not quite. I'll have to try harder to erase that melancholy she wears.

"How do you come by your love of hockey?"

"I was raised on it. Hockey rinks were my Disney World and Zambonis were my roller coasters growing up. My older brother worked at the local rink and gave us free rides. I'm from a hockey family. Both my brothers play and my father... used to play." I hate thinking about the fact that the only place I ever saw my dad on skates was in old photos. But the car's gone quiet, so I brighten. "The good old days." I go for a wistful smile and hope it works.

"It couldn't have been too far back—you're still very young."

I don't respond because this is too obvious, almost embarrassing to be such a child compared to everyone else in the party. A self-conscious blush creeps up my neck to my cheeks in a warm wave.

"How old are you? If you don't mind my asking. Just curious."

She must be dying of curiosity to be so bold. Or maybe Quinn takes after her.

"I'm twenty-two." I answer her even though I mind very much. I can't turn her down.

She nods and the radio goes silent as we pull up to the curb for valet parking at Buttermilk & Bourbon.

Quinn jumps out and gets my door, reaching a hand in to help me out. I take it and a shock of awareness jolts me. I freeze as I meet his gaze.

I talk under my breath as he leads me inside the door being held open like we're someone important—though, I guess he *is* someone important. That makes me even more nervous. "Are you sure this is a good idea?"

He laughs softly. "Depends what you mean by good. You'll be a good distraction for me and a buffer between me and my brother. We're more likely to stay on best behavior with you—a newcomer—around."

"Well, when you put it that way... Just don't come looking for me if I disappear into the ladies' room for longer than expected." I'm half-kidding and he laughs as we gather with the crowd at the host's station.

"We'll have your table ready in one minute, Mr. James." The maître d' is dressed better than all of us. He sends off a couple of the serving staff into the dining area, presumably to make our table ready.

Quinn helps me out of my coat, adding to my illusion that we're together. Lenny checks everyone's coats and we head to the bar area.

Quinn's mom heads straight for a handsome knockoff of Quinn except he's slightly older and a few inches shorter.

"Chris, I'm sorry for the delay. Quinn had to talk to some press," she says.

"Of course he did." Chris hugs his mother and then nods at his brother.

I wait for a hug or a fist bump or handshake, or even a smile to soften the cool stare, but... no. It's worse than I thought and my protective instincts go on alert as I stand a smidge closer to Quinn while he says hello to his sister-in-law and two wide-eyed nephews. At least he treats *them* to a grin and fist bumps.

I look around to see if any of the patrons are paying attention to us. Other than a few looks of recognition, some whispers behind cupped hands and small gestures in our direction, the crowd here is cool.

"Sara, let me introduce my brother, Chris," Quinn says. He doesn't elaborate about who I am, leaving his brother to make whatever assumption he wants, so I jump in.

"I work with the Brawlers organization," I say, a bubble of dismay at my identity. It doesn't sound quite right, but I don't know what else to say.

Chris smiles, making him look more like his brother and not so bad. But I'm not ready to let down my defense of Quinn yet.

"This is my wife, Jennifer," he says. The pretty woman at his side, perfectly put together and polished to within an inch of perfection, smiles at me with pearly teeth.

"Nice to meet you."

"And this is Tyler." Chris ruffles his son's head.

Tyler gives me a goofy grin.

Him, I can handle. He looks about ten years old and full of mischief.

"No alliteration for you," I say, giving him a goofy grin back.

"I'm lucky," he says, surprising me. I was sure the alliteration reference would go over his head. "I was almost named Jimmy James."

I laugh and Jennifer gasps. "You most certainly were not."

"Where'd you get an idea like that?" His dad asks.

"Uncle Quinn told me—"

"Figures." Chris throws a dagger-like scowl at Quinn, which surprises me because the reaction is so over-the-top. And when I glance at Quinn for his reaction, I expect an unapologetic smirk, but no. For an instant, I see hurt and regret and grief. But then he replaces it with a mild version of his game face and turns away. When he winks at Tyler, I'm relieved. A little. But I can't forget that hurt and pain I saw on his face. I may never forget it.

Tamping it down, I know I should try or... I'll feel that swelling need to do something about it. I can't afford to start feeling animosity toward his brother after meeting him only five minutes ago. It's that stubborn, Italian loyalty-to-the-point-of-destruction, the implacable maxim in life of treating any enemy of my friend as my enemy. Anyone who would do harm to my friend I have a disturbing blood lust need to do harm to. Crap. I can't let that ridiculousness run free.

I haven't felt this kind of animosity since I was a kid and I beat up Wally down the street for teasing Paul when he was only five. I've always been protective of him, even from my parents whenever they come close to hinting that he was their surprise child. He's five years younger than me and it always seemed like a big gap until now because, at sixteen, he's taken quite a growth spurt and can grow a legitimate beard if he wants.

"And this pipsqueak is Timmy James," Quinn says, giving his other nephew a playful nudge.

Timmy sports a toothless grin and nudges his uncle back. A bout of lopsided roughhousing between an adult and kid ensues.

Their mom looks horrified and nudges her husband to say something.

"Settle down now. Time and place." He scolds his son.

Quinn gives him a look that I would bet translates to *f-you*. He's about to say something when the maître d' approaches with menus and clears his throat.

"Please follow me to your table."

"Thank God," Quinn's mom murmurs and I catch her eye, unable to squelch my smile. She winks.

I almost stop walking because I've seen that wink before, that exact expression—from her son. It's uncanny because she doesn't have his bright blue eyes or look that much like him, but there's something about her, from deep down, that they share, that reminds me of him exactly.

"We're going to get along, you and I," she says, looping her arm through mine so that Aunt Mary, her, and I walk in Quinn's wake to our table.

Eyes turn stare at him. He nods at anyone who speaks to him —which is quite a few. "Good game" or "Glad to have you on the Brawlers" and the like.

Lenny sticks to his side, running interference.

"No one's asked for his autograph, thank God," Aunt Mary says under her breath. "Last time we went to dinner with him, it took us an hour to get out of the restaurant."

"Oh, don't exaggerate," his mom says before looking at me. "You must be used to this kind of thing."

"Who, me? No one's ever asked for my autograph." I snort.

She laughs. "I mean putting up with all the interruptions whenever he's out in public."

"Oh. Aah..." Thanks to the restaurant gods, the maître d' interrupts us as we reach the table to seat us. We're at a round table in a private corner and I'm seated between Quinn and his mom, with Aunt Mary next to her. Lenny sits on the other side of Quinn. I want to kiss him because Jennifer almost sat there and something tells me that wouldn't be ideal. The kids are across from us and Chris is on his wife's other side.

Our server takes over and asks Aunt Mary, "Can I get you something to drink?"

"I'll have a margarita," she replies.

"I'll have the same," Quinn's mom says.

He smirks at me and that's all the encouragement I need.

"I'll have the same."

Jennifer orders white wine and Chris orders some kind of ale, with soda for the boys.

"I'll have an ice water," Lenny says. "I'm driving."

"And for you, sir?" the server asks Quinn.

"I'll have what he's having, but with lime, thank you." He grins at Lenny.

Chris raises his brows as the server walks away. "Since when don't you drink?"

"Since the season started."

"I've seen you drink during the season before." His brother doesn't let it go.

"This is the season we're going to win The Stanley Cup." Quinn's stares at his brother, as serious as a priest. After two beats of silence—during which I watch Quinn's jaw muscle twitch—Tyler finally breaks the tension.

"How can you be so sure you're going to win, Uncle Quinn?"

"Because I'm going to give everything I have and so is everyone else on the team. We have an awesome team."

"Yeah, you do," Tyler says.

"Does that mean we get to go to more games?" Timmy asks.

"Absolutely," Quinn says. "As many as you want."

"We'll see about that," Chris says. "We don't want to make promises we can't keep." He directs a pointed look at Quinn.

"No, but we do strive to do our best to make things happen," Quinn says to Timmy, who's now become the unfortunate proxy for the brothers to argue with each other.

"Oh, look, here're our drinks," Aunt Mary says with undisguised relief as the server approaches with a tray filled with assorted drinks.

The drinks get sorted out while the boys talk hockey with Lenny, and the server takes our dinner order. It takes me a few big gulps, trying to keep pace with Aunt Mary, who's slogging hers back like there's no tomorrow. And then she orders a second *one.*

She nods at me. "She'll have another, too. And how about you, Natalie?" She waves without waiting for a response from Quinn's mom. "Bring us another round of margaritas."

"Are you sure—" Jenny starts but Quinn cuts her off.

"Don't worry about Aunt Mary." Quinn winks at his aunt. "She's an original Irish drinker. Was born with a hollow leg like her dad, Gramps." They grin at each other and raise their glasses in a toast.

His mom joins in and Quinn looks at his brother in invitation. "How about it, Chris? To the original old man."

Chris pauses a beat, glances at his mom, then raises his glass. "To the old man's old man."

They clink glasses and take sips. Warmth runs through me as if I'd witnessed something special. Something sad and happy at the same time, the connection between them all wrapping around them in a reminder they all acknowledge.

I sigh.

The boys go back and forth with their mom and dad about how hungry they are, and Lenny, my new hero, engages Jenny in conversation. Natalie and Mary laugh about some memory from their childhood about their dad. That leaves Quinn to turn to me with those wicked blue devil eyes that make my panties blush and that irresistible dimple that speaks volumes, things like, *You turn me on* or *Let's spend the night together...*

I must be in some kind of hypnotic state that makes me think in terms of campy seventies love songs. Which is ridiculous even for me so I shake myself out of it.

"What are you thinking?"

"About you and how irresistible you look." His voice is soft.

"You can't say that." Which is crap since I was just thinking the same thing about his dimple.

"Why not?" He raises a brow. "I can't wait to hear your answer."

Me, too. "Because that would be flirting and..."

"And?"

And my mind is temporarily disheveled by those eyes that are rummaging through the drawers in my mind. Crap. I clear my throat and let the margarita ease through me.

"And we're not on a date. We're not... like that. We're friends. Right?" Crap. I didn't mean for that to be a question.

"We are supposed to be friends. You're right. I'm out of line." He looks at his water glass, shaking his head and drawing a circle in the frost. "You make it hard."

I snort. "Hardly. I make it hard to take me seriously. I'm a disaster."

He chuckles. "Funny, I was thinking the same thing earlier." He moves his hand to mine and draws me in with his electric blue stare. "But the thing is, it doesn't matter. I can't pretend away the attraction." He leans in, lowering his mouth to my ear and whispers, "Which is too weak a word for the size of my dick right now."

My whole body seizes up in the female version of a stiff dick as I suck in a breath and grip the seat of my chair so I don't launch myself into his lap to go for that promised ride.

"You sure know how to turn a girl's head," I say, dredging up a random line from an old black-and-white movie because my brain has clearly gone haywire.

Predictably, he laughs. "See? How can I resist a girl who always surprises me? Who makes me so fucking excited just anticipating what she's going to say next?"

"That's a rhetorical question, right?"

"No. The right answer is, 'Why, Quinn, of *course* you can't resist me so you should stop trying.'"

I laugh, a bubbly, borderline out-of-control laugh like I may need a strait jacket soon.

Since we're in public at a restaurant, it shouldn't be a surprise when the server returns with his minions bringing our meals and I look around as if I've just stepped from a movie theater into the bright daylight, blinking back to reality. Quinn's mom is looking at me with a kind smile and I smile back, wondering if she's over-heard or can somehow read my mind.

Crap. She can probably read my face since I'm notoriously transparent, especially when I'm drinking and double-down especially when I'm flummoxed by Quinn James and all my flimsy defenses evaporate like the steam billowing from a Zamboni.

We settle into eating and talking about the meal—or the others talk and eat while I try to fork the same piece of food repeatedly while my mind spins around in a loop, repeating the same question. What the heck is going on with Quinn? Is he really flirting? What does that mean?

And, most scary of all, how the heck do I explain being at dinner with him and his family to Delaney tomorrow?

Because—judging from the pops of cell phones around the room—I won't be surprised if there isn't a pic of us somewhere on social media by now. And Delany will have her minions ferret it out.

Except—lightbulb moment—Billie Mae and I are her new minions. So maybe, just maybe, she doesn't have to find out...

"It's a shame you have a game on Thanksgiving," Quinn's mom says. "But I don't mind having Thanksgiving dinner the day after if you have it off." She holds her breath, pleading with her eyes for Quinn to say the right thing.

I don't know what else I've missed in this conversation, but I've regained use of my faculties in the nick of time and I nudge Quinn's leg with mine. The contact sends all kinds of sparks running through me and I pray they don't show.

He darts me a glance. Then winks.

"I do have that day off, Mom. I'm yours for a Day-After-Thanksgiving dinner." He grins and his mom reaches her hand over to clasp his.

I glance at Chris and Jenny to see stony silence.

"That's great," Lenny says. "We can resurrect our traditional game of street hockey if you're up for it."

"You're on." Quinn fist-bumps with Lenny, and the boys bounce in their seats.

"Cool! Can we play, too?" Tyler grabs his brother's arm to include him. Their eagerness and brotherliness warm me.

"Of course you can," Quinn says, fist-bumping each of them.

"We'll see," Jenny says.

"Finish up, boys. It's time to leave," Chris says. He turns to his mother. "I'll check the schedule to see if we can rearrange things."

"Thank you, Chris." She nods and I give a silent cheer for Natalie James. Yay!

The server removes our plates. The boys argue with their mom about going to the men's room, and Quinn's mom turns to me.

"I would like you to join us for our Day-After-Thanksgiving dinner, Sara. Will you?"

The sheer graciousness of her invitation, the natural and genuine warmth of it, makes it impossible to say anything else. "Yes. I'd love to."

It's not until I'm in an Uber on my way to home when the ludicrous enormous mistake of accepting that invitation comes to mind.

What the heck am I doing? I can't have Thanksgiving dinner with Quinn's family—without even telling him? What was I thinking? What am I still thinking as I run through my wardrobe options and make plans to bake a pie to bring with me?

No way is this cool to have a holiday dinner with a man's family who I'm not even dating. Who I'm technically not even flirting with, let alone getting to know all his relatives as if we have an actual relationship.

Crap.

CHAPTER 16

QUINN

*F*uck. I slam the hotel suite door behind me. I can't believe Mom invited her to Thanksgiving without checking with me. Even more unbelievable, I can't believe Sara accepted the invitation without checking with me.

I stride to the bedroom, tossing my jacket and tie onto the floor, followed by my shirt. My frustration has me pacing as I get to my boxers, not giving a damn about the expensive Italian suit and shirt strewn on the floor. I flop onto the king-sized bed and check my phone. It mocks me with the time—midnight.

Frustration gets me out of bed to pace. What the hell am I going to do about Sara?

Hell, I'll just treat the Thanksgiving dinner like a date between Mom and Sara if that's how they're playing it. This absolutely doesn't count as fulfilling my promise to Mom to bring the right girl home for Thanksgiving dinner. Absolutely not.

Lenny—the traitor—dropped me off first at the hotel so I didn't have a chance to discuss my relationship—or lack thereof —with Sara with Mom. But we'll definitely have a talk later.

Exactly what I'll tell her, I'm not sure. I push my hands through my hair.

Fuck. There *is* no relationship between us. Isn't that the frustrating part? Maybe I should drive to Portsmouth in the morning to see Mom, but I've got a morning skate with the team and then I'm meeting with the realtor to finalize the paperwork for the house. Then the team bus leaves for our road trip.

I'll have to call her—but when? I can't have this conversation with all the guys around.

And what about Sara? When the hell am I going to talk to her about it? More importantly, what am I going to say that won't hurt her feelings... the truth?

What the hell is the truth?

Pacing around the hotel room sucks because even though it's a suite, there's no space to unwind. I can't wait to get out of here and move into the house. A walk along that beach would be perfect about now. The salty ocean breeze would help me calm down enough to sleep.

Tonight, it's about more than hockey and more than the weight of guilt over my family or disgust with myself for the stupid glam lifestyle I allowed myself to get sucked into. The strain of keeping the soul-crushing hurt at the loss of my father at bay is wearing me down.

I pick up my phone and wonder who I can touch base with at this hour.

Scrolling through, my thumb lands on one name and I click. Shit. Am I stupid or what?

I still don't know what the appropriate thing is to say to Sara, but my thumb had a mind of its own, apparently and doesn't care about appropriateness. There must be a straight line from my dick to my fingers right now as they start texting.

Me: Are you safe at home now?

Sara: If the lock on my bedroom door holds.

Who's asking?

ME: Your favorite hockey player.

Sara: The one with the big head?

Me: The one with the big stick.

It takes a while before the three dots appear on my phone and I let out a breath. I should not be flirting with her. In fact, I should probably apologize.

But my dick has control of my fingers, so. I settle on the couch because said dick is squirming around and making it impossible to pace. I lean back and wait for the results of those flickering dots, holding my phone with two hands, resisting the urge to shove one hand into my pants. *Do not go there.*

Her reply finally appears.

Sara: The forbidden stick?

I laugh and my *stick* takes notice, stiffening and begging me to turn up the volume on the flirting. But, damn, what kind of ass would that make me? I'm not going to be the guy to toy with the likes of Sara Bellagamba. I never was that guy and I don't care how much she begs me, I'm not going to start now. I need to shut this down.

Me: That's right. There are no sticks among friends. I'm leaving for a week of away games tomorrow.

Sara: Good. I deserve a break from you.

Me: You're right. After tonight.

Sara: What about Thanksgiving dinner? What will you tell your mom?

I have no idea what I'm going to do about Thanksgiving dinner except that Sara can't be there. We can't carry on the charade and allow my family to think there's something between us. Because there's not. Plus, it would be career suicide if the press thought there was. But I'm not going to resolve the puzzle of our relationship in a text tonight, so I kick the can.

Me: Don't worry about it. Thanksgiving is five weeks away.

Sara: That's right. A lot can happen between now and then. Maybe you'll find a real girlfriend to invite to dinner.

Shit. The last thing I want to do is make her feel rejected, like she's less than.

Me: No. No girlfriends for me.

Sara: Just puck bunnies who work with you?

Me: You're no puck bunny.

Sara: What if I want to be?

Fuck.

Me: You're not puck bunny material. You are definitely the serious girlfriend type.

Sara: Except not for you.

Me: Poor me.

Sara: Boo-hoo. I'm going to sleep now.

Me: Sweet dreams, Sara.

I hold onto my phone for a while in case she comes back on, but there are no more dots. No more texts. And I'm left feeling restless and unsatisfied like I was just getting into a good book and someone ripped it away.

The need to finish my story with Sara gnaws at me.

CHAPTER 17

SARA

*I*t's impossible to go through my boring work day and not think—okay, *dream*—about Quinn. I shouldn't, but I keep my cell phone out where it can taunt me with its silence. Meanwhile, the computer screen filled with numbers that I usually embrace and turn into fine productive reports looks like an impossible mess. Or maybe that's just me projecting myself onto the screen. Crap.

Billie Mae looks at me from her cubicle for the hundredth time. She suspects there's something wrong with me—beyond the usual—but I'm putting up a brave front by not admitting that I'm a fool by hoping Quinn will toss aside good sense and contact me. Oh, who am I kidding? I'm hoping he'll swoop in and finish the job he started that night and then... I shut down any thought of what could happen next.

"Oh, for cripe's sake." Billie Mae glides her rolling chair over to my cubicle. "What is your problem?" She looks around and lowers her voice when I shush her. "If you want him, go after him. What's the worst that could happen?"

"I could get fired and, worse than that, I could ruin Quinn's reputation and career."

She waves a hand. "No, not that—you're both too smart to get caught. I mean to you—emotionally."

"Oh that. Only complete and utter humiliation by a flat-out rejection, followed by desolation."

"Exactly. So what?"

I blink. "That's cold."

She rolls her eyes. "Because from where I sit, you're already there, girlfriend. You may as well go for broke because you have nothing to lose."

I'm not sure she's right, but I shut down my pesky good sense and go for optimism. It's my natural state, isn't it?

"Maybe you're right. What's the harm in sending him a good luck text before the first game of this grueling west coast road trip? I'm sure he can use the moral support."

"It's a start," she says, unimpressed with my plan to go for it.

Martha walks by wearing a new Brawlers' hat and Billie Mae slides back to her cubicle with a wave.

"Nice hat, Martha."

She smiles and scurries past me.

I don't waste any time executing my newly-formed plan with my newfound courage because it's as fragile as it is new. Snatching up my phone, I tap in my message fast and then, for a brief second, I prevaricate, holding my breath. There's no harm in telling him good luck; I can't get fired for that and the media won't make mountains out of that small molehill.

Letting out my breath, I hit Send.

Then my vigil starts. Waiting for the response is excruciating.

And maybe... a little... desperate? After all, Quinn could have any woman in the world he wants. Hell, even a gorgeous princess is after him, yet, he's not interested. And he'd told me that he's not interested in anyone, so why on Earth would I expect him to care if I text him or not?

My eyes pop as three dots appear on the screen.

An instant later, the world *thanks* appears.

I wait… but no more dots.

I huff out a breath and shove the phone into my bag. That's it.

The short response doesn't encourage me to send another message and I know better than to push it, to distract him when he's trying to not be distracted.

He needs balanced and I'm the opposite of balance. In fact, I'm thoroughly unbalanced.

AFTER THE GAME is over and I'm bouncing up and down in my bed because the Brawlers win, temptation to reach out to Quinn again curls around my heart and squeezes.

My text is innocent enough with a "Congratulations!" him. for scoring his first Boston Brawlers goal in the third period, sealing their 4-1 win.

Then my phone rings—it's him!

I pounce to answer it. "Hey."

"What the hell are you doing texting in the middle of the night?" His words are lazy and full of mischief.

"Besides watching you play hockey?" The loaded question pops out and a vibration of excitement runs through my entire body—not for any other reason except that I think I've finally learned how to flirt. I can tell by the tense silence on his end that my flirting is working.

"Okay, I'll bite. What are you doing besides watching me play hockey? Being a naughty girl?"

"Depends on what you call naughty," I say, having no idea where I'm going with this because the truth is a big fat dead end and I'm not much at making up stories.

He gives a breathy chuckle into the phone that sends a chill of need through my body and an impulse to my hand as my hips arch up reflexively.

"Tell me what you're up to," he says, "and I'll let you know if I think it's naughty."

Holy moly. This could get really hot really fast. I try to think about if that's good or bad or what could go wrong, but my brain power has been seriously curtailed on account of all my blood flow hitting my lady parts right now. I can feel the unmistakable tingle.

Then it occurs to me that it's my turn to speak.

"I…" have no idea what to say.

"That's what I thought." He sighs. "You're too good to be naughty."

"You forget that night at Billie Mae's…" I shouldn't be reminding him of that debacle, but I'm desperate not to be cast as too good to be naughty. What a horrible thing for him to say.

"That night you were Lola. And she does have a naughty streak."

"You realize there is no Lola, right? Not anymore. We agreed—"

"We agreed we'd be friends. Didn't we?"

"Yes."

"So why did you text me tonight, Sara?"

Is that accusation in his voice? Defensiveness spikes in me.

"Friends can text, can't they?" Can I tell him the truth? That I don't want to be just friends, that I want to have a fling and finish what we started?

"They could, but… Look, I'll be honest. There's something about you that… I have a hard time leaving alone. You intrigue me. You interest me. And I find you sexy as hell. So being friends is a challenge." He lets out a breath. "But it's a must."

"Remind me why we have to be just friends." My mind is fried, completely blown by his words. I don't understand anything right now except my overpowering desire for this man, which has been blown up exponentially after hearing him say he finds me *sexy as hell*. Either we're having phone sex right now or I'm hanging up and grabbing my vibrator. Not that it'll be very satisfying in the end when what I really want is Quinn. In the flesh.

He chuckles again, this time sounding resigned. "Because I'm not having flings. I don't need the distraction, remember? Besides, you're not Lola. You're Sara and even if you didn't work for the Brawlers—which is a large fucking red flag by itself—you're not the kind of girl to toy with. You're a keeper girl, not a fling girl."

"But how can you decide that if I say I'm most definitely a fling girl."

"Because you have no idea what a fling is, what the implications are, or what it would do to you."

"*Do* to me? I think I know what it will do to me. It'll give me some Big O relief with a slamming hot guy. How's that for implications?" I'm delirious and words are flowing from my mouth from a well of desperation.

"Have you ever had a fling before, Sara?" He says the words softly.

I wince. "No." There's no way to fudge the truth.

"Right. Good night, Sara. I'll see you sometime after I get back."

I have no choice but to end the call and now I don't even feel like keeping my date with the vibrator. How am I supposed to have a fling if *not* having a fling disqualifies me from having a fling? It's a mean catch-22 and I should have made that point.

Next time.

THE NEXT DAY, I decide to call instead of text. The injury report said Quinn's thumb is still a problem and they're playing the toughest team of their road trip today.

I hunch over my phone to tap in his number and hold my breath until he answers.

"Hello. Who is this? Sara or Lola?"

I laugh, pleased at the playful sound of his voice.

"Sara since I'm at work," I whisper. "I wanted to tell you good luck tonight."

"You're being very naughty today. I appreciate the sentiment, but you shouldn't be calling from work. I don't want you to get fired."

My heart warms, but the feeling is short-lived when I'm interrupted.

"Drop everything."

Delaney just *has to* ruin it, doesn't she?

"Delaney's there, right?" he asks in a normal tone of voice.

"Shh!" I put my hand over the mic, but I can still hear him laugh.

Delaney glares at me.

"I gotta go now."

"No kidding?"

I just can picture his dimple from the laughter in his voice.

"I'll call you after tonight's game."

"Fine. Bye." I hang up.

Delaney clears her throat while glaring at me and Billie Mae. "I have a special assignment for you two. The Brawlers organization annual charity gala is coming up and you will need to be there. Your assignment is to take video clips of all the important attendees for social media. We want to get all the content we can and make the most of the good publicity." She looks between us. "Got it?"

"Absolutely," Billie Mae says.

I nod

"Good."

"Can I bring a guest?" Billie Mae asks.

OMG, is she crazy?

Delaney delivers her most withering stare. "You aren't attending as guests, Ms. Stoddard. This isn't a party for you. This is a job."

"When is the event?" I ask.

LATER THAT NIGHT, I can't turn down the invitation to watch the Brawlers game with my family and have to admit it's fun to share the hockey excitement with them. We then watch the post-game show and their company helps keep my nerves calm because anticipating Quinn's promised call tonight has me on edge. I have no idea what to expect.

Fidgeting with my phone, I'm ready to escape to my room, so I get up.

"Where are you going? They're about to interview the coach," Mom says.

Crap. I always watch those interviews—mostly because I'm waiting for a glimpse of Quinn, hoping to see him, to see that dimple. But, tonight, I want to be anywhere but here with my family when he calls.

If he calls.

"Can't a girl go... get a drink of water?" What the heck kind of lame excuse is that? They all look at me like they know I'm hiding something.

"What's up with you?" Paul says. He gets excited and uses his taunting voice. "You're hiding something, aren't you? It has to do with Quinn James, doesn't it?"

"What insanity are you talking about?" I toss back, well-practiced at defending taunts from my brother.

"Be quiet, the both of you," Mom says. "Why would she have anything to do with that old man?" she asks Paul. But before he can answer, while I'm turning blue holding my breath, she shushes him. "Quiet. The coach is on." She rivets her eyes to the TV and Dad smiles—who knows why?

I use the distraction to leave the room. It was a close call, but Mom's words have a calming effect on me. Not because I suddenly agree with her that Quinn is an old man—i.e., too old for me—but because she's right that he's not an immature inexperienced boy like Jonas, who doesn't have any appreciation for how women feel. If he says he's going to call, he'll call.

Turning on the TV in my room, I change into my sexiest night gown, which is actually the top to a pair of pajamas that I misplaced the bottoms to. So what if it's sprinkled with kittens? It shows my legs which are my best attribute.

Throwing myself onto my bed, I shake my head at my absurdity. It's not like he's going to facetime me. But if he does, I'm damn well going to be ready.

CHAPTER 18

SARA

*W*hen the phone finally rings, I rouse myself from that half-asleep stage where the day dreams are fading into dream-dreams and this one was a good one. By the second ring, I'm alert enough to scramble in my sheets for the phone. Picking it up with shaky hands, I clear my throat and put on a smile. Dad always told me that, if you smile, a person can hear it even if they can't see it.

"Hello there." My heart beats too fast and I reason with the panic that I'm too young to have a heart attack.

"Hello there," he says, a sexy gravel to his voice, made thicker because my imagination is on overdrive, thanks to the remnants of that dream. I want to ask him when he got such a sexy voice, but my natural reserve rebels in horror at the idea. *Way to go with the flirting.* "Did you catch the game?"

"Of course. Congratulations on the win." I don't mention the fact that he was in the penalty box when Vancouver tied the game on the power play with five minutes left in the game. And then he wasn't on the ice in the final seconds when O'Rourke scored the winning goal.

He snorts. "No thanks to me. O'Rourke bailed us out."

"That's why they call it a team sport." I wish I could be more encouraging, but he didn't have a great game and I'm a tinge worried about it.

"No need to sugarcoat it, sweetheart. I sucked tonight. But you're right, it's a team sport and I'll bail the team out on another night. Enough about hockey. Tell me about you. What are you wearing?"

Boom.

Even if I'm not much at playing the game, I know a flirty line when I hear one. My heart almost stops and I touch a hand to my chest as it doubles down, pattering all over the place.

He chuckles. "Sara? I'm sorry. Forget—"

"No, no." I'm not about to forget that sexy question or the low suggestive note in his voice. "I'm wearing a t-shirt. And panties."

"Your *bellagambas* are bare," he says like he's stroking my legs with his words, his voice silky smooth and appreciative.

"You've picked up the Italian really fast," I say, then squeeze my eyes shut because it's a decidedly non-flirtatious piece of nonsense.

He laughs. "That's what I like about you; I'm always surprised by what you say and can't wait to hear it."

I snort, then I clap a hand over my mouth, then squeeze and try to redeem my unsexy self. "I mean, you'd be a party of one in that club."

He laughs again. "I don't mind. Matter of fact, I'm glad."

Heat flames from between my legs all the way up my body like I'm a rope on fire and he lit the match. He's showing signs of possession and I know that means interest. Real interest. Holy crap.

But it's my turn to talk again and I don't know where to go from here.

Of course, he bails me out. He's a natural at bailing people out.

"Is that what you usually wear to bed, or did you leave your legs bare because you knew I'd be calling?"

"I confess. I dressed for you."

He groans. "You shouldn't have told me that. Now, I'll feel guilty. We're just friends. "You know that, right?" He lets out a long breath and I'm turned on by the gritty need in his voice, the raspy texture.

"Yeah, I know." I lower my hand to my panties and slip my fingers inside. My skin is hot and I hold my breath as I slide a finger through my folds to feel how wet I am. I knew I would be, but the sensation on my fingertips makes it officially hot—and I'm past the point of no return. I want to make myself explode with the sound of his voice in my ear.

I just need him to keep talking. "How about you? You sure we're just friends." My voice shakes and I move my finger up and down over my swollen pussy.

"I'm sure. You okay?" His voice is low.

I nod, breathing heavier, speeding my fingers up, circling my engorged clit. "I'm… great." I bite my tongue. My voice is too breathy.

"Sara?"

His voice goes even lower and the vibration of it sends a wild thrill through me, making me arch into my hand and flick myself wildly. I bite down hard on my lip to prevent the moan that wants to let loose into the phone.

"Sara," he says again, the question gone. "Are you… pleasuring yourself?"

His voice is hoarse now and a rush of heat swamps me, setting off the explosion in my pussy, making me spasm and the moan escapes in a strangled, "Yes… yes," as I answer him. My hips pump and I ride the throbs of my orgasm, shaking and too caught up to know what he's saying.

"Sweet Jesus. If it weren't for my fucking conscience, I'd be right there with you, sweetheart. But…" He covers the phone and his words are garbled.

"Oh my God. I'm so sorry." It dawns on me what I've done and that he's been trying to be a gentleman and I've ruined that for him.

"No you're not," he chuckles. "I bet *sorry* is the last thing you feel right now."

"No, really. I mean, I feel… good—well, great—but I'm sorry that you—"

"Don't go there, honey. I'm not joining in this game. It's bad enough I opened the door by flirting; I should know better that there's no such thing as harmless flirting with you." He pauses, takes a shaky breath while I pull my hand from my soaked panties. "I shouldn't have called you."

"Don't say that. Then I wouldn't have had… my big O with you. It was my goal, after all."

"Technically you still haven't," he says. "Forget I said that. I'm glad you had your big O." He mumbles something that sounds like, "At least someone's getting action."

"Not that it was nearly as satisfying as it would be with you in person."

"Not nearly. But that's not happening. Sorry, sweetheart."

"Then you'll have to stop calling me *sweetheart*."

"Sorry. You're right."

"Does this mean we won't be talking on the phone anymore?"

"Probably not. Unless it's business related."

"What if it's friendship related?"

There's a long pause. "I'm not sure I'm up to it. You're testing my conscience as it is."

I laugh. "I'm confident your conscience will hold out. You're a tough guy. Besides, I'm only talking about a phone call. What could happen?"

He laughs and I turn pink. "Oh yeah, besides that. I mean, I can promise it won't happen again." I tangle my fingers into a double cross and I'm sure my face is crimson now that I've turned into a no-conscience tramp.

This is a classic example of a big ol' fat genie being let out of a bottle and the bottle being smashed to smithereens, never to be repaired.

Besides, phone calls are safe. No one at work can ever find out if we keep the calls out of the office.

"You're right," I say. "No more naughty phone calls."

"Back to co-workers?" he asks.

"Sure." *Is* there such thing as co-workers with benefits?

We end the call and I'm exhausted. With my heart still pattering faster than it should, I fall asleep.

NOT SURPRISINGLY, after our call I have a dream-filled night and a big-O filled shower before work. I get through the day in a good mood, and even though Billie Mae is suspicious, I manage not to share my secret. Besides, she's too caught up in her romance with my brother, Bobby. Not that she's admitted it's Bobby. She's referring to her new heartthrob as Mr. Mysterious.

But the dead giveaway is all the phone calls—and I can guess exactly what kind of calls they have at night, given my recent experience. Not that I want to imagine her and my brother—No. But she's seemed deliriously happy all week.

Tonight is the last game of the Brawlers' six-game road trip and Quinn has been true to his word not to call.

It's three a.m. my time and I'm ready to talk to him. I can't go another minute without consoling him, giving him a virtual hug of support after the disaster of tonight's game. The game was in L.A and the media made a big deal of it. He didn't play well and some of the local and national press were brutal. I'm not sure if he'll be in bed or out with his L.A. friends, but in spite of the shake in my hand, I hit the button and let it ring because I want to tell him something supportive, like a friend would. Of course. The phone rings twice.

"Sara. Your sweet voice is exactly what I need tonight."

"Is that right? I wasn't sure if you'd mind me calling. Sorry about the game."

"Let's forget about the game. What about you. How was your day?"

I laugh. "No way are we talking about my day. You'll fall asleep in ten seconds."

"You called me in the middle of the night. What did you want to talk about?"

I don't miss his suggestive tone. Heck, I'm already halfway there thinking about it. I lick my lips, tighten my grip on the phone, and lower my other hand down into my panties. I should have learned and come prepared without panties, but I hadn't planned this.

"Let's talk about what I'm wearing." I proceed to make up the most outrageous outfit I've ever seen in a porn video.

He sucks in his breath. "You're being naughty. You called to torture me?"

"Anything to keep your mind off the game." There's a teasing note in my voice that I hadn't planned and it surprises me.

It surprises Quinn, too. He groans. "Fuck. Okay. Let's say you really are wearing a red rubber bustier... tell me, does it cover your nipples?"

I look down at my nipples and they are hard and straining for attention through my t-shirt. I put the phone on the pillow next to my head and give them something to remember.

"They're popping free and so hard." There's a strain in my voice and he groans again under his breath.

"You're determined to kill me, aren't you? To crush my resolve." He takes a deep breath. "But one of us needs to be good. Funny, I thought it was going to be you."

And my big O desire has now been crushed. "I'm sorry. You're right. I'm out of line calling you. It won't happen again." I keep my cool and mean the words. "Except for business."

Now what? Do I back off and try to be cool, keeping it just friends when he returns as promised? Or do I really test him, press forward, run with the momentum, and go all the way to the promised land?

Do I dare take the risk of rejection or getting found out? Can I see myself breaking all the rules, sneaking around, and hiding a fling from everyone—Delaney, my family, and his family too?

Because there's no way I want him to get in trouble over a little fling with me.

And what if it's not a little fling? What if it's a big *fling?*

Because chances are my falling heart will tumble all the way. Am I prepared for that?

Yes. Because that's when I quit my job and save us all from the clutches of disaster.

That's when I move onto my next job and the next chapter of my life with a clean break, wiping the slate of my romantic life clean. Like nothing ever happened.

Right?

Right. Sounds incredibly painful. And lonely. Crap.

"Look, I should go," he says. Thank you for the call to cheer me up. It was a sucky game tonight. No way to sugarcoat it or try to pretend otherwise," he says.

"Everyone's entitled to a lousy game now and then. The team and you will bounce back when you get home. It's been a long road trip."

I adjust to the role of friend and it feels right. My chest feels heavy and my belly hollows out like his unspoken words have sucked all the energy out of me.

"Sorry if I'm a downer. You're right; we'll bounce back. But it'll take a fuck load of hard work and attention to every little detail. More attention than I've been giving."

"Okay." My voice sounds small and I try to smile to make myself speak normally. "I'm sure you're right."

"I'll be back home tomorrow. No more phone calls. You ready for that?" he asks.

"As ready as you are."

He laughs softly and I picture his dimple and the soft crinkles at the corners of his beautiful blue eyes, and my uterus whimpers.

"We can do this. We can behave like two professional adults. You have a job to do and so do I. I need to focus."

I know he's disappointed about his so-called six-game scoring slump, but it can't be because of me—can it?

"You're right. Of course."

"You're a young woman, a truly hot young woman with a lot to offer. You'll have no problem finding someone else. A younger guy."

"You don't mean that, do you?"

"Which part?"

"About finding a younger guy."

"I should mean it, but I hope you don't mind if I'm a little jealous of your future young man."

"Stop talking like you're old. That's ridiculous."

He laughs. "You're right. I'm not old, but I'm too old for you. And I'm unavailable."

"That sounds final."

"It is."

Crap. "I understand." I take a breath, but it doesn't help. My voice is still shaky. "I hope your focus pays off, Quinn. I hope you score the winning goal in the seventh game of the Stanley Cup finals and you celebrate with your family, and your brother congratulates you with a big, heartfelt hug."

There's a beat of silence on his end and my heart beats fast—too fast.

"That's a kind and beautiful thing to say, Sara. And so like you." He clears his throat. "I wish you all the hockey tickets you can handle and one lucky young man to sweep you off your feet."

"Thank you." I make my voice as strong as possible.

"Good night, Sara Bellagamba. Have sweet dreams and a sweet life."

CRYING all night didn't help, so I slather on some makeup and get into work early today, determined to make Quinn's wish for me to come true. Billie Mae listened to my story last night and let me cry on her shoulder over the phone. She didn't say one word about Bobby—her Mr. Mysterious.

But this morning, hiding behind my fake reading glasses, hunkered down in my cubicle, I'm determined to be a grown-up woman, not a pretender. It's no wonder Quinn thinks I'm too young for him. A girl with a crush. Someone he almost, but didn't take advantage of in spite of me throwing myself at him repeatedly.

Billie Mae stops at my cubicle before taking her coat off. "At least it's Friday," she says rubbing my back.

Delaney walks in and Billie Mae scurries to her cubicle.

"That's right. It's Friday and tomorrow is Saturday. And the gala. I want to make sure you're prepared. It's black-tie. Do you own evening gowns? Or forget that—dressy cocktail dresses? Maybe something with sparkle?" She's looking between us, her hands on her hips.

"Of course. I have just the thing," Billie Mae says. She grabs my arm. "For both of us."

I can't speak, but not because I truly have nothing to wear to this event, but because, somehow, I'd forgotten all about it. And all about the fact that I'll be seeing Quinn there. Dressed up and the object of affection by every woman there. I wish I were exaggerating.

Delaney walks out of our cubicle space and I deflate.

"Don't worry, Sara. I have several dresses that'll look great on you."

I slump forward to take a minute to regather my spunk. When did I turn into such a wimp? Crap. I've always been a wimp when it comes to guys and social situations. And especially when it comes to Quinn James, apparently. I force myself to sit straight.

"That's perfect. You're a lifesaver. I'm… looking forward to the event."

She pats my back again. "Sure you are." She leans over and whispers, "If nothing else, we'll make him drool. No reason you should be the only one out of sorts."

I laugh and it feels good. Good enough to continue working right up until quitting time when my phone rings. At five past five. My coat is half on and I stare at the phone, willing it to stop ringing. But then a fit of conscience forces me to do the responsible thing and I pick it up.

"Brawlers Ticketing and Public Relations Office." There's a beat of dead air and I'm ready to hang up when a familiar voice shocks me.

"Well I'll be damned," Sheila the puck bunny says.

CHAPTER 19

SARA

"**S**heila?" I squeak. It can't be. "How did you get this number?"

She laughs. "Jonas gave it to me. I hope you don't mind. I would have bet my mother's house he was playing with me. So, you really *do* work for the Brawlers."

"Yes, but I..." I lower my voice. "You have to keep it quiet. I could get into big trouble if—"

"No worries, sister. I know. No fraternizing with the players. I was calling to invite you to come out after the next home game. I promise to keep your secret."

Crap. We finally earned our game ticket privileges and that's the game Mom, Dad, Paul and even Bobby are going to. Billie Mae, too, of course. "I'm not sure. I—"

"Don't tell me you have a date with Hollywood Hockey? Girl, you go."

"Please don't call him that. No, I don't. I wish. How's Mindy doing?"

"Jonas is hot and cold with her. Now that her baby bump is showing, she convinced him to take the paternity test before he left for the road trip. The results will be in on Friday and she's meeting to talk to him after the game because he doesn't want to see her alone. Guess he thinks he needs witnesses."

"That's so crazy. If you think she needs moral support—"

"The truth is, she needs you to play his conscience. You make him feel guilty. Having you there might help him make the right decision."

"Okay. I'll be there." I squeeze my eyes shut against the image of my mother's wagging finger of disapproval like she's my conscience. I must take after her.

Before I let that horrifying thought set in, I switch to worrying about logistics. I'll need to disappear after the game. How the heck am I supposed to transform from Sara Bellagamba to Lola before I get to The Tea Party without anyone knowing about it?

"You're the bomb. I know you're busy. You have a big shot career with the Brawlers, not waitressing at a diner like me and Mindy."

"Who me? You're kidding, right? If you're trying to say I'm too good to be hanging out with you guys, then you couldn't be more off base. My mom is a waitress and I... work in a cubicle crunching data. It's a boring job that pays next to nothing."

"Really? I thought you went to college—the way you talk."

I laugh. "The way I talk is like I need a strong dose of cool."

"So, what about you and Hollywood Hockey—I mean, Quinn?"

"What about us?"

"What's going on? I could swear he's got a thing for you the way he eyed you."

"Umm..."

She laughs. "I'll see you at The Tea Party after the game next Friday."

CHAPTER 20

QUINN

*A*s soon as I get off the plane at Logan airport, I take a minute to thank the gods that I'm back on the East Coast where I belong. Even after living on the West Coast for ten years and being absorbed into the culture, I'd still felt like I was on another planet, especially when we played in L.A. and the media had made a big fuss over my so-called return home.

Home had never felt so far away. Moving east and joining the Brawlers was the best decision I've ever made. Now I need to follow through on the rest of the promise to myself and play hockey undistracted by anything. Especially women. Especially one particular woman named Sara.

Calling her that first night had been a mistake. I'd thought we could be friends, but that was stupid. And I have no excuse—and no idea what compelled me to slip.

Whatever the fuck my thing is for her, I need to shut it down and keep it shut down. For both our good. I don't need to get her into trouble—or, heaven forbid, break her heart—and I do have something to prove to my team and my family. Most of all, to myself.

There's a lot of baggage in me that needs unpacking before I'm fit for anything else but focusing on hockey and family.

Hefting my actual baggage over my shoulder, I book it to my car, waving to the guys. All I'm focused on now is crashing at home in my new bed to sleep for a century.

❦

SITTING in the locker room taking my time undressing after practice, I can't believe it's only Thursday. It's been a tough week. I worked my ass off in practice and the result was one fucking assist in Tuesday's return home game. Damn discouraging and I need to do better because I'm working hard at limiting distractions. It takes everything I have to ignore Sara. Responding to her texts with one word feels mean, but I warned her and we agreed, didn't we?

Who am I kidding? She's too young and vulnerable for flirting with the likes of me. I'd be a heel to take advantage of her. I led her on and I need to fix that—somehow without encouraging her further.

Problem is, anytime I engage with her, even in a normal polite friendly way, I get derailed. Why? My subconscious is begging me for a distraction, that's why. Now my conscience has gotten in on the action.. I give myself a mental slap. It's time I dealt with my issues straight on.

Coach peeks his head in the door and looks straight at me. "James—in my office as soon as you're dressed."

That doesn't sound good. "Yes, Coach."

"What did you do?" Jonas pokes me as he walks by on his way to the shower "Can I talk to you after Coach gets through with you?"

"Yeah, sure."

Dressed in jeans and a Brawlers t-shirt, I fling my jacket over my shoulder and head for the door.

Finn stops me. "You okay?"

"Sure. Why do you ask?" It's a stupid thing to ask and I suck in a breath. "Nothing winning The Stanley Cup won't fix."

He smiles, but shakes his head. "Tell me it's not that girl from the front office?"

My eyes widen . "What are you talking about?"

"You're in a scoring slump. I figured maybe you're going too hard on the extra curriculars."

"Fuck no. Jesus. Give me some credit."

"No judgment. I fooled around with an intern when I definitely shouldn't have."

"Yeah? How did you get away with that?"

"I married her." He grins.

I snort-laugh. "Quite the solution." I take a hard look at him. "But you're happily married, aren't you?"

"Yes, I am. Mostly because of her. I'm a lucky man. Just saying. Maybe you ought to think about a serious relationship."

"Fuck no. She's far too young—"

"I didn't necessarily mean with Sara," Finn says in a low voice. "But with someone."

"You sound like my mother."

"I'll forgive you for that comment only because I don't believe in kicking a guy when he's down." He smacks my shoulder.

I give him the finger. "Thanks for the pep talk. It's not my first scoring slump and it won't be my last."

He nods and I leave, walking at a brusque pace to get this talk with Coach over with. I'm not looking forward to it.

Knocking on the door jam, I wait for him to look up from his computer and wave me inside his small office. It's spare in furniture with not much else—no photos, no shelves, only a white board and a large wall monitor. I sit in one of the two sturdy chairs in front of his desk.

"I'll get straight to the point, Quinn," he says as he gets up to close the door behind me, then comes back and sits. "We need to get to the root of the problem that's causing this scoring slump. We can't afford for it to linger."

"Yes, sir. I'm working on it. I—"

He waves a hand. "I don't mean extra shooting practice. I mean figuring out where your head's at because it's not on hockey."

Boom. I didn't expect his accusation, but I should have. I haven't been focused even though that's been my goal, my aim, and my intention from Day One. I sit and stare back at him, unsure what to say. Since he didn't ask a question, I say nothing.

"I expect more production from you. Is there a problem?"

"Hell no." The image of my father's grave stone pops into my head and I close my eyes.

"You lost your father recently, didn't you?"

Fuck. This is not what I need to talk about. I can't open that box of shit. Not now. But I can't lie either. I nod.

"A loss like that is a funny thing. You think you have it under control, but find out you don't at the oddest times. It messes with your concentration. Believe me, I know something about it. Lost my wife not long ago."

"I'm sorry. I didn't know."

He shrugs. "The point is, you need to deal with it. You have someone to talk to?"

I have no idea how to answer the question. My mind wanders, the faces of people I know popping in and out, none of them fitting the role. Until I come to one face with a sweet smile. Sara Bellagamba.

"Yeah."

"If not, I'd suggest a professional. I have a couple of names of people who've worked with players in the past. Whatever you do, don't ignore it. Don't push it away without dealing with the loss and everything that it might entail, all the feelings, not just sorrow."

"Shit, Coach. You moonlight as a therapist?"

He scoffs, "Son, being a therapist is a requirement for coaching." He stands and so do I. "Carry on. Let me know if you need a name." He clears his throat and adds in a gruff voice, "Or if you want to talk to me."

I thank him and leave, my gut riled up and a sharp pain stabbing me between my shoulder blades. As I leave the office, I see Jonas waiting for me at the end of the hallway. When I reach him, he steps in line with me and we head for the garage.

"Everything okay?" he asks. He might even sincerely care.

"Sure. Nothing I can't handle. Scoring slump. I'll get through it. What about you?"

He looks down as we walk. "I took the paternity test."

I stop and grab his arm. "Slow down. This is serious shit. Are you—"

He shakes his head. "I don't know the results yet."

He knows deep down; I can see it in his eyes. "When do you find out?"

"Friday. After the game. That's why I wanted to talk to you."

He stops talking and I wait him out. He looks miserable. His problem helps me keep what I have going on in perspective. I can handle my family and hockey. *A kid?* That's a whole different thing.

"Whatever you need, bro," I say to encourage him. He obviously needs something from me.

He takes a deep breath. "Mindy wanted to meet in public and read the results together." He snorts. "She doesn't trust me not to bolt or ghost her if we're not face-to-face with witnesses. Her words." He looks at me, confusion, guilt and panic warring it out.

I take his arm. "Whatever happens, you'll be fine. I'm sure there's a way to handle things so that you can have your career, and your life *will* go on. Probably better than before."

He barks. "Thanks. She wants to meet at The Tea Party after tomorrow night's game for the reveal—that's what she's calling it

—the paternity reveal." He shakes his head and looks like he wants to cry.

"You want me to go with you?"

He nods. "Yeah, man. That would be cool." He looks up again. "I'd really appreciate it. I mean, I'm sorry I'm dragging you into all my shit, but you kind of asked for it when you started giving me shit about Mindy."

"I did. It's no problem. I'll be there."

He nods and smiles with some relief. "Thanks, man." He turns to walk away to his car, but then turns back. "And, for what it's worth, I'm sure you'll figure out your scoring slump." He gives me a smirk like he already has it figured out.

I'm not sure what it says about where my head is when I have to stop myself from asking if Sara will be at the paternity reveal.

I need to avoid her and it's easy enough not to cross paths with her—except in my dreams. I shouldn't be having those dreams. They're just perpetuating my lust for a woman I can't touch. It's bad enough I let things go as far as they have.

Fuck.

Hockey and family. Focus. Deal with Dad's death.

Fuck no. Not now. Not in the middle of the fucking hockey season.

Filing into the locker room after Friday's game, I walk with Finn. It's become our ritual.

"Congrats on the two assists," Finn says, tapping my pads with his stick.

I take a seat to undress. "It's step in the right direction," I say, but I really need to make the goals. Next game. As long as I keep my head into hockey and block out all other distractions.

After I shower and dress and talk to some media, I catch up with Jonas near the exit.

"You ready?" he says.

"I'm fine. What about you?"

He snorts and we head out the door.

The tension ratchets up the closer Jonas and I get to The Tea Party. Him, for obvious reasons. Me? Because I'm hoping Sara will be there—which makes me a dick.

I know she's the distraction killing my game and I don't know how to deal with that.

"Thanks," Jonas says after a few beats while we walk. It's only a couple of blocks and we have our hats down and scarves covering our faces.

I blow out a cloudy breath of air into the cold. "You know what you're going to do if it's a positive match?"

"No. I'm fucked either way."

"Or you could make the best of it and it could turn out to be the best thing that ever happened to you."

He gives me a skeptical look and I challenge him with a raised brow. "It's obvious you care about her, man. Just admit it."

"I'm too young for this. She's… all wrong."

"Whatever plans you had or timeline you thought was best, forget about it. None of that matters. As for Mindy being all wrong, I'm not sure why you think that, but I'd say you're at least conflicted on the point." I pause until he looks at me. "Besides, you don't have to marry her to do the right thing by your child."

I can't blame him for being concerned and afraid. I nudge his shoulder. "You could end up with a little hockey player; someone who'll look up to you."

He gives me a lukewarm grin. "Didn't think of it that way."

We arrive at The Tea Party's glass door and stop outside.

"This is it," he says.

I glance inside and can't see if Sara's in there because it's pretty crowded. I'm a fucking idiot. I can't even focus on my teammate's important problem for five minutes without her distracting me.

I follow Jonas to the back of the bar. Mindy and Sheila are huddled together when we approach and disappointment drops like a lead puck in my gut. No Sara.

That's a good thing.

Jonas takes a seat, pulls his ball cap lower and doesn't bother taking off his jacket or scarf.

I do the same because I'm not anxious to be recognized. I haven't been out since the last time I saw Sara here.

"Let's get this over with," Jonas says.

Mindy starts crying, accusing him of being cold hearted and I can't disagree.

I kick him under the table.

"Sorry," he says. "How are you doing?" He stares at her belly and she sits up, a tentative smile showing.

"I'm good. I got pictures of the baby from my last ultrasound."

"Never mind that. Let's get to the paternity test results."

"Not yet. We're waiting until Lola gets here," Sheila says, squeezing her friend's hand.

Mindy nods while I light up with surprise.

I quickly subdue my reaction because *what the hell?*

Mindy slides a grainy picture of a tiny curled-up baby across the table toward Jonas.

He doesn't look at it.

"Lola?" Jonas snorts and I nudge him. "Don't you dare say fucking anything that will give her away as Sara. Got it?"

He nods and starts bouncing his knee, his anxiety level amped up.

I glance at Sheila.

She wanted Lola-Sara to be here to act as a super conscience.

And it's working before she's even here because Jonas's anxiety just skyrocketed.

He picks up the photo of his baby and stares, trying to be disinterested, but I can see that he is.

"There's Lola now." Sheila waves in the direction of the door.

It takes everything in me to not turn around, but when she arrives at our table, I stand to help her into the seat next to me.

"We meet again," I say.

She gives a nervous smile. "Sorry I'm late. I was at the game with my family and—well you know." She waves a hand, stopping herself from telling the no-doubt funny story about how she escaped from her family to come here.

I want to encourage her to go on, but I don't.

"Are we ready?" I ask Mindy.

Jonas' hand shakes as he returns the photo of the baby to Mindy. "I'm ready," he says, deadly serious, no smirk.

Mindy pulls her bag onto her lap and rummages through it.

Jonas bounces his knee up faster.

Sara watches Mindy like she's a magician about to pull a rabbit from her bag and Sheila wraps a protective arm around her friend.

Finally, Mindy pulls an envelope from the bag and puts it on the table in front of her.

Jonas snatches it. "Let me open this. You're taking too long."

"No way." Mindy pulls the envelope back from him and holds it against her chest. "This is my baby and it may—or may not be—yours."

"I thought you said—"

"Of course I did. I *know* it's your baby. You're the only one who doesn't believe it. So, as far as you're concerned, it's my baby until after the reveal."

Jonas glares at her.

"She has a point." I say it at the same time Sara does, too. We look at each other and laugh. Some of the tension eases, or, at least, some of *my* tension.

Jonas sits back and folds his arms over his chest looking like he's waiting for his sentencing.

Not a good way to receive this information.

"Time to open the envelope, honey," Sheila says.

I nudge Jonas to sit up and prepare himself.

He unfolds his arms and pulls himself from his slumped posture.

Mindy pulls a single sheet of paper from the envelope and reads it silently.

"What does it say, goddamn it?" Jonas asks, leaning forward.

I hold his arm to prevent him from snatching the paper away from Mindy.

She looks up and meets his eyes. "It says you're the father. Of course." She hands the paper to him.

He grabs it and speed reads through to where it says his name in bold print. Even I can see it from over his shoulder, plain as day. Not that I ever doubted it.

Sara vibrates with excitement and tension next to me. She covers Mindy's hand with hers and offers an encouraging smile.

"This is fucked up," Jonas says, throwing the paper back across the table at Mindy.

He's about to get up, but I keep him in his seat.

"I'm not marrying you," he says to Mindy, leaning forward. His eyes are wild and he looks like a trapped animal.

I'm about to say something, but Sara stops me, putting a hand on my arm.

"That's fine with me," Mindy says. "I wouldn't want you to. You're terrible husband material."

"What the fuck is that supposed to mean?" Jonas asks, "I'd be a great husband. I'm a catch. And I'll be a great father, too." He's breathing heavy and staring at Mindy. There's a beat of silence between them while they stare and I'm holding my breath, prepared to restrain him if necessary.

"I know you'll be a good father," she says.

"How would you know?" Jonas asks.

"I can tell. You have enough bravado to put the fear of God into a kid, and yet…." She gives him a knowing smile. "You have a soft underbelly. Especially for animals and people you care about. I've seen it. Glimpses."

"Me, too," Sara says. "I mean I've seen glimpses."

Jonas scowls at her and I scowl at him until he turns away, muttering, "Sorry."

Jonas and Mindy bicker back and forth, making tentative plans to get married, with Sheila refereeing.

I half listen and order a pitcher of beer from the server without interrupting the conversation.

"Good call," Sara says. "Have you been listening?"

I shake my head.

"We're all invited."

"Great." I turn to Jonas. "Are you sure about getting married?" It's a question I have to ask as his friend and teammate.

Mindy glares at me.

Sara answers for him. "He's sure."

Jonas doesn't object and he continues arguing with Mindy about where it's going to happen while the server delivers the pitcher and I gratefully give her a fifty-dollar bill.

"Keep the change."

Sara's eyes widen and she smiles.

I shrug.

"Then it's agreed," Sheila says. "The ceremony will be at city hall where Mindy lives."

"No parents," Jonas says. "We keep this small and quiet."

"Fine. But we're going to have to tell our families afterward," Mindy says.

"Sure."

"Where do you live?" Sara asks, typing into her phone calendar. "Boston?"

"No," Mindy and Sheila both say and laugh. "We live in Revere."

"That's where I live," I say. That's a convenient coincidence—but then I glance at Sara.

She's turned white and has let go of her phone.

She's worried about this charade being so close to home.

I squeeze her hand, and she turns to me. I smile and she relaxes. I'd love to take her into my arms, but let go of her hand instead. We don't need any scrutiny. The team is going to get enough publicity once Jonas and Mindy's story gets out.

"Great," Sara says without admitting she lives in Revere, too. "I have to go now."

"Don't let us keep you," Jonas says and this time I don't hold back at all as I kick his shin good and hard under the table.

"Fuck. That hurt," he says, reaching down to rub his leg.

In truth, I'm lucky he doesn't kick me back. Except he knows he's wrong to be rude to Sara.

She stands and smiles warmly at everyone, making my chest tighten and an empty feeling pangs in my gut at her leaving.

"I need to go, too," I say and stand. Every one of them nods and smiles with that look that says they know my secret. Hell, they probably do.

I wish I knew what it was that makes me want to follow Sara when I shouldn't.

Outside, she turns when I push through the door and join her on the sidewalk.

"Can I get you a ride?" I ask.

"Déjà vu much?" She laughs. "I don't think I can afford to re-live the experience."

I stare at her, then shove my hands in my pockets and move closer. "I have my car this time. No strings. No need for you to take the train this late at night."

"You realize I do it all the time, right?"

"Then consider this a treat. Come on." I put a hand on the small of her back and walk with her, holding onto her warmth as we head back to the Garden's parking garage. We don't talk, maybe because the crackle in the air between us is too loud.

As we reach the private entrance where staff and players park, she finally speaks. "I always wondered where this door went."

"You don't park here?"

She laughs. "I'm not high up enough on the corporate ladder for a parking space. Correct that—I'm not even on the ladder."

"Don't sell yourself short. Delaney seems to rely on you. I've seen the IG and other social media. You do a great job making me look like a saint."

"It's easy to make you look good," she says. If any other woman said those words, they'd sound fake or cheesy, but the way she says them, infused with her passionate brand of sincerity, sends a rush through my body that chases away any residual tension I have.

"This is my car," I announce, clicking open the doors, glad to have something to say besides what's on my mind. Like *Spend the night with me*. Shit.

"It's you—I mean, the *real* you, not the Hollywood version," she says as she gets inside my tooled-out Jeep Rubicon.

I'd duplicated Finn's custom version but in steel gray. I did it partly to annoy him and hear him give me shit and partly because it spoke to me—because it feels like the real me.

"Thank you." A rare, no-holds-barred grin takes over my face automatically.

We get to route 1A north and the silence is tense and calm at the same time. I want to talk to her, but I can't trust myself to keep inside the lines we've drawn—the lines I've drawn for her benefit. Mine, too. *Remember hockey. Family.*

"How's your family?" she asks as I pull off the highway and wind around the side streets toward her house. Thank God for navigation.

"My mom joined a widow support group and I think it's helping her. I haven't talked to my brother. But I text with my nephews and they can't wait to go to another game."

"They're so fun."

"You like kids."

"Who doesn't?"

"You'd be surprised. Just about every woman I've dated for the past ten years." The truth of the words silences me. The slicing pain through my shoulder blades returns in full force.

She looks at me, shocked. "Seriously? That's so... unusual. I don't know any women who don't like children. I can't wait to have—" She turns away and waves a hand. "Don't mind me. Off topic."

"No, it's not. I asked, didn't I?"

"Yes, but—

"No *buts*. Don't apologize for who you are. Own it. You're a child lover and you'd beat the old woman in the shoe in a child-rearing competition any day. I'd put my money on you."

She laughs. "I don't think it would be hard to beat that old woman seeing as how she didn't know what to do."

I laugh and pull up in front of a double-decker house with a tiny well-kept front yard. "Your house?"

"Yes. Such as it is." She sighs. "Better than an old shoe, I suppose." She smiles apologetically.

"Own it, Sara. It looks warm and genuine." *Like you. Like home.* "You live upstairs or down?"

"I'm downstairs with my parents. Grandma Zanetti and Aunt Yolanda live upstairs. I know—it should be the other way around since Grandma has a hard time with the steps, but we can't get her to move."

I smile at the family picture she paints and my chest tightens. "Sounds like a great place to live, surrounded by family. No wonder you haven't moved out into the cold, cruel world."

She snorts. "I'd be out of here in a nanosecond if I could afford it." Her smile goes soft and she sighs. "But you're right. I wouldn't go far. I'd miss them too much."

"Amen to that."

She puts a hand on the door latch and looks at me. "Thank

you for the ride—and for the company." Then she turns away and shoves the door open.

"Not so fast." I pull her back into the seat before her feet hit the ground. Glad those lightening reflexes are good for something these days, because they've been failing me on the ice.

She turns and lets her face ask the question. *What are you doing?*

I give her my answer, leaning in, without thinking, my heart rate kicking up and blood rushing as my mouth touches hers, pushing into the soft warm cushion of her lips and tasting... parting them with my tongue and taking what I can in the moment I allow myself.

Then I pull back, watching the dark pools of her eyes and stroking her soft, smooth cheek with the back of my hand.

"Something to remember," I say.

She sucks in a breath and nods. "I'll see you tomorrow night at the gala."

She jumps from the car while I take in her words, my whole body reacting reflexively with the primal need to have more of her, to take her home with me and ravage her like she's never been ravaged before. *Something to remember?* I want to give her something she'll never forget.

Something *I'll* never forget.

As I put the Jeep in gear and pull away from the curb, my dick is as hard as granite with my runaway thoughts about Sara Bellagamba, the forbidden one. I curse myself for kissing her.

Everything about her is exactly what I need to forget.

CHAPTER 21

SARA

"*W*hen are you going to call his mom and tell her you're not coming to her Friday-After-Thanks-giving-Dinner?" Billie Mae asks as she zips my dress. We're in her bedroom to get ready for the gala because I need to borrow a cocktail dress from her.

I'm watching in the mirror, amazed that this dress fits because she's a size smaller than me.

"I've never seen you in this dress. Does it even fit you? I bet it swims on you. Why would you even buy it?"

She rolls her eyes. "Never mind that. Look how gorgeous and sexy you are." I do what she says and she's not wrong as I feel the warmth of a blush creeping up my neck. The dress is definitely her style—fitted, low cut, and short. The satiny black material glitters with rhinestones and I hope the thin straps will hold against the strain of my boobs. But I can't help being suspicious that she bought it for me. It wouldn't be the first time.

"Are you sure it fits? It feels a little tight." I tug on the bodice. "It barely covers my nipples."

"Don't exaggerate. It looks perfect. Quinn will drool when he sees you."

I spin around to eye her. "I thought we agreed my fling with Quinn is history? Right?"

She shrugs. "Doesn't hurt to rub it in and send a message about what he's missing."

I laugh. "About Thanksgiving dinner—I don't have his mom's phone number. I'll have to ask him to to tell her I'm canceling."

"Bummer, you'll have to have another conversation with him. A non-work conversation. Oh no." She's mocking me.

I swat her arm. She thinks I'm too worried about the repercussions of a fling.

She also thinks I could change Quinn's mind about it in a nanosecond if I really tried. I don't want to bring up my failed attempt that time over the phone, so I let her think what she wants. Either way, we have the specter of the Friday-After-Thanksgiving-Dinner looming in less than two weeks. And I need to deal with it.

"I'll talk to him tonight."

WE ARRIVE at the BC Club high up overlooking the city through 360-degree walls of windows and rush by the entrance to the impressive room to the back where the Brawlers' party is. We're in the nick of time and Delaney puts us to work greeting people and checking their invitations to make sure they're supposed to be here. A security guard in a tux stands by in case anyone doesn't agree with our policy.

We give each guest a gift bag stuffed with hockey-related decadence, like a specially-made full-sized chocolate hockey puck.

"After most of the guests have arrived," Delaney says, "I want you both to mingle, making sure the guests are enjoying themselves. You are official Brawlers organization hostesses. But I also want you taking plenty of photos and videos. Got it?"

"Yes, ma'am," Billie Mae says. She's on best behavior because she promised Bobby half a dozen Brawlers tickets for his high school friends and she's nervous about asking.

Me? I nod like a puppy. Then I stop myself and try a professional smile. It's still me and I'm still eager to please, but I'm no puppy. Not anymore; I'm a grown-up dog—I mean, woman.

"Good," Delaney says, hands on her hips. She's wearing an elegant, full-length gown in black, with gold embroidery around the neck-line and waist, but she still manages to carry off her drill sergeant routine like she owns it.

I have to admire that in her. She knows who she is and isn't afraid to go with it at all times.

She hands us fancy Brawlers Hostess name tags. "Put these on where people can see them." She eyes my dress skeptically. "The players, their guests, and people from the Brawlers' organization will be coming in the back, so you won't have to worry about them."

A mountain of tension that I hadn't realized I'd been carrying lifts from my shoulders.. But it's no sooner gone than it's replaced by disappointment. Because, yeah, I'm that messed up, confused girl. Crap.

Delaney leaves us with the chocolate-filled bags and I'm itching to pilfer a puck and swallow it whole.

"Don't even think of taking one of those," Billie Mae says. "All we need is someone complaining that they're missing a puck."

"I wasn't going to," I insist. I wasn't; I'd only thought about it. But since Billie Mae knows my penchant for nervous chocolate eating, or sad chocolate eating, or hell, let's face it, chocolate eating in general, it's a reasonable assumption. "I don't want to stain your dress because you're going to return it right after this event."

She rolls her eyes.

"I know you bought it for me."

"Shush. There's a group of guests getting off the elevator.

We're on. Let's greet the hell out of them and be the best goddam hostesses that ever lived."

It's my turn to roll my eyes, but I take up the challenge. We're a team of two and we're out to reach our goal by winning the game and defeating the opposition: Delaney-the-ball-buster.

It's easy to smile and be pleasant because everyone is happy to be here, even me.

"I LIKE THIS JOB," Billie Mae says. "I just wish Bobby was here."

"Why? We're not guests, remember?" I do a Delaney impression and she laughs.

The next group of guests approach from the coat room and I gather up three bags, one for each of them. It's been over an hour and the stream of guests has trickled down to barely any. My belly flutters with anticipation as we start mingling, hoping I'll run into Quinn.

When I turn to greet the guests and take their invitations, I freeze mid-motion because I'm looking into the face of the last person I ever wanted to see here—or anywhere.

"Princess Romanov," I murmur.

Billie Mae takes the invitations from her extended hand.

"It's you again," she says. "I'm sorry, what was your name?" She stands straighter and taller than ever in her silvery, full-length gown that glitters all over, matching her crown.

She's wearing a frigging crown.

"Her name is on her name tag," Billie Mae says, bordering just this side of the polite-rude line.

"It's Sara Bellagamba," I say, restoring my voice to its full volume. I wish it didn't have that pesky nervous vibration.

"Of course. You're Quinn's little friend."

I hand her the gift bag. "Have a lovely evening, Princess." I smile the sincerest smile I can muster. I can't blame her for being miserable about being rejected by Quinn, can I? Maybe we have more in common than she realizes. Maybe she's not my enemy.

As long as she leaves Quinn alone and doesn't cause him any more grief.

My mission as hostess just got super-sized. I'm a hostess who needs to protect the welfare of one Quinn James, super star hockey player. I bite into the role like Popeye with his spinach and I seriously eye the chocolate puck peeking from one of those bags.

When the princess and her entourage of two body guards—because she didn't treat either of them like a date—head into the room, Billie Mae huddles with me. "She's some sparkly super-bitch, isn't she?"

I laugh. "That just means we'll need to be extra stealthy super hostesses."

She snorts. "Whatever that means."

"It means I need to watch out for Quinn's back. She has a grudge."

Billie Mae nods. "Of course. The spurned woman syndrome. I've seen it before. She has it bad."

Which is just confirmation that I need to be the avenger-protector super hostess.

So, when Delaney swings by and tells us to go forth, take pics and make sure everyone is having a great time, I'm more than ready. She hands us each official Brawlers-issue digital cameras and we head into the depths of the party jungle to protect the guests from boredom—and worse.

I'M TAKING a video of Finn and his wife, Vicki, on the dance floor, while surreptitiously looking around for Quinn when I feel a hand—a large one—land on my shoulder. Finn grins and I stop the camera and turn around.

"Quinn."

"Want to take a break from picture taking for a minute? I'll buy you a soda."

I look around for Delaney and she's nowhere in sight. "Make it an ice water and you're on," I say. "It's been a long night and we still have an hour to go."

"Maybe you can leave early. I plan to," he says while we walk to the bar. He orders two ice waters.

"That's it? What happened to the vintage whiskey?"

"I haven't been drinking much since I came back East. Some habits are better left in L.A."

"You're probably right." I don't know what to say now, maybe because I'm too nervous Delaney is going to pop out of nowhere and shout, "A-ha. You're both fired."

"Who are you looking for?" He sounds concerned.

"Delaney. Why? Who did you think I was looking for?" The ice princess pops to mind and I wonder if he knows she's here. All at once I'm ashamed because I haven't been watching out for him. "Have you seen Princess Romanov yet?"

His face changes and he rolls his eyes. "Yes. We had an encounter. It was short, though not very sweet. It was, at least, polite."

Relief floods me. "I'm glad. I was worried she was going to cause a scene."

"No worries. I can handle it."

"Right, I forgot. You have plenty of practice with women throwing themselves at you. Even me." Now why on Earth would I remind him of that?

He laughs. "You're the one woman I'm having a hard time handling."

"I'm sorry. Truly. The last thing I want to do is make your life more difficult."

His face softens, but before he has a chance to say something that I'm sure will melt my heart, the princess returns, invading our space near the bar.

"Is it too much to ask you to buy me a drink?" she asks Quinn, attaching herself to his side and ignoring me.

"Aren't you afraid I'll get you a glass of poison?" He smiles at her and I almost laugh, but I hold back for once.

"You're so charming. I'd forgotten about your sense of humor. Seriously, Quinn, I've missed you. A lot's happened since... Paris."

"I hope that means you've moved on—"

"Of course. I only ever thought the best of you, thought we had something special." She shrugs. "Can I help it if I still think we could—"

"We can't, Anica." He's gentled his voice.

She stares at him, then abruptly turns to me. "How about a picture at least, for old times' sake. Would you mind?"

I smile and raise the camera, suddenly remembering that that's what I'm supposed to be doing. I check around for a Delaney sighting.

"Please don't take a photo of us, Sara." Quinn says quietly. Something in his voice and face, like he's in pain, makes me stop.

The princess laughs. "Come on, Quinn. What are you worried about?" She waves a hand around and points to another photographer. "There are a dozen other people in the room taking photos. Why so camera-shy now?"

"I don't want to start any gossip about us." He grits the words out and I can sense his anger winning out over his earlier sadness.

"How about if I take one and I'll make sure it's appropriately captioned so there's no misunderstanding that you aren't anything but acquaintances. We'll keep it gossip-free." I take a few shots with her hanging off him and him looking like he's barely putting up with an overzealous fan. I make sure I catch her in the most unflattering angle because that's the one I'll post. Everywhere.

"Who knows what might happen now that I'm staying here in the States for a while, Quinn?" She pauses to make sure she has his attention. "Especially since I joined the board of the Brawlers' Foundation."

He says nothing and keeps his face a blank mask. It's his game face, the one he wears to intimidate.

When I see a muscle in his jaw tic, I decide I need to pick up the conversational ball and be a big girl by keeping it civil.

"Speaking of that, why *did* you come to the States?"

"I'M GOING to grad school at Yale and came up for the charity event. And, of course, to see Quinn." She's looking at the camera and speaking pleasantly, but then she snatches the camera from me. "Let me check those photos."

Crap.

Quinn removes the camera from her hands in a move so quick I need a replay. Then he hands it back to me.

"Why did you do that?" the princess asks, surprised.

"Sara is in charge of the camera. She works in PR," Quinn says "by day. But by night—"

"By night I'm studying … photography." I kick his foot and grab the princess' arm, though I do keep my camera away from her as I walk her away from the bar.

She resists at first but then relents.

I bring her to Finn and his wife, introduce her then walk away. Fast. I check the camera quick and—Crap. It's still running. I'm going to have to delete this clip as soon as get the chance.

I don't know what Quinn was going to say about what I do by night, and hope to heaven that he wasn't going to say that, by night, I'm a puck bunny, because that would have been disastrous. What had he been thinking? I need to find out.

But he's no longer at the bar and Delaney's heading in my direction, so I resume doing my job.

CHAPTER 22

QUINN

*F*uck. That did not go well.

O'Rourke comes over and hands me a beer. "You want to drink this one for me? An overzealous fan got ahead in their drink orders. I only escaped because she and her friend had to run to the ladies' room."

"Where's your wife? Isn't she supposed to be running interference?"

"She's at home growing twins in her ever-growing belly. No way did I have any bribe big enough to get her to come to this event tonight."

I laugh and take the beer as my eyes wander the room in search of Sara. I last saw her ditching the princess with Finn. Then she'd taken off. Probably to the ladies' room.

"You look distracted. I saw that Princess Anica Romanova found you. She asked me all about you like she has a thing for you—like she knows you."

I snort. "You don't read the gossip rags I take it?"

He shakes his head. "Spill it. I could use some good gossip to liven this night up."

"We dated briefly in L.A., but I broke it off and she went back

186

to Romaldestan." I end the story prematurely when I see her coming this way. "Shit. Speaking of the she-devil."

He turns and sees what I'm talking about. "You need me to run interference for you?"

"If you do, I owe you my firstborn."

He puts up a hand. "No, please. No more kids."

We laugh and I bump his shoulder with my fist. "I owe you, man. You have no idea."

"You can tell me the rest of the story another time."

I nod and take off for the exit. There's a ladies' room in that direction and I may as well start looking for Sara there. When I step out into the elevator lobby, I see her near the coatroom and head that way before she sees me because I have a feeling that, if she does, she'll run the other way.

Stopping at the coat check closet, I ask the woman for my coat. Sara spins around and stares at me like she doesn't know what to say or do. Like she hadn't planned to run into me. I take my coat and sweep her up. She has her coat on so I escort her to the elevators.

"Where are we going?" she asks,.

"Somewhere private. To talk," I say. We manage to get an elevator to ourselves and, as the doors slide closed, I turn to her. "What happened back there with the princess? What's wrong? What did I say or do to upset you? Or... was it her?"

She huffs and stares at the diamond-encrusted football tiepin on my tie.

"It was you. What you said. *By night*? Really? Nothing good comes of a sentence that starts that way. What could you possibly have planned to say I do *by night* that was going to be okay?" She peeks up at me. "Not that I have room to criticize, since I often say things that are the opposite of okay. I suppose I should be more understanding."

She pauses and her chest is heaving with the effort of breathing and taking in enough oxygen to keep her talking so fast and furious, to keep up with all that passion and the expenditure of all that emotional energy.

"Okay," she says. "Go ahead and explain." She folds her arm across while skepticism wars with hope on her face, that ever-present, heart-squeezing hopefulness.

Glancing at the digital readout above the elevator doors, I see I've got four more floors to straighten this out. I clear my throat and go for the truth. "I was going to say, 'By night, she's my muse.'" *More like my distraction. Or, if I had my way, "My woman. The one I want to bring home to bed and make sweet love to until the dawn forces us to stop."* Fuck. Is that the truth? Or wishful thinking.

She snorts then covers her mouth.

I look at her hand.

She takes it down and laughs. "Some muse. Explains your scoring slump."

The elevator stops and the doors slide open to the main lobby.

"I'm going to leave now," I say, looking around at all the people coming and going from the gala. Many smile at me. Shit. "Wait ten minutes, then leave—I don't care if you have to call Delaney and tell her you're sick to get out of here. Then go out the front door and cross the street and walk a block. I'll pick you up. Don't tell anyone. Not even Billie Mae." I hold my breath, waiting for her response. It's a crazy plan, but something's got to give. I need some time with her. My chest is so tight from holding back all the emotions of guilt and fear. But it's the sorrow that's crushing me. Searing pain slashes through me as I watch her face, waiting.

The story her expression tells brings me back, gives me life with the need to protect her, to make her smile and laugh and scream with pleasure. It's filled with caution and hope and then finally resolve.

"All right. I'll call Delaney, then meet you." She clears her throat and backs up a step. "Good night now," she says in a comically loud voice, giving me a wave. Then she turns and walks to the other side of the lobby with purpose in her step as she pulls her phone from her purse.

ON THE WAY TO REVERE, I settle into the silence which has a strange quality of tense calm. Sara doesn't ask where we're going and I'm not sure if I'm driving to her house or mine. I should be taking her home.

In fact, I shouldn't be taking her anywhere, but that ship has sailed and sunk. When I pull into my driveway she finally speaks.

"Your house. It's…unbelievably beautiful. Is it on the ocean?" She waves. "Don't mind me. Of course it's beautiful and on the ocean; where *else* in Revere would you live? A double-decker? I don't know what I was expecting, but this is exactly what—"

"Sara."

She looks at me.

"Stop talking."

I give her a smile and she sighs.

"Sorry. I'm nervous and I don't know why I should be—"

I pull her into my arms, and plant my lips on hers. None of which is easy because of the Jeep's wide console. The rush of warmth makes me feel like I've come home, like I'm where I belong.

Before I get too sucked into the kiss—literally—I let her go.

She's breathless and looking at me like I'm a dream.

Damn it. She's too young and vulnerable for this.

"No you don't." She grabs my lapels and kisses me as if her life depends on it. Like she's proving a point. Like she's an expert and can arouse me in less than two seconds.

Breathing heavy, I break away gently on a long, hungry sigh. "Well, fuck," I say catching my breath. "That was some kiss. And I don't believe I'm saying this, but we need to talk before…"

"You're right. I have questions."

"How about if we go inside?"

"I'm dying to. You know, a person's home says a lot about them. Let's see what yours tells me about you."

"Hopefully none of my secrets," I say reflexively. Then I realize I'm not worried about sharing secrets with this woman. There's no fear, only total trust.

And I don't remember the last time I felt like that with a woman.

INSIDE, I show her around and she's impressed, but mildly disappointed at the sparse furnishings in the living area. Nothing but a large screen TV that came with the house and an old couch that my realtor had donated after she dropped by to welcome me to the area and found the place empty.

"The couch is comfortable enough." I shrug. "I've been busy. I'll finish furnishing the place during All-Star break." I motion for her to sit on the couch and sit next to her, not too close, but close enough so I can feel her warmth.

"What about the furniture you already had from your previous home?" She waves as if the previous home was in outer space somewhere.

It may as well have been. "I didn't want to bring anything from L.A. back here with me."

"Purging all the baggage?"

"Literally and figuratively," I admit. "The literal baggage is a lot easier to get rid of, I'm finding."

"Is the princess part of your pesky lingering baggage?" she asks.

I nod. "It's a long story." It's a story I've avoided telling anyone except my mother—and I only told her because she deserved an explanation about where I'd been when my father had passed. I never even explained to my agent, Ham Jett, that the princess is why I'd wanted to go into free agency and sign with the Brawlers.

But looking into Sara's compassionate and spellbinding green eyes, I find myself leaning in, wanting to share.

"I'd like to hear it. What is it between you two?"

"How about a drink before I tell the sordid tale?"

"Sounds like maybe I'll need one."

Rising, I cross the open space to my kitchen and grab the bottle of Courvoisier—a congratulation gift from Jett that's gone untouched until now—and the only two glasses I own, and bring them back to the couch. I pour us each half a glass, put the bottle on the floor, then wrap an arm around her and lean back into the cushions.

"Hmm. You're right. This couch is comfy," she says, making me smile.

"We're staring at a blank TV screen and an empty fireplace, yet, somehow, you make the place feel very comfy," I say.

We clink glasses and I take a long sip of the smooth liquid, letting it warm my throat.

Sara takes a short sip and then coughs and her eyes start watering.

I take the glass away from her, but when she gets control of her cough, she gestures that she wants it back.

"Let me try again. That stuff is good."

I laugh and give it to her. "The trick is to hold it in your mouth for a second, then swallow slowly."

She nods and tries it, then closes her eyes while a slow smile takes shape on her face, making her look like an angel. But my eyes wander over her, taking in the creamy mounds of cleavage and the satiny black dress over her shapely hips and down to those legs. Those magnificent legs. She's the sexiest angel who ever lived. She opens her eyes and immediately blushes when she sees the way I'm staring at her. No doubt I look like a hungry wolf and she suddenly feels vulnerable.

I clear my throat. "You ready to hear the story about the princess and the hockey player? Fair warning, it's not one of those happy fairy tales. More like a horror story."

"I'm ready. Though I already want to slap her in the face and I haven't heard one word yet."

I laugh. "It all started out innocently enough. You might even call it exciting. We met in L.A. at some opening and went to the after-party, where we were the darlings of the paparazzi all night. Then I brought her home with me."

"I see," she says, staring at me.

"We saw each other for dinner a couple of times, had a few more nights together, but it was time to move on because the media—not to mention my teammates—were starting to make a big deal out of us. Social media was wild with stories of an impending marriage. So, I decided to put on the breaks and blow the whistle on the relationship. I told her I needed to focus on hockey and couldn't see her anymore."

"Sounds familiar," Sara says. "I'm feeling sorry for her so far and I don't want to feel sorry for her."

"Oh, don't worry, her feelings weren't hurt. We didn't have much of a connection really."

"Not even in bed?" she has the surprising nerve to ask.

I laugh.

"Sweetheart, I can find a connection with almost any woman in bed, but that doesn't make for a relationship."

"Got it. You were a man-whore."

I snort. "Thank you for using past tense." I clear my throat and take another sip of the brandy. "Back to Princess Anica. She didn't take me seriously and showed up at the next game which was in Tampa, and invited herself to stay over with me."

Sara's eyes widen. "What did you do?"

"I couldn't kick her out and didn't want to create a scene for the media that was constantly following us around. I was the hockey playboy and she was the jet-setting beautiful princess; a perfect made-for-Hollywood love story they didn't want to let go of. And neither did she."

"I remember the coverage. I didn't like the story."

I laugh and squeeze her shoulder.

"So, what did you do?"

"I let her stay and then had a heart-to-heart talk with her the next morning. Told her I never wanted to see her again and that, if she forced it, I would break up with her in public, making a huge scene." I shrug. "I felt like a Class-A asshole telling her and making her cry for Christ's sake, but she needed to leave me alone."

"I bet the tears weren't real." She put a hand to my face, caressing my cheek in a comforting sexy way that makes my dick stir in my pants. I lose track of my story for a second, staring into Sara's eyes, drinking in the beauty of her face. Of her soul.

"So, she left you alone and you lived happily ever after?" she prompts.

I laugh. "*Not*. The next time I heard from her was a phone call from Romaldestan."

What did she say?"

"She told me she was pregnant and asked me to come to Romaldestan to take care of it."

Sara sucks in air like she's about to drown and clutches my arm. "Oh. My. God. I had no idea. I'm so—"

"Let me finish the story. When I got there, she took me to Paris to supposedly see her doctor. We were seen together everywhere for two days, *except* at the doctor's office. I started getting suspicious and more than agitated because my dad was sick and I wanted to get home to see him.

"When I questioned her, she then pretended to have a miscarriage. I was more than suspicious now—more like livid—because, well, let's face it, she is who she is. So, when she was on a call supposedly with the doctor's office, I eavesdropped. She was

talking to her mother and her conversation confirmed that she'd
fabricated the whole thing."

"Oh my God. Crap." She vibrates with emotions, her face
paling.

"Oh yeah."

"How did you not strangle her on the spot? If I'd been
there—"

I laugh and wonder if she might just have done some damage.
"I confronted her and she was forced to admit she'd never been
pregnant. But it was too late. I got a call from my brother that my
dad had passed, literally as I was making the arrangements to go
home."

Sara throws her arms around me, hugging me like I'd needed
back then, consoling me. And even though it should have been
too little too late, her warmth and shaky arms holding me tight
give me a measure of relief. In this moment, I feel lighter, less like
a terrible person, less undeserving than I've felt in a long time.
We separate and I brush her cheek because she's shed tears of
empathy, making me feel something I can't remember feeling.
Tight-chested, yet not in a bad way.

I take a deep breath. "Let me finish."

"There's more?" her voice vibrates and she braces herself.

"After I made my arrangements to return home too late,
almost wishing I could delay going home now because it would
be a different, foreign place without my dad. It would never be
the same and I knew it would take a chunk of my soul to see my
family, to confront the sadness, the judgment, and guilt.

So, I wandered Paris alone, shoring up my defenses and
emotional numbness before I went home for Dad's funeral."

"I'm so sorry," she says, her green eyes shimmering with
unshed tears reached inside me.

She gives me strength rather than drains me, so I continue
even though I haven't allowed myself to think of any of this, let
alone talk about it all these months.

"My brother barely talked to me, but his accusation came across loud and clear all the same. Lenny stood by me, but there wasn't much talking, mostly drinking and ignoring the mammoth elephant in the room. After less than a week, and after a brief apology to my mother for not being there when I should have—which included telling her the story about Anica—she was more forgiving than she should have been. Than I am for my own mistakes. She'd said she'd already known about the princess when she saw photos a friend from church had shown her." I exhale because the guilt lingers. Anica's damn lies are emblematic of my entire lifestyle for the past ten years.

"No amount of willful blindness can shield me from the enormity of my mistakes, from the stark reality and infallible indictment against the stupidity and shallowness of my life in L.A."

"It can't be that bad." Her voice rises in my defense as if she's my lawyer pleading to the jury of my conscience, not a battle she can win.

My head buzzes from the emotional toll and sudden tiredness, but I need to finish, to purge it all. Especially this next part because I'm not sure I'll take it and I'm tied up in knots with no easy answers.

"Mom gave me an edict and I have no choice but to pay attention, because she's always been my rock, the one who's always understood me best." I pause, my gut churning because Mom's words had been like a real pronouncement of guilt, knocking me to the ground, to the lowest point I've been in my life.

"What did she say?" Sara whispers. It's hard. I'm having trouble working up the courage to bare this last vulnerable underbelly of my soul."

I take one more deep breath and plunge forward, feeling like I'm taking a knife to my chest. "Mom said my life was a wasteland of meaningless relationships and mirages, unreal and, ultimately, destructive." I snort.

Sara sucks in a breath and squeezes my hands.

"I knew this deep down, but hearing it, especially from Mom, cut deep, and shame bled out, almost taking me out at the knees. I honestly don't know how I kept standing. The implication that Dad knew and thought the same thing about me before he died still twists the knife in my gut."

"Oh my God—"

I put a hand up because I need to finish this. If I don't, I'll never be able to get over it..

"She said I need to settle down and find the right girl. No more starlets and princesses, no more arm candy. She told me to bring home someone real, someone right for me—for Thanksgiving."

Sara claps her hands against her mouth, but I go on, forcing every ugly ridiculous detail out.

"She implied that I shouldn't bother coming home otherwise." I shake my head. "My brother had been less subtle with his dissatisfaction and anger, and, therefore, easier to dismiss.

"I gave her a nod that she took as agreement. It wasn't, but it took all I had to withstand her judgment and all the guilt and overwhelming sadness of losing my dad, of not being there for them the past years and especially in the end.

"As soon as the words left my mouth, I knew they were wrong. That I had no business making a promise like that to my mother, that she's bound to be disappointed in me yet again. Even if I don't need the distraction when I'm starting with a new team and trying to make a run for The Stanley Cup, my head is too unsettled for me to be legitimate relationship material."

The tightening in my chest threatens to asphyxiate me, so I give her a quick hug and leave without saying another thing to anyone. All kinds of festering wounds remain open, but I take all the baggage with me, the heavy dark guilt of unsettled shit burdening me with every step, right or wrong.

But one thing was always clear in the hurricane of my emotional state. I needed a change from my L.A. lifestyle. I needed to try to get back on track and focus on the most important things—my family and hockey.

As I tell her about my epiphany, I re-live it, feeling the churn of emotions down to the sensation of my ass hitting the gutter, and knowing I have to pick myself up.

"When I gathered my strength, thinking she was finished, she added one last edict. She said wouldn't it be the perfect Christmas gift if I were engaged by then."

"How could she make such a demand?"

Outrage on my behalf infuses Sara's voice and I find an unexpected smile make its way through my tension.

"She has a right. In the end, I promised her no more arm candy. That was all I could do. I convinced her that I need to concentrate on hockey and couldn't promise I'd find the right girl by Thanksgiving in the middle of hockey season. She asked me to at least promise her I'd try. That it was for my own good." Remembering her softened words cut through me, stabbing all my vital organs with the slash of guilt.

"Oh no," she says. "That's worse than being unreasonable and crazy."

I snort and shake my head. "How do you get me when you don't even know me?"

"It's my superpower. I feel people, feel what they feel, understand all too well the deep, emotional pain."

"Well, fuck," I say. It's true. I know it is. I've felt the connection. But knowing she's like this with everyone deflates me. I scoff at my idiocy, thinking without thinking that we had a special connection.

"But I have to confess," she says, turning a deep pink and breathless. "With you, that connection goes to another level. Something I've never felt before..." She trails off and turns away.

Instant lightness returns to my soul like I just had a shot of some kind of super drug that powers me to take her in my arms. She feels our connection the same way I do. My face forms the deepest, most sincere smile I've ever felt, the kind I can't stop or erase even with an effort, even if I think of kittens drowning or losing The Stanley Cup.

"It's all so impossible," she says. "You can't possibly put both your family and hockey first. You can't have everything."

Fucking bingo. A whoosh of relief removes a chunk from the knot of tension in my gut like scoring a goal in sudden death overtime. I'm ready to get everything out.

"On the way to the airport after I left my mom, , I called my agent, Hamish Jett. He'd been at the funeral, but I hadn't bothered talking to him because I hadn't had it in me. I hadn't had anything for anyone. The whole thing was a major low point in my life." I look away from her, but I keep talking.

"In spite of my obligation to comfort my distraught family and deal with the media, I didn't have anything to give. I was empty, like a shell of a person. Not even my slick, star persona showed up. I felt like I'd lost everything, my very soul." I clear my throat, admitting the hard truth. "But I still had hockey."

She presses against me and puts her hand over mine but keeps silent while I travel back to that day I'd last left home, and I keep talking.

Last summer

Resting my head against the plush in the back seat of the limo, my legs sprawled out, I will Jett to answer the damn phone.

After two rings, he does.

"What's up, Quinn? You okay? I'm so sorry—"

"I don't want to re-sign with the L.A. Shooting Stars—"

"Are you fucking with me?" he asks in a *how's the weather* tone of voice. "They're giving you everything you wanted."

"Get me a deal with the Boston Brawlers. I want to play back

East. Back home." There's only one beat of silence on the line before Jett comes to a complete understanding like I knew he would. He's a smart man and he knows me better than anyone, including my teammates in L.A. None of them were at the funeral though they had all sent condolences. To be fair, it had been quick notice—one day. But Jett had shown up.

"Okay. I get it," Jett says. "For what it's worth, I think the change will do you good. Especially after—"

"Do you think the Brawlers will go for a deal?"

He snorts. "You're shitting me, right? You may have to take a pay cut, but we can make it happen."

My pay cut doesn't matter, but that means he's taking a pay cut, too. "Thank you, man. I owe you."

"Just get your head straight, heal your soul, and keep playing hockey. I'll be fine."

I laugh and end the call. I swear this flight back to L.A. will be my last except to travel with my team. No more Hollywood Hockey, no more shallow glamour, and no more fucking arm candy.

Now

"I'm so sorry for all the emotional turmoil you've been through, Quinn. That you're *still* going through." Sara strokes my arm, her deep concern overriding her innate shyness.

I snort. "It's all of my own making." The last thing I want is her thinking I'm blameless, that I'm innocent. I'm anything but. And I'm definitely nothing like her—the opposite, in fact. The kind of guy who's seen too much—enough to spoil everything good about her.

"Not exactly," she says, undaunted. "You can't be blamed for a devious-minded princess or for your dad dying more quickly than expected. You're too hard on yourself. You're a human being and you're not perfect."

My heart lifts like it's taken hold of a balloon named Sara Bellagamba. And I don't want to let go.

"You have a point." I wink, feeling her admiration down to my soul.

She sucks in a breath. "I guess I'm glad I don't qualify as arm candy," she says, her wry smile emphasizing the small spray of freckles across her nose. I'm coming to have a thing for those freckles.

"In what universe are you not the exact definition of arm candy, *Lola*?"

She blushes deeply like I knew she would, and my dick takes notice. My dick has a definite *thing* for her blushing.

"In the Sara Bellagamba universe." She crinkles her nose like her universe stinks.

"That's a powerful universe you have there, sweetheart."

She sits up. "You called me sweetheart."

She looks surprised and I laugh. "Problem?"

"No, it's just... No one ever has—if you don't count Grandma Zanetti, which I don't."

"Then I won't count her either. I like the idea that I'm the only one."

"Why is that?" She has a tentative smile, like she's hoping she knows the answer and she's crossing her fingers behind her back.

"Because I'd be jealous if you had another guy somewhere who could claim you as a sweetheart."

"Does that mean...? Never mind." She sighs and turns away, shifting in her seat to create space between us.

"Yes, it does mean exactly what you think it means. I want you to be my sweetheart." As I say the words, I realize they're true and not just a line. I've never said the words this way before.

She waves. "You're just saying that—"

"I mean it. I wouldn't toy with you."

"Wouldn't you? I mean, that's exactly what I asked you to do. What I wanted..."

Her eyes turn that an intense green that sucks me in until all I see is her beautiful soul…

"No—I mean, yes. I *do* want to give you what you want. But I meant what I said. You're a sweetheart and I wish you could be mine." Fuck. I'm backtracking and confused. She's so out of my depth. Because she has depth, the kind I'm looking for in myself. But I'm not there because I still care more about hockey than finding a sweetheart.

Or that's what I'm telling myself while my heart beats hard and my chest tightens, sending me a different message.

"You wish… but I can't." She sounds so wistful and defeated. Turning away, she goes on, rushing her words. "I get it. I knew that. You have hockey. You said it right from the start. No big secret. Hockey and family are what you're all about and I can't blame you. *Whew*—you've been through a lot—"

"Shut up." I pull her in and take her chin in my hand, forcing her to face me. "You're right and you're wrong because it's a goddam struggle to keep my priorities straight. Because of you. Because I crave you. Not just physically. Everything about you." Moving close until my lips are a breath from hers, I whisper, "Especially your perfect, pouty mouth."

Holding my breath to give her a chance to pull away, I stare at her, and she stares back, saying everything in that visceral language that can't be confused. There is no confusion about the want in her eye,

I touch her lips with mine and let the soft sweet sensation sink in.

Then I ravage her mouth.

She moans and I'm all out of noble self-control to save her from my less-than-perfect devilish intentions and confused tumult of emotions. Because the one thing that's not confused is my dick. And it takes control in the vacuum of power.

CHAPTER 23

SARA

*H*e breaks the kiss off and I want to cry with the loss of his powerful lips against mine, the way he makes me feel like I'm the real princess, a queen of the universe. Abandoning any sense of restraint—because why?—I hold onto him, needing him to continue.

"Let's go to my bedroom," he says in that rumbly voice that vibrates through me, sending a shiver of pleasure to my pussy.

"Do you have a bed?" My brain is haywire. I didn't mean to speak, didn't know I could. Nerves of raw passion have disconnected my brain from my body. Panic sets in.

Until he laughs, a deep quiet laugh with his dimple deep and calming in a panties-melting way.

He lifts me to stand and I'm like a magnet against his body. That's when I realize he may have a hard time walking from here to the bedroom because he has a dick the size of a baseball bat in his pants.

And it wants me.

He wants me.

I moan and take his face in my hands, pressing my mouth to his, letting my greed for his lips and tongue have its way.

He groans—no, make that, *growls*—and that sends a zap like an electric current to my pussy as I press into his solid-as-petrified-wood cock.

"Sweetheart, you're killing me. Let's—"

I release him. "I'm sorry, I lost my head. I mean—"

He covers my mouth with his hand and it shouldn't be such a sensual experience, but I taste his salty flesh as I lick his finger and breathe in the manly spicy sent of him. When I realize his hand is shaking, I want to faint with the heady power, knowing I make him shake with need.

Wrapping an arm around me, he leads me down a hallway to the double-door to his bedroom. There certainly is a bed. It's gigantic.

I stop and stare at it, the bed clothes messy, a thick charcoal comforter trailing onto the floor, and I don't know how many pillows heaped in the middle.

"It's so big."

He laughs and tugs me onto it, pulling me on top of him as he lands on his back.

"You haven't even seen it yet."

I laugh. "No, but I've felt it." The heat of a giddy blush rises to my cheeks at my bold flirting.

He squeezes my bottom to emphasize my point and my breath catches. My face is close to his so that when I see the look in his gorgeous eyes, my heart races as if it's running for its life.

"Do I need to bring you home? Will your parents be worried?"

He shakes his head while I bite my lip, wondering if I can get away with lying that I'm living at Billie Mae's.

"Those are words I never thought I'd be saying again. I haven't had to ask about worried parents in way too many years to think about."

"I know. It's ridiculous. Of course I don't need to go home. No need to worry about my parents." I lie my ass off because Mom will be livid. But it's worth whatever grief I get because I'm an adult and I need to act like one.

"Won't they worry about you?"

"No. I spend the night at Billie Mae's all the time." It's a partial truth. When I do that, I usually bring a bag and let them know I'm staying out. Crap. "But I'll send Mom a text to make sure."

"Good girl," he says like he's an old man and I bite my lip again. Maybe he is too old for me. But the flood of sensations protest the idea that he's too old. And if he is too old then too bad because I want what he has, everything, all of it, even the more mature parts.

What about him, though? Maybe he'll regret being with a girl too young for him?

What the heck am I thinking? He's only eleven years older than me. That's nothing. Dad is older than Mom, isn't he? And they're perfectly happy. Sort of.

I get up and get to go find my bag for my phone and he latches onto my dress.

"Hey, where are you going?"

"My phone—"

"Use my phone." He reaches into his pocket which is a feat because his pants have become impossibly tight, and pulls out his phone.

"How'd you fit that in there with your giant…"

"Cock?"

I nod.

"We have to work on your dirty talk, sweetheart." He grins like it won't be a hardship and hands me the phone. "I assume you know your mother's number, right?"

I nod, suddenly becoming mute as my eyes dance between his dimple and the straining fabric of his pants. That's what's waiting for me. All I need to do is send this text.

I quickly tap a note to Mom that I'm staying with Billie Mae and I'll be home in the morning. When I hand the phone back to him, he tosses it onto the floor into a pile of clothes.

"You're a slob, aren't you?"

The instant furrow between his brows in puzzlement is almost as adorably sexy as his dimple.

"I'm sorry, I mean, you're not a tidy person—"

"I know what you meant."

His voice is mock menacing and he pulls me down on the bed, then covers me with his body, but the last thing I feel is menaced. In fact, I want to get out the pom-poms and cheer him on on his way to ravishing me. I giggle and that heady combination of desire and power, that mutual need for that same thing from each other, the anticipation of reaching that goal together, sends a shiver through me until I feel like all my nerve endings have been disconnected temporarily and then reconnected.

Everything is brighter. Clearer. *More*. He touches my shoulder with his hand and I swear I see a spark—I know I feel one.

He slides the strap of my dress off my shoulders.

"You have the creamiest skin." He drags his fingers down my collar bone to my cleavage as my chest heaves with anticipation.

I'm not disappointed as his thumb slips under the top of my dress and pushes under the straining confines of my bra to find my nipple.

"Oh God." The words shoot from my mouth in a breathy moan as he circles and flicks my nipple.

His mouth follows, his rough tongue laving a hot trail between them.

I squirm and run my fingers through his hair, pulling him closer, *needing* him to be there, to feel his scalding tongue on my nipple.

Tugging my dress down to my ribs past my boobs, his strong hands reach back, leaving my breasts momentarily forlorn and I hold my breath. When I feel the release of my bra, I gulp, expectation winding my nerves into a tight ball waiting to explode. *God, he hasn't even touched my pussy yet.*

"You are so fucking beautiful, so sinfully tempting."

His whisper scrapes my skin, provoking every hair follicle and nerve ending as his mouth glides toward my nipple. Then he sucks it into his mouth as he presses my breasts together, flicking it with his tongue, then moving to the other.

I call out his name and convulse, my hips rising, my back arching up instinctively. "Quinn, I want you. So much." I pant the words.

His teeth tighten against one nipple and I cry out, but not with pain, the ecstatic pulsing at my center begging for more as my lust-honey flows from my throbbing center. *Lust-honey?* Oh my God, I'm going to Hell.

Breathing hard and fast, he lifts his mouth and looks me in the eye, his stare intense and his intent is as clear as a wolf at night in a forest. All of a sudden, I feel like Red Riding Hood. And it feels damn good.

"I need to get this dress off you."

"Rip it off." My mouth spews the words on orders direct from my pussy.

Thank God he obeys. With one hand, he tears the dress off me, tossing it aside with a self-satisfied look of determined power on his face—and lust. Lots and lots of glorious lust lights his eyes.

"Your panties are next," he warns.

I answer with a smile, trying to disguise my eagerness and he moves over me like a marauding Viking.

As he kneels over me my pussy melts even further as his intoxicating dimple overpowers me.

"Do you know how devastatingly sexy you are?"

He whispers the words and if I wasn't so drunk on his touch and the look in his eyes, I'd scoff at his words.

"Don't stop," is my greedy response.

He gives me a slow smile as he lowers himself between my legs. "One track mind. You're a greedy girl."

I start to protest, to take my thoughtless, selfish words back, but he stops me with a finger to my lips.

"Own it, Sara. You want what you want and pretending otherwise won't change anything."

A breath *whooshes* out of me and my hips reflexively pop up to meet his face as he lowers himself, treating me to one last glimpse of that hypnotic dimple. And then, sliding his arms under my thighs, he takes holds of my rear, one cheek in each hand and lifts me off the mattress.

"What—"

"I'm eating you like a proper feast," he rasps like a hungry wolf in man's clothing. My heart beat ratchets up as it pumps all my blood to my pussy which is throbbing, hot and waiting for Quinn's mouth.

Up on my elbows I watch as he takes me in, kissing my lower belly and then my inner thighs. I widen my legs reflexively, inviting him in for more, holding my breath in excruciating anticipation, every nerve tingling. His hot breath fans my pussy as he inhales and lets out a puff of air.

"You smell so intoxicating. I want to get drunk on your juices."

His hoarse words snap my restraint and I dig my fingers into his hair and push his head down onto my pussy.

There's no resistance as he opens his mouth and sucks everything, all the swollen folds and my throbbing clit, pulling so hard I see stars and nothing else.

I hear a scream of pleasure and realize it's mine when he lifts his mouth. My entire body vibrates with impending release and a flash of triumph lights his eyes before he lowers his mouth again. I suck in a breath.

This time his tongue assaults me, licking a circle around my clit, through the folds and into my opening. My hips pulse with need and my back arches as I try to press my clit into him, to find that nirvana of release, that ever elusive big O.

"Please." The word comes without provocation.

He flicks his tongue oh-so-close to my clit and I jump reflexively.

"Please what, sweetheart?" he says in that gravel voice as he goes back to kissing my inner thigh, way too far from that promised land.

"Please stop torturing me. I want…"

"Say it. Tell me what you want."

He blows a breath on my hot pussy and I squirm, needing him so bad.

"I want you to make my pussy explode with a mind-blowing orgasm." The words rip from me in a passion-filled voice. I grab the bunched muscles of his shoulders, urging him back down.

He growls then waits a beat.

I hold my breath.

Then he lashes his tongue across my clit and I convulse, letting out a scream, but he doesn't stop. He flicks his tongue, presses down hard and repeats it over and over as I jolt and a giant wave of orgasmic release pulses through me. My hips rise and my thighs clench around his head as all my muscles seize up until my nerves coil into an impossibly tight ball and the world turns black, like I'm suspended in nothingness. For a moment? Forever? I don't know.

Until I unravel in a series of shuddering waves, still clenched tight, my hands pulling at his face, needing to see him, to kiss him, to worship him, and hold him.

"Oh my God. You shattered me and I finally understand what that means."

He moves up my body, shaky and sweaty and I feel the diamond-hard length of his cock between us as he takes my face in his hands and kisses me. First, my lips and then my chin, then my forehead.

"You are so beautiful. Do you know that? Do you even understand?"

"You..." I don't know what to say, but I need to give him everything I have because I can't stand to hold back on whatever is pouring from my heart and soul for this man. "I adore you. You are the most giving and sexiest man alive. I never dreamed how absolutely and utterly heart-melting you could be. Never dreamed there was a man as good and as bad as you." My eyes are on him, trying to infuse my words with everything in my heart and I see his pupils dilate as he takes in what I'm saying.

"Good and bad?" he asks, sounding ragged, like he just skated a twenty-minute turn in overtime.

"That's all you got from what I said?"

"No." He presses a light kiss to my lips, then takes a possessive nibble. "That's the only part I don't understand. Maybe the only part I believe."

I push his shoulder and he rolls us to our sides. "I meant everything. Good and bad means the best of both. You're good, as in thoughtful and kind and decent, and bad, as in irreverent and naughty and so damned experienced at lovemaking that it's scary."

His face softens and he kisses me deeply this time, like he wants to know and possess every part of me down to my soul.

I grab onto his face and open myself up and take him and give him everything in me because that's all I can do with this man. No matter what the consequences.

Meanwhile as his face softens, another part of his anatomy hardens against my belly and I reach down to squeeze.

He groans, lifts his mouth from mine and grits his teeth. "Jesus, sweetheart, don't do that unless you mean it. I don't know how much more restraint I have."

"We can't leave you in this state."

He laughs, a real, eye-crinkling, full-dimpled laugh, the one that gets to me with a pang so strong that my chest tightens and I'm worried my heart will pop from the pressure.

"Don't worry. I have no intention of remaining... pent up."

It's my turn to smile. "What do you have in mind?"

"Seriously?"

I don't know if it's mild alarm I see in his eyes, but I renew my squeeze of his cock. "You want a hand job?"

He covers my hand, stopping me from moving it. "That's not what I had in mind," he says. Then he reaches for his nightstand drawer and removes a foil packet. He turns back to me and holds it between us so that I can see very clearly what he has in mind.

I gulp. It's not that I don't want to go all the way, it's just that he's so big and it's been so long and my experience is so... not good—okay, disastrous—that I don't know if this is a good idea.

"What is it, sweetheart? You know your expressions are like reading a children's book on your face, right?"

I swat his arm as a flush of embarrassment heats my face. What do I tell him?

The truth and don't be such a chicken all of a sudden.

"It's just that you're so..." I wave a hand, losing nerve.

"Big?"

I nod and look away.

He cups my chin and forces me to face him.

"I'll go easy. It'll be okay. I promise."

"That's a big promise."

He gives me a big smile.

I laugh and let go of him as he hands me the condom. I don't want to tell him that I've never done this before. The last thing I want to do is disappoint him. Besides, how hard could it be? I can handle this.

I rip open the packet and pull out the condom, praying to my statue of the Virgin Mary—and not caring how ironic that may be—that I'm up to this, *and* that this thin film of latex will hold up.

He turns onto his back and lifts me on top of him so that I'm straddling his hips, sitting squarely on the cushion of his balls.

My pussy screams back to life with a vengeance, prodding me with a jolt of dizzying need to get on with the show.

"Roll it on from the tip, sweetheart," he says, his cock tall and solid, jumps when I look at it and lick my lips.

Holy mother. When I figure I should be bone dry, my pussy leaks more lust honey and I make my move.

With shaky hands and his intense sex-starved eyes watching, I roll the condom down his shaft. I don't mean to be painstakingly slow, but I guess I must be because he covers my hands and helps me with the few couple inches. It was a long freaking way to go. I don't know if I should gulp with trepidation or wipe the drool from my mouth at the prospect of him inside me.

"I'm ready," I say and do a mental sign of the cross, a flash of my family's bathtub-enshrined statue coming to mind.

"Let's see if you are." He lowers his fingers to slide them between my thighs at the base of his cock.

I jolt to attention and pour myself all over him like I'm weeping in thankful pleasure, squirming to get everything I can out of his touch.

He chuckles softly. "I guess you are."

"Told you," I say and smile as I lean forward, kissing him because his mouth is so tempting.

CHAPTER 24

QUINN

*H*er tantalizing kiss encourages me, so I take her by the hips and lift her up because—God have mercy—I need her like fucking air right now. Like I'll die if I don't have her. Really die. Heart-stopping dead. I glide her onto my cock as I watch her face and feel her tight pussy suck me in, pulling me deeper so that my arms shake with the strain until she finally sits, wholly impaled, on top of me, sunk to the hilt.

"Oh my God, Quinn…" Her eyes roll back.

I squeeze her. "You okay?"

She snorts and the tightness causing me to shake snaps.

"*Okay?* Seriously?" She exhales and wiggles her hips, sending all kinds of dangerous sparks through me, the kind that could set off an explosion, so I still her.

"I'm in heaven," she says, opening her eyes. "And I have the most magnificent view possible." She stares at me, communicating so much with her eyes. Her pussy clenches for emphasis and I nearly lose it.

"Take it easy," I say, my voice like gravel. My throat's parched and I pull her toward me, reaching for her breasts like I need a drink.

But she aims her lips at mine and I drink, instead, from her to quench my thirst, to calm me. But the calm lasts only a moment until the sensuous feel of her tongue tangling with mine registers with my cock.

"You are so sexy, sweetheart. I'm having trouble hanging on."

"Is that right?" She tests my words with another wiggle of her hips.

I groan and can't resist, can't hold back any longer, as I take hold of those hips again, trying to wrest back some control. Holding on, I move her up my shaft and then lift my hips to meet her as she comes back down.

"Jesus." I grit my teeth and repeat the motion, struggling to keep it slow and easy.

"My God, that feels so good," she says breathlessly. "You have no idea."

"Oh, I think I might have an idea," I grit out.

I repeat the motion again.

But, this time, she pushes up from my chest and comes down hard on my hips, letting out a deep moan in the process.

Whatever control I had snaps and, this time, I lift her and slam her back to my thrusting hips hard and fast and then again. I keep doing it as I listen to her moans and her heavy breathing. My motions become frantic and I'm lost to the wild rhythm, racing to the end and prepared to head over the cliff, praying to reach it in one piece, needing to shatter apart and lose everything like I've never done before, holding back nothing.

As I slam her hips to mine, thrusting inside her one last time, her scream killing the frenzy of energy around us, I lose everything in a spine-breaking gush inside her, spasms of ecstasy collapsing me on top of her as I wrap her up like she's my life raft, like she isn't the person who just stole everything from me— my mind body and soul are hers forever. The feeling of devastation is outweighed by the ecstasy, mingling together in an impossible explosive mix, fueling aftershocks when I should be unable to breathe.

She holds onto me and strokes my back. It's a while before I become aware that my racing heart has slowed, that its beating perfectly matches hers under me, thudding together in synch. The sensation is something I've never experienced before. The other-worldly quality has me mesmerized as I kiss her face and hold her, trying to hold onto that out-of-body feeling, the one that keeps the real world at bay.

"You are so blazing hot, you're dangerous." I'm not sure if it's physical or whatever else she does to me, but I feel the shield that's kept me from indulging in anything beyond the physical before coming to Boston is shattered.

I brush a strand of hair from her face and tracing her brow, then lean in to kiss her forehead.

"I'll take that as a compliment," she says. "Because those are the kinds of words this girl doesn't hear very often. Or ever, if I'm honest." She strokes my chin with a touch that makes me shiver... But also makes me afraid because it's the kind of touch that's authentic and heartfelt, the kind a guy can't hide from or gloss over as meaningless.

Taking her hand in mine, I move it to my chest. But the warmth only makes my heart thud harder. I'm in trouble.

My mind floods with the prospect of the seventy-plus hockey games still ahead of me and all my teammates, Coach, and the fans counting on me. The Stanley Cup is what I want and if that's selfish, then...

What? Does that make me bad? Is that what my family thinks —that I've been a selfish bastard all these years focusing on myself, my career, my money, and, most of all, having fun?

Well, fuck, that's what I'm still doing, only worse.

I'm playing with an innocent girl, the unlikeliest puck bunny who ever lived, no matter how much she aspires to the role.

"Your heart is so strong," she says. "Like everything else about you. Except your heart is soft and kind and—"

"You don't know me very well," I say. It hits me that this is a problem. If she knew the real me—the bastard I've been for the past ten years, she would run the other way like she should.

She laughs, of all things. "I know you better than you do."

"You're crazy." I let my smile fade because it's time to get serious. "Sara," I take her chin in my hand, trying to ignore the soft skin of her impossibly creamy face. "Look at me closely. Those wrinkles you see? They're real and the way I earned them, along with the rest of my tough-as-nails hockey rep and the cool play-boy-at-large rep, is not through being soft and kind. I don't rescue kittens and I'm not—and never was—anyone's idea of a boy scout."

We stare at each other and I wait for her to say something, to give me some sign of her understanding, an inkling of disillusionment. But her eyes only soften more and the adoration radiates from her undiminished.

"Look at that. You even have a humble, self-deprecating side that I'm sure a lot of people would be very surprised to see." She smiles.

"Fucking almighty," I mutter and force myself to roll away from her naïve Pollyanna sunshine.

"Don't worry, Quinn. I was half-kidding. I know you're not perfect. I heard your story."

She leans over me, her breasts almost making me forget my frustration and my conscience.

She whispers, "That's why I'm here. Because I empathize with you. Because I know how hard it is to come to terms with who you are and try to do better. I know how it is to want to escape your family to see who you are without them, to feel guilty about neglecting them. And I know how it feels to lose someone you care about."

My gut churns at the last thing—about her losing someone—because I didn't know, had never even asked.

"Who did you lose?" I pull her down to my side, where she rests her head on my shoulder.

"It's not important—"

"The hell it isn't. Your loss is as important as mine. *You're* important." I glare at her and squeeze her shoulder to emphasize my point. "Say it, Sara."

"That's silly—"

"Say it."

"Okay. I'll say it—if you admit to being kind."

I can't help the laugh and doing so drains the tension from me. Shaking my head, I sit up and drag her up with me so that we're sitting against the pillows and the headboard. This is going to be a serious conversation and I'm determined to have it.

"I'll admit to being kind—if you admit that you're important and," I pause to make sure she understands that I'm perfectly serious. "You tell me all about your loss. All about the person and your relationship and your feelings."

Her eyes widen and her mouth opens and whatever I thought before was her look of admiration just got surpassed by the stars she has in her eyes now.

Am I the stupidest fucking idiot by making this worse, or what? I'm supposed to be disillusioning her, not letting her think I'm some unicorn who... listens to girls talk about their feelings. Well, fuck.

CHAPTER 25

QUINN

"My loss... isn't the same as yours. It's not—I mean my dad didn't die; he just went away one day and when he came back months later, he was different, a diminished version of himself. Like someone had let half the air out of the tires and welded the valves shut so he can never be filled up again."

What the fuck? "Something bad happened to your father? I'm so sorry, sweetheart." I ask softly, "What happened?" I stroke her hair and trail my hand off as it reaches her breast, reminding myself there will be no touching of a sexual kind while she's talking.

She takes a minute, her eyes down and one of her hands wanders to my thigh.

Jesus. Does she even know how sensual she is?

"I'm sorry," she says, looking up at me. "This isn't something I usually talk about."

"I'm the one who should apologize. I didn't mean to make you uncomfortable. You don't have to tell me anything if—"

"That's the thing, Quinn. I do want to share it with you.

You've shared so much with me and I appreciate it so much. I'm really glad you did. So now I need to be brave and do the same." She lifts her chin and smiles unconvincingly. "After all, I'm the one who opened the can of worms when I told you I had a loss. The least I can do is not leave you hanging."

"I admit I'm curious. But most of all, I care." I should qualify that and tell her I care as a friend, but, right now, I'm too confused about the truth of that. I have no idea why I care about her, only that I do. Very much. And I have no business caring.

"My father was in the Iraqi war. He married Mom before he went overseas and she was thrilled when he came back with all his limbs intact. He was fine… for a while. They had Bobby and then me and then Paul. But, by the time Paul was three or four, Dad had started having a hard time getting out of bed and couldn't take care of us. I started taking care of Paul and my dad when Mom was working and Dad stopped going to work. Then, when I was nine, he went away. I remember the day clearly because he looked so helpless. it was the day before my birthday and he was so sad that he was missing it.

"Mom promised to send him photos so he'd stop crying. We were all crying that day, even Bobby who was a tough guy. I'd never seen him cry before or since."

"Shit. That sucks. Where did he go?" I have an idea, but I don't want to make assumptions.

"To a mental health facility. He was on drugs and needed to dry out and get treated for depression. To this day, I don't know how the heck Mom handled it all."

"It must have helped that her mother—your grandmother— lived upstairs."

She looks at me surprised. "It's true—you remembered that detail?"

"Of course. I don't think I've forgotten a word you've ever said. You're a pretty memorable lady, you know."

"Sure, that's what they all say—and they mean it—but not necessarily in a good way." She gives me a smirk and then sighs. I laugh and hug her to me.

"Anyone who doesn't appreciate you for the unique woman you are doesn't deserve you, sweetheart. Remember I told you that if you remember nothing else about me."

She snort-laughs. "You think I'm going to forget anything about you? You're crazy. This is the kind of story that's going to be a legend in my family among my grandchildren and their grandchildren. I'll tell them their granny had a fling with a famous, handsome hockey star when she was young. They'll insist I'm making up fairytales."

We share a heartbreakingly sweet moment until her smile fades and she clears her throat.

"Where was I? Oh yeah, Dad left for the mental hospital and we kids had no idea how long he was going to be gone. Mom didn't say, but I got the impression that it was for a couple of weeks."

"How long was it?" I ask.

"Six lousy months. I swear I thought he was never coming back, that he was sucked up by an alien spaceship and kidnapped, never to return. I thought he was dead on my worst days. But, no matter what, I never talked about Dad to Mom or to anyone when she was around. Bobby, Paul and I talked among ourselves. Bobby said he'd be the man of the family. Paul didn't worry because he had most of Mom's attention. I pretended not to worry, but all I *did* was worry. At least I had Grandma Zanetti and Aunt Yolanda's attention."

"It's amazing that you had your family nearby to help you through it."

She nods and keeps talking.

It's like I turned on a spigot and it turned into a firehose because she can't stop now. She tells story after story about hearing her mom crying at night, about Bobby acting like her father and taking her to a father-daughter event at school, and about how her mom spoiled Paul and worried about him most of all because he was so much like his father.

"Then when Dad finally came home, he wasn't the same. To this day, he's like a kitten in a jungle. He never goes out. Doesn't work except publishing poetry now and then." She stops talking and leans against me, spent and yawning.

I wrap an arm around her, wishing I could make up for all the bad stuff, make her world as bright and shiny as she is.

We lie back together in silence, all the tension released and I yawn. The sun glows orange on the horizon outside the bedroom window, sparkling off the waves in a bright streak all the way to the sand. I pick up my phone from the night stand to check the time, while trying not to disturb Sara.

She stirs, bolting to alertness, then snatches the phone from me to see the time. "Oh my God. I've kept you up all night. What time do you have to get to practice?"

"In two hours," I admit.

"You still have time to sleep," she says as she scrambles off the bed.

Every muscle in me wants to stop her, but I can't. I need to let her go. For good. I have no business being with a girl-woman like her. Not now anyway.

Who am I kidding? By the time I get my shit together, she'll probably be married with five kids.

"I'll drive you home," I say, getting up. "It'll only take twenty minutes round-trip."

She stops dressing, with her panties halfway up her legs.

I should look away, but I can't.

There's a look of sheer panic on her face. "No. You can't drive me home."

Yeah, I'm right to let her go because she's not an independent adult yet since she's still living at home and having to sneak out. Me? I hadn't been home in six months before this move back, and, before that, it'd been two years. I'm past independent and well on my way to being estranged from my family.

"I get it. No worries. Let me call you an Uber," I say.

I pull on some boxers and follow her through my bedroom door. She's carrying her shoes to the living room couch where she left her bag.

"I'll get it. I have the app." She pulls her phone from her purse and taps away.

"So, this is it," I say, partly to make myself believe it.

She looks up, a puzzled smile on her face.

Shit.

"Our fling," I say. "You accomplished your goal." I smile.

"What do you mean?" Her brow furrows.

"I mean, this was only a one-night stand for us. For a million reasons."

Her face falls and I see everything there—all the sadness, disappointment, and lost hope. I see what that little girl looked like when her dad left that day. Jesus fucking Christ. I'm a bastard.

Fisting my hands against the instinct to hug her, to tell her I didn't mean it, that we can be something, I stand stock still because anything else would be mean.

"Right," she says, gulping down her emotion and struggling to control her expression. She looks away, then bends down to pulls on her heels.

I take a deep breath because I want to do this right, to make certain she's clear and knows what's going on—or *not* going on —between us.

"Whatever you think of me, Sara, you have to understand one thing. I'm no good for a relationship. I have a lot of baggage to unpack and goals to conquer."

She straightens and looks at me, her heart on her sleeve and brave determination vibrating from her. She looks exactly like that brave puck bunny she was that first night I saw her at The Tea Party.

A vicious knife of pain stabs me between my shoulder blades.

"What about your mom—"

"No matter what my mother thinks, I can't have a relationship with you or any other woman now. I'll have to make her understand that, but that's another problem for another day."

I'll have to fucking disappoint my mother yet again and hope she forgives me. But one thing is for certain. I'm going to be there for her, including the dinner the day after Thanksgiving.

"What about the day after Thanksgiving dinner?" Sara says, pulling on her coat, her voice quivering with the exertion of holding her emotions back.

"I'll talk to her about the dinner. Don't worry about it. You don't have to be there or explain it. I'll handle it."

Sara nods, her brave face falling steadily into disappointment, the bravery and sunshine diminishing, and I wonder exactly how big a horse's ass I can become? If I keep seeing her, I'd be afraid to look in the mirror. I'm already not liking the man I see much.

I have no idea who the hell Sara sees when she looks at me, but it's not who I am. He's a figment of her imagination.

"The Uber will be here in a minute." She looks at me with glassy eyes, her voice wobbling, but she doesn't cry. She walks to the front door, bag in hand.

I follow her, running a hand through my hair.

"I'm sorry," I say when we stop at the doorway.

She turns away, pretending not to cry, trying to hide her tears. "It's my own fault. I always have expectations—a side effect of my optimism that can bite me in the butt at times, but it's always worth it." She sniffles then meets my eyes.

"Or, rather, it always has been worth it until now," she says.

Then she opens the door and dashes outside. The car pulls into my driveway. giving a wide berth to my Lamborghini.

It's unfortunate that I couldn't sell the car. Like everything about my past L.A. life, it's not that easy to get rid of. Jett had it shipped here once I moved in. Now it sits like a giant 3-D representation of my selfish past and doubles as a thousand-watt jolt to my guilty conscience every time I look at it.

CHAPTER 26

SARA

"*I*t's a nice sunny Sunday, isn't it?" the driver, a young man with an eager smile, says to me.

A good excuse to throw on my sunglasses before I smile at him in the mirror which is all I can manage. Pulling out my phone, I call Billie Mae. There's not much time, but the ache is eating me alive and I have to say something to someone. Like what?

Like, I've been such a fool? Like, why didn't I believe him when he said this wouldn't go anywhere? Like, why did I believe myself when I said that was fine?

Because I'm an idiot—otherwise known as a hopeless romantic—and too full of unbridled hopeful optimism.

Normally, I'm cautious enough not to test myself, but, this time, this *one* time, I had just enough bravery in me to give it a shot. It all started with that terrible puck bunny incident. Combine a big bully jerk making a girl cry with a couple margaritas and I turn into the avenger. The Puck Bunny Avenger. So brave I thought I could do some avenging for myself.

Well, it didn't work for me, but maybe, just maybe it'll work out for Mindy.

Billie Mae answers her phone after I finally hit the call button.

"It's early," she says. "What time are we meeting at the Garden?"

Crap. I'd forgotten. The hockey game. "Oh no." My tears start leaking again.

"What is it?"

"I can't go. You take my family."

"What the hell is going on? Tell me." She sounds panicked and we're turning down our street, so I talk fast.

"I went home with Quinn and had my big-O-virginity-crushing-dream come true and now we're done. Never again. It's all over between us." If there'd ever even been an *us*. I realize there wasn't and a fresh spout of tears streams down my cheeks.

The driver looks in the rear view and I put up a hand to stop him from being concerned or, heaven forbid, asking me what's wrong.

"Oh, baby, I'm so sorry. I thought you knew—"

"I did, but it still hurts." The car pulls to a stop. "I gotta go. I'll call you back later. I just got home." I end the call with a stab before she can ask because I don't want to tell her I'm just getting home from Quinn's and about to try to sneak into my house unnoticed. Fat chance of that. It's past eight a.m. and Dad's always up by six.

When I walk in, Dad is standing at the kitchen counter pouring coffee and asks, "What's wrong, sweetheart?"

I try to be brave, but when he calls me sweetheart, I burst into tears and collapse into his arms.

He holds me and rocks me in his arms like I'm five years old again. He says, "There, there. It'll be okay. Everything will be fine, sweetheart."

I cry harder.

He gives me a tissue from his pocket—unused thank God—and I get myself under control enough to blow my nose.

"I don't know what the problem is, sweetheart, but I don't

think it's something I can make go away like I did when you were a kid and that neighborhood bully threw a rock at you and hit you in the arm and we had to get you stitches."

"You remember that?" I wipe my eyes and separate from him, feeling silly, and he lets me.

"Of course I do. I remember lots of things. Don't like to talk about most."

I nod. "You're right about this problem, Dad. It's something I need to deal with on my own." I exhale then blow my nose again.

He gives me a look and nods. "Boy problems."

It's not a question so I give him a watery smile and wave him off. The last thing I want to do is confess to my dad that I've been a fool. "They're the worst."

"The worst is never having a boyfriend or someone who you think is special," he says. "You're a brave girl to take chances and better for it, no matter how bad things seem now."

He stares at the ceiling like he often does and I think he's gone back into his faraway world where he lives most his life until he speaks up again, surprising me.

"Most of life is like that, but you got to live, don't you? No such thing as a safe life, so you may as well live a good life and take some chances."

I nod. That's the most he's said to me in a very long time—since I went away to college and he'd given me a speech. Now that I recall, it was a similar one. He'd encouraged me to put myself out there and have fun, meet new people, take a few chances. "Thanks, Dad. I love you." I kiss his scruffy face. He feels frail and it makes me sad, but it puts my problem with Quinn into perspective.

"No problem, sweetie. Hey, at least we have the Brawlers' game today to look forward to. That should take your mind off your troubles." He smiles bright and it takes everything I have not to stumble and collapse right then and there.

I'd forgotten that today was the day I got tickets to take the family to see the Brawlers. They've been looking forward to it for a week, well, actually, forever. Which means I have to go —crap.

There are worse things in life, like not living it or letting it waste away—like Dad, sitting in his rocking chair, dishing out his cautionary tale.

BOBBY COULDN'T MAKE it because he's on a road-trip to Baltimore, but the rest of us pile into two cars including Mom, Dad, Paul—who drives—Aunt Yolanda, and Grandma Zanetti. Billie Mae meets us at the game and keeps giving me concerned looks and mouthing questions… Like I can answer her.

I never had a chance to call her back after my talk with Dad because I'd been too busy holed up in my room, trying to make myself look presentable with ice packs on my eyelids all morning. Dad had promised he wouldn't say anything—not that I'd told him much—and ruin the day.

So, I let Billie Mae drag me to the ladies' room before the first period is even over and I tell her the longer version of what happened last night and what Quinn said. I manage to keep my emotions down to a quiver in my voice and no tears.

"He needs to focus on *hockey?*" she shouts.

"Sshh." I look around in panic, but only one older woman gives us a glance and shakes her head like she's been there, done that. I feel ridiculous.

"He's right," I admit. "I've been a distraction and he's been in a wicked scoring slump."

"The bastard better score a goal today or I'll wring his—"

"Shush already. I appreciate your outrage on my behalf, but he's not the bad guy."

"No? It sure looks like it from where I sit. He took advantage of you. He knew you were inexperienced—"

"I convinced him—badgered him really—to…" I look around

and wave a hand in lieu of saying out loud what I'd badgered him to do. My face heats up, remembering it.

She snorts and remains skeptical as we go back to our seats.

Quinn scores not only one goal, but *two*, and performs like the super star he is on the penalty killing line. I don't know if I'm proud and happy or extremely disappointed. Then I scold myself for being a jerk. How can I begrudge the guy for finally scoring his goals? It's exactly what he needed. He's a great player and a decent human being; he deserves his success.

And I need to move on.

It's near the end of the game and the crowd erupts as Quinn takes a wrist shot from close in. The goalie barely saves it and the place applauds the team as they regroup for a face-off with only twelve seconds to play. The fans chant, "Hat-trick! Hat-trick!" and I can see the grin on Quinn's face from here. Or maybe I can imagine it, right down to the devastating dimple.

Paul and Mom talk about him like he's the second coming as time runs out and the team piles together in mutual congratulations.

"Too bad he's so old, Sara." Mom reaches over and jiggles my knee, giving me a sly smile. "He'd be the best catch of them all on the team."

As we file out of our seats, Paul insists that I should use my employee badge to go down to the locker room area and get an autograph.

"You must know at least one of the guys," he says. "You can introduce me and I'll get my jersey signed. Maybe I can get the whole team to sign it."

"I'll bet that nice Quinn James will sign it for you," Grandma Zanetti says. "He seems like a really nice man."

She winks at me like we have a secret, and a bubble of panic threatens to close off my windpipe. I cough.

"How do you know he's a nice man?" Billie Mae asks, not hiding her scowl.

"We've seen him interviewed dozens of times," Mom says. "He has a killer smile."

I want to chime in and agree, but I keep my mouth shut as we descend the stairs and Paul helps Grandma Z. We get to the point where we either turn toward the garage or toward the locker room corridor.

"How about it?" Paul asks. "You must know someone." He looks between me and Billie Mae.

"I know Jonas Bergman," Billie Mae says, bailing me out—though she couldn't have picked a guy *less* likely to do me a favor. "I'm sure he'll sign your jersey."

"The rookie?" Paul is less than impressed.

We all take the turn toward the locker room then go past the security guards with our badges to the crowded area seething with press and family members. I feel like an outsider.

Paul keeps his eye on the locker room door and, as soon as it opens, he pushes forward.

He grabs my arm and pulls me front and center as he corners none other than Quinn.

Of *course*.

"Hi Quinn, you know my sister, right?"

"Congratulations on the two goals," I say, coming to an abrupt stop.

He looks down at me, his hair dripping and his eyes brilliant, looking happy. I beg him with my eyes to be understanding. He stares, his eyes lingering a second longer than is comfortable and I forget to introduce my brother while Quinn forgets to take his eyes off me.

"I'm Paul Bellagamba. I play hockey for Revere High. I heard you moved to the city."

I cringe and telecommunicate my apology, hoping he doesn't hold our non-relationship status against my brother.

To my surprise, he grins at Paul, dimple and all, and shakes his hand. Okay, I shouldn't be surprised because I know Quinn is a nice guy and good with fans. Why else would I have fallen for him? I wouldn't feel this way if he were an a-hole, would I?

"You heard right," Quinn says. "How's your team doing?"

"Good enough. Still hitting our stride."

"A lot like the Brawlers," Quinn says. "Want me to sign that jersey for you?" He nods at the jersey Paul's holding.

"That'd be great. It's for our team's fund-raising auction. Signed by you, it'll be worth a lot more."

"Is that right? Well how about if the whole team signs it?" Quinn waves a couple of the other players emerging from the locker room over to sign the jersey, telling them it's for the Revere High hockey team.

"This is Sara's brother," he says to Finn who, to my shock, gives me a big grin.

"Sure, you're Sara Bellagamba from the front office." Finn grabs the jersey and felt tip pen from Paul.

O'Rourke comes over and gives me a friendly nod and signs the jersey next. After Paul explains the fundraiser, O'Rourke takes the jersey into the locker room to get more signatures.

"That was really nice of you, Quinn," I say. You didn't have to—"

"Of course I did. It's the least I can do." His blue eyes are intense and, after a beat, he turns to Paul. "Your sister is excellent at her job and a very kind young lady, always helping others."

"Sure," Paul says, sounding anything but sure.

Jonas comes over and I hope to God he doesn't call me out as a puck bunny in front of my brother.

Quinn gives me a look like he senses my tension and throws an arm around my shoulder.

"This is Sara's brother, Paul." He waves a hand in Paul's direction. "This is our new bad ass rookie—"

"I know. Jonas Bergman," Paul says and then goes on to recite his stats.

Jonas is impressed and they talk hockey.

Crisis averted. Meanwhile, Quinn's arm is still around my shoulder.

I sneak a look at Mom and the family, and they're watching, open-mouthed, from a respectful distance, not making a move toward us for introductions, which I think is strange except... Mom's holding them back.

Crap. She thinks I have something going on with Quinn.

I slide away from his hold. "It was nice of you to take care of Paul. I gotta go... get Grandma Zanetti home."

Quinn's face looks wistful, his eyes sad, and I stop for a fraction of a heartbeat.

"Go ahead," Paul says. "I'll take the other car and catch up with you at home later." He leans in.

I punch his shoulder, wave to Jonas, then, without another word or backward glance at Quinn, I rush back to the family and herd them toward the garage.

I try not to read too much into the looks he gave me, like he's wistful or something. I'm proud of not taking the bait, not even when his dimple showed and my panties wanted to melt. I clench my jaw instead of my thighs and remember that he'd said, "There is no us." He has hockey and his family and he doesn't want a relationship with me.

I ride home with Mom, Dad and Grandma Zanetti. Aunt Yolanda said she'd wait for Paul because there's not enough room in one car for everyone.

"You make any progress on hooking up with that hot player I saw you talking to?" Grandma Zanetti asks.

Dad watches me in the rear-view mirror while Mom drives.

I try not to give anything away, but I'm worried he sees more than he lets on.

"It's against the rules, Grandma. No dating the hockey players because I work for the team."

Mom snorts. "Don't worry about those rules. They can't fight Mother Nature. The heart wants what the heart wants."

I zip my mouth shut as Mom goes on about the virtues of dating a hockey player and Grandma argues that football players are better and then Dad joins the conversation. Me? I keep my mouth zipped and jump out of the car as soon as we get home.

When I finally crawl into bed after this draining endless day, I do the one thing I know better than to do. I check my texts because I'm a fool and I seem to require multiple doses of disappointment before I'm cured of my delusions.

Nothing. My gut feels like I had a bunch of organs removed and the surgeon left a big gaping hole there.

To compound my gluttony for punishment, I scroll through our text chain and stare at his name and the call icon longingly.

In the end, I'm not brave enough or stupid enough to turn into that girl—the stalker who won't leave her celebrity crush alone.

Am I a puck bunny after all?

MONDAY MORNING, I slog into the office, determined to make it business as usual. The fact that the team left this morning for a three-game road trip makes me optimistic that I can carry it off.

Billie Mae comes in ten minutes after me and gives me a hug before she takes her seat and spreads out in her cubicle.

I'm humming along, answering calls while I tap on my keyboard and stare at the columns of numbers on the screen, kicking butt on this multi-tasking deal.

Hanging up from one call, I answer the next one, feeling good about myself and my happy, productive roll.

"Hello. Brawlers' ticketing and public relations. How can I help you?"

"Is this Sara?" a familiar woman's voice asks.

. . .

"Yes." My mind buzzes around trying to place the voice and getting nowhere.

"This is Mrs. James—Natalie James—Quinn's mom."

I try not to pee my pants, kicking myself for that second cup of coffee.

CHAPTER 27

SARA

*M*y heart races and I finally gather in the crazy thoughts zipping around in my head. "Hi. Hello." Why the heck is she calling me here? It can't be an issue with Quinn's tickets.

"I hope you don't mind that I tracked you down at the office, but I didn't have your cell phone number. We can correct that problem now, can't we? Quinn is, of course, too busy for me to bother him with details now that he's focused on hockey."

"He played great last night. Two goals," I say, glad to have something positive to say to his mother besides *Did you know your son broke my foolish heart?* That's unfair since it was all my fault. I threw myself at him. Repeatedly. He tried to tell me no, but I, the ridiculous optimist, refused to believe that he... what? Doesn't have a heart? Wouldn't sweep me into his vortex and make me fall for him so hard? Wouldn't get past my crush and become so much more to me?

"Will you be driving up with Quinn for our dinner? We're so looking forward to having you."

He hasn't told her yet. Crap. *Well, duh, when did he have the chance?*

"No, I don't think so…" I try to stall and stay neutral because this is not a conversation I'm prepared to have. I have no idea what to say, what she thinks there is between me and Quinn, or what Quinn has told her about me.

"Well, I'll have to call him and make sure he doesn't make you drive up on your own. That would be silly and wasteful."

"Yes, you should definitely call him." Please. He said he'd take care of it, and she's his mom, not mine.

"If you talk to him first, tell him dinner is at two and I said you should drive up together. And tell him to call me. Okay?"

"Okay."

"I can't wait to see you again, Sara."

I think she actually means it. "Okay."

"I'll let you get back to work. Bye now."

"Bye." I slam the phone down and jump from my seat like a cherry bomb went off under my butt.

"What is it?" Billie Mae rushes over to me and even Margaret looks at me, concerned.

"Nothing." What a ridiculous lie that no one believes.

Billie Mae takes fast-walks me to the rest room.

I stare in the mirror while she rubs my back and I suck in a breath. What am I looking at here? A big baby. I straighten.

"That was Mrs. James – Quinn's mom. She said I should ride with Quinn to their house the day after Thanksgiving."

Billie Mae snorts. "Oh, that's all? I thought your doctor called to say you were dying of cancer." I elbow her, but I agree; it shouldn't be a big deal.

"I can't help it sometimes. I'm hypersensitive when it comes to Quinn. He's… I'm…" I don't know what to say that won't sound ridiculous, so I wave a hand. "I fell for him, you know, because he's a good person on top of the fact that he's fun and funny and sweet and gorgeous—"

"Let's not forget that he's a walking aphrodisiac."

I elbow her again, but this time I laugh. "Truth?" I say. "That's the least of why I fell for him. I think it's because, deep down, I connect with him." I don't mention that he's a lost soul, looking to fit back in with his family like some prodigal son because that's something he told me in confidence. And I don't tell her how much pain he's in and how I empathize and how he believes in me and is so supportive of who I am and loves my quirks.

"I'm sure he's a wicked nice guy when he's not taking advantage of vulnerable young women," she says, hands on her hips now. "Get over him. And get over his mother."

Wistfulness whispers by and I let it go like a pesky mosquito. But the buzz remains underneath everything, giving me that uncomfortable anticipation of a bite. for the rest of the day.

For the rest of the week and all the way until the Monday before Thanksgiving, I limp around metaphorically with the buzz of anticipating some kind of bite, something bad besides not seeing or hearing from Quinn. Not even a text.

In the void of Quinn-related stimuli, I should feel calm and settle down back to my old routine before we'd met that night in the bar, but I can't make it happen. He's playing well, better than ever—he's on a scoring streak that more than makes up for his slump.

That's a good thing. Every time I watch him score, I get a little thrill, followed directly by a blast of disappointment.

Sitting at my desk, I stare at my computer screen, trying to emulate his focus on work, but all I see are the still-available VIP tickets for the Thanksgiving matinee.

Mom had wanted the family to go because Bobby is home for two days, but I'd lied and said there were no tickets left.

Billie Mae had gone along with it because she's just as happy to spend the time with Bobby alone—which I prefer not to think about.

My cell rings, startling me from the grip of my overactive conscience—which must be working out because I swear it's stronger than I ever remember it. I grab it. "Hello?"

"*Lola?* It's me, Sheila, calling instead of texting. Surprise!" Her voice is peppy and very unlike her.

I smile. "A really nice surprise." .

"I'm calling with great news." She stops and I hear a commotion in the background and another voice. "Mindy wants to talk to you." She giggles.

I never thought I'd hear Sheila giggle. She's def not the giggling type.

"Lola? This is Mindy," Mindy says. "Is it okay if I'm calling you? Sheila says you have some kind of important corporate job—"

"No problem at all. It's a slow day."

"We're really getting married—me and Jonas. Do you believe it?"

"That's great, Mindy. I never doubted it for a minute."

"Sheila will be my maid of honor and a few other puck bunnies will be there. They're all wearing Brawlers' jerseys. My mom will be there, too. Jonas refuses to tell his parents because he doesn't want to make them fly all the way in from Minnesota for a ten-minute ceremony."

"That makes sense," I say. My heart isn't sure if it should jump for joy or break in two with wistful envy, but my natural romantic tendency rises up to dominate whatever else I'm feeling because, no matter what, I really am happy for her. "I'm really truly thrilled for you and glad that you're getting this chance to make a happy family."

"I owe you everything. I don't know how you did it, but you really brought out the best in Jonas. I would be honored if you would be my bridesmaid."

"I would be honored to. Thank you so much for asking. Did you set the date?"

"Yes, we're getting married right away. The day after Thanksgiving."

Boom.

My belly bounces around at the mention of that infamous day and I crash onto the arm of the couch. But heck, Mindy's wedding is a better distraction than sitting in the office pretending to work. There's no question that I have to go to her wedding and see this thing through. Only thing is, this time, my partner in the mission of holding Jonas accountable won't be there. No Quinn.

"Will you be coming with Quinn?"

"No. He's having dinner with his family up north," I say, my voice steady and calm—and grateful for a good excuse. I can avoid the humiliation of telling her that Quinn won't be going anywhere with me. That, in spite of her impression otherwise, there has never been anything between us.

"That's too bad. Jonas wanted him to be his best man." She huffs a breath and I hold mine. A jolt of fear shakes me. He's not going to bail on his family's dinner. He couldn't. Not even for a wedding. Not even if he's supposed to be the best man.

But there's no doubt that Jonas's request for him to be best man will put a strain on him, forcing him to make a difficult decision and disappoint his teammate.

The priorities of hockey and family were bound to clash at some point and this decision puts him squarely between that rock and a hard place I've heard tell of. Crap. My chest tightens like I'm the one being squeezed by the proverbial rock.

CHAPTER 28

QUINN

The day before Thanksgiving, Coach barges into the dressing room, blowing his whistle and I stop pulling off my shirt halfway.

"Listen up. Before you dress, PR is having us re-shoot our team photo." He gestures to the carts being wheeled in by our equipment manager, Zeb Standish, packed with plastic-covered uniforms hanging from the rod. "Some bullshit about including our newest player up from the junior league, Chase Kondorski." Coach casts an accusing glance at the kid.

I nudge Chase's shoulder. "Welcome aboard."

To his credit, the kid laughs.

Quinn whispers, "Coach isn't known for his tact, but he's a good soul and a hockey genius."

"And he has damn good ears," Coach says, not completely covering his smirk with a frown.

But the locker room laughs and we get dressed in our brand-new classic Brawlers' uniforms

We mill around outside the rink, waiting for the photographer while the Zamboni finishes up.

Delaney appears around the corner and asks, "Where's the photographer?"

Coach yells back, "You're the one in charge of this fiasco, Delaney? You tell me where he is."

"It's a *she*. I'll find out now." She stares at me like I'm the one to blame and puts her phone to her ear.

"This better not take long. We have practice for an important game coming up." Coach bristles while Delaney cups a hand over her phone and has a vigorous conversation with some unlucky bastard on the other end.

Chase says something to me, but I miss it because that's when Sara shows up, her long, killer legs in black tights and impossible platform heels. Her sinfully short skirt spikes my already surging heart rate and her green eyes stare straight at me, daring me to change my mind and throw in the towel and succumb to the weakness deep inside me that answers to her, that craves her and every fucking little thing about her.

Fuck.

Her pint-sized friend is holding on to her like she'll kill anyone who tangles with her—meaning *me* if the snarl aimed in my direction is a clue.

Sara clutches a sheet of paper, clears her throat, then says, "Let's line up while we're waiting for the photographer to arrive." She turns to Coach. "You don't mind, do you?"

The old bear smiles at her like he has a heart of mush. "Great idea. Do your thing." He turns to us, any trace of the smile gone and shouts, "You heard her, men! Onto the ice and follow Ms. Bellagamba's directions."

O'Rourke leads the charge as the captain

I hang back. "Are you going out on the ice with those shoes?"

"Do you think I'm crazy to? Wait—don't answer that." A moment of real panic crosses her face before she grins. "I'll call directions from the bench."

I grin and nod. "Good idea. Not that I wouldn't love to see you on skates."

"I can skate." She lifts her chin. "Wouldn't be a full-fledged member of a hockey family and fan since birth if I couldn't."

Delaney storms toward us, shoving her phone back into its holster, usual grimace in place.

"I better get out there." I nod in the direction of Delaney and Sara turns then scrambles into the penalty box. I keep my laugh to myself because she won't be able to call anything from inside that glass.

She seems to figure that out and opens the door onto the ice.

"What are you doing?" Delaney asks.

"I'm going onto the ice to make sure the guys are lined up," Sara says bravely.

Billie Mae stands nearby, horrified, but not brave enough to come onto the ice to rescue her friend.

"You're going to—" Delaney sounds truly alarmed.

"I volunteered to help," I say.

Coach raises an eyebrow.

Delaney narrows her eyes.

Billie Mae frowns like she's holding in a growl and my team-mates snicker.

Not surprisingly, a few of them expected it. I hear muted comments from Finn and Jonas, like, "Of course he's going to help his girlfriend."

Looping my arm through Sara's, I walk her to center ice and she directs the players where to stand, consulting her sheet of paper, and calling out names. I don't let go of her or leave her side until she turns to me.

"I'll be all right if I stand still. You can take your place now." She gives me a wistful smile and my friendly dagger almost splits my shoulder blades in two.

The answering wistfulness buried inside me cracks the surface of my stone heart and I feel every bit of the pain.

Skating to the end of the first line, I put up with some hoots and whistles.

Jonas stands behind me and nudges me. "You never fooled me for a minute," he mutters for my hearing only.

I grunt and elbow him back. Maybe I'm the only one being fooled because he and my own mother have a different idea of my relationship with Sara—maybe more in line with Sara's idea.

She looks at Delaney who nods her approval and shouts, "The photographer is on her way!"

While we're waiting, Sara slips out her phone and starts taking photos of her own. "Might as well take advantage of the moment," she says. "These photos are for social media, so make them interesting."

With that, the team jumps into action with shenanigans like stupid faces, finger horns over guys' heads, nudges, punches, shoves, and even a dance step or two.

When the photographer arrives with her camera and Sara helps her set it up, I whistle so we organize into our original neat line-up.

AFTER IT'S OVER, the guys skate off the ice and I escort Sara to the gate.

Jonas meets us on the other side and says to Sara, "Not bad for a puck bunny."

When Sara freezes next to me, I notice Delaney on her phone nearby. Shit. She couldn't be paying attention, could she?

Her head shoots up and she frowns at Sara. "What's this?"

Well, shit. Of *course* she is paying attention.

"It's nothing," Sara shakes her head, her face pink.

I could strangle Jonas right now—yet again.

"He said something about you being a puck bunny?" Delaney points at Jonas, demanding an explanation.

I don't trust Jonas to give it to her. "Don't pay any attention to him. Sara is no puck bunny." I put my arm around her and pull her to my side for extra protection, like I can shield her from gossip by owning her, or owning up to having a relationship with her.

"Is there something going on between you two?" Delaney shifts her eyes to me, then Sara with a tense, skeptical stare like she can see through us.

Maybe she can.

Sara is about to answer her, saying who knows what, likely something that'll get her into trouble because she's not a good liar, so I step in. "Yes and no," I say in all honesty.

Sara tenses and I automatically pull her closer. Shit. I'm not sure it's a good idea, but I'm running with it because that's all I have left, and all my stabbing conscience will let me do.

"Explain," Delaney says, more curious than angry.

I look around and all the guys except Jonas have gone back into the locker room. As for Jonas, he's watching our scene like we're the newest reality TV series.

"I wanted to go out with her, but she turned me down flat. I'd still like to date her because she's a wonderful lady, as I'm sure you know, except I'm pretty certain she turned me down because she's too good for the likes of me."

"Are you serious? You expect me to believe that bullshit?" Delaney asks.

"As a priest."

Jonas snorts. "Wait. Didn't you tell me she was invited to go to Thanksgiving dinner with your family?"

Fuck. That's what I get for confiding private matters in a locker room—guys like Jonas overhear them.

"No, I didn't tell you that." I glare at him and avoid looking at Sara whose eyes I can feel burning a hole in my soul because who knows what she's thinking right now. As soon as I let go of her, she's probably going to run the other way, fast, and be thankful that she dodged the Quinn bullet. Fuck.

"You still didn't explain what all is going on with you two. Are you a couple or aren't you?"

"No," Sara says.

"Yes," I say.

Jonas cackles and Delaney takes her time examining us like an inquisitor deciding on the best torture.

"For the record," I say, clearing my throat in the interest of total honesty and to give Sara an out I suspect she desperately wants, "Sara declined the invitation to Thanksgiving dinner."

Delaney's eyes pop and she aims her beady eagle eyes at Sara "Is this true?"

Sara nods.

"Well, I'll be damned." Delaney says, "You're crazy not to take him up on his offer."

"You should definitely go for Thanksgiving dinner," Jonas jumps in, probably thinking he's doing me a favor.

Sara looks at me. Delaney and Jonas are watching her and waiting for her to respond.

I look at her and I'm not sure what my eyes are saying, not sure what I want her to say or do, but, after a few tense beats, she finally responds.

"Okay. I'll go." She says to Delaney, "You talked me into it."

She doesn't look at me, studiously avoids my gaze, so she doesn't see my grin.

Jonas slaps my back and whispers, "You can thank me later."

Delaney says, "Enough bullshit. You boys get your asses into the locker room. You have an important practice I'm told."

CHAPTER 29

SARA

*R*unning up the stairs from the practice rink to the corporate office floor three flights up might have been a bad idea with my heels, but I have too much pent-up energy to wait for the elevator and I needed to get some distance between me and Delaney while she was distracted on her phone. When I reach the office, I waste no time tracking down Billie Mae and rip her from her cubicle. Luckily, she had time to hang up the phone or the phone would have been coming to the ladies' room with us.

"What the hell?" she says under her breath while Martha pulls down her gold-and-black knit hat and gives us a curious look as we rush past her, again standing at the file cabinet doing who knows what.

"The hell is, I told Quinn I would do dinner with him and his family." My heart pounds with exertion and the strain of confusion as I tell myself to calm down. I take a deep breath as Billie Mae scowls. Her face says *Don't be a fool.* Or that could be my conscience talking, my rational mind.

"You're serious? I left you back there with the jerk because I figured Delaney would make a great chaperone. What the fuck happened?"

"I know, but she was the instigator. And Jonas, that brat. He set Quinn up."

She shakes her head while I explain how Quinn came to my rescue from Delaney.

"None of it matters because even though I said I would, I'm not going to dinner. I have a wedding to attend."

She gives me a *you're a terrible liar* look. "That's the lamest cover I ever heard, but whatever. You go with that." She pats my shoulder.

"The crazy thing is that I don't even care about my job. Delaney can fire me tomorrow and I wouldn't care—okay, I might care a little about being fired because it looks bad on a resume or when someone checks references—but I would quit in a heartbeat if I thought I was going to get Quinn in trouble and Delaney…" I take a deep breath while Billie Mae stares at me like she'll die if I don't finish my sentence. "Delaney didn't care a whit about us having a relationship. She said I'd be crazy not to go with Quinn."

"What? That sounds—" She stops short and clamps her mouth shut.

"What? It sounds like what?"

"Like maybe she's trying to get rid of you," she says quietly.

"Rid of me? Why? I work my butt off—"

"Well not *you,* necessarily, but I overheard someone in personnel say they needed to trim the staff in our office."

"Crap. I swear to God, Billie Mae, I'll quit and you won't need to worry—"

"I'm not worried. Dad will pick up the slack in an emergency. Besides, you're right about this job. It sucks—except for the game tickets." She grabs me by the shoulders as someone comes into the ladies' room and pulls me outside to the corridor.

"That doesn't solve your dilemma with Quinn. You can't continue this non-relationship with him. He's using you."

"No, he's not. I almost wish he was, then it would be easy to forget about him." I let out a sigh because I know what his problem is. "He's confused. Overwhelmed really. He has too much unpacked baggage and too many important things to focus on. I'm one more thing—a monkey wrench in his already too full plate."

"I have no idea what you're talking about—"

"I can't tell you because it's confidential."

"No problem, but if it has anything to do with the princess and her aborted pregnancy—"

"What?" For a split second, her words vacuum my brain and I get dizzy. Then my avenger instinct kicks in like a tsunami. "Where did you get that rumor? There was no aborted pregnancy." I feel a little nauseous because I know the answer.

"Social media. I was working on burying the rumor because it's too close to home—and by home, I mean our man Quinn."

"*She's* behind the rumor."

"The thought crossed my mind." She clamps her mouth shut and looks at her wrist as if she's wearing a watch, which she isn't.

"You're not telling me something. What is it?"

She huffs. "The gossip implies that Quinn forced her into the abortion."

Stumbling back against the wall, I can't imagine how the rumor would hit Quinn if he found out.

"How far has this gotten?"

"Not far. Only a few hundred views on Twitter."

"Twitter?"

She shrugs. "No one said the princess was a master at social media. I've reported the tweets and called the source disreputable —not with the official Brawlers account. It hasn't caught on yet."

"It will if we don't do something big to counter it. This kind of crap goes viral all the time, especially if the mainstream media gets hold of it."

"What do you suggest?"

"A juicier story—one that she won't like."

THANKSGIVING DAY BILLIE MAE comes to my house for dinner because she said she couldn't get a flight home. I know, and so does everyone else at the table, that it's because she wants to spend time with Bobby. He's the only one pretending there's nothing between them, the jerk. I'm just glad she's here because I'm all nerves about tomorrow's wedding as if it were my own.

Plus, I have more work to do on the Princess Matter. That's what Billie Mae and I are calling it. She's handed everything over to me because she still has mixed feelings about Quinn. But since she detests the princess, she's on his side.

From the minute Billie Mae walks in the door, she looks for my big brother Bobby and doesn't take her eyes off him. At the dinner table, we sit on either side of her and he soaks up all her attention like butter. It's cute. In a disgusting way.

Thanksgiving dinner includes the usual turkey, plus antipasto and a pasta course. I help Mom serve the food as is tradition, while the boys do their best to eat it all. Also tradition.

"See what a good wife you would make some lucky man?" Grandma Zanetti says. "What about that handsome hockey guy who had his arm around you? Any progress with him?"

Bobby looks up and squints. "Who's this?"

Paul answers, "Quinn James. He likes her." Paul grins at me. "She likes him, too. I could tell. There was a vibe."

I swat him. "This isn't kindergarten. There was no vibe." I lie my ass off. No one believes me because I am, in fact, a terrible liar.

"You should have brought him home for dinner," Aunt Yolanda says.

"They have a game today, Yola," Mom says and she changes the subject to the food. She gives me a wink like she knows something and doesn't press. I love my mom.

"You have tomorrow off?" Mom asks.

"No," I say, looking at my plate while I lie.

"Yes," Billie Mae says. Then she looks at me and shakes her head.

She still thinks I'm going to Thanksgiving dinner with Quinn tomorrow. She doesn't believe I'm using work to cover for going to the wedding. The last thing I need is for my family to know that I'm one of the puck bunnies. They wouldn't understand. They would be shocked. My brothers would shoot me.

Billie Mae shrugs while I'm trying to figure how to appease the suspicions of my family.

"I wanted to save my vacation time, so I'm working," I say.

"I thought they were shutting down since the team had to play today?" Paul says. "Which reminds me—I'm having dessert in the living room because the game starts in twenty minutes."

Mom argues with him and the subject changes to the Brawlers like it always does at some point at a family dinner during the season. Then the discussion turns to Bobby's new team. He was traded to Rochester, which is closer, so Mom is thrilled—but not as thrilled as Billie Mae was when she broke the news to me. The fact that she got the news before me was my first clue that there was something more than a flirtation going on between them, but I left it alone because, frankly, I didn't want to know.

"Now that you're with Rochester," Dad says, "any chance of getting called up to the New Jersey Devils?"

All eyes turn to Bobby and I hold my breath. Only Dad could get away with asking him that, but only once. The last time someone prodded him, Bobby stormed out and didn't talk any of us for two weeks. Guess the answer was *no* at the time, but, now, he seems less tense—dare I say, even mellow.

I glance at Billie Mae and my emotions swirl around, changing colors, and I don't know how I feel. Like I'm losing her? Or maybe like something good is about to happen.

But I don't dare think that as I wait with everyone else while Bobby wipes his mouth with a napkin before answering.

"As a matter of fact, I wasn't going to say anything because it hasn't happened yet, but I was told I'd be first up as soon as the Devils need someone."

Paul punches his arm, whooping while Dad's smile fills his face.

Billie Mae continues to gaze at Bobby adoringly, and not surprised at all—she already knew, the rat.

Aunt Yolanda and Grandma Zanetti gush and come to tears, doing the sign of the cross in thanks.

Mom goes over to him and gives him a big hug and kiss while he pretends to squirm.

Me? I'm stunned. Not about Bobby maybe getting a chance to play in the NHL at long last, but about the bomb of realization that not only has Billie Mae fallen for him, but maybe it's mutual.

My big bad brother Bobby is smitten with my best friend.

"Too bad you're working tomorrow, Sara," Bobby says. "You could take a ride down to Jersey with me and Billie Mae to scope out the area."

"Take the day off and come with us?" Billie Mae says.

She still thinks I'm going with Quinn's for his family dinner. I give her a look that says *Please trust me*. "I can't possibly do that. I have that thing to do at work. Remember?"

"Forget the thing," she says.

Now, I want to shake her and then smack Bobby and ask him what he's done to my friend.

"I can't forget the *thing*." *The thing is a friend's wedding* I want to shout at her.

"What thing?" Grandma Zanetti asks.

"A work thing," Mom answers. "It's short hand for crap we wouldn't understand."

Grandma nods. "Aah. Sara is a smart girl. They're lucky to have her. She understands all that crap."

In the morning, as I pretend to get ready for work, I make a pot of coffee and Bobby appears.

"That coffee smells so good."

"Good morning, future NHL player."

He grins, gives me a one-armed squeeze and pours the first cup. Then he hands it to me.

I'm surprised as I take it, then he pours a second one for himself.

"You ready to handle the *work crap* today?" he asks.

"Billie Mae said something, didn't she?" The taut wire of my nerves loosens a fraction. No need to pretend with Bobby anymore—one less thing to worry about.

He shrugs. "I don't know why it's a big secret."

"Because I don't want Mom and Dad to know. Plus, if work knew, there'd be hell to pay. There was a video of me with the puck bunnies that went viral and we had to handle with it. They didn't know it was me, thank God."

"Wait—what the hell are you talking about? Because I don't give a crap about some puck bunnies. Billie Mae told me you were going to dinner with Quinn James and his family—"

Crap. "You don't believe that, do you? I told her I wasn't going. I'm texting him this morning to let him know."

"What's going on with you two?"

"Nothing." Is it a lie? I'm too confused to tell, frankly. He stood up for me and seemed okay with telling Delaney I was invited to his family's Thanksgiving dinner, but wasn't that all because he was put in a difficult situation?

"Oh *there's* something going on between you two. It's just a matter of what it is. And I'm very curious to know because if he's taking advantage of you, I'll need to—"

"It's nothing like that. I mean, what makes you think he's taking advantage of me? Maybe I'm taking advantage of him." Stupid thing to say.

"He is, isn't he? The fucker is a player, Sara and you're... not." His words are tight and all the cheer has gone from his voice.

"I'm—"

"You're as innocent as they come. I know you." He gives me that look that brings me all the way back to our childhood and those shared secret discussions about what happened to Dad and if we were ever going to see him again. My chest squeezes because I love my brother.

"Maybe you don't know everything," I say and it's unquestionably a legit act of bravery to say this. "Either way, you're going to have to trust me. Trust that I can handle him because I'm a grown woman. Don't you dare think of interfering—as much as I know you mean well—or..." I don't know what. My indignation subsides because I feel the caring behind his words.

Bobby studies me for a few beats then softens up, huffing out a breath. "Okay. For now, I'll trust you. But first time I hear he's made you cry, all bets are off. I'm in his face and I bet you anything I'm tougher than his fancy old ass."

I don't say what's on the tip of my tongue—that ship has sailed and sunk. Instead, I swat him, half playfully because I appreciate his protective streak, but the other half of me doesn't like him casting Quinn as a bad guy when that couldn't be further from the truth. He doesn't know that Quinn is also trying to protect me—from myself.

CHAPTER 30

"Great game, men," Coach says as we file into the locker room. "Rafe volunteered to do media duty, so all you reprobates can get home to your Thanksgiving dinners. Report back on Saturday. Don't over-indulge because we have a game Sunday."

He leaves to a disjointed chorus of "Happy Thanksgivings!" shouted from all over the room.

"I can't wait for the pie," Finn says, bumping me on my pads with his stick as he lumbers by. It's become a tradition. His cubby is two down from mine.

"What kind of pie?" I ask as I undress, in no particular hurry when everyone else seems to be moving in fast motion to get home.

He tells me, but I'm only half-listening. I went into the game feeling good, with a clear conscience for telling the truth to Delaney about Sara. Now, it doesn't feel real. Should she be coming to dinner with my family? Am I giving them the right impression—or better yet—am I giving Sara the right impression?

I thought we had a real relationship, but after seeing the players greeted by their wives and girlfriends waiting outside the gate, I realize how far away I am from a real relationship, how foreign it still seems to me. It takes some level of commitment that I don't have, that I'm not capable of.

Should I have that relationship with Sara? Right now, we have nothing like that kind of commitment between us—no matter how many secrets I've shared with her, no matter how different or intimate sex felt with her. No matter that she spent the night and the only other time I spent a night with a woman it was with Anica and only because she'd tricked me into going to Paris.

"Great slap-shot goal there," O'Rourke says as he passes by, the first man down to his boxers and heading for the shower. No doubt he's dying to get home to his wife and three kids.

"Don't sound so surprised," I say.

Jonas is right behind O'Rourke and he smirks. "And there's the Hollywood Hockey player with the unapologetic ego we've all seen everywhere for the past however many years it's been." Jonas's voice booms, getting everyone's attention.

I give him the finger.

O'Rourke laughs. "We'll let him have this moment of glory. You know how those Hollywood stars fade fast—"

I tap his butt with my stick. "Fuck you."

He laughs harder and I grin.

Finn shakes his head. "So, what *is* your favorite pie?"

JONAS IS WAITING for me just inside the door to the parking garage. I'm not surprised because he's still a bundle of energy though I would have thought the adrenaline from the game should have worn off by now. Eh, maybe as he becomes a more experienced player.

Or maybe I just have too much on my mind personally right now to dwell in the high of the game.

As I walk toward him, I scroll my texts and find one from Sara.

I won't be going to dinner with your family tomorrow. I have a wedding to go to. Tell your mom I'm sorry.

I look at Jonas, shooting accusation from my eyes and wanting to punch him—yet again. "Is Sara going to your wedding ceremony at city hall tomorrow?"

He smirks. "What if she is?"

I suck in a breath and push through the door.

He follows me to my car. "What's up with you and Sara?"

"Nothing. We're friends."

"Bullshit. I know the look when I see it. I've seen it in the mirror often enough."

"What the hell are you talking about? Cupid hijack your brain? You in some kind of wedding day spell?"

"No. I'm for real."

When I reach my car, I turn on him. "I don't need you to keep throwing us together right now. I'm—we're not in a relationship and it would probably be best if it stays that way." I'm not sure if I'm trying to convince myself of this or him. I shove my hand through my hair, resisting the urge to pull every strand out by the root.

"Not in a relationship? Are you sure? Because it sure looks like you are to me. Every time I see her, there you are. And not just casually. I see you sticking up for her like you'll murder the guy who does her wrong."

"Your point is?"

"You have feelings. Admit it."

I huff, but the truth stings a hole in my chest that won't quit. "Maybe I do, but so what?" I pull out my phone to Sara. I'm the one who needs to apologize for the confusion I created with the Delaney encounter, but I felt a need to bail her out with her boss.

I dash off a text while Jonas stands over my shoulder like a defenseman pinning me to the boards.

She texts back right away saying she understands.

I wish I did, but I'm as confused as fuck.

"Look, I can't go to your wedding, man. My mom is having dinner for the family tomorrow and is too important. I promised her I'd be there." I watch his face fall and he may as well have punched me in the gut. "But I'll be your best man in absentia," I say.

"In what?"

I try to laugh. "I'll throw you a bachelor party after the dust clears and invite the team. Your decency is worth celebrating even if it is newly found."

He punches me. But I can see that he's trying to cover his disappointment.

"I don't see why you can't do both," he says, losing his battle and sounding like a pouty kid.

I know he could use the moral support and I feel like a fucking heel.

"You're getting married at the same time as my mom's dinner. I wouldn't arrive until everyone else was ready to leave." My brother would give me worse than a barrel of shit if I walked in late after promising to be there. He'd accuse me of bailing on the family again—and he'd be right...

"How about if I change the time of my wedding to ten a.m.?" Jonas asks. His face is smirkless and he looks uncharacteristically vulnerable, like he's desperate for moral support. He probably *is* desperate since he'll be the only guy there surrounded by Mindy, her mom, and her friends. Fuck.

"You could do that? At the last minute? Wouldn't Mindy have a problem with changing the time?"

He shrugs. "I'll explain it." He smiles. "She would do about anything for me if I ask nice." He ducks his head like he's embarrassed.

I'm seeing another whole side to the Jonas Bergman I thought I knew.

"It's why I'm marrying her," he says, lifting his chin.

I nod. "Good reason." Sara is the same way, but I keep that thought to myself. "If you change the time to ten a.m. and I'll be there. I'll need to leave by eleven, though. Does that give you enough time?"

"Shit, yeah." He smacks me on the back and grins, relief and unabridged joy finally showing on his face.

"Confirm it with Mindy and text me later," I say, fist-bumping his shoulder. "Looks like I'll be seeing you in the morning."

On the way home, I call my mother to let her know what's going on.

"What did you think of the game? That last goal was all for you," I say and she laughs. "I might be a few minutes late for dinner tomorrow."

"That won't be a problem. I'll make dinner for two-thirty. What about Sara?"

"I'm not sure if she'll be able to make it," I say. The response is as true and genuine as it can be. I should have told her Sara cancelled, but I can't make myself give up on us. Maybe it's the influence of the bastard Jonas. A smile stretches across my face. Pretending there's nothing between us doesn't work. Insisting she's not right for me hasn't convinced my feelings. And even though I've been playing my best hockey of the season, I don't care if she's a distraction or not. I don't even care that I have too much baggage to be in a relationship. I need to give my feelings a chance.

Because I've never in my life have I had these feelings before, not for any of the women I've been with. That has to be worth paying some attention to.

"She has to go to a wedding," I say.

"A wedding?" Mom laughs. "That's an inventive excuse," she jokes. "She has a habit of saying delightful things, doesn't she?"

"Yes, but her excuse happens to be the truth. I'm going to the same wedding."

"You are?" She laughs and then goes silent. "Quinn?"

"God, no. It's not *my* wedding, Mom. It's one of my team-mates. No worries there."

"Oh. Okay.."

"The wedding is first thing in the morning and we should be able to make it to dinner by one. Sara will be there." What made me make that prediction is pure insanity. Or maybe I'm deter-mined to face the demons in my luggage finally.

THE WEDDING PARTY is assembled outside of City Hall when I arrive and my eyes go directly to Sara. She takes my breath away, standing there with a bouquet of carnations and looking like the jewel among all the ladies.

I take my place next to her, not caring about what the protocol might be.

Mindy introduces me to her mom who titters, saying of course she knows me.

"Let's get this show on the road," Jonas says and leads us inside.

The clerk tells us to wait in the lobby for a few minutes and I take Sara's arm. "Can I talk with you a minute?" I move us away from the group.

She goes along and doesn't say anything. The tension shows in the stiffness of her smile that should be soft.

"Come with me to my family's for dinner after the ceremony."

"I told you—"

"Please." Pain releases the plea from me and stays to constrict my chest.

She gives me a long studying look and her face softens. Then she looks down.

"I can't go like this."

At least she didn't say she wouldn't go.

"You look nice." I grin, because nice isn't the right word. She's dressed in a tight, low-cut pink version of the team jersey with my number on it, a short black shirt with tights, and tall boots.

She blushes, but she stays quiet.

I don't rush her. I want to convince her so fucking bad, but I don't want to force her.

"If I can go home and change, I'll go."

"You have a deal."

AFTER THE CEREMONY we head to the lobby from the courtroom and I can feel the joy in the air. I hand Jonas an envelope. "Put that in your pocket. It should be helpful for your honeymoon when you get a chance to have one."

"I don't know when that'll be with the baby coming," Jonas says, his grin faltering.

"You'll manage," I say and point to the huddle of the bridal party, all smiles and giggles and hugs as they give Mindy their well-wishes and gifts. I watch Sara, with her kind, sad smile, make Mindy feel special as she hands her a small gift. "You have plenty of potential baby-sitters there. Heck, even I'd help you out if you go on the off-season."

"You? Take care of a baby?" He laughs.

"Sure. I have a couple of nephews and I'm pretty good with them. I like kids."

Mindy and her entourage join us and I automatically reach for Sara, pulling her to my side.

"This reprobate just volunteered for baby-sitting duty," Jonas says to Sara. "I might let him if you help."

"That would be wonderful," Mindy says.

Sara gives me a smile. "I bet Quinn would be great at taking care of a baby. He's a natural at giving comfort."

Sheila and the others volunteer their services and Mindy laughs, shining with joy.

Sara makes her the center of attention as they talk about the baby, but then the courthouse door swings open and three people walk in.

This is not going to go over well.

CHAPTER 31

SARA

*I*n walks my mother, Bobby, and Billie Mae. My mouth opens all by itself. I feel dizzy.

When Mom scans the crowd with a faint smile, my knees give out. But Quinn catches me.

"What's wrong?" he whispers.

When Mom's eyes lock on mine, I freeze. Guilt darkens the edges of my mind, but it shouldn't because I'm not doing anything wrong. I'm attending a friend's wedding.

"Sara?" She finally gets past the disorientation of seeing me here dressed in a racy pink hockey jersey with a group of similarly dressed ladies and two hockey players. I smile. It could be hysteria setting in. I straighten my spine to ward it off.

"What the hell are you doing here?" She sweeps her gaze up and down. "In that getup?" Her eyes dart to Quinn's and widen so far that I worry she's going to lose them.

Bobby grabs Mom's elbow as she moves toward me.

Billie Mae rushes to my side.

"Did you just get married?" Mom asks in a high-pitched voice, looking at the flowers in my hand.

"No." Mindy steps from behind me. "*I* just got married," she

261

says, grinning and hanging onto Jonas, who's smirking from ear-to-ear like he doesn't mind so much after all.

"What are you doing here?" I ask Billie Mae, as it finally dawns on me that she's here with Mom and Bobby and that's very strange.

Pink floods her face and I can hardly believe my eyes because in the history of our entire friendship, Billie Mae has never, , ever blushed. I'd always assumed she was genetically incapable.

Then my brain kicks in. *Crap.*

"You—you're not—"

She nods. "I am. We're here to get a marriage license."

I let out a breath, but Mom is still glancing uneasily between me and Quinn and the arm he has around me. I try for a little space between us, but he pulls me closer. Crap.

"Wait here while we take care of business," Mom says and waves Bobby and Billie Mae to follow her inside the clerk's office.

"I'm sorry. I need to wait and talk to Mom," I say to Quinn. "I don't want to make you late. Your family dinner is important—"

"I can wait," he says. "You're not getting out of it that easy."

"We have to go," Jonas says, holding onto Mindy tightly.

Another round of well-wishes ensues. Once Mindy and Jonas are gone, I promise the puck bunnies I'll see them soon.

Sheila is about to walk out the door when she, "You don't have to pretend. You're not one of us. It doesn't matter if your name is Lola, or what you're wearing, you're not a fun-and games-kind of girl." She rushes to catch up with her friends.

"Wait! That's not it!" I start after her, but Quinn, the only one left in the lobby with me, holds onto my arm.

"She's right," he says.

"But that doesn't mean we can't be friends." I don't want to lose them.

"You can talk to her later," he says, caressing my back. "We need to deal with your family first."

"Right." I settle down for a millisecond before my heart seizes up again when Mom, Bobby, and Billie Mae emerge from the clerk's office.

"I wanted to tell you," Billie Mae says, rushing to my side and ripping me from Quinn's hold.

"Why didn't you? You can tell me anything."

She turns an accusing glare on Mom who surprises me by looking contrite.

"I thought it would be best because you... were having a hard time. With him." She points at Quinn.

"Wait—how did you know?" I'm so shocked I forgot to be embarrassed that Quinn is getting an earful of my family drama.

Mom snorts. "It's not hard to figure. You still have his poster hanging in your bedroom for pity's sake and now he's on the team. Then, I saw you with him and I figured, well, maybe there's some hope." She shoots daggers at him now, squinting her eyes as if she has the old Italian lady power to curse him. She doesn't or my one and only boyfriend would be dead by now.

I turn to Bobby. He's been quietly sizing Quinn up as if he's measuring him for a coffin.

"Why didn't you tell me?" I'm more hurt than mad because he had his chance and we've shared so much.

He looks down and shrugs. "Same reason. Besides, I figure it was Billie Mae's place to tell you."

"Besides, you have secrets of your own," Billie Mae says, but the bite of her accusation is muted by her guilt.

"I told you I was going to a wedding."

"You told me a lot of things," Billie Mae says. "Like that you were done with him." She jerks her head at Quinn.

"She *was* done with me," Quinn says. "But I'm not done with her."

"Is that right?" Bobby steps forward with menace in his voice.

"Yes, sir. Bobby." Quinn puts his hand out . But I can tell he's nervous underneath because his jaw ticks just under his left ear.

It's a tell I've seen before, usually around Jonas who gets under his skin.

Every instinct in me shouts to intervene, to protect him, but I meet my mother's eyes and I read her loud and clear. Don't let him off the hook, don't rescue him, give him room to sink or swim—any one of those pearls of wisdom that my mother has preached over the years in an effort to encourage independence.

Has she been keeping me at home all this time or have I been holding myself back? And just because I leave home doesn't mean I'll lose my family, does it? *Dad came back, didn't he?*

"In fact, I talked her into coming to my family's day after Thanksgiving dinner up in Portsmouth, New Hampshire

"Is that true, Sara?" Bobby asks.

"Yes." I'm done lying and pretending to myself and my family. Everyone here cares about me.

Quinn wraps an arm around my shoulders, reclaiming me from Billie Mae's grasp. I stand straight and then lean my head on his shoulder because I want to and it feels right.

"I would love it if you would all join us," he says, a genuine note of excitement in his voice.

At first, I'm thinking he's being polite, but then my head slaps me into reality. He means this.

"Seriously?" Billie Mae asks with serious skepticism.

"He's just being polite," Mom says.

"No, I mean it. My mom would love to meet you. She's been dying to see Sara again. I really mean it." He holds up his right hand as if he's taking an oath.

"We can't go off and leave my husband and Paul and Yolanda and Grandma Zanetti behind," Mom says.

I shake my head. "Mom—"

"Bring them all. Your whole family is invited," Quinn says and I feel compelled to shake him, but I'm in no position to shake anyone.

I snort. "That's crazy talk," I manage to say.

Mom waves me off like I'm the crazy one. "Call your mom right now to ask if it's okay and you're on."

Quinn gives Mom a respectful nod and pulls out his phone. Right there, in front of us all, he tells her he's bringing seven more guests to dinner.

I can hear his mother's excitement on the other end of the line as she says, "Fabulous" and asks who.

"We'll surprise you. I gotta go if we're going to get there for one-thirty." He ends the call and Mom gives him a return nod of respect.

"You're a ballsy one," Bobby says.

Quinn throws his signature dimpled grin and I don't know if I want to jump him or slap the smugness off his face. Wow. That's some progress. A couple of days ago, I'd never have dreamed of such a thing. Now… I want him— all of him—for all the right reasons, but with my eyes open and my soul ready to handle him.

The question still lingers about what he wants from me.

AFTER WE MAKE a pit stop at my house so I can change and update the rest of the family on our new dinner plans, Bobby drives Billie Mae, Mom, Dad, Aunt Yolanda, and Grandma Zanetti to Portsmouth while I ride with Quinn.

We make it to the highway before I burst out with the question that can't be contained.

"What the heck are you doing with me, Quinn? What do you want?"

CHAPTER 32

QUINN

"*E*verything. I want everything." I chuckle and shake my head because I have to say this right no matter how difficult or impossible it is. "A lot of things," I say. "But what you need to know is that I want a relationship, *not* a fling, *not* a friendship, and *not* an acquaintance." That much I'm sure of. What a *relationship* with a woman feels like, I'm not so sure of. I've never had one. But I've seen it with my parents and my brother and his wife. I know what it's supposed to look like.

She nods and I wait for her response as I pull onto I95 north. It's an hour drive and after a minute or two I'm worried I'll have to wait the whole hour before she talks again.

"What do *you* want?" I ask.

"Same. But more."

"More?" I keep the car in the lane.

"Don't worry. You asked what I want, not what I expect."

"You should expect everything you want, Sara." I put a hand over hers and she turns it over and holds on.

Driving to my childhood home is instinctive, , my driving muscles take me where I need to go without my mind's involvement. That's how we found ourselves on this back road, a short-cut home from the highway. A road that goes directly by the cemetery.

Shit. Why did I take this route? *Fuck.* My eyes flicker to the side of the road, grazing past the wrought iron fence and the headstones beyond, nestled among trees and grassy knolls. The car slows down like someone else is at the controls. Probably my buried baggage spontaneously unburying itself and taking over.

Re-gripping the steering wheel, I hold on tight to make sure I don't turn into the cemetery's driveway, and I press down on the gas.

Except my foot hits the brake. The car comes to a stop at the side of the road near the gate.

"Your father is buried here," Sara says, putting a hand on my knee and staring at the side of my head because I keep it facing straight ahead. "What are you thinking? You want to visit him?" she says quietly, like she doesn't want to spook me.

"I wasn't thinking," I say, honestly, every bone and muscle in my body stiff so that I don't think I can't move.

"Let's go inside," she says, her words soft and musical like a little bird.

"I haven't been since…" I don't bother finishing my sentence, but I turn and I look at her. I *need* to.

"Since you buried him."

I nod. When we buried him in the ground, I buried everything about him deep down under my bones because it felt like the pain of facing the loss, of not having a chance to tell him—to *show* him—I cared, and to have him tell me he still cared… it was more than I could handle. It was that one last devastating blow that knocked me out.

I turn the car off, but stay planted in my seat, turning my body to face her. That much I can do.

She faces me, taking her hand off the door handle, getting the cue that we're not getting out of the car. At least, not right now.

Maybe not ever.

"Around the time he got sick, it seemed everything was falling apart. In the playoffs that year, I'd lost a step. I wasn't as fast as the young star on our opponent's team and we got knocked out first round of the playoffs."

"I remember that game," she says.

Of course she does.

"The kid deked you out and scored." She takes a deep breath. "I can see why that would feel like a failure to you, but it wasn't your fault. You shouldn't have been the one back on defense. If it wasn't for you, it would have been a breakaway. And then you dove to try and stop him. You did everything. The defenseman who was supposed to be there wasn't and the goalie who should have stopped him didn't. It was a team loss, not your fault."

I listen. She's not wrong. I've heard it all before. "The thing is, a few years ago, I could have made the play. My team always counted on me to be able to do it."

"And that's on them. It goes two ways. They let you down when you needed to count on them." She takes my hands. "Look, it's a team sport. Everyone has to man up. There's a reason you never made it to The Stanley Cup finals. It wasn't you. It was your team."

I shake my head because I've heard all this before, but I can't accept it because it feels too much like blaming others and not taking responsibility for myself.

"Leaving the Shooting Stars wasn't an easy thing to do," I say. "I felt like I was letting them down, letting the fans down. Management was going to bring in some new players and really try for a Cup run. If my dad hadn't been sick, I don't know if I would have left."

"I thought you left because of the Princess Anica scandal."

"I did in the end. But I'd already thought about it. I'd already felt the pull to be home again, to be there for my mother, especially. When Anica pulled her stunt, that was the straw that did me in. Jett was the only one I told about it and he helped me keep the lid on the scandal. I don't know what kind of threat he made, but it worked.

"The problem was that there'd be a good chance something like that would happen again if I kept going the way I did. Jett told me he thought I was damn lucky Anica was the first one to *misbehave*, as he called it, given the string of starlets and models and other bootstrappers—his term, not mine—that I'd tangled the sheets with."

Her face flickers at that, like a fire almost getting blown out and my chest tightens so hard I'm worried about breathing.

I force a deep breath in and out. "Sorry. It's the way it was." I give her a sad wry smile. "No sense sugarcoating it since you already knew."

"*Everyone* knew." She smiles and touches my face like she adores me anyway.

I take her hand and pull it away because I don't deserve it. "Don't be so quick to forgive me for being an immature asshole."

She laughs. "You were a guy taking life by the horns, having fun, working hard, and enjoying the fruits of your labor."

I snort. "Nice spin. I was a shallow shit who all but ignored his family for ten years."

"Stop beating up on yourself. You were an independent adult who had some living to do. Your family was always going to be there."

"Now, it's my turn to be there for my family," I say and shove my door open. Even if it is too late for Dad, it's time to deal with my issues and ask for forgiveness.

"I'm coming with you," she says and scrambles out of the passenger side, catching up to me.

I walk fast as if I can somehow make up for lost time.

She takes my arm and the instant warmth gives me strength to face my demons as we wind through the rows of graves.

We reach a tall, newly- chiseled headstone and I stop.

Standing on top of the dirt that covers my father, I squat down to read the gravestone.

Joseph James
March 5, 1951 – May 15, 2022
Loving father and husband

Fucking simple words. His name. His birthdate. The date of his death.

My hands fist and anger seethes through me, helping to ward off the excruciating sadness.

Her hand is on my shoulder, then she squats down next to me. "I can feel your tension, your anger and sadness. It's so mixed and volatile."

I snort. "Yeah. I know." My voice breaks. "Fuck, this is hard." I have no idea what to do or say, but I have so much pent-up energy coursing through me I feel like I'll snap if I don't let everything that's bottled in me get out.

"I feel like I'm going to crack in two and I don't…" I can't talk or I'll choke. Emotions well up like lava in my throat, burning and stopping everything in their path.

She holds onto me, not saying anything, her arms vibrating with her passionate emotions, letting them rule her.

"Goddam it, Dad." I spit the words from my soul. "I wanted to be there. I wanted to say goodbye, to tell you how I felt—how I feel…" I can't say the words. I'm shaking.

"Go on," she whispers. "I bet he's listening."

"I wanted to tell you I love you, that I always wanted to make you proud. I'm not sure I ever did. Not really. Not the way it counts—with the family."

She wraps her arms around me tighter, but doesn't say anything and I'm glad. I don't need her to tell me he was proud. Those words have been said by Mom, by Lenny, by Mr. Derico…

by everyone. Except Dad. I needed to hear them from him. He loved me. I know that.

But was he proud? Did I do what I needed to do to make him truly proud?

"It's never too late," she says, answering the question in my head. I stand and lift her with me, staring another minute at the grave. Dad's name blurs.

Tears stream without me realizing it, not until she wipes my cheeks with her gloved hand and kisses my eyes.

I take in a ragged breath and the afternoon rays of the sun strike me through the bare tree branches. "Shit. We're going to be late to dinner." The weight and the pain fade into the background, descending into that place buried beneath the moments of everyday life—where I've always pushed them.

We walk back to the car and we get inside. When I go to start it, she stops me.

"Take a minute. I'll text your mom to let her know we'll be late."

"If I don't keep moving, it may take more than a minute," I say. Trying to bury the unanswered questions back where they belong, relegated to the unsolved problems box, the one that maybe should never be opened if I don't have the solution.

"I'm glad he wasn't cremated," I say out of nowhere. "Mom's friends pressured her to cremate him, but she couldn't do it. She said she wanted to be able to visit him. An urn wouldn't be the same. And her family and Dad's are all buried here. She wanted Dad here with them."

"It's so peaceful and beautiful here."

"You should see it in May," I say as if we're having a casual Sunday-after-church discussion, as if she's part of my past, part of my hometown life, the life I left more than ten years ago for the big time. "You fit in here," I say and she furrows her brows. I laugh. "Not the cemetery. I mean here, in Portsmouth, my home town. I haven't fit in for a long time. Since I left for college."

"For the big time," she says and I snap my head around to look at her like she's somehow found a way to read my soul.

"That's what everyone called it—what Dad called it—the big time. Except…" I stop, remembering that day in the bakery when he'd been telling the guys in the back that his son had hit the big time. I'd gone in because Mom had told me the guys wanted autographs. She'd had to push me out the door because it felt odd that my dad's friends would want *my* autograph. I was just Joe's son. I'd also thought Dad would think I was being too cocky—he'd often thought that.

"The day after I got drafted, I went to my dad's bakery," I say. "I didn't want to, didn't think he'd want me there signing autographs for the guys. But when I got there, he was telling them I'd made the big time and… he'd said it with pride and a great big grin on his face." I turn to her. "I was surprised. They all wanted me to sign their L.A. Stars shirts and he laughed, but tolerated it. I remember being uneasy, wondering when he was going to shoo me out because he had *real* work to do, but he didn't that day." Well, damn. I'd forgotten about that day. That *one* day. One hell of a day.

I cup her chin and raise her face to see into her eyes. "How did you know?"

She looks confused. "Know what?"

"About *the big time*? About my dad?" I laugh because I know I sound ridiculous. "Never mind." I pull her in for a kiss, the kind that comes from down deep, that needs to connect past the physical.

As I taste her sweetness and soak in her warmth and generosity, my irrepressible dick—where she's concerned—threatens to take over my intentions.

"I knew your dad was proud of you," she says.

Her words slam me with truth and, for the first time since he died, the mention of my dad doesn't slice me in half with guilt and pain.

I feel a wave of deep sadness, of loss, and it's not pretty, but it's what I need,.

"Dad would have liked you," I say, taking her face in my hands and kissing those lips as she turns that delicious pink that never fails to rile my dick.

Letting her go, I shake my head and start the car before I make us later than we are. "I don't know, my little puck bunny. What *am* I going to do with you?"

"I've been wondering that myself." She pauses and then, as if deciding to go for it, she turns to face me. "You say I fit in here, but the problem is you don't exactly fit in here, at least not comfortably." She stares up at me, her words turning into whispers. "That's the problem, isn't it?"

"It's a temporary problem, sweetheart. This is where my roots are, where I'm from. I'll fit in because I belong here and because I want to be here. I want the peace." I'm sure about that much. I feel like I've been through hell right now, but I feel whole enough to move ahead even if I'm limping.

"Temporary?" she says. "What do we do in the meantime while you're shoe-horning yourself back into the genie's bottle?"

I snort. "It's not like that. I'll fit in. I'm already feeling the pull of my roots."

"It's exactly like that. You think that, after you make it to the big time, you can come back and feel the same as before you left?"

"Probably not, but better than I have in a long while." I stop at a stop sign with no traffic. A simple thing to do, basic and calming. The absence of other cars, the quiet, jiggles loose any remaining tightness in my chest. "I was lost, Sara. I needed to come home."

"How long before you leave again when the big time comes calling?"

"Never. The big time will have to come to me from now on."

She laughs and says, "You're right. You've made it so big, you can live life on your own terms now."

"I always could." I pull her in and whisper in her ear, "So could you."

She shivers and goosebumps rise on the delicate skin in the hollow beneath her ear.

We drive by a strip mall on the right and I swerve to pull in the parking lot.

"What are you doing?" she asks.

"Living life on my own terms," I tell her. There's a jewelry store in this mall and I'm going in.

e're parked in the fire lane in front of a jewelry store. I get out of the car and follow him in, reluctant to leave him alone. "Did you forget to buy your mom a gift?"

"No." He reaches for the door and pulls me in with him. "Not for my mother."

He stares at me. That jelly feeling takes over my belly as he kisses me. The kiss sparks through me like an electric shock, doing nothing to calm the jelly.

"How much do you like your job?"

He pulls me inside the store and my mind scrambles to figure out where he's going with this question and how I should answer him. But then I realize I don't need to figure out *how* to answer him; I need to give him my honest answer, regardless of how I think he'll react.

I stop in the middle of the busy store, noticing the plush carpeting while he shows me that dimple. I exhale, then set the truth free. "I love everything about it. Even the boring stuff. Even Margaret and her knit Brawlers hats."

"Margaret?"

"She works with me and is always wearing—it doesn't matter. Why are you asking about my job?"

"I had a suspicion you like it more than you've let on. That your complaints are more, let's say, a defense mechanism."

"Maybe you're right, but why are you asking?"

"Because… I want to see you. I want to go for a relationship between us, but without causing you any problems. Without causing problems for either of us," he says as if it explains everything.

"And?" I wave my hand, waiting for more because I can't for the life of me puzzle out what my job and our relationship have to do with a jewelry store.

"I have an idea."

Everyone in the place is openly gawking at him, but he doesn't seem to notice as he steers me to a salesclerk.

I, however, *do* notice that we're a sideshow right now.

"You're Quinn James," the manager says. "How can I help you?"

"Thank you… Mr. Rosen, is it?"

The man nods.

"Well, I'm in a hurry, but I'd like to buy a diamond ring. To take with us."

I register Mr. Rosen's delight and the buzz in the room and Quinn asking me if I have a preference, but, somehow, I feel like I'm still missing a big piece of this puzzle. I want to ask him why he's buying me a diamond ring, but, at the same time, I sense it would be the wrong thing to say. Not that I can figure for the life of me what the right thing is.

Mr. Rosen sets a velvet-lined box with five giant diamonds in front of me after exchanging a few quiet words with Quinn that I don't hear.

I look around and there are a couple of older women smiling at me. They wave. I'm about to wave back when Quinn gets my attention.

"Do you have a preference, sweetheart?"

"Preference?" I look up at him.

He leans in and whispers, "It's okay. I know it's a surprise, but trust me, okay?"

Is it okay? My belly flips when I allow myself to think about what's really happening once I take the willful blinders off—the ones protecting me from expecting too much.

When I look down at the tray of diamonds, my heart leaps to my throat because they are *real*. Quinn James is really—for-honest-to-goodness-real—buying me a freaking diamond ring.

His eyes are on me, then nuzzles my temple. "Do you need help choosing?" he asks.

I laugh because it's the most absurd question that anyone in the history of the world has ever asked me. "Heck, no. I want this one." I lift the brilliant square-cut rock from the middle of the tray, forcing myself not to ask the price. I want to know because he shouldn't spend an obscene amount, but I can't allow myself to be that awkward girl. I need to do better.

"Excellent choice," Mr. Rosen says politely.

"Put it on your finger, Sara."

Quinn says the words and they mean so much more than he's saying. There's so much missing from this moment.

My heart drums fast and I look at the diamond ring in my hand, so sparkly and real, wondering how there could be anything wrong.

I slip the ring on my finger. It slides to the side, a little loose .

"It's a half-size too large," Mr. Rosen says. "Maybe less. I can fix that."

"We'll bring it back to have it fixed. I'll arrange it with you later," Quinn says. He hands his platinum credit card to the jeweler who nods and grins broadly, then disappears into the back room.

Quinn takes me by the shoulders as I stare down at the ring, mesmerized. "Sara."

I look up at him, ignoring the open stares and whispers getting louder all around. I see someone slipping a phone into their bag and my stomach clenches. Crap.

"What are we doing, Quinn?" I whisper, trying to keep the panic from my voice. Because I suddenly realize what's wrong with this picture. He's buying me an engagement ring, but he's never asked me to marry him, not even asked… anything. Never said he loves me, never… anything.

Mr. Rosen comes back with the receipt and a velvet bag.

With a hand on the small of my back, Quinn escorts me out of the store, oblivious of all the people watching us, smiling, and, yes, taking pics with their phones. Crap.

In the car, I let out a long breath. "Tell me you didn't just buy me a diamond ring."

"But I did."

"Why? Why did you do that? Are you trying to fulfill my every fantasy? Because I don't feel like I'm in the real world right now. I feel like I'm in some light-and-fluffy rom-com and the cameras are going to stop rolling any minute."

"Maybe I do want to make your fantasies come true," he says, pulling me across the console. "Do any of them involve you getting naked?" His grin goes deep and his playfulness is infectious. But we're still in the parking lot so, when someone beeps as they drive by, he starts the car then waves.

"Luckily, this is my hometown crowd," he says, "so they'll leave us alone."

"Seriously, what's this all about, Quinn?"

"It's about us being engaged."

"For real?"

"Look, I know it was unconventional for me to spring it on you."

"Almost like you took it for granted that I'd go along."

"I'm sorry. I don't want to take you for granted, but I thought you feel the same way I do, that you want a relationship."

"Yes, I do. But jumping from a relationship to being engaged —I don't know if we're ready for that."

"Someone once told me you need to play the part to feel the part."

"Was that someone a Hollywood starlet, by any chance?"

He laughs. "Maybe. But it's true. Act the part until it's not a part means the same thing is fake it until you make it. And as the saying goes, sweetheart, I want to make it with you."

He brushes some hair off my cheek and it's all I can do not to lean into that caress. Because I can't. Not until I know exactly what he wants and, more importantly, *why* he wants it.

"But I mean this, Sara. I *do* want to make it with you—a relationship, a life, a family... a home."

His voice is low and raspy and reminds me of *that night*. The one we spent together. The frisson of danger and excitement he generates runs through my entire body leaving me on some kind of edge, uncomfortable and exhilarating like the top of a mountain. And I only need to choose which way to go.

"You know I care about you," he says.

I hear the vibration of emotion in his voice and my heart leaps into my throat and my insides dissolve into jelly and then hot molten lava.

"I care about you, too." I mean the words and I think he means them, too. But I have no clue what all that meaning-the-words adds up to. Does it add up to the kind of romantic love you need to get engaged and then married? I've always pictured things differently, that a guy would get down on one knee and swear his undying devotion and love.

But then there are couples like Mindy and Jonas. They care about each other and I was perfectly happy to see them get married without a smidgeon of down-on-one-knee romance. Who am I to think I'm better than that?

I smile and sigh. "So we're engaged now."

"We'll keep it quiet for a while," he says.

I nod. That'll give me a chance to fake it 'til I make it, too.

🍂

We arrive at Quinn's mom's house on the heels of my family to find Mrs. James already welcoming the whole clan, taking their coats and getting them drinks.

Quinn stows our coats, then introduces me to his extended family as we make our way through the dining room to the great room. The space is massive and I can see why they need it—there are no less than two dozen people there and all seem excited to meet my family.

Until we walk in.

"Everyone, this is Sara Bellagamba. My fiancée."

That, I didn't expect. He knew it, because he's ready and waiting to hold me up in a standing position before I collapse to the floor while my family and the entire James clan watches our performance.

Are we acting the role, or are we pretending, kidding ourselves into something neither of us is ready for, but too foolish and in lust to admit?

Either way, the stakes are high.

If we're engaged, the Brawlers will accept our relationship as serious and the media and fans will embrace the romantic story. The fact that we were breaking all the non-frat rules to get to this point will get glossed over.

Plus, this is the ultimate social media gossip to put Princess Anica in her place and keep her out of Quinn's business. Maybe, now, she'll look for someone else to haunt.

Until we're not engaged.

On the other hand, if we *don't* get engaged—pretend or otherwise—the organization's lawyers will come down on us with who-knows-what kind of threat. Delaney may be okay with a Thanksgiving dinner between friends, but the Brawlers organization has traded players for less. I made it my business to know this when Quinn got traded here.

Which will then give the mighty Princess Anica a clear shot at harassing Quinn with nasty rumors, causing who-knows-what kind of problems to her heart's content.

I had been planning to post a photo of me and Quinn on social media, not as Lola, but me as me, wearing his diamond, and *that* would be next-level-times-ten more effective than her silly rumors.

Family collapses around me, holding me up in their huddle and I get through dinner, but only because Quinn stays with me. Literally. Some part of him touches a part of me at all times. You'd think I was devastated by some horrible event, but maybe being traumatized by the surprise of your wildest fantasy coming true is just as bad.

I talk Billie Mae, then Mom, then Quinn into letting me stay at Billie Mae's place tonight. Bobby's going back to Rochester and Quinn has to get up early for a morning skate, so Mom is the toughest sell, but she lets me go.

Quinn drives me into Boston to drop me at Billie Mae's. I can't talk him out of it.

He stops the car at the curb in a no-parking zone, then turns off the engine.

"Living dangerously," I say.

"Why stop now.? He blows out a breath. "You've been quiet. It's been an eventful day."

"For both of us," I say. "The stop at the jewelry store was—"

"Unexpected," he says. "The stop at the cemetery was—"

"Unexpected," I say and smile.

He squeezes my hand. "I needed to do it. To face the loss and start unpacking the baggage." His voice is heartbreakingly raspy. "I couldn't have done it without you."

He caresses my face and he lowers his mouth for a kiss.

I get that giddy feeling in my belly again and run my hand

through his hair like I own it, sinking into his kiss and taking all he has because, if this is a fairytale, I'm going to live it to its fullest. All the way to the ending, whatever that may be.

His breathing is heavy when he lets me go. "Good night, sweetheart."

I jump from the car, feeling too much like Cinderella and wondering when the clock is going to strike midnight.

BILLIE MAE and I change into pajamas. I borrow some from her, covered in pink poodles.

She hands me a margarita, then joins me on the couch. "Give it to me. What the hell is up with this sudden engagement?" She studies me.

"I wish I knew."

"That's not an answer."

"I'm worried." The words fall from my mouth and I take a long gulp of my drink.

She follows suit.

I don't wait for her to prompt me because, suddenly, all the worries come tumbling out, all those things that make the engagement feel not right, that have been piling up behind my wall of hope.

"I'm worried he's doing this for his mother and to give us cover at work and not really because he wants to marry me. I'm worried he's forcing our relationship past where it's meant to be to make his life seem better before it really is."

"I get that his mother is pressuring him, but what are you talking about regarding work?"

"He thinks if we're engaged, we won't have to worry so much about the non-frat policy. But mostly, I think the engagement is to please his family. His mother and brother have wanted him to stop being a playboy and settle down, so the engagement will appease them."

"Plus, it gets Princess Anica off his back," Billie Mae throws in. "The jerk is using you."

I laugh.

"It's not funny, Sara."

"He's not using me. I went along with the whole thing and… he cares about me."

She gives me a skeptical frown. "I suppose he wouldn't have bought you such a ridiculous rock if he didn't care somewhat."

"Still," I say, "even if it's true that he wanted to get engaged for all the wrong reasons, I still feel that connection between us, still trust him enough to share things." And he trusts me enough to take me to his father's grave. But I keep that to myself. It's too private, too intimate to tell anyone else.

"What does that mean?" she asks. "Is he *the one*? I mean, the *real* one, not just some hot hockey crush."

"How did you know Bobby was the one?" I ask.

"Easy. My heart nearly explodes in my chest every time I see him. And not just because he's a hunk—sorry, I know he's your brother, but that's the reality. He's so much more. He's decent and strong and has that alpha streak I can't resist."

I wave a hand. "Half the guys on the Brawlers would meet that description. What makes Bobby *the* one?"

"He gets me, honey. He's there for me, knows what I'm thinking, and I know what he's thinking, how he feels. And he's *wicked* nice to me."

"I'm sorry, did you just use the word *wicked* in a sentence?" I laugh and so does she. She always swore she'd never say *wicked* no matter how long she lived in Boston.

"It's Bobby's influence." She sighs the way a girl in love does— long and happy.

"I think I know how you feel," I confess. I understand about the connection, and the understanding. "Quinn is thoughtful and kind, truly kind. Look at what he did for Jonas."

"That was a spectacular success story. You both rock for accomplishing that bit of matchmaking. When you told me the story, I kept thinking it would be unbelievable if I hadn't seen those puck bunnies dressed in pink Brawlers jerseys myself."

We laugh and I tuck my feet up under me as I sink into her couch. "And this couch," I say.

"What do you mean?" she says.

"That night I came here with Quinn."

She squeals and slaps her hands over her eyes. "Please don't make me remember that night I found you two here *naked*."

I laugh. "But he did cover me with the blanket."

"He did. I noticed that." She rolls her eyes. "Maybe he is a decent guy."

We fall quiet for a moment and I drain my drink. My head swirls. But it's not the tequila. My vision clears and I swear if Billie Mae's tiny apartment had a view of the Atlantic, I'd be looking at London Bridge right now.

"So, what are you going to do?"

"I'm going to quit my job and break up with Quinn. Then I'm going to take control of my life, find a new job and be independent. I'm going to move out on my own and I'm not going to be afraid of losing the closeness with my family."

"Bravo. You go, girl." she claps and fist-bumps me.

"I'm especially not going to be anyone's Cinderella. She's my least favorite Disney character."

"Ooo-kaay."

We laugh.

"But I have one tiny little problem with your plan." Billie Mae tips her drink my way.

I cock my head; I know what she's going to say. "Go on and say it."

"What if Quinn *is* the one and you're throwing him away?"

"I'm not throwing him away forever. I'll get him back."

"Then why bother throwing him away at all?"

"I need to know he's the right one and I won't know until I can stand on my own and act like a grown-up." I pause and my belly flips around so much I'm afraid I'm going to lose my cookies, but I take a deep breath and go for it, say the scary thing. "And I want to know that I'm the right one for him. I want him to want me enough to wait for me, to come for me when I'm ready."

"Wow. A real, honest-to-goodness epiphany." She hugs me. "You're taking a big chance. You're a braver woman than I am. But then, you were always the courageous one."

"I was?"

She nods. "I know you'll stand up and be everything and have everything you want. You're too good not to."

Her words calm the tremor in my heart because I'm oddly certain and determined about what I need to do, yet, it's still scary as heck and hard as crap.

MONDAY MORNING when I get to work, I leave my coat on, tap out my letter of resignation, then print it. Emptying my desk and drawer of all my personal crap, I stuff it in a bag and stop at Billie Mae's cubicle.

She stands. "Are you sure I can't talk you out of this?" She hugs me, not waiting for the answer because she already knows it.

Margaret gives me a questioning look as I walk past her. She's wearing the pink version of the Brawlers knit cap today.

"Cute hat," I say and I mean it. "Good-bye Margaret. I won't be coming back."

"Why not?"

"I'm quitting."

Her eyes go wide—and then she surprises the crap out of me by giving me a big hug.

I hug her back and try to keep my eyes from leaking.

"You'll do well out there," she says, jutting her chin toward the window as if the outside world is outer space.

My belly rolls, agreeing with her assessment—about the outer space.

Billie Mae comes over and throws an arm around Margaret. "It's just you and me now, Margaret."

But Billie Mae winks at me and I escape from the cubicles to head down the hall straight to the office of the Brawlers Corporation V.P. of Public Relations.

Delaney's office.

CHAPTER 34

QUINN

I meet Sara at my front door as her Uber ride drives away before she has a chance to knock. "Delaney told me you quit today."

"Well, that takes the wind out of my sails. Or the sting out of my bee or ..." She looks down and flaps a hand. "I'm sorry, I shouldn't be so flip about something so big and important."

My "*But*" sinks because I know she wouldn't be this upset if this was her only news. Plus, she's been semi-ghosting me since dinner at my mom's with uncharacteristic minimalist responses to my texts and unanswered calls.

"I have a feeling your resignation isn't the only thing you have to tell me about today."

She looks up and flashes those crazy green eyes showing all her emotions like a telescope to her heart and soul.

Gripping the door frame, I stand through a wave of gut-clenching pain, so different from the guilty stab through my shoulder blades and no less intense.

"Come inside." My voice sounds like it belongs to a man who needed to quit his four-pack-a-day habit years ago.

She steps past me, careful not to touch, but it doesn't matter because I feel her warmth, the cord of energy connecting us.

It takes all my strength to keep from gravitating to her, from embracing her and swallowing her whole like she's the magic pill I need to make me alive, like an addict who needs a hit.

Fuck.

"You got some furniture," she says, but she doesn't go past the entryway before she stops and faces me.

I keep a distance, struggling between self-preservation and going to her, but then I throw all caution aside. "Look, I know we were supposed to have dinner, but I have something to tell you. It's important."

I clear my throat so I can sound human. "You know you can tell me anything." *Except the one thing I have a bad feeling you're going to say*. My heart thuds loud in my ears like it's trying to shield me from hearing something terrible as I wait for her to do just that.

She stands there looking at me, looking small and vulnerable, but straight and strong at the same time. Her eyes are bright and her chin quivers and I'm about to break in two and sweep her into my arms.

But she stops me by yanking the ring from her finger, then holding it out to me.

"Jesus, Sara." I croak the words.

"I don't want a fake-it-til-we-make-it engagement, Quinn. Truthfully, I'm not ready for *any* engagement. I want to start a new job, move into my own place, and stand on my own. Be a real adult. My own person. I need to be an independent adult before I'm ready for any kind of relationship."

Her words pelt me like fireballs, their truths branding me with each strike. I can't argue with her. I understand her completely. But my heart pleads with the reality gods for mercy, for hope, because it won't let go.

"This must be what it feels like to be in love." The words

seep from my bleeding soul, my voice sounding normal through the pain and gratitude and muck of my leftover baggage.

She laughs a watery laugh and sniffs. "I think so. I'm feeling it, too," she says.

I bite down on my tongue to keep myself from shouting, "Then why?" because I know why.

A person can't make it no matter how much they fake it until they have the muscle power to see it through.

"No pain, no gain," I say.

She nods because she gets it.

"So, dinner is out?" I say to break the tension, to loosen the grip of pain in my gut before my spine snaps and I can't stand, can't hold my course steady and give her what she needs—her freedom and my support.

She smiles, tears streaming now. "No dinner. No... anything."

I see stars like I've blacked out from a shot through the heart. Like I've exploded from the inside out. "Sara—"

"I know. But I can't... I'm not strong enough to do this any other way. Not now."

I grasp onto the thinnest thread of hope she offers. *Not now.* "Maybe... someday?"

She nods. She's still holding her diamond ring in the palm of her hand, open and vulnerable.

It's like she's handing me back my heart.

I take the ring from her palm and squeeze like I'm trying to hold myself together.

"I'll see you sometime," she says as she passes by me to the door.

"Sometime soon," I say.

She turns in the doorway. "Hopefully."

She shuts the door behind her, shutting me out from her foreseeable future so she can create a new life for herself.

I hope to God there's a place for me in her new life. Because I sure as hell am going to be around to find out whether she believes it or not.

❀

I MISSED a week after Thanksgiving because I turned into an automaton to get through the three games we had right after Sara handed me my heart back in a bloody mess—well, that's not fair to put on her because I deserved it for putting us out there in such a ridiculously clumsy way.

My cell rings on my dashboard.

"Hey, Mom. I'm on my way. I should be there in twenty minutes." I haven't told her or anyone else about the un-engagement. No one would even know Sara and I were ever engaged if it weren't for social media. A clip of us at the jewelry store went viral and the guys were low-key on their congrats since I hadn't said anything.

Or maybe they don't believe the fake bull shit.

One good thing that's happened is that Anica has stopped sending me texts, and, more importantly, has stopped mentioning me in social media. Coincidentally, the nasty rumor posts about me have stopped also. As silver linings go, it's a shallow one.

I'd promised myself that, today, I'll let my family know what's going on with me and Sara—or, rather, what's *not* going on.

I haven't told anyone about the breakup yet. I'm toying with the idea of returning the diamond to the jewelry store and letting social media finish the story they'd started. That's about as real as the engagement was, so it would be fitting.

When I pull in the drive, a calm settles in and it actually feels good to be home. The tension and guilt about my dad not being here has dissipated, morphing into a sad melancholy, with a stab sharper than I like, but, that, I can handle.

I get out of the car, expecting to limp to my the door like I've been wounded by Cupid in the romance wars, but my body seems to be better able to recover than my heart.

Mom opens the front door and greets me with a big smile and a hug that never gets old no matter how old I get.

My mother's dinner table doesn't need the extension to seat Chris and his family and me.

The food is delicious and my nephews keep a genuine smile on my face, not like the half-ass one I've been sporting all week.

"I'm so excited that the whole family will be over again for Christmas," Mom says. "Do you think there's any chance that Sara's family will—"

"No chance," I say, and take a deep breath. "We broke it off." I close my eyes a second and go for the real truth. "She broke off our so-called engagement."

"I'm so sorry." Mom covers my hand with hers.

"Sorry to hear it, bro. That's tough."

"Too bad," Tyler, my older, more sophisticated, nephew says. "I liked her. What'd you do to mess it up?"

His mom immediately shushes him by stuffing a roll in his mouth and Chris glares at him.

"It's okay," I say with a half-grin because I can see where the kid is coming from. "I did mess up. I rushed things before we were ready. Now... I don't know."

"Do you think there's a chance for you two in the future?" Mom asks.

I shrug and Tyler and Timmy start a fight over the last roll, changing the conversation. I owe those kids more than they know.

Even though I didn't want to have the conversation at dinner about a possible future universe where Sara and I might have a chance, I do need to talk about it with someone I trust or I'll explode. Preferably someone with female insight. Which leaves Billie Mae or my mother.

Carrying a pile of dirty plates, I head into the kitchen where my mother is loading the dishwasher. My sister-in-law is helping her and I tell her I'll take over. She's not an idiot, so she nods, gives me an encouraging smile, then leaves.

"You look so sad, Quinn." Mom stops loading dishes and invites me to unload my heart with her sympathetic smile. She's the only one on the planet who can get away with giving me that look.

I grunt. I have no idea where to start or what to say.

"Guess you jumped the gun on the engagement ring," she says.

I grunt again.

She nods. "You really care about her?"

"I love her." The words fly from my gut and my heart and my head without effort.

"I could see that." She pauses. "If Dad was here, he'd tell you to go for it."

My eyes sharpen, my senses and every muscle in my body go into alert like this means something special. Because it does. And I think she and Dad are right.

"Problem is, she wants me to leave her alone. To give her a chance to become an independent adult."

Mom nods. "She is a young one."

"So, what do I do?"

"You've done things backwards, Quinn. You need to do all the things to make her understand how you feel deep down, all the things that add up to making her know on a visceral level that you love her. And, when she's ready, she'll take you back."

"I've done things to let her know," I say, knowing she's right.

"I'm sure you've done plenty, Quinn. But Sara is the one who gets to decide how much convincing she needs. And you have to accept things at her pace."

"I get it. I can be patient. I know how to stay with something for the long haul before the payoff."

Mom rolls her eyes. "Please don't compare romancing a

woman to preparing for a career in hockey. Not in Sara's hearing."

I laugh. "Believe me, romancing Sara will be like heaven. There will be no resemblance to the hell of two-a-days."

She laughs.

"But seriously, when the time is right, I want to do something really special. Something completely unforgettable."

"Of course you do. You always were a showman." She softens her look and takes hold of my arms. "There's nothing wrong with a grand gesture and nothing like it to convince a girl you're serious." She winks. "As long as you've done all the right things, all the little things, the groundwork that makes it real, you'll have your moment with the girl you love."

I HEAR THROUGH JONAS, of all people, that Sara got a new job and found an apartment. We're at practice on Monday after my talk with my mother and I stifle the urge to hug Jonas's smelly ass.

"How do you know this?"

"She talks to Mindy all the time, man. She was serious about the babysitting gig and being into kids."

I nod, my chest tightening with empty longing. Maybe it's not too soon to make a move.

THAT NIGHT I send her a text.

I heard you're moving to an apartment soon. I have a badass SUV and a few muscles to help you with the move when you're ready. Say the word.

THANKS FOR THE OFFER, but we have the family van, and Bobby and Paul are helping with the muscle. Good luck for tomorrow's game.

. . .

FUCK. We're playing our arch-rivals, Montreal, tomorrow and if the leaden feeling of disappointment doesn't improve by then, I'll need all the luck I can get.

AFTER THE GAME—WHERE I score *no* goals, but the team wins so I'm happy anyway—I come out of the locker room to see Billie Mae. My eyes immediately search the surrounding area for Sara since they go to games together all the time.

But there's no sign of Sara and my gaze collides with Delaney's instead. She's standing with Billie Mae. Delaney zeroes in on me and drags Billie Mae over.

Fuck.

"And here's the heart-breaker," Delaney says. "Billie Mae tells me you broke off the engagement."

Billie Mae looks at the black rubber-matted floor like it's turned into a magic carpet, refusing to meet my eyes, but I don't correct Delaney's story about who broke off the engagement.

"Guilty," I say with no need to elaborate.

She grunts. "About what I expected from Hollywood Hockey." But it doesn't hurt when she says it.

Billie Mae's head snaps up. "Don't call him that."

"If the skate fits," Delaney says, challenging me with her stare and an evil grin.

Is she bating me?

"It doesn't fit." Billie Mae comes to my defense which is odd after blaming the breakup on me. "He's not Hollywood. He's a decent guy."

"Good girl. Make sure all the fans see it that way before it hits social media." Before she blinks again, Delaney takes off in search of another victim with balls to bust.

"I'm sorry," Billie Mae says. "My first allegiance is to Sara."

"Of course," I say. "How is she?"

She grins. "I knew it was only a matter of seconds before you'd ask. She's great. Her new job is mega and she's killing it in the salary department."

"I'm glad. I hear she's got a new apartment."

She rolls her eyes. "I know. She told me you texted. Let me guess who has a big mouth—Jonas?"

I nod and grin. "Don't hold it against him. He has a big heart, too, underneath it all."

"If you say so." She squints at me. "You *are* a decent guy, aren't you? Sticking up for a guy like Jonas, making him a better person."

"Not me. It was Sara who convinced him he had a conscience."

Billie Mae nods. "Right. So, you're such a loyal guy you wouldn't rat out a girl if she let it slip that Sara was moving on Friday, right?" Then she mutters the address and my mind manages to catch it like a steel trap because I know a lifeline when I see one.

PAUL AND BOBBY are at the apartment and we almost get into a fight, but Sara stops it.

I back off, then walk back to my car. "I didn't mean to cause trouble."

She follows me. "I know. Those two lugs I have for brothers don't speak for me—and I say *thank you.* I appreciate that you showed up for me today."

Trying to control the puffing-up of my chest because I don't want to get ahead of myself, ahead of her all over again, I nod. "Good luck in your new apartment. Call me when you're ready to see me."

. . .

She waits two days to call me.

"I want to see you."

"How about for dinner after the Saturday matinee game." I hold my breath.

"Your place?"

"I'd have dinner on the moon if you wanted."

I cook, but we let dinner get cold. Neither of us are hungry.

"Are you ready to date me?" I ask her as I hold her in my arms, tangled in the sheets.

She laughs. "Okay. We can move beyond the hook-up stage to dating."

Pacing around, I'm nervous as fuck. It's a big game today. The Christmas Eve game always is, but this one is bigger for two reasons.

First, we can clinch our spot in the head-to-head standings against Montreal, our biggest rivals. My family, Lenny's family, and Sara's family are all coming to the game.

Second, I have a big surprise set up for Sara after the game. Shit.

"What's your problem, old man?" Jonas asks. The team is lined up in the hall outside the locker room busting each other's balls to loosen up before the game as usual. Jonas has taken to calling me *old man* more and more now but I don't mind, though I pretend to because it gives me an excuse to shove him around and show *him* who's old.

"I've got something going on after the game." I keep my voice low.

He raises his brows and pulls me aside. "What are you doing?" He looks worried, like I'm meeting a fence to sell stolen goods or worse.

I laugh. Jonas is always good for breaking my tension. But

only when Sara's not around because she is my number one tension-breaker. Sara's world-class for tension-breaking and everything else I can imagine. Yes, that's my dick talking.

"I'm going to propose to Sara," I say, leaking the secret to him because I'm busting with nervous energy.

He gives me a sound smack on the shoulder, grinning wide. "Good for you. Finally. Don't worry—she'll say yes. Where are you taking her to pop the question?" he asks.

"Center ice."

I ARRANGED for two security guards to bring Sara onto the ice at the end of the game. The Zamboni driver agreed to wait before he goes out there to clear the ice. By the end of the second period, all the guys on the team have heard about my grand gesture thanks to Jonas having a big mouth. But I don't mind. Not even when Finn starts calling me Hollywood again.

When the final horn sounds, we've won four-two and all the guys stay on the ice because they know what's going on and don't want to miss the show.

"If you stay on the ice, then you're part of the show and you need to behave," I say as I join the circle around Finn at the redline. They agree and line up at center ice, the same way they did that day for the team photo Sara had directed. That's how tight our locker room is, that's how much I trust them.

I watch Sara's confusion as she's reluctant to go with the security guard but my mom and hers practically push her into the aisle. Since I know my shy puck bunny, I consulted with both moms and they were over the moon with my idea.

Coach gives her a double-take as the security guards walk her out onto the ice.

The trio doesn't look steady, and before I move off my spot at center ice with my glove and helmet dropped at my side, Rafe and O'Rourke skate over to escort her the rest of the way.

She looks terrified as she reaches me and she's rambling about how no one seems to know what's going on and hopes everything is all right and how the cameras are on us and people are still in their seats and the crowd seems to be buzzing louder instead of going home.

"What the heck is going on, Quinn?" She takes my hand, hanging on for dear life as she takes the last step into my orbit.

I hold onto her and steady her. "Don't worry about a thing, Sara. Everyone is here for you. Especially me."

The furrow in her brow deepens and I smile. Then I slip my hand into a small pocket I had sewn into my pants, hoping to heaven it's still there, and pull out a ring. A new one, sized properly to fit her in karats and finger size. I keep it fisted in my palm as I get down on one knee.

That's when the place erupts and Sara starts shaking, but I hold onto her hand and keep my eyes on hers, showing her everything in my heart.

"Sara Bellagamba, I love you more than anything. Even more than hockey." I pause because the crowd rears up in protest and applause.

Tears stream down her cheeks as she laugh-cries and frantically swipes them. "Oh my God, my make-up is smearing and I'm on camera."

"You look beautiful. You'll always be beautiful to me, inside and out, Sara. I want to spend the rest of my life with you." I clear my throat and then belt out the line that will convince her I've left everything on the ice for her.

"*I want to make it with you.*" I belt out the words as loud and heartfelt as I've ever sung them before and hold out the ring to her.

She stares at me with a stunned look on her face.

The crowd goes crazy and my team applauds me.

"Will you marry me, Sara?"

Her mouth drops open and she throws her arms around me, screaming, "Yes! Yes! Yes!"

Lifting her in my arms as I stand, I swing her around. "I wanted to buy you a proper ring and give you a proper proposal and, more than anything, I want to marry you, sweetheart. I want to spend the rest of our lives together because I love you."

She's crying and I put her down and wipe her tears as the team crowds around, congratulating us and the organist plays "Here Comes the Bride." I can't stop grinning like a giddy kid who won the biggest jackpot ever imagined, better than shooting the winning goal in The Stanley Cup finals.

I end up carrying her off the ice because she's too shaky to walk.

"You okay?" I whisper in her ear, nuzzling the delicate skin there and wanting to take a bite.

"I'm so much better than okay. I'm in-another-galaxy-okay. But don't put me down anytime soon because my bellagambas are not okay."

AFTER THE TEAM gets through with me in the locker room, alternately roasting me and congratulating me—and having a fucking good time at my expense—I make it out to find Sara still surrounded by family and friends and a few media. I don't want to think about how many pictures and videos were taken of the spectacle, but it should put to rest any rumors that might have started up—by the princess no doubt—that I'd never intended to marry Sara.

The idea that I do anything but spend my life with her is absurd. *And* unthinkable.

"Can I tear you away from your admirers?" I ask her as I pull her into my arms away from Billie Mae and Bobby.

"That was some show," Bobby says. "I heard what you planned to do and I didn't think you could pull it off. You sang to my sister, you fucking nut." He laughs and pulls me in for a bro hug, bumping my back with his fist and murmuring congratulations.

Before he lets me go, he whispers, "Don't ever let her down. I don't care who you are, Hollywood." He gives me a stony-eyed stare for a split second and I nod, giving him the same stare back to let him know I'm more than a Hollywood-style hockey player who can sing.

"Leave him alone, Bobby," Sara says. "He has an incredible voice."

"You have to say that," Chris says, "now that you're stuck with him. Be careful what you wish for."

Everyone in our combined family circle laughs, including me.

"Watch out. I still haven't decided if it's you or Derico for my best man," I say, having every intention of including them both in that role.

Derico steps in. "Don't worry on my account. He'll probably want karaoke for his bachelor party and I want no part of that."

"As much fun as it is to listen to how much you all adore me, it's time for me and my bride-to-be to get out of here."

"I second that," Sara says. "All of a sudden, my bellagambas are feeling great, like I could run all the way to Revere." She takes my hand and tugs.

I give my mother a quick hug and wink at my soon-to-be mother-in-law, then let Sara drag me to the exit.

From the minute I close the car door, I can't stop kissing her.

"Should we call a limo and get someone else to drive us?" I suggest, my breathing heavy and my dick harder than her new diamond.

"No way am I making it with you in the back seat while the

driver knows what's going on. But I do have an idea." She straightens, pulls down her Brawlers jersey and pushes me back behind the wheel. "Start it up and drive. Let's test your nerves."

I start the car and pull out of the garage.

"What do you have in mind?" There's a crazy sexy look on her face, looking far from the innocent Sara Bellagamba and reminding me distinctly of Lola. "Should I be afraid? Don't you think my nerves have been tested enough tonight?" I'm mostly joking and more than curious. *Titillated* might be the right word if I used that kind of word.

"This is a special test of your self-control," she says, licking her lips in a way that jolts my cock to strain against my zipper.

Fuck. I'm way past titillated now.

"I think you're already testing me, sweetheart." I shift in my seat and try to keep my eyes on the road. "What happens if I don't pass your test?"

"Oh, you will."

The way she says the words churns my blood and I step on the gas as we pull onto the highway. "I can't wait until we get home."

"You won't have to," she says.

Fuck.

She unclips her seat belt and leans forward.

"No..." I growl the word as she takes hold of my cock and then unzips my pants.

"Yes. You keep your eyes on the road and your hands on the wheel."

"I can't concentrate when you're... Fuck!"

She has my cock free from my pants and her soft hands caress me tip to base. Fuck, fuck, fuck. My hands tighten on the steering wheel and I wish to God auto-pilot was an option in this obscenely expensive piece of junk right now.

"Sara—"

301

"Keep your eyes on the road." She licks my tip. "And your hands on the wheel."

Then she sucks the head of my cock into her mouth long and hard, and it takes everything in me to stay on the road while I struggle to breathe and my hips pulse against her.

She works her mouth and hands, and I watch the road, my hands and legs tense and my heart ramming my rib cage.

"Fuck... Sara..."

Her hands pump faster, her tongue swirls, and she sucks hard.

The rumbling of my breaking point starts from deep down. My hips come off the seat and I grit my teeth with the tension of keeping control of the car and letting go of the monster explosion from my cock.

"Jesus... Sara..." I see stars and I pant and hang onto the wheel as my hands shake and the car slows down because my foot is off the gas.

I pull over to the side of the road.

She lifts her head, breathing hard and a sexy smile on her swollen wet mouth.

"Did you fucking swallow—"

"Every last drop. I want everything you have to give, Quinn. And everything I can rip from you, screaming and kicking. Every last drop." She catches her breath, her chest heaving as she leans against me, my hands still clenching the steering wheel.

I'm mesmerized by her stare, her mouth and her words.

Then I throw the car into park and wrap her in my arms. "You are crazy—if you think I wouldn't give you everything I have, everything I never knew I had."

"And you have me. All of me. The awkward, the loving, the loyal, the shy, and the crazy sex-tiger you've brought out in me..."

I laugh. "I don't even know what part of you I love best. Fuck, all of it. Every crazy, awkward, sexy, sweet part." My mouth takes hers in a deep kiss, the kind where I feel like I can touch her soul, where my lips mold to hers and our tongues fight and make up and taste everywhere.

The kind that will bring my dick back to full attention if I don't stop.

Pulling away from her, I say, "We have to get home."

"The sooner the better," she says.

I slip my hand under her skirt, cupping her pussy over her panties and suck in a breath. "Jesus your panties are soaked." I look at her. "Do you—"

"Not here. Take me home with you. Right away before I touch myself."

"Fuck. Now I'm conflicted."

She gives me a playful swat and puts the car in gear for me.

I GROAN when I see that it's almost three in the morning, but I can't complain. Because I wouldn't trade sleep for a single minute of our lovemaking. She's laying with her back to me and I pull her closer, feeling my sleepy cock nestle in that perfect crevice of her backside.

"What could possibly cause you to groan here and now in heaven on earth," she asks.

"Are you staying the night?" I ask again.

"I can't." She sits up and sees the bedside clock, then groans. "Oh crap. I have to go."

"I could drive you to your parents' in the morning before practice." I repeat my earlier offer.

"Thank you, honey buns, but I don't want you dropping me off in the morning at my parents' house. Even if he knows better, Dad's old-fashioned and I respect that."

"What happened to that independent woman?"

"She promised to have breakfast with her dad." She kisses me, then leaves my bed.

"Someday, you'll have to have breakfast with me in the morning." I'm not sure if I'm warning her or asking her to promise me.

"I know." She caresses my jawline, running her hand over my morning beard. "That's all the more reason I need to make the most of these breakfasts with him. We've grown close in the last month. It's been one of the other beautiful things that have happened while I was falling in love with you."

My chest tightens with her words because they still seem impossible. She seems like an impossible combination of everything I had no idea I wanted and needed. "Before you go, I have a question."

"Another one?" She laughs and collapses back on the bed against me.

"This is serious." I take a breath. "Now that the dust has settled, tell me if you loved my mid-ice proposal or if you'd rather I waited until we were alone, like now?"

"Honestly?"

"There's no other way to answer," I tell her.

"I didn't need the theatrics or the over-the-top ring. I would have been yours no matter how you proposed."

"Did you mind?"

"Of course not." She laughs. "It's who you are. I know that. You have—"

"Don't say it." I put a finger over her mouth.

She nibbles it so I snatch it away because this is important.

"I'm always going to have some Hollywood in me." I shrug. "It's who I am, but only on the surface. There's a whole lot more underneath. You know that, right?"

"I think I like those under-the-surface parts best—but you know I love all of you just the way you are because you're a good, kind, generous, knock-out of a man and I love you to the moon. Even the showy part of you, and I will always worship the ground you walk on because you cherish me the way I am, too."

"You're killing me, sweetheart." It's all I can do to keep the emotions from choking me up.

"I love you, too," she says. "Always." She lifts her hand with her new diamond ring and watches it sparkle in the light.

And I watch her sparkle in the light of my love, the kind of love that comes from the most real and true places in me, the kind that isn't for show.

EPILOGUE

QUINN

ockey fucking rocks. The Brawlers rock and I'm the luckiest fuck in the locker room. We're in the playoffs and I'm still scoring goals while scoring in bed every night with my one-and-only puck bunny.

The locker room buzzes with a high frequency energy I've never experienced before. Because this is the fucking seventh game of the Stanley Cup finals.

"My boyhood dream is going to come true tonight, guys. I'm going to make the winning goal."

Finn spits out his water and O'Rourke barks out a laugh. Rafe scowls and gives me the finger. The others jump in with laughs, lewd gestures and a couple of Hollywood Hockey insults. All in good-natured banter among teammates. I laugh as my heart thunders with determination.

Finn says, "Other than a goalie, what hockey player doesn't have that dream?"

"And I'm going to score that winning goal in the dying seconds of regulation."

"Who do you think you are?" O'Rourke says, "Babe Ruth

calling out his final home run when he points to the wall on his last at bat?"

"He did it, didn't he? I'm calling it now." No one can knock me off my high horse because my high is life and feeling the satisfaction and doing the hard work to prepare, all coming together. And it's having everything because I have Sara, my family and this team. Knowing they're all with me no matter how obnoxiously Hollywood I act sometimes, because they know I'm with them down deep, always.

Even Jonas, who snorts and laughs the loudest, as usual, slaps me on the back as we file out of the locker room. The ruckus dies down. The time for serious game faces and focus descends and I tune everything else out except hockey.

IN THE THIRD PERIOD, Montreal scores late, tying the game. My blood pumps hard and fast and my adrenaline pumps faster. I skate by Finn and tap his pads.

"No worries man. I got this."

His face is grim, but he nods and taps me back. All the guys rally around him as Montreal celebrates their fucking goal.

I take a rest on the bench, hyper aware of the clock ticking down until with less than two minutes to go the ref blows the whistle, calling Jonas for a penalty. Fuck. Our team is short-handed for the remainder of the game.

I jump over the boards to play the penalty killing line with O'Rourke and Rafe and our best defenseman. It's a bold call for coach to call for three forwards and only one defensemen, but I like it because we need to score.

One of Montreal defensemen is set to pass the puck to his center, but I dive in and intercept the puck, managing to shuffle it to Rafe.

If anyone can get it down ice for a scoring chance he can. I

307

race to the blue line with him when I see only one defenseman from Montreal going back. Rafe passes it over to me, and in a reflexive move born of practicing the shot thousands of times since I was five years old, I snap my wrist, shooting the puck at the net to win the game.

But the fucking puck doesn't go in the net. I watch Montreal's hot goalie deflect my shot with his pads as I'm knocked into the boards. But Rafe muscles his way in front of the net for the rebound. The son of a bitch lifts the biscuit over the goalie's sprawling form. I watch as the puck heads for the back of the net. My heart stops. Everything stops like my life is riding on what happens in the next millisecond.

The puck hits the back of the net and the goal light flashes red. My fucking heart starts up again like I've been jolted with a thousand megawatts. My legs thrust me to a stand and into the air so high I land on Rafe's shoulders and we fall to the ice in a heap of mindless euphoria, shouting and pounding each other as if to make sure we're not dreaming.

After we parade around the ice with the Cup raised, we stop to talk to the TV sportscaster. He asks to speak to me first and I take my place next to him with the cameras aimed at us.

"I understand you predicted you would fulfill your boyhood dream of scoring the winning goal tonight. Does it make this win any less sweet because that didn't happen?"

With everyone looking on as the team stands at center ice, I answer the sportscaster.

"First of all, you realize that's every hockey players boyhood dream, right? Even Finn's whether he admits it or not." The sportscaster laughs along with the crowd. "But to answer your question, I don't give a crap who scored the winning goal." The crowd cheers and I'm grinning with the truth of the words. "We won the Cup!" I heft it above my head one-handed even though the son-of-a-bitch is heavy. I lower it and finish saying what's on my mind. "More importantly, I'm part of the best team I've been on since I was a child. And most importantly, I get to celebrate winning the fucking Stanley Cup with my family, and dedicate the game to my dad who is still with us in spirit." My voice breaks, but I don't care.

The applause is deafening. The sportscaster nods, pats my back and is about to take the microphone away to move onto Rafe for comments, but I hold the mic in place because I have one more thing to say. These words need to be said before they burst from me if I don't let them out.

"Hold on—one last word." People laugh, especially my team-mates. I clear my throat and the Garden goes quiet and I search the stands for where I know Sara's sitting and my eyes zero in on hers.

"Last, but most definitely not least, I want to say that I'm the luckiest fuck in the world to be celebrating my dream with the love of my life, Sara Bellagamba." The Garden erupts and I raise the Cup in the air one more time before I pass it on to Rafe.

I throw her a kiss. A glance at the jumbotron shows me the camera found her and she's covering her mouth in shock and her eyes are streaming with tears.

I know the words are true and I think she believes me. She *can* believe me because this is no Hollywood act no matter how cheesy it sounds. And I intend to make sure she understands how I really feel if it takes the rest of my life to prove it.

THE MAYHEM in the locker room explodes exponentially the second the coach let all the friends and family in. The media and the team were already doing a pretty good job of popping cham-pagne corks and guzzling down the bubbly and whatever else the Brawlers had carted into the space to celebrate the team's fucking Stanley Cup win.

It's been a long time since I got drunk on champagne with my brother. Probably not since his wedding when I was in college because the lucky bastard got married young, had no problem knowing who he was and who he loved and what life was about.

"Here's to the scrappy stupid little brother who's finally grown up," he says, lifting a freshly popped bottle to his lips. His kids are hanging on his sides and staring and his wife is laughing. Mom and Sara are toasting to something and I wonder if they're trading secrets about me.

Not that I'm worried about hiding anything these days.

Not when I'm with the most loving, giving, real and sexy little puck bunny on the planet. Sara Belagamba hasn't changed in the most important ways, but she's grown in confidence and independence. Every time I see her my chest tightens because my heart swells so big. And I say a silent thank you to dad for being there as an example to me all my life, for knowing what's important—a happy loving family and living life well.

* The End *

**To read the BONUS EPILOGUE
join my newsletter!
HERE**

Thank you for reading my book. ❤ *Stephanie Queen*

Look for the next story in the *Some Girls Like It Cold* series, *The Groupie* - a hockey rom-com.
Read it Now!

HERE's a Sneak Peek of *THE GROUPIE*:
While I'm trying not to cry in my beer, I feel a draft and a zing

of something run down my spine. I look up and see a woman walk into the bar. My mouth opens and goes instantly dry.

A woman?

I mean a fucking vision. If someone spied on my wet dreams and created the ultimate hot sexy lady for the sole purpose of tempting me into doing anything and everything she wants, this would be that woman.

She flicks long, lush dark hair over her shoulder and checks out the place with brilliant dark fringed eyes. And her body? It's the kind that would make Barbie dolls jealous. Last but not least, by anyone's score, she has a fucking sexy world-conquering attitude that I can see in the tilt of her chin, the glint in her eye, and the way she carries herself with perfectly squared shoulders. She has the kind of confidence a lot of women don't have when walking into a bar alone—make that no woman I've ever met.

That's who just walked in the fucking door. *Shit.* She's heading this way.

Keep your fucking butt in this seat, and do not flirt with her. Do not even look at her.

No more complications.

No fucking flirting.

READ MORE...

NEW Boston Brawlers Spin-off Books!

The Puck Bunny The Groupie & The Do-Over Girl

Delicious Hockey Rom-Coms!

Steamy College Sports Romance

Big Men on Campus Series

Big Men on Campus

Best Man on Campus

Bad Man on Campus

Notorious Man on Campus

St. Paul U Players Series

I Want to Know What Love Is

Your Kiss Is on My List

Best Things in Life

ABOUT THE AUTHOR

***USA Today* Bestselling Author Stephanie Queen**

The compulsion to write stories has been

with me always. I've written for fun since I was in second grade. In college, I started to work seriously at writing, and have been writing ever since (a wicked long time!) (I'm from the Boston area).

Improving my craft remains a constant goal, but I finally couldn't wait to share my stories, ready or not. And here I am now, 50+ books later, sharing all over the place and loving it!

Writing romance is me sharing my heart and my deeply held view of the world. An enthusiastic optimist, needing to envision the best in humanity, I bring this view to life in my stories, where the good guys always win and two people fall in love and live happily ever after.

What else besides writing? Ready for chocolate, morning,

noon and night, I also adore kittens even though I'm allergic, love dancing like a maniac, bright sunny winter days that make you go snow-blind, and UConn Women's Basketball (go Huskies!).

Every December I take the month off from writing to enjoy my all-time favorite holiday. I'm one of those people who goes crazy at Christmas, decorating, cooking, connecting with family and friends, and soaking up every minute of the fun, giving, loving spirit of the season.

Socializing may be distracting for some writers, and down-right scary for others, but I *thrive* on it. So, write me any time at Stephanie@StephanieQueen.com and I will reply. Can't wait to hear from you!

Join my Newsletter HERE!

Join the Stephanie Queen Team HERE!

Find Me Everywhere

Printed in the USA
CPSIA information can be obtained
at www.ICGtesting.com
LVHW041004050923
757271LV00024B/113